*Keeping You
Close*

BOOK YOUR PLACE ON OUR WEBSITE AND MAKE THE ARABESQUE ROMANCE CONNECTION!

We've created a customized website just for our very special Arabesque readers, where you can get the inside scoop on everything that's going on with Arabesque romance novels.

When you come online, you'll have the exciting opportunity to:

- View covers of upcoming books

- Learn about our future publishing schedule (listed by publication month and author)

- Find out when your favorite authors will be visiting a city near you

- Search for and order backlist books

- Check out author bios and background information

- Send e-mail to your favorite authors

- Join us in weekly chats with authors, readers and other guests

- Get writing guidelines

- AND MUCH MORE!

Visit our website at
http://www.arabesquebooks.com

Keeping You Close

CELYA BOWERS

BET Publications, LLC
http://www.bet.com
http://www.arabesquebooks.com

ARABESQUE BOOKS are published by

BET Publications, LLC
c/o BET BOOKS
One BET Plaza
1900 W Place NE
Washington, DC 20018-1211

All Kensington Titles, Imprints, and Distributed lines are available at special quantity discounts for bulk purchases for sales promotions, premiums, fund-raising, and educational or institutional use. Special book excerpts or customized printings can also be created to fit specific needs. For details, write or phone the office of the Kensington special sales manager: Kensington Publishing Corp., 850 Third Avenue, New York, NY 10022, attn: Special Sales Department, Phone: 1-800-221-2647.

First Printing: May 2005
10 9 8 7 6 5 4 3 2 1

Printed in the United States of America

*To my mother, Celia Mae Bowers Shaw Kenney,
and to my aunt, Dorothy Kirk.*

ACKNOWLEDGMENTS

I would like to thank the following people for giving me support, and encouragement:

Melody Alvarado, my most voracious reader, thanks for keeping me on track.

To my new writer/reader friends, Darlene Ramzy, Valencia Bradshaw, Cindi Louis, and Eulanda Bailey, thanks for all the information and other helpful hints about government agencies and children.

To my editor, Demetria Lucas, thank you for being so patient.

To my family, thanks for all your love and support.

To my friends, thank you and bless you for the times I told you I was too busy writing to go out, and you understood.

To the Arlington K/A Writers' Group: Diane, Gay, Urania, Simon, Charles, and Cecelia, thanks for the insight to the writing world. To my friends at Writer's Block, get ready for the next critique meeting!

And a big thanks to the man who inspired this story.

To anyone else I have forgotten, please forgive me.

Peace.

PROLOGUE

Fort Worth, Texas

Kasmira Brenton entered the Village Savings and Loan with awe. This wasn't the usual branch she and her mother had banked at for years. The upscale bank reminded her of a something out of a European travelogue. The building stood regal and proud along the backdrop of north Fort Worth's strip malls, bookstores, and retirement villas. It looked like something straight out of a Renaissance painting.

The Italian tile floor, cathedral ceilings, and marbled countertops made her think of Rome. Or what she thought the inside of one those exclusive villas would look like in the romantic city.

As she walked toward the information center, a plump, mature woman greeted her with a smile. Kasmira informed her that she needed to enter the secured area of the financial institution. The woman looked her up and down before finally relenting and summoning the security guard.

In a few minutes, the young man, dressed in a crisp black uniform, was leading her down a dimly lit corridor, away from the main area of the bank. They approached a series of barred doors. He took a plastic card out of his pocket and swiped it through the electronic reader. After it beeped at them, he motioned for her to enter.

Finally the guard spoke. "Your key," he said without casting a glance in her direction.

She watched him still. Was he asking for the key or did he just want to make sure she had it? "I'm sorry," she said.

"Your key, ma'am," he explained. "You will need your key to enter the next door. I can't enter that area."

The light finally came on in her brain. "Yes. I have it."

He nodded and they stopped at a massive steel door. He swiped the card again and beckoned for her to use her gold-plated key. She was granted entrance to the room that should have the answers to the questions that had plagued her all of her twenty-seven years.

She looked at the key in her hand again. It dangled from her mother's favorite gold cross chain. She walked to the appropriately numbered box and opened it with trepidation. What could her mother have at this bank, and why hadn't she told her only daughter about it before?

Kasmira shook her head, fighting back the memories of her mother getting shot in her front yard.

She could still see her mother playing with her only grand-daughter, Reese, as she did every day while she waited for Kasmira to get home from work. It was a miracle they weren't both killed in the freak act of violence. Although their neighborhood wasn't the safest, there were never random shootings. Everyone in the neighborhood knew the three generations of the Brenton women: Helen, the grandmother, Kasmira, the daughter, and Reese, the granddaughter.

Kasmira unlocked the large metal box and went through the assortment of papers. She glanced at insurance policies and baby pictures, hoping to find a picture of her mysterious father, but no such luck. She had asked her mother about her father when she was a teenager, and the question almost brought her mother to tears. She said she didn't want to discuss her one reckless act of abandon that occurred many years ago.

Noticing an official-looking brown envelope, Kasmira hoped it wasn't a wad of bills her mother had neglected to tell her about. She opened the envelope and took out the contents. A small, black savings-account book fell out. Her birth certificate was scattered along with other important papers. Finally, she would at least know her father's name. She quickly scanned the paper. But as usual, life laughed at her. Her father was listed as unknown. "Momma, why didn't you tell me?" she asked as tears fell down her honey-hued face.

Kasmira stood, gathered the contents of the envelope, shoved them in her oversized purse, and exited the room. She walked the few steps to the door, ringing the bell for the officer to escort her out of the secured area. Walking to the tellers' counter, she decided to close her mother's account. This bank was too far from her house, anyway. She opened the savings-account book to check out just how much money her mother had saved over the years and gasped as she noticed the amount her mother had penciled in. "Momma must have been doing some wishful thinking, adding all these zeroes to her balance," she muttered as she approached the counter.

"Can I help you?" the woman asked in a snooty voice, pushing her half-rimmed bifocals further up on her very prominent nose.

"I'd like to close this account. It was my mother's," Kasmira said, handing over the diary of broken dreams.

The teller took the book and grinned at her. "I'll just enter this account number into the computer so I can get the proper balance."

Kasmira heard the sarcasm in the woman's voice and rolled her eyes. She hated snobby women.

"This can't be correct," the woman muttered, just loud enough for Kasmira to hear. "Miss Brenton, please step into Mr. Roberts's office. He's the bank president and should be able to help you. It's just down the hall to your left."

Mira nodded and walked in the direction the women pointed. "This is a lot of trouble for fifty dollars," she muttered to herself.

A tall man with gray hair came out of his office to meet her. He extended his hand as he approached her and plastered on a smile so wide it had to be fake. "Miss Brenton, I'm John Roberts, the bank president. Please, come in."

After Kasmira was seated comfortably in his large office, John continued speaking as if he had known her mom personally. "Helen was a valued customer for over twenty-five years. Are you sure you want to withdraw that amount in cash?"

"Mr. Roberts, I know my mother couldn't have had much money in the bank, considering that I have been the breadwinner of the family for the last five years. I don't see what the problem is. Since I am on the signature card, just let me cash out her savings, and I'll be on my way."

"Well Miss Brenton, that's a lot of money for a single woman to be carrying around. I would prefer to send the money to your bank by wire transfer."

"Just how much money are we talking about?" *And where did it come from?* Something wasn't sitting right with Kasmira, and she couldn't figure out what it was.

The bank president studied her intently before he finally spoke. "We're talking about a little over half a million dollars."

CHAPTER 1

Laredo, Texas

Patrick Callahan opened his eyes. Bright fluorescent lights blinded him, but he forced his eyes to adjust. His last conscious memory was a ten-year-old kid aiming a nine-millimeter pistol at him.

Memories of a failed operation flittered through his mind. Two years of living in Mexico, learning Spanish, infiltrating Paulo Riaz's inner circle, all gone because he let his guard down and a kid got too close. She had simply walked up to him and shot him point-blank. Paulo got away again, untouched. *Bastard.*

Patrick knew he was in a hospital, but had no idea where or how long he'd been there. He hoped he wasn't still in Mexico. He felt movement in his feet and hands, always a good sign. Something was in his mouth; he realized it was a tube.

"Mr. Callahan," a voice called.

Slowly Patrick turned his head toward the sound. It came from the nurse standing next to the hospital bed and changing his IV. She had nice eyes and a comforting voice.

"You have a visitor," she announced. "He's been waiting for you to wake up."

He couldn't answer with the tube in his mouth. He nodded, hoping the nurse could see the miniscule movement of his head. He watched as the visitor came into view. Why couldn't he have amnesia, so he wouldn't remember this man's face?

Harlan Reynolds took a seat near the bed and watched the

various computer screens that monitored Patrick, then let out a loud grunt. "They got you wired for sound, don't they? I know you got that damn tube in your mouth, so don't try to talk." He leaned back in the uncomfortable chair. "Well, according to the doctor, you got some liver damage, and some innard problems," he added in his Southern drawl, rattling off the rest of Patrick's injuries like they were ingredients to a recipe.

Patrick didn't hate Harlan just because he was his boss. He hated him because he was the self-proclaimed Southern Rebel. He hated him for the fact that he had to listen to Harlan drawl on about phase two of the plan that almost got him killed.

Harlan leaned closer to the bed so the nurse wouldn't hear. "We found a detail in Paulo's past. He has a daughter in the United States. He's never seen her, and we know he wants to. We're thinking he might want to give her the family business."

Patrick spun his free hand in the air, silently telling Harlan to hurry up.

"Okay, okay, I'll get to the point. Well, she's never met him, and the mother wanted nothing to do with him. Now, since the mother's dead, we figure he'll try to get in contact with the daughter. He may have already; she's recently came into a large sum of money. She's his only heir, and since Paulo's days are numbered, we want his drug business to be, too. If we could get her cooperation, we could be rid of him once and for all.

"Since you will be inactive while you recover, why don't you take some classes at Fort Worth University, so you can keep a discreet eye on her?"

Again Patrick raised his hand in question.

Harlan laughed—that obnoxious laugh that grated on Patrick's nerves. "For a guy that can't talk, you ask a lot of questions. For your information, Kasmira Brenton just enrolled as a freshman for the fall semester at Fort Worth University."

Kasmira rolled over in her king-size sleigh bed and felt a familiar figure beside her as she reached for her digital alarm clock, which beeped annoyingly. Her six-year-old daughter, Reese, had crawled into her bed sometime during the night. She smiled as she shook her daughter awake.

"Reese, we talked about you sleeping in your own room. Did you have another bad dream?" She stood, putting on her silk floral bathrobe, and then sat on the bed.

"Yes, Mommy. I miss Granny. Why did she have to go to heaven? Didn't she want to be with us anymore?" Tears welled in Reese's big brown eyes as she hugged her mother.

"Honey, she loves us and is looking over us right now. Don't worry, Granny misses us as much as we miss her." She wiped her daughter eyes, pulling back the mass of black curls from her face. "This morning, little girl, we both need to get dressed for school."

Reese's tears disappeared as fast as they had started. Kasmira, known as Mira to almost everyone, ushered her daughter down the hall to her bathroom. "You get dressed, and I'll meet you downstairs for breakfast."

"Okay, Mommy."

Mira stood in the middle of her large room and sighed. For the last six years, she had shared a room with Reese, but she now had her own room, as did her daughter. As she took her shower, her mind floated back to her life as it had been. Memories of her mother fluttered to mind. She always thought the cancer would have taken her mother, but she was actually getting better with chemotherapy. It was just a question of being in the wrong place at the wrong time that ended her life.

Mira dressed in jeans and a white cap-sleeved blouse that tapered at her waist, then blow-dried her naturally curly hair to make it straight. It flowed gently over her shoulders and midway down her back.

She knew exactly why she was going to all this trouble. Patrick Callahan. When she had enrolled in college, she would never have thought the most gorgeous man in the world would be sitting right behind her in her sociology and English classes. If she closed her eyes, she could imagine smelling his cologne and looking into those luscious green eyes of his. She couldn't believe that for the first time since her divorce, a man had her taking great care in getting dressed.

She examined her attire in the full-length mirror and smiled. "You don't look twenty-seven," she said to the reflection. Mira laughed and headed downstairs to fix Reese's breakfast. *Watch out, Patrick,* she thought. She vowed to make him notice her that day.

Mira pushed the sexy thoughts of Patrick Callahan from her mind and concentrated on her daughter. She took special pains to make sure Reese's home life was as normal as it could be. If that meant cooking elaborate breakfasts, she did. She fixed omelets, bacon, toast, orange juice, milk, and pancakes, if Reese so desired, every morning. She poured orange juice in a glass as the phone rang. She knew without looking that the caller was her best friend and former coworker, Tashara Hilliard. She usually called Mira every morning. Mira picked up the phone before it rang a second time.

"Hi, Shara." Mira covered the mouthpiece of the phone with her hand and shouted, "Reese, honey, breakfast!"

Shara laughed. "Are you still fixing those Ozzie and Harriet breakfasts for Reese? It's been a few months, I thought you would have stopped by now."

Mira smiled as she heard Reese stomp down the stairs. "Not hardly, we've been living out here for three months, and she's still having nightmares. I thought a different atmosphere would help her to forget, but I'm taking your advice and taking her to see a counselor. Her first appointment is today. Are you free for lunch? I could stop by after class before I pick up Reese from school."

"Okay, girl. Everybody at work still asks about you, since you deserted us to go to college and be a full-time mom. I don't blame you. If I could give my kids a chance at a better life, I'd do it, too. I still can't believe all that happened to you in the last six months."

"Sometimes, I can't either," Mira agreed.

"I gotta go. My kids are ready to go to the Donut Hut. Remember, we used to go there every morning with the kids before you moved out to the 'burbs?"

"Bye, girl." Mira hung up the phone as Reese walked into the kitchen.

Reese was dressed in her school uniform—a khaki skirt, white blouse, white socks, and black shoes. Her full head of curly black hair was pulled back in sloppy ponytail Mira would have to fix before they left for school. Sometimes it looked like Reese's hair weighed more than she did. She plopped down in the wood chair and began eating her omelet.

"Mommy, why can't I wear my other clothes?" She took a gulp of milk, then an equally large gulp of orange juice.

They'd had this same conversation every day for the past three months, ever since they moved to their new house by the lake in west Fort Worth. It had been a period of adjustment for both of them.

Mira sat down and began her usual answer. "Because at Kirkstone Preparatory Academy, you have to wear either blue, black, or khaki shorts, skirts, or slacks. We talked about this before we moved here." She sliced her own omelet and took a bite. Heaven. "Would you rather be back at your old school?" Mira knew the answer.

"No. I like this school better and my new friends. I like this house better, too. We never hear loud music or the police cars anymore."

She's right about that, Mira thought. She had heavily weighed the option of moving from the less desirable side of town. Her daughter would have all the advantages Mira didn't: better school, better neighborhood, more stability, and a chance of making her wildest dreams come true.

Since discovering the money, she'd decided to make both their lives better. After quitting her dead-end job downtown, she'd bought a two-story house and a new car, and had decided to get a college degree. All the things she had thought would never be possible when she was the sole support for herself, Reese, and her cancer-stricken mother.

Now her life was full of scheduling study time for herself and quality time for Reese. They had settled into their life in the burbs, as her friends referred to the location. Although she missed her childhood friends, she knew she had made the right decisions.

"Mommy, I'm done."

Reese snapped her mother back to the present. Mira looked down at her daughter's empty plate. *Where does she put it?* Reese's slender frame was a gift from her father. The Brenton women traditionally had a daily battle with the scale. Usually the scale won.

"Okay, honey."

Reese left the table and headed to the living room, leaving Mira to finish her breakfast alone. By the time she finished eating, she heard Reese nearing the kitchen again. She laughed as her daughter entered the room lugging both her small canvas backpack and Mira's heavier leather one.

"Thanks, honey. You shouldn't carry mine; it's too heavy for you." Mira picked up her backpack and they headed to the garage.

After she dropped off Reese at school, she headed to Fort Worth University to begin her day.

Patrick walked into the sociology classroom with a smile. After healing from the gunshot wound, he was on to his next mission of surveillance, or baby-sitting, as it was commonly known throughout the agency. Although he already had a master's degree in sociology, forging his academic records to underclassmen status proved no problem for Harlan.

After six weeks of sitting in two of Kasmira's five classes, he still wasn't any closer to her than he was at the beginning of the semester. He knew he was good looking. In his thirty years on God's earth he hadn't gone a day without a woman hitting on him. Being blessed with the genes of both Irish and African ancestors certainly didn't hurt. But for all his good looks, Kasmira still hadn't given him more than a casual glance, which was less than he gave her.

The first day of class, her beauty had him tongue-tied. He had the DEA notes on her, but the file photo didn't do her justice. Patrick didn't think of her as a suspect, he thought of her as a woman. And that meant trouble. He sat his tall frame at the too-small desk and watched as the other students filtered in. Reaching into his bag, he retrieved a miniscule tape recorder and placed it on his desk.

Patrick knew the exact minute Kasmira entered the room. The same thing happened every day. His heartbeat accelerated and his palms sweated, making him feel like a sixteen-year-old virgin.

When Kasmira walked into the room, he saw her naturally curly hair was straightened and flowed gently over her shoulders as she strode to her seat directly in front of him. Her honey-brown skin, a tribute to a black mother and a Hispanic father, looked as if the sun from the previous weekend had toasted it. He cleared his throat as she took her seat. Nothing. She didn't even notice him. The professor spoke, ruining Patrick's opportunity for small talk.

"We're going to do something a little different for your next project. As I call your name in groups of two, this will be your study partner for the rest of the semester. You will analyze each other's study habits, rituals, etc. Then you will report on how to improve them. The downside to this is that it will count for forty percent of your grade." The professor laughed at the groans heard in the room. "Now, there are three more tests, so you'll have plenty of time to analyze. Did I mention your analysis would appear in a five-page report?" More groans were heard.

"I hope I get her," the student next to Patrick whispered. He pointed to Kasmira as she reached into her book bag. "We'd probably never study," he said with masculine innuendo.

The room became quiet as the professor began calling names

in pairs. "Samantha Hathsburg–Taiwana Stanley, Hannibal Zenderhaus–Amin Al Jabid, Patrick Callahan–Kasmira Brenton, Brian Piazza–Joi Chin."

Patrick smiled as the professor continued. His late-night computer hacking had paid off. By switching names around, he was now Mira's partner, providing the opening he needed. Harlan would be proud.

She turned around and introduced herself to him officially. "I'm Kasmira. You know, like cashmere, but with an *a* on the end. Please call me Mira," she said, smiling her dazzling pearly white teeth at him. "Our next test is in two weeks. When did you want to study? I've already started going over the chapters."

He hadn't realized by pairing himself with a mature student she'd want to study right away. He should have known. "How about later today? I'm a little behind in my notes."

Mira huffed her instant disgust with him. "Don't tell me you haven't been taking notes or studying since the beginning of the semester?"

"No, that's not it," he remarked, feeling that he had to defend himself. "I record the lecture notes and I haven't listened to the last two, that's all." He couldn't tell her he'd been gazing at the back of her head during class and studying her profile instead of paying attention. "How about we meet around lunchtime?" he offered, showing he wasn't a total slacker just because he didn't have his notes in order.

"I can't today," Mira said quickly. A little too quickly for his taste.

She took her Palm Pilot out of her leather backpack. She frowned as she tapped on the small display screen with a metal stylus. "Sorry, I have an appointment I can't miss."

Patrick needed to establish contact, and Mira wasn't cooperating in the least. He tried a different approach. "How about later in the afternoon?"

"Later isn't good," she said with no explanation. "How

about Wednesday at lunchtime? That way you could get your notes in order and we can focus on the test."

He nodded. She would be studious, wouldn't she? After they decided to meet in the university center for lunch, she turned her attention to the professor. So much for first impressions, he thought. *She probably thinks I'm here trying to catch some eighteen-year-old college chick.*

After class ended, he watched Mira leave the campus with a group of women. He followed them at a discreet distance as they headed for the parking lot. His phone rang, distracting him. He flipped opened the tiny cellular wonder. "Callahan," he answered.

"Harlan here. Have you made contact? I have some info for you. I'll fax it tonight."

"Contact still hasn't been established, but I will complete my mission. Did you send me the bugs?"

"On the way." Harlan cut the connection.

Patrick snapped the phone closed, stuffing it into his jeans pocket, and then looked for Mira, but he didn't see her. *Where did she go?* He watched several cars leave the parking lot, but she wasn't driving any of them. Then he saw her. He watched her cherry-red PT Cruiser motor down the street. That wasn't the kind of car he thought she'd have. He was expecting some kind of four-door sedan, not a retro-mobile!

Patrick jotted down her license plate number in a hurry. Whistling, as he neared his baby, a black convertible Mustang, he got inside his car and sighed. He had some major computer hacking to do.

CHAPTER 2

Mira parked in front of her former place of work. As she got out of the car, she smiled. She didn't miss working at the O'Shannon Corporation one bit. She had been in a catch-22 situation when she worked there. It seemed the only way to advance was to have taken college courses, be enrolled in college, or have a college degree, and since Mira was the breadwinner of the family, she didn't have the time or money to go to school.

Although she was a senior trainer, she was stuck in the firm's call center until she found the money. Now, anything was possible.

She walked into the reception area and smiled at the mature woman behind the desk. Had it only been six months since she'd left this place? "Hi, Georgia. How are you? I'm here to see Shara."

"Mira Brenton!" Georgia plucked the headset from her head. She walked from behind the large desk and hugged Mira with enthusiasm. "It's so nice to see you." She stepped back from Mira and took in her outfit. "You look good! How's my baby?"

"She's fine. Growing like a weed. I miss you guys," Mira admitted. "Not the job, mind you, but the people. Your baby is keeping me busy."

The phone buzzed, signaling Georgia to return to her desk. "Well, you look good. Considering," she added in a motherly tone. Georgia picked up the phone, answering as she took her seat.

Mira walked to a sofa and plopped down. As she took a moment to relax, she glanced around the lobby, positively giddy with joy over not working here anymore. She was planning the rest of the day in her head when she heard her friend's voice.

"Hey, you're late!" Shara smiled, walking into the lobby. "So, this is how you dress for college now."

Mira stood and hugged her friend. "You're dressed the same as I am. Jeans and a blouse. I must say, I don't see how you're walking in those tight jeans."

"I know, but one of us needs to get married. You're at a college with lots of guys."

Mira knew where the conversation was headed. "Come on, Shara, you have only an hour. Are we going to spend it here talking about why I don't have a man?"

"No, let's go eat. We can always talk about men. Let's go to Cleo's. You used to love eating there."

"Yes, and I remember Momma getting mad when she cooked the same thing that I had already eaten." She smiled at the memory of her mother quizzing her about her lunch.

The women walked out of the office building and across the street to a restaurant that served home-cooked food. Mira looked around the room, noticing the change in clientele as well as the decor.

The friends joined the long line of customers for the buffet. After Mira had loaded her tray with all her favorites, she looked for Shara. Laughing, she spotted Shara talking to a guy by the checkout counter. She walked to her friend, shaking her head as the guy retreated.

"This place looks so different," she murmured as they looked for a table. "What happened to that ratty wallpaper? Those plastic chairs? When did Cleo's go upscale?" Mira nodded at the tray she was holding. The plastic trays were also gone and replaced with wooden ones; paper napkins had been replaced with cloth napkins. "Has everything changed in the few months I've been gone?"

"I know," Shara commented as she led them to a table in the center of the busy room. "A lot of people eat here from that investment firm on the seventh floor of our building. When the clientele went upscale, so did the restaurant." Shara glanced around the room. "Luckily the prices didn't increase, or we wouldn't be eating here today." She leaned toward Mira. "I heard one of the partners is married to a sister."

"So?"

"She works at O'Shannon, or she did. I hear she's pregnant and she was in the hospital for awhile," Shara commented.

Mira knew exactly whom Shara was referring to, but didn't think that was any of Shara's business. "Really?" She tried to sound interested in the gossip, but that part of her life was gone. "She didn't work in the call room, did she?"

"No." Shara started eating her lunch. "Any cute guys at college?"

"Yes, and they are all eighteen. But there is this one guy. He might be cute to you; he's not to me," she lied. "He's too good looking. There's something about him that doesn't sit right with me."

"Maybe you could introduce him to me," Shara hinted.

"I don't know. Maybe I'm just overly suspicious of good-looking men. He doesn't seem like he belongs in a college classroom, but now he's my study partner for the rest of the semester."

Shara smiled. "Well, now you can find out what it is that unsettles you about him, and why. You're still coming to Keisha's party, right?"

Mira pretended to concentrate on her dessert. "I don't know."

"Mira, why? She rescheduled it so you could go."

"I'd feel guilty leaving Reese with a sitter. Uncle Harold offered to keep her so I could go out sometimes. But I feel that I should be with her. And I don't want Aunt Tilda around Reese for one second!"

Shara nodded. "I know things haven't been good with your aunt for a long time. I think she was jealous of the relationship your mom had with your uncle."

"What do you mean?" She knew, but didn't want to think her aunt could be that hateful.

"You know, when your uncle always came over to help you guys in a crisis. He treats you and Reese likes daughters instead of nieces. I think she was jealous of that."

"I offered him some of the money Momma had saved. He said I should put it to good use for Reese and me. When Aunt Tilda found out, she hit the roof. You know how materialistic she is."

"Yeah, I remember. At your baby shower, she had to make sure everybody knew how much that infant car seat cost."

"Forget the fact that it came apart before I had Reese." Mira laughed at the memory.

"Well, Mama said she'd be happy to keep Reese for the night of the party," Shara said. "You know she doesn't really baby-sit the kids much anymore, but she really misses Reese since you guys moved away. She's an angel compared to my kids. She could spend the night and I'd bring her home Saturday morning."

It would be nice to have an adult conversation again, Mira thought, and not just conversations about trust funds, investment accounts, and private schools. "I'll talk to Reese about it tonight and see how she feels about me going out."

Shara leaned back in her seat and laughed. "See, that's how we differ. I don't discuss nothing with my kids. I *tell* them."

"Well considering all we've been through, I don't want her thinking I'm trying to get rid of her."

"I know, but you need your space, too. Mira, you've got to start dating at some point in your life. We're already twenty-seven, girl."

"I know, but only if Reese approves."

Later that afternoon, Mira nervously flipped through a magazine. She sat in the office of Sidney Goldberg, pediatric counselor, waiting her turn at the hot seat or, more accurately, the hot couch.

Reese had been in with the doctor for over thirty minutes. Mira hadn't heard any screams, so she assumed all was well. She glanced at the secretary as she watched her. "Is this normal, him wanting to see me as well?"

"Yes, Dr. Goldberg always talks to the parent after he talks to the patient."

Mira didn't like Reese being referred to as a patient. It brought to mind images of sanitariums and medications that a child shouldn't endure. Maybe Reese could have worked through this on her own. The door opened, and Reese ran to her. "How was it, honey?"

She shrugged her shoulders. "Okay. He asked about Granny."

"Ms. Brenton, you can go in," the receptionist called.

Mira nodded. "Sit here, honey. What are the rules?" She stood and watched her daughter as she got comfortable on the leather sofa.

Reese exhaled and recited the rules for her mother. "Do not leave this spot unless you tell me to. Nobody else. If someone tries to make me leave, I should scream."

"Very good. I'll be right back." Mira walked into the office. She was surprised at the decor. Cartoon characters decorated each wall. Instead of a couch, there was a small table and chairs. The table was littered with coloring books, games, and puzzles.

"Ms. Brenton, I'm Dr. Goldberg. The kids call me Dr. Sid. Please, sit down."

She was about to ask where when she spotted an adult-sized desk and chairs in the corner of the room. She quickly took a seat and watched as he took the seat next to her.

"I like the informal method," he explained, waving his

hand at the room. "I find if a child's attention is diverted, the information is easier to obtain."

Mira nodded. "Did you find out why she's still having nightmares?"

"Yes and no. She needs more than a few months to recover from her grief. She lost her grandmother, her caregiver in your absence."

Again, Mira nodded. "I know this will take more than one visit to treat. I'm prepared to do whatever needs to be done."

Dr. Sid looked at her for an uncomfortable amount of time, then wrote something in the chart. "Are you prepared to attend sessions with her?"

"If that's what needs to be done."

"Good, I'll see you next week."

Patrick rubbed his tired eyes. Hacking into the county record system should have taken a few minutes, but an hour had passed since he'd turned on his computer. He looked around his apartment. It was suitable for the job he had to do, but it was not like his digs in Turner's Point, Virginia.

The place he now called home didn't have his elaborate stereo sound system or his plasma TV—he had to make do with a thirty-six-inch color TV. What he really missed was his king-size heated water bed. But Harlan, being the idiot he was, had rented Patrick a queen-size bed instead.

A loud beep attracted his attention. He hated pop-up ads. He had been meaning to tinker with the computer to get rid of them, but hadn't had time. *Why is this taking so long? Easy*, he thought, his mind just wasn't on the job.

Finally, he got the information he wanted. He knew he could have just asked around for Mira's address or maybe followed her home, but he didn't want to take the chance she'd recognize him. Patrick wrote down Mira's address and then looked up directions to her place.

"How's she living by the lake with no visible means of

income?" he asked the computer. But the computer didn't answer him.

"That's how," he muttered as he looked up her financial information. *Where did she get over half a million dollars?* Her mother's insurance policy was his first guess, but further investigation proved that Helen Brenton's meager insurance policy wouldn't provide those kinds of funds; it barely covered the funeral expenses. With his thoughts turning to Mira, he was also reminded that he was supposed to meet her the following day for lunch and studying time.

"I'd better be ready for our study session, or she'll think I'm wasting her time," he muttered as he turned off his computer. He walked over to the tape recorder and started listening to the lecturer.

A few hours later, the phone jolted him awake. It wasn't his landline, or his undercover cell phone; it was his special phone, and only one person had that number.

"Hi, Mom. Is everything okay? How's Dad?"

"He's fine. We're fine. How about you? How's the liver? I think you went back to work too early. Surely that ass of a boss you have should know that gunshot wounds take longer to heal than just a few weeks," his mother added in her no-nonsense fashion.

Patrick laughed at his mother's tone. Amelia Callahan had been a nurse for thirty years and never bit her tongue. She'd told Patrick repeatedly to get out of his line of business. "Mom, I'm doing fine. I'm still under the doctor's care. Stop worrying. I'm just taking classes, that's all."

"For a degree you already have. Don't give me that bull. Save it for your father. Besides, he agrees me with me on this. I just wanted to hear your voice."

He also knew what his mother wasn't saying. "This is my last job, I just need to tie up some loose ends."

"Does this mean you'll be home for Christmas?"

"I can't say."

"I know. Have you met anyone?"

"Mom, I'm on assignment."

"That's never stopped you before. Why now? I recall the girl from Barcelona, and that poor girl who about died because I offered her roast beef. You should warn me when those girls don't eat meat. I don't mind the different women you meet; that lets me know that you're not just thinking about your job."

He had to stop her before she rambled on and on and divulged some critical information. Although the phone was supposed to be secure, nothing was absolute. "Mom, one disaster at a time. I have to finish this."

She took a deep breath, which was a hint that a lecture about his choice of occupation was due. "Patrick, you can't bring your cousin back from the dead. Yes, he shouldn't have been taking drugs in the first place. You promised me three years ago you'd quit. I just don't want you to end up being a casualty trying to get this guy. It's bad enough you're mentally scarred."

"How?"

"If you don't know, it's better left unsaid. You just finish this job so you can have a normal life with a damaged liver."

"I promise. This assignment is a no-brainer. No violence, promise." He knew that wouldn't satisfy his mother.

"There's always the danger of being discovered."

"I'll be careful. Goodnight, Mom."

Patrick pushed the "end" button on the phone and threw it on his bed. This was the second time he'd been shot in the line of duty. There would not be a third. Company policy. Three strikes, and you're at a desk. Paulo was getting under his skin. But for Patrick to quit the agency, Paulo would have to be killed, and his business, destroyed.

CHAPTER 3

San Juan-Jimenez, Mexico

Rico Suarez went about his morning duties, overseeing the cooks as they prepared his boss's breakfast. He watched them carefully from his seat on the barstool near the island in the middle of the enormous kitchen.

The cooks prepared the omelets with precision, and the air was soon filled with the aroma of the coffee Paulo loved so. The scent of coffee was Rico's cue to start assembling the gold-plated tray. He reached for the brasserie dinnerware and began his task. After he decorated the tray with its customary red rose, he took everything upstairs.

He walked to the end of the second floor, knocked on a door, and waited for Paulo's answer.

"Come in."

Rico entered the large bedroom, placing the tray on the nightstand near the bed. Paulo sat up in a custom-designed king-size bed, dressed in silk pajamas and drinking water from a crystal goblet. He had just taken the last of his morning medication. He glanced at Rico.

"Good morning, sir, I bring good news today."

Paulo nodded, reaching for the tray. "I see the cooks have done me proud today." He reached for the Lombardy flatware and cut into the omelet with the gold-plated knife. "What is your news?"

Rico cleared his throat, hoping the man he thought of as a

father would not see through him and know he was lying. "You said last year that you wanted to see your daughter, and that her mother was preventing that. I've just received confirmation Helen died several months ago."

Paulo stopped eating and stared at Rico. "How?"

Again Rico coughed. "She died from cancer, sir. It took her suddenly."

"And the girl?"

"There was a small child," Rico said.

"No, I mean my daughter. Where is my daughter?"

Rico pretended to search his pockets for notes he knew weren't there. He shrugged. "I'm sure the small child must be hers. Why do you want to see a daughter who never once wanted to see you?" With that sentence he knew he had overstepped the boss/employee relationship. Paulo's temper was legendary, and he wouldn't tolerate those kinds of questions. Rico's life probably hung in the balance.

Paulo pushed the tray aside and slid easily out of the king-size bed. "Don't you ever ask me anything like that again. I will kill you. But since I know you've got aspirations, I will tell you. I don't have much time left; she's the only child I have. All this will be hers. Now get out."

Rico nodded, left the room, mentally kicking himself for getting Paulo upset. It had taken him over ten years to get to be second in command. Now there was no way he'd ever be in charge—unless something happened to Paulo's daughter, who either didn't know or care that Paulo existed.

Mira navigated through the busy cafeteria, searching for Patrick. She decided to get out of the line of fire, not knowing if her body could take one more hit by hungry students not looking where they were going. She started to exit the cafeteria and wait for Patrick outside in the hall, but changed her mind when she smelled the delicious aromas from the kitchen. She stood at the end of the lunch line and pondered her food choices. Fast food or healthy? Did she want Patrick to think she was a pig or not? Did she care? Of course she did. She decided on healthy.

Mira picked the baked chicken and mashed potatoes special, and then she looked for a table. The healthy side, as most of the students referred to it, didn't have all the noise of the fast-food side. Mostly older students were on the healthy side, and she was grateful for the quiet. Being around people was enjoyable, but she treasured silence every now and then. Hopefully, Patrick would figure out which side she was on. She laughed, figuring he was probably knee-deep in eighteen-year-olds!

She had just taken her first bite of chicken when she noticed him walking toward her with a confident stride. He smiled as he neared her. Whether she was suspicious of him or not, he had a nice build. Athletic, but not bulky. Usually an orange shirt made men look feminine to her, but on him, it looked good. It seemed to light up his green eyes and it complemented his honey-beige complexion.

He sat down with his tray. "Sorry I'm late. I was working out at the university gym and lost track of the time."

Mira instantly noticed two things. He didn't have one piece of meat on his tray, and he attracted the attention of almost every woman on their side of the cafeteria. She took a sip of tea to steady her nerves. "Are you on a diet?" She looked down at her own plate and could only imagine what he thought of her meal.

Patrick smiled at her after he took a long drink of milk. "I'm a vegetarian."

"Religious or health reasons?" Mira shook her head. "Look at me, getting all in your business. I'm sorry."

"It's okay. Actually, my job took me to some countries where the meat wasn't always safe to eat. What can go wrong with veggies?"

Mira thought he seemed disciplined and had the physique of a military person. "What branch of the service were you in?"

He took another long drink of milk. "Have you been studying?"

"Ulcer?" Mira wondered why he didn't answer her previous question. She didn't think she was being overly nosy.

"No," he answered, "I have a sensitive stomach." He took a few bites of salad before continuing the conversation. "I went over my notes last night. I think I'm ready for this test."

"My daughter was sick last night," she admitted, remembering how she previously had accused him of not studying. "I lost my study time to a tummyache."

"Y-you have a daughter?"

Mira sighed. "Yes, Reese is six going on sixty. She won't often interfere with my studying, if that's what you're worried about."

"No, I just wasn't aware. I-I mean, I've never heard you mention her in class."

She thought he was too quiet when she and her classmates chatted before class started. "No, I'm here to learn, not brag about my daughter."

Patrick nodded. "I guess bragging rights belong to your husband?"

"I'm not married anymore. I have been divorced about five years. But bragging rights used to belong to my mother. In her eyes, Reese could do no wrong, and of course, she was the smartest child around the neighborhood." She smiled at the memories of her mother.

"I bet your mom is proud of you, too."

"I hope so. She passed away six months ago." Mira glanced away. "I'm sorry. Sometimes, it seems just like yesterday when—"

"Why? I'm the one that's sorry," he apologized. "I didn't mean to dredge up unhappy memories." He reached across the table and caressed her hand. "I know what's it's like to lose someone close to you. I'm sure she's proud of you."

Mira nodded. "Where would you like to study? Here or upstairs in the study room?" Mira rose to put her tray away.

She surprised him by taking his tray as well. As she returned to the table, she caught him looking at her. *Surely this very attractive man is not checking me out!*

"We can study here." Patrick retrieved his backpack and got out his study notes as she did the same. He watched as she took out her cell phone and checked the display. "I always check to make sure the school hasn't called," she explained.

"I'm sure Reese is all right," Patrick reassured her. "Why don't we start with the notes?"

Mira nodded and pulled out her brightly colored folder, placing it on the table. She assembled her papers and giggled. "I know I shouldn't use so many different-colored highlighters, but I was playing with my daughter. If it's highlighted in pink, it's definitely on the test. Yellow is something the professor stressed in class. Green means someone asked about it in class, and blue means it was interesting to me."

"Why don't you use a tape recorder? It would be easier for you, and you wouldn't have to write out all those notes."

"I like to write things down," she explained as she thumbed through her papers.

After two hours of smelling Patrick's cologne and looking into his dreamy eyes, Mira announced she had to leave to pick up her daughter. He volunteered to walk her to her car. "I'm parked in that area."

"H-how did you know where I parked?"

"I'm sure you're parked in commuter parking, right?"

Mira relaxed. "Yes, I am." She gathered her backpack, and they exited the building.

As they walked through the maze of students, she knew this was her chance to dig up some dirt on him and maybe ease her own curiosity. "Where are you from?"

"Virginia."

"Were you in the military?"

"Yes."

"Married?"

"No."

"Kids?"

"No."

"Can you speak in more than one-word answers?"

He smiled. "Yes, I can. Sorry. Occupational hazard."

"What did you used to do?" Mira asked, hoping for some real information.

"You could say I was part of the police," he answered vaguely.

Well it wasn't a one-word answer, but the result was the same, she thought. "Why did you come to Fort Worth?"

He shrugged his broad shoulders. "Just picked a place, I guess. Seems nice enough. What about you?"

Mira couldn't imagine living anywhere else. "This is home. I was born here. My roots are here. My uncle and his wife are here, and so is my best friend." They neared her car, and she disarmed the alarm. To her surprise he did the same, since he was parked next to her. She should have known he had a sports car, a convertible no less. Probably trying to hang on to his youth, she supposed. "Nice car."

"Yes, it's my baby," he said proudly. "You have Reese. I have this." He rubbed his hand against the rooftop of the car. "Hey, I have an idea," he said casually. "Why don't you show me around this city? I pretty much know how to get to class, then go back to my apartment, and that's it."

She wanted nothing more than to be in his company, but she had responsibility in the form of Reese. "Maybe another time." She hoped he'd offer an alternative, but he didn't.

"Maybe." Patrick nodded and slid into the sports car, taking off without another word.

Mira watched him as he drove away. For the first time since her brief courtship, marriage, and ultimate divorce, she was thinking about a man. But she had so much going on with Reese and trying to get settled in their new life, did she really have time to devote to dating?

The prospect scared her out of her mind.

* * *

Mira watched Reese as she ate her dinner. They sat in the dining room and occupied two of the eight chairs at the large cherrywood table. The room also doubled as their study area. But that night, Mira had a different agenda in mind. She made all of Reese's favorites for dinner. A sure sign of guilt, she knew. Reese was on her second hot dog when Mira broached the subject of the party.

"Reese, how would you feel about me going to a party?"

Her daughter shrugged her shoulders and continued eating.

"Would you like to spend the night at Shara's next Friday night?" Mira picked at her salad, wanting a hot dog smothered in chili, cheese, and onions, and accompanied by a plate of French fries, more than anything, but her latest battle with the scale was not in her favor.

"Why can't I go with you?"

"Because honey, this is a party for adults only. Children are not allowed inside the club. You can see Angela and John." She mentioned Shara's children, hoping it would make Reese more agreeable. "Don't you miss them?"

Reese shrugged. "Who will protect you?" She reached for another hot dog. After she slathered it with ketchup, she began eating it.

Mira watched her daughter in amazement. "That's your last hot dog. You'll have another tummyache if you eat any more."

Reese looked at her with big brown eyes and then nodded. "My teacher sent a note for you on my backpack."

Mira's heart started racing. "And you just thought to tell me now? We've been home three hours. You know better than that, Reese."

"I'm sorry, Mommy, I forgot." She took a drink of milk and set her glass down. She let out a very unladylike sound and giggled, leaning back in the chair and laughing harder until she saw Mira's look of displeasure. "Sorry," Reese said in a quiet voice.

"Where did you learn that disgusting sound?" Mira tried to keep a straight face, but lost the battle and started laughing, remembering her own beer-induced burps from her younger days.

"At school. This boy in my class was showing us to how do it today. He got in trouble for it."

"I'm paying top dollar for my daughter to go to a private school so she can learn how to burp?" Mira tried to be stern but understanding. "That is not a very nice sound. Young ladies shouldn't do it, anyway. I don't want to hear you do that again." Mira knew that was just the beginning of things she didn't want her daughter exposed to but had no choice in the matter.

"Yes, Mommy."

"Where's your backpack?"

Mira watched as her daughter pointed toward the living room with one hand as she put another French fry in her mouth with the other. *It's a good thing she's got her father's metabolism*, Mira mused as she rose.

She spotted the tiny bag on the floor by the spiral staircase. Shaking her head, she went through Reese's things. But the note was just as her daughter said, pinned to her backpack. Why didn't she see it when Reese got into the car that afternoon? Her mind had been on Patrick's conversation, or lack thereof, as they walked to the parking lot.

Mira opened the letter and read it quickly. She sighed. Relief flowed through her body. The first grade was going on a field trip to the Dallas Museum of Art and needed volunteers to accompany the class. She was going to be a room mother, one of those women she always envisioned with no job and no life. Now she was one of them.

She giggled as she entered the dining room with the note in her hand. "Yes, I will go with your class on the trip. The museum should be fun, huh?" She could imagine twenty six-year-olds being bored out of their minds at the museum. "I'll call your teacher tomorrow."

Reese nodded. "Mommy?"

"Yes, honey."

"Can I have another hot dog?"

* * *

Patrick spotted Mira chatting on her cell phone. It wasn't their study day, but he had thought he would take a chance that she would be in the student center. The fact that he didn't have class that day meant nothing.

As he walked toward her, he overheard her conversation. It was concerning Reese. As any mother on this earth, she was defending her child.

"I don't want you telling my daughter anything about babies, parents or otherwise. Her father and I are not together, and I know I'm not the only single parent. It's better that she is loved by one parent than not loved by two."

Patrick wondered about Reese's father. Was he in their life now? He continued watching her from a discreet distance.

"I just don't want her thinking she's unloved," she continued, "especially with all she's just been through recently. I'm not asking for special treatment for her, just for respect since she's still grieving. Thank you." She pushed the button on her phone and set it down on the table with a thud.

He watched her run her fingers through her curly hair in frustration. He knew she did that in class whenever the professor called on her. Maybe nervous frustration, he surmised. He took the chance and walked toward her. She was surprised to see him, but still welcomed him. A good sign, he hoped.

"Patrick, what are you doing here?" She smiled, motioning for him to sit down.

He noticed her Palm Pilot on the table and tried to discreetly read the display screen upside down. "I just noticed you sitting here," he offered as a lame excuse, sitting down before she could answer.

"Just trying to get organized." She noticed him staring at the PDA and turned it off.

Patrick nodded, trying to mask his disappointment. "You can never be too organized." He picked up the small computer and examined it. "I have one, but it's a different brand.

How do you like this one?" He opened the case and played with the display panel. She had one of the top-of-the-line models that also had downloading capabilities, which was what he needed for his plan to work. "I like the feel of this one." He placed it back on the table.

"It's idiot-proof," she confessed. "When I first got it, I hated it. Reese had to show me how to work it. I'm always amazed at how fast she catches on to anything related to the computer. Now I'm lost without it." She demonstrated some of the functions to him. "It reminds me of everything. When I need to pick up Reese, her appointments, and stuff like that."

What kind of appointments could a child have? he wondered as she continued talking. What had Reese been through that any other child hadn't? The answers to all the questions would take time, he reminded himself, and he'd have to get lot closer to Mira to find out.

He noticed another woman from their class walking toward the table, ruining his opportunity.

"Hi, Mira. How's Reese?"

"Pretty good." Mira's expression didn't quite match her answer. She stuffed the Palm Pilot in her bag and rose.

"I just stopped by to tell you about the gymnastics class for kids. It would be a great way for her to channel her . . ." The woman glanced in Patrick's direction. "Anyway, it's wonderful. They meet at three o'clock three days a week. I'll call you later with the information. I gotta run. See ya."

Patrick watched as Mira wrote down the scant information and then returned her attention to him. He wondered why she didn't volunteer her phone number to him when they became study partners. He had it, but he wanted her to give it to him. "So, how about showing me some sights today?"

"I'm sorry, I have an appointment." She looked at her watch. "Maybe later in the week." She picked up her backpack and purse, and abruptly left the dining area.

Patrick watched her leave and exit the building. *What am I going to have to do to get a date with this woman?* He'd never had two refusals before. Why was she so protective of Reese and her feelings? Or was she just one of those mothers that couldn't let her child grow up? He looked down at his watch and noticed the time. He would have to speed up to get to the Dallas branch of the DEA to make his appointment. He also needed to make sure that the bug he'd placed on Mira's PDA worked.

CHAPTER 4

Patrick walked into the Justice Building in downtown Dallas, thankful for the contrast of quiet to the noise on the street. He nodded to the receptionist and headed to an unmarked elevator. After he pushed the button, he counted the seconds until its arrival. Twenty seconds exactly.

Not bad, he mused. He stepped into the empty elevator car, and the door closed. With a swipe of his ID card, the car jumped to life. The doors didn't open again until he reached the tenth floor.

A familiar scene hit him as he exited. Gun-holstered agents were scattered along the hallway. He felt naked without his Glock, his standard-issue DEA handgun. It had become a part of him.

Finally, he spotted a vacant office and slipped inside. He had just gotten comfortable at the computer when he was interrupted. *Damn!*

"Patrick Callahan!" A tall man with shocking red hair that only made his white skin look even paler walked inside the office and closed the door. "I heard you were baby-sitting," said Danny Flanagan.

Patrick laughed at the phrase his friend used, but it was true. "Yeah, Flanagan, you know they sometimes say it's an easy assignment, but it never is." Patrick smiled at his friend. "I haven't seen you in about two years. We'll have to get a drink or something while I'm here, which I hope isn't long. You know how to reach me."

The man nodded and left Patrick to the computer. A smile twitched on his face as he watched the blip on the computer screen. It was Mira. The bug worked perfectly. Every time she stopped for more than five minutes, her location would pop up on the screen. She had stopped at Kirkstone Preparatory Academy, the screen told him. "I bet she's giving Reese's teacher a piece of her mind," he muttered.

"Callahan," another voice called.

Patrick turned away from the computer screen. "What's this, homecoming week? I just saw Flanagan, and now, here you come." He stood and walked to the tall man in the doorway and shook his hand. "I heard you were in Bogotá."

Sean Harris nodded. "Barely got out alive. Those bastards are getting smarter and more computer literate." He paused and stared at Patrick with sympathy in his eyes. "I heard about Mexico. I'm glad to see you're doing okay."

Okay wouldn't have been the word the Patrick would have used after being on the receiving end of a nine-millimeter gun; *broken* would be a better term. "Yeah, somewhat. Just can't go on those benders like we used to do when we killed one of those bastards. It's milk now."

"Oh, no. Well, you could always be the designated driver." The man laughed and left the room.

Patrick returned to his task and wrote down some necessary information on Mira. Maybe he'd get her phone number officially the next time they studied together. He turned off the computer and walked down the hall to his appointment with the deputy manager.

Carlos Salvador greeted Patrick with bad news. "Rico was picked up by the border patrol at Laredo. He was promptly sent back to Mexico. You know, he was just playing with us. We know he's not stupid enough to get caught by the border patrol by accident." Carlos shook his head. "Not when Paulo has a jet and could fly him to the States undetected."

Patrick nodded. Rico wanted Patrick to know that he was

coming. "Yeah, and hopefully this will be his last time to think he can outsmart me," Patrick added with confidence.

Carlos watched Patrick with an uneasy gaze. "How's the liver? Harlan said you were still under the doctor's care, and not much else."

Of course, Patrick thought, those weren't Harlan's guts splattered on the street in Mexico. "You know Harlan. A head wound is just a minor injury to him. But I'm doing okay, Mom." He laughed at Carlos's shocked expression.

"How's the assignment going? Any connections? Has Paulo attempted contact?" Carlos paused his questions and grinned. "How's school?"

"Very funny. I could teach that class." Patrick stood. "It's difficult to feign ignorance." He stretched his tired body. "I need to install the chaser on my PC. Does it work the same as the old program?"

Carlos nodded and handed Patrick a tan, sealed envelope. "This came today from Virginia. Let me know if you get in any trouble at school." He winked at Patrick.

Patrick ignored the sarcasm and left the office to do a little more research on Mira and Reese. When he was satisfied, Patrick exited the Justice Building.

Once he returned to his apartment, he tried to form a plan to get closer to Mira. He could always pretend he was lost in her neighborhood. But she wouldn't be that gullible.

Patrick fixed shrimp scampi, his favorite meal. He wasn't supposed to eat the dish full of hearty spices due to his wounds still healing, but he loved it. He looked over his notes for the upcoming test as he ate.

He didn't really have to study to keep his cover as a student, but if he didn't do well on the test, Mira might think he was not studying. For some reason, what she thought of him made him want to do his best. As he glanced at the notes, he found his concentration wavering. His mind was on San Juan-Jimenez, Mexico, the home of Paulo Riaz and Rico Suarez. He knew that Rico had a flair for the dramatic and loved an audience. What was his next act? Getting caught at the border was nothing. He had probably planned it, had enjoyed playing hide-and-go-seek with Patrick.

He walked into his makeshift office. Another Harlan-inspired room. The small room held a desk, chair, computer, printer, fax machine, scanner, and little else. Mostly boxes of information Patrick had on Paulo and his drug operation. The room didn't look lived in, as his mother called it. Actually, it reminded him of a hotel room.

He turned on the computer and installed the tracking program. As he watched the blip on his screen, he noticed something strange. "Why is Mira at my condominium complex?"

Patrick crossed the small room and stood by the window. He looked onto the parking lot and noticed Mira's red PT Cruiser was pulling into a parking spot across from his condo.

He smiled as Mira got out of the car. The passenger door opened and a much smaller, very thin version of Mira popped out. He smiled as he watched Mira and Reese walk to a condo hand in hand.

Grabbing his night-vision binoculars, he turned off his bedroom lamp so that he wouldn't cast a shadow. He walked back to the window and noted that they went in to apartment 1522 and noticed the resident as the same woman who spoke to Mira about gymastics earlier that day.

About an hour later, he watched Mira and Reese leave the condo and get into their car. He smiled every time he saw that car. Initially, he had thought that it wasn't the car Mira would drive; it didn't seem to fit her personality. Now as he had learned a little more about her, it seemed exactly the kind of car she should have. Something a little off the beaten path.

Too bad her father was a drug lord in an impoverished country and used children to do his dirty work, he reminded himself.

A beep from the fax machine attracted his attention. He turned on his lamp and went to his desk. As he pulled paper from the machine, he swore. "I don't feel like decoding any messages tonight, Harlan. I would have the only boss in the agency that followed procedure," he muttered.

With a sigh, he walked back to his computer. It didn't take long to decode the message, but Patrick knew Harlan's only joy in life was to make his life harder.

Mira walked into the Student Union, instantly noticing Patrick sitting in the lounge. He sat in an oversize plush chair, reading a magazine, attracting attention from the other women in the area. Mira thought he looked especially sexy that day—or was that her hormones in overdrive?

He was dressed in a blue short-sleeved sport shirt and khaki pants, with casual leather shoes. He looked like a model. Mira was about to approach him when a very young and thin African-American woman approached him. Her tight, short denim skirt flattered her slender figure. Her two-inch high heels made her legs look very sexy. She reminded Mira of a very young Tyra Banks, breaking Mira's spirit and her will to study. *Well*, she reflected, *he's not going to want to study sociology if he can study biology with the latest Playboy pinup!* She turned to leave the building, but his voice attracted her attention.

"Mira, wait," he called.

She turned around and saw him sprinting toward her.

"I-I saw you were busy. It's okay if you don't want to study." Why did she feel rejected all of a sudden?

Patrick smiled. "She wasn't my type. She's nineteen, young."

Well at least he's thinking with his bigger brain, she thought. "That's good to hear. I-I-I meant that you still want to study." Why couldn't she think and talk at the same time in his presence?

"How about let's eat first?"

The way he smiled, Mira thought she was the only woman in the lobby. "Lunch sounds great. I'm starving today."

"How about we eat somewhere away from school? You promised to show me some sights."

Mira still didn't know him. He was virtually a stranger. Lunch off campus would be reckless. "We'd better stay here. I study better at school," she lied.

"I didn't mention anything about studying, but okay." Patrick winked at her. "I'm still going to hold you to your promise."

Mira knew that. He had the persistence of a child. He reminded her of Reese when she really wanted to do something that Mira didn't. She was relentless and wouldn't give up until she got what she wanted. "I know, but our test is next Friday, so that has all my attention." Another lie.

"Okay, let's eat here," he said.

They walked in silence toward the cafeteria. Suddenly, Patrick's cell phone rang. A very different Patrick answered.

"Callahan," he barked into the phone.

Mira walked ahead of him, not wanting to eavesdrop. To her surprise, he pulled her back beside him. She watched in amazement as he rattled some orders into the phone, then disconnected.

"Sorry," he apologized. "Boss, er I-I mean ex-boss." He nodded at her and they resumed their trek to the cafeteria.

"What was your job? Were you in the military or what?" She studied him as she waited for an answer.

"I was in the military."

"Military Police?"

"Okay."

Mira knew that wasn't the truth. He was hiding something—or someone. But she probably would never pry that information out of him. Especially if he was in military intelligence or something of that sort, he'd probably die before divulging any vital information to her.

After they got their food and settled down at the table, they resumed their conversation.

"You weren't in the MPs, were you?"

"No."

She hated those one-syllable answers. "So what was it? Were you undercover or something? I have a six-year-old. I can smell a lie, and you won't like it if I do."

Patrick knew he had to give her something to chew on or his mission would be over before he could get to Paulo. "I was in military intelligence." A half-lie.

Mira continued questioning him as she ate grilled pork chops. "What branch?"

"I was in the Navy. I was honorably discharged last year." Lie.

Mira squinted her eyes at him. "There's no ocean around here. You just picked Fort Worth, Texas, out of all the cities in the United States, and moved here? Where do you work?"

"I'm getting my bachelor's on the military's dime." Another lie.

Mira nodded and took a sip of water. He knew the wheels were turning in her head as she took in his answers. With any other assignment, the lies would have flowed naturally, and he would have already gotten what he wanted and left town. What was so different about this woman? *Think, Patrick! Stop looking at her face and think, Patrick!*

"How about you? Where do you work?"

Mira smiled. "Well, I used to work at O'Shannon Corporation in downtown Fort Worth. They own Irish pubs all over the U.S., but I quit after Momma passed away."

"Well," he smiled. "I guess we're both unemployed." He nibbled on his soy burger as he contemplated his next round of questions. "Since our evenings aren't cluttered with work, how about a study session later? That way you won't have to rush off and get Reese. You could relax."

She tossed her head back and laughed. "Obviously, you've never been around a single parent. After I pick up Reese today, we're going grocery shopping. Then after we get home and settled, we do homework until I start dinner. After dinner, we usually do something together before she goes to bed at nine."

Patrick didn't remember any of his siblings doing all that.

On the other hand, his two brothers and three sisters all had spouses or significant others to help. "I guess I never understood the plight of the single parent. I'm sorry." He felt bad and didn't know why.

"That's okay, Patrick. You don't strike me as domesticated."

"I just might surprise you," he said confidently. "I'll just have to show you, won't I?"

She smiled at him. "Maybe one day."

He forced himself to think, which was hard when he focused on her smile. It made him think of her in not-so-studious positions and doing acts he knew he shouldn't have been thinking about, considering she was part of an ongoing investigation. *Think boring*, he ordered himself. Investments. His parents' anniversary. His niece's birthday. Finally getting Paulo. Keeping his vow to his dead cousin. Slowly his mind focused on something other than getting to the next level with Mira.

"Patrick?"

"Oh, sorry."

"You were staring straight through me," Mira scolded him.

She was still smiling, so she couldn't be that upset, he thought. "Why don't we go upstairs to study?"

She nodded as she finished drinking her water. "Sounds good. It will probably be a lot quieter."

They went upstairs to the study lounge. Usually Patrick sat across from her just to steady his nerves. That day, he sat next to her. Only after he inhaled her perfume did he realize his mistake. But it was too late. He couldn't have moved if he had wanted to, and he didn't want to.

Patrick leaned closer to Mira as she discussed the test. If only she'd lean in just a little closer, he thought, but she didn't. All through their study session, Mira kept a discreet distance from him, but stayed just close enough to drive him crazy.

He glanced at his watch. It was almost two o'clock. Mira would have to leave soon to pick up Reese from school. He scooted closer to her.

"Patrick, what are you doing?"

"W-what?"

"Are you anxious about our first test? You know this stuff cold. It's almost like you already know all about sociology. I'm the one that needs more study time," Mira said.

That was his chance. "Hey, if you want to study on the weekend or something, here's my number." He hurriedly wrote his home number on a piece of paper and slid it to her. He knew this would be an easy way for her to give him her phone number.

But she didn't. She hesitated taking his, but she finally put it in her backpack. "If I did want to study this weekend, which day would be better?"

Was she asking his plans for the weekend, or was she trying to see if he was dating someone? "Either day is fine with me. You're the one with the child."

She took a deep breath as if she was actually relieved he had no pressing plans. "That's true. If I decide, I'll let you know." She started gathering her items and rose. "Well, I'll see you Monday in class, if not before."

Patrick rose as well. "I'll walk with you." He began stuffing his notes in his bag. He slowed when he noticed that she had sat back down and was waiting for him. After they exited the building, he fought the urge to put his arm around her shoulder as they walked to the parking lot.

When she reached her car, she unlocked it, threw her bag and purse inside the car, then faced him to say good-bye. Patrick saw his opening. Her brown eyes met his as her mouth hung open in surprise.

"You're doing it again." Her voice was thick with apprehension. "You're staring straight through me."

He couldn't deny it. He wanted to sample her sweet lips more than almost anything, but a familiar face had come into view. Dressed like an undertaker and hiding behind the large oak tree was none other than Rico Suarez, and he was watching them.

CHAPTER 5

From a discreet distance, Rico watched the couple from across the parking lot. They stood by a few parked cars. He was concentrating so much on the woman's face he almost didn't recognize the man. What was *he* doing in Fort Worth? For a corpse he looked pretty good, and why was he with the one woman that Rico wanted?

But that was how it always ended up. Dorian Martinez had been a thorn in Rico's side for the last two years, and now he had tracked down Paulo's daughter before he could get to her. Showing him up once again. It was bad enough when his girlfriend had left him for Dorian and then dropped off the face of the earth.

Rico watched the couple. Dorian had his arms wrapped around the woman and looked like he was going in for a kiss, but then he looked up and into Rico's line of vision.

He had to do something. What? He could just play it cool, hurry back to the car, head for the landing strip, and hightail it back to Mexico. He wouldn't dare think about reporting this little incident to Paulo. Especially when Paulo had been told Dorian had been killed and Rico had done the killing.

He would kill Dorian before Paulo found out he was still alive. But for now, his only objective was getting Paulo's daughter out of the way. No one was going to stop him from his goal of taking over the business. He already had a plan forming in his mind; he just had to work out a few particulars and get his men in place.

His contact with the IRS had given him Paulo's daughter's name, but that's all he'd gotten. Once he'd revealed a part of his plan, the contact had been severed. It seemed no one had the stomach for cold-blooded murder of an innocent woman.

Mira drove to Shara's house for John's birthday party on Saturday. Her pulse raced as she neared the old neighborhood. Reese had become quiet, almost trancelike.

"Reese, honey. Talk to me." She reached across the console and rubbed her daughter's slender arm. "I know you miss Granny. I do, too."

Reese looked at Mira with those teary brown eyes tugging at Mira's heart. "How did they know who she was?"

"What?"

"The bad men said 'That's the one, Helen' and one of them aimed at Granny and shot. Then Granny fell down." Her little voice trailed off into silence.

Mira gripped the steering wheel tightly so she wouldn't swerve out of control. "What bad men? I thought you didn't see who it was."

Reese wiped her eyes with the back of her hand. "I never said that. Nobody asked me. I miss Granny."

Mira wanted to change the subject so Reese wouldn't be upset. But she made a mental note to mention this to Dr. Sid on their next visit. "Honey, I'm sure she misses us, too." She caressed her daughter's face, wanting to take her pain away. "Why don't we do something special tonight after the party? Just the two of us."

Reese's whole demeanor changed. "Just us? No Angie or Aunt Shara tagging along?"

"Of course," said Mira. She would have agreed to almost anything just to get her daughter to smile. "Just you and me. Kind of like a girls night out."

Reese faced her mother with an excited gleam in her eyes. "Can we go to the movies and ice skating?"

Mira knew that Reese would want her to skate as well. She didn't like the thought of falling with an audience watching, but Reese's smile made it all worthwhile. "Okay."

Mira realized she'd been so busy trying to fill all of Reese's spare time with activities so she wouldn't think about her grandmother that they seldom spent any time alone on the weekends anymore. Saturdays were filled with trips to the mall, movies, museums, and the library.

"Do we have to go to Aunt Shara's?"

"It's John's birthday party, honey. We'll leave after he opens his presents. Don't you like seeing Angie?"

"John is mean. He always pulls my hair and follows me and Angie everywhere we go."

"Oh, honey. That's just what little boys do. Later on, you'll be wanting that attention from boys."

"Not me." Reese folded her little arms across her chest to emphasize her point.

Mira laughed. She continued driving, noticing the changes in the old neighborhood in the few months since her last visit. The house she had shared with her mother had already been sold, but no one had moved in yet. A few new cars dotted the street. She parked alongside the curb and they got out of the car. Mira noticed a man sitting in a black Lincoln Navigator and watching her.

Not only did the vehicle seem out of place, but so did the Hispanic gentleman sitting inside of it. He looked more like he belonged on the cover of a fashion magazine than inside a black SUV.

Although the neighborhood was predominantly African-American, other minorities also called it home. But the man didn't seem working class, and he was parked in front of old lady Tucker's house. She wouldn't be entertaining a man like that. Or a man, period. Cats, yes; humans, no.

Reese attracted the attention of the stranger. The next noise Mira heard was the screeching of the tires as the man drove off. *What is he doing here?* Mira shook all those thoughts from her head. "Who do I think I am, a detective?"

Mira felt a sense of something she couldn't quite put her finger on as she and Reese reached the house. She had called this frame house her second home most of her life, since she and Shara were best friends and were often at each other's houses. She missed her old friends, but she was also beginning to enjoy her new life. Was she a sellout?

She felt like it sometimes, like today.

Mira and Shara watched the children as they played. Reese was laughing with Angie, Shara's daughter. Mira wondered why Reese didn't want to see Angie more since they moved. In the months following their relocation, Mira recalled Reese asking to see Angie only once or twice. Shara's voice startled her, pushing her out of her deep thinking.

"Girl, who you thankin' about?"

"Shara, it doesn't always have to be about a man. I was thinking about Reese." It was a half-truth. She was really thinking about Patrick and him not kissing her the day before.

"What's wrong?" Shara set her margarita on the table. "She looks fine." She waved her hand at Reese. "She's having a good time. Maybe she just misses Angie and John. Why don't you bring her out here more often? I just can't afford to make the trip out to your house; you just live so far away. You know how it is when you're on a budget. Or you used to."

Here we go. Mira hated when Shara brought up money. "I'm still living on a budget, Shara. That money has to last us a long time, and I'm paying for Reese's private school while I go to a private college full-time. I don't get child support like you do. I'm trying to make good choices for both Reese and myself."

"I know. I just miss you, I guess. You just seem different now. With you going to college and making new friends, I just feel like I'm losing you. You're the only sane friend I have.

You have the most drama-free life of any of us." She wiped her eyes. "I didn't mean to let loose on you like that. Why don't the kids and I come over next Saturday when I bring Reese home? We could make a day of it."

"I'm sorry, Shara, but Reese has a playdate Saturday and a birthday party Sunday." Mira felt awful for not having time for Shara, but she also wanted the best for her daughter. "How about the next weekend?"

"Never mind," Shara whispered. "What is a playdate? I ain't never heard of that."

"It's like a date for kids."

"See what I mean."

Mira was tired of having to defend her choices. Why did she think she had to have Shara's approval? "Shara, we've been friends forever. We'll always be friends, nothing will change that." Mira couldn't believe Shara was acting more like a jealous lover than her friend. *A friend is supposed to be happy for you,* she thought.

"I guess. I was just hatin' on you. I'm sorry. We have been through a lot together. Single parenthood, no-good men. Speaking of, how's the study partner?"

Mira blushed but remained silent.

Shara studied her face and gasped. "He made a move on you!"

"He almost kissed me yesterday."

"What do you mean, almost?"

Mira shrugged, not wanting to admit she was a little hurt when Patrick didn't kiss her. "He had that look in his eyes, but something happened and he kind of got distracted."

Shara leaned back in her chair. "Details. Did he ask you out on a date? I guess you're not suspicious of him anymore?"

"No, he didn't, but yes, I'm still suspicious of him. He asked me to show him the sights of Fort Worth. Was that his way of asking for a date?"

"Is there blond hair under all that curly black mane? I always thought you had too much hair, and now it's cutting off the oxygen supply to your brain." Shara laughed. "Of course that was his way of asking you."

Mira shook her head. "It's been ages since I have even thought about a man."

"You've been divorced over five years. What you did took guts. Not many women with a newborn would leave their husband."

"I know. I tried to make it work. We married too soon, but he had swept me off my feet. But all that changed when I found out I was pregnant with Reese. Then he became someone else, claiming he didn't want children. I didn't want her growing up feeling unloved and unwanted. It was for the best," Mira reflected. Now she could smile about it. "I don't regret Reese, she's been a joy. I just wish—"

"He told you he didn't want Reese?" Shara asked, shocked.

"Yes. But that's over. Patrick is like Jonathan. Too good-looking for his own good."

"Sounds like Patrick wants you," Shara teased.

Mira shook her head. "No, it's because we study together, and he really doesn't know anyone else, that's all." Mira wanted to get off the subject of Patrick Callahan or she'd start having those hot flashes that had nothing to do with the unseasonably warm weather. "How's John enjoying his fourth birthday?"

Shara stared at her son. "Like any other kid, wanting more gifts. You and Reese bought him way too much stuff. Mira, you have been more than generous to us."

"You're like my sister," Mira said truthfully. "Your family is my family. You have to give me some advice on Patrick."

Shara stared at her. "Like what?"

"You know, should I call him tomorrow? He wants to get together and study for the test. Should I? Was that him trying to ask me again?"

Shara didn't answer her, but gave her a look of disbelief. She rose, stood behind Mira, and began running her hands through Mira's hair.

"Shara, what are you doing?"

"Looking for blond roots!"

Mira playfully slapped her friend's hands away. "I know I'm slow. It's from lack of practice. I don't think I'm calling him." Mira knew she would and hoped Shara would talk her out of it.

Shara returned to her chair and stared at Mira. "I know you, Kasmira Brenton. You have a good heart, you deserve a man with a big—"

"Shara!"

"Heart," Shara laughed boisterously. "I was going to say you deserve a man with a big heart."

After Mira and Reese left the birthday party, Mira hoped Reese had forgotten about their plans and that they could go home and take a nap. She decided not to bring the subject up unless Reese did.

"Mommy, are we going to the movies?" Reese asked, destroying Mira's hopes.

There went the nap and the dream of a nice quiet evening. "Of course," Mira sighed. "How about at the mall near the house?"

Reese nodded and settled in her seat. "Okay. Can we eat there, too?"

Mira shook her head. "Didn't you eat at the party?"

"Yes."

"We'll eat after the movie, okay?"

Reese nodded and continued looking out of the window at the scenery as Mira drove. "What do you think Granny's doing in heaven? Angie says she's watching us."

"That's true, honey. She's watching over us, making sure we're fine and nothing bad happens to us." Mira wanted to get Reese's mind off her grandmother. "Did you have fun at the party?"

Reese shrugged her small shoulders. "I guess. Sometimes

I miss Angie and John, but I think I'd rather play with my new friends."

"Why?"

"Because Ashley likes to go skating, and we play on the computer and stuff like that. Angie wants to talk about boys. I don't like them."

Mira noticed Reese was changing and talked to Ashley, her new friend at school, almost every night. "Honey, I don't mind who you're friends with as long you like them and they don't get you into trouble."

Reese nodded.

Mira wondered why she couldn't follow her own advice.

As they watched the latest kid movie, Mira's heart swelled at Reese's joyous laughter. Maybe she was slowly on her way back to being her usual cheerful self. Mira could only hope.

When they walked out of the theater, Mira thought she saw Patrick in the crowd. "I'm just crazy," she muttered to herself. He probably didn't live out there anyway. *Where does he live*?

"Can we eat there?" Reese pointed to the pizza stand. "We haven't had pizza in a while," she hinted.

"You should eat something healthy. You had nothing but junk at the party." Reese's big, adorable eyes tugged at her heart, like they always did, making her a soft touch for whatever her daughter wanted. "All right," Mira gave in, "we'll have pizza tonight, but tomorrow, we're eating healthy food. Nothing but vegetables," she threatened.

Reese agreed, already knowing Mira wouldn't live up to her threat.

After they got their food, Mira was amazed as Reese ate three large slices of pepperoni pizza. Reese had also eaten a hot dog during the movie.

An hour later, Mira held her breath as the attendant sized her feet for ice skates. She must have been crazy, letting her energetic daughter talk her into this. Reese was already out on the ice, skating.

"Your daughter is pretty good. How long has she been

skating?" the attendant asked when he returned with her skates.

Mira smiled. "This is about her third time on the ice. She does seem to enjoy it."

The attendant finished lacing up the skates and helped Mira to stand. "You might think about getting her into skating classes. She's got the build for it and she has a natural grace about her."

The attendant left Mira watching her daughter glide across the ice as if she had been born on it. Mira knew that Ashley's father had brought them skating a few times and that Reese had gabbed on and on about how much fun it was. Maybe it was a hidden talent? Soon Reese was at her side helping her onto the ice.

"Come on, Mommy. It's fun."

"Mommy hasn't skated in a long time, and I've never skated on ice, so I'll just stand here and watch you." She hung on to the wall in fear of falling on her face.

But Reese wasn't about to let her mother be a wallflower. "Ashley's dad taught me." She demonstrated some steps for her mother. "See, it's easy."

She made it look as natural as walking. Soon Reese was back on center ice and skating her little heart out, twirling around like Surya Bonaly. Mira swallowed her pride and attempted to skate. The ice was very cold, but falling wasn't as bad as she thought it would be. A nice man helped her up.

"Are you okay?"

She stood and brushed the ice off her jeans. "Of course not. I must be crazy."

The man laughed. "The things we do for our kids, huh?"

Mira liked his natural laugh. "Yes."

He pointed to his child. "Mine is the one with the Dallas Stars hockey jersey on. Where's yours?"

Mira looked around, but didn't see Reese. "Oh, no. She was just there in the center. Where did she go?" Her eyes scanned the crowd, and she didn't see Reese anywhere. "Oh, no. She's gone." Panic. "Where's my daughter?"

"Calm down. I'm sure she's just lost in the crowd. What did she have on?"

Mira's mind was a complete blank. She couldn't remember anything. "I-I can't remember. Reese!" She yelled her daughter's name. Mira looked around at all the children skating by her, but she still didn't see Reese. Where could she have gone? Did someone snatch her?

"Mommy!" Reese ran to her mother. "What's wrong? I had to go to the bathroom."

Mira hugged her daughter. She caressed her face. "Don't ever leave my sight without telling me."

"Mommy, the bathroom was right there." She pointed. "I saw you were getting on the ice."

In Reese's defense, Mira realized it would have been more time consuming for her daughter to come tell her that she was going to the bathroom than to just go. "It's okay, honey. You scared me, disappearing like that."

"Mommy, you're choking me."

A masculine chuckle startled her.

She relinquished her death grip on Reese and shook the man's hand. "Thank you for your help. I appreciate you not treating me like some crazy woman who couldn't keep up with her child."

"It's understandable. I would have reacted the same way. That's why we're out here on the ice in the first place. Our kids."

CHAPTER 6

Patrick walked down the desolate street. No one roamed the plaza. Out of the corner of his eye, he noticed little children playing a game down the alley. He knew Rico was hiding in one of the buildings; he just didn't know which one. A door opened and closed behind him. He couldn't decide which building to enter first. It felt like a setup orchestrated by Paulo and carried out by Rico. Patrick's brain told him to get out of there as fast as he could.

As he gave in to his senses, he turned around to leave. Patrick was surprised by the small girl, but didn't feel threatened; after all, she was just a child. Her hands were behind her back. She was hiding something.

"Why are you alone in the marketplace?" he asked the tiny Mexican girl in fluent Spanish. With her long dark hair and brown eyes, he thought she looked like an angel.

An angel with a nine-millimeter gun, which was what she hid behind her back. She took a step forward, pointing the gun at him. "That man told me to do it."

Patrick knew whom. And he knew why. "But you don't want to, do you?" He took a step back, knowing what a point-blank shot would do to his intestines and to his life expectancy.

The little angel only smiled. "He said you'd get up." She pulled the trigger.

Patrick sat straight up in bed, dripping with sweat. It had been a dream. The phone was ringing. He reached for his undercover phone, but it was silent. It was his landline. "H-hello?"

"Patrick, it's Mira, from sociology class." She hesitated. "I was wondering if you wanted to get together for a quick study session today."

He was silent, trying to sense her mood. Then he decided, what the hell, at least she called him, and it was a start. "Sure, sure, Mira. What time?" He tried to calm his voice so he wouldn't sound like the overexcited man he was. She didn't mention anything about the near kiss on Friday. *Why?* That had been some of his best work until he had caught sight of Rico spying on them.

"I'm taking my daughter to the bookstore for story time about one o'clock, and it usually lasts an hour, how about then?"

Patrick smiled as he heard the small child in the background. "That sounds fine. Where is this bookstore?"

"Oh, I forgot you're still learning the streets here. Do you know where the West Hill Mall is?"

He knew exactly where the upscale mall was. The three-building shopping center was the talk of Fort Worth and boasted some of the pricier stores in the area. "I think I might have seen it."

"The Bookworm is a block down from the mall. You can't miss it."

"I can find it. See you at one." He hung up the phone, smiling. It was almost a date. Maybe he hadn't lost his touch completely.

As Patrick entered the bookstore, his pulse began to race. A little girl ran in front of him and almost bumped into him. "Hey, kid. Watch it," he said harshly.

The little girl looked up at him with tears in her eyes. "I'm sorry, mister."

He felt like a heel for making her cry. "That's okay. Just watch where you're going, someone might run into you." *Or you might shoot me,* he thought, his memories fading back to that dreadful day in Mexico months before.

She nodded and took off running in another direction. He shook his head and headed for the children's section until he heard someone call his name from the café. Patrick turned around, smiling as he spotted Mira and her daughter.

Mira was dressed casually in jeans and a light sweater. He liked the way the jeans molded to her full hips. She was all woman. Her long, curly hair hung loose and fell well below her shoulders. Reese was the spitting image of her mother. The little girl had on jeans and a sweatshirt. He wondered about Reese's father. She must have gotten her physique from him. She was thin as a stick, he thought.

"Patrick, this is my daughter, Reese. Reese, this is Mr. Callahan." Mira smiled as her daughter offered to shake his hand.

"Please call me Patrick."

Mira gave him a look of disapproval as she shook her head. "I prefer that she call adults "Mr." or "Mrs." as a measure of respect."

"How about Mr. Patrick?"

Mira nodded in agreement. "That sounds like a compromise to me. We were just getting ready to have some lunch. Why don't you join us?"

When she smiled at him, his whole world tilted. "I'll probably just have some tea or something."

"Oh, I'm sure they have some kind of vegetarian meals."

He didn't bite at her sarcasm and watched as Reese dragged her mother inside the café. He was amazed at Reese's appetite. She picked out a ham and cheese sandwich, chips, and cookies. She ate as much as an adult.

Patrick settled on tea and a scone. As he buttered his pastry, he watched Mira as she tended to Reese and ate her food. "You're a doter, aren't you?"

Mira wiped her mouth with a napkin. "Yes, I guess I am. She's all I have. I want to make sure she's a balanced adult when she grows up, not like so many kids these days, thinking the world owes them something."

Patrick nodded. He watched as a little blond girl approached their table. He reached his hand behind his back, grabbing for the pistol that wasn't there.

"Hi, Reese," the little girl said. "Hi, Ms. Brenton. Can Reese go to story time?"

"Hello, Ashley. Yes, that's why we're here." Mira looked at Reese as she finished her meal. "Okay, honey you can go. You go straight to story time. When it's over, come back here."

Reese finished her milk in one gulp and hastily wiped her mouth. "Okay, Mommy." She glanced at Patrick. "Will you be all right with Mr. Patrick?"

Patrick was surprised at her question. "I promise I will watch her," he said, winking at Mira.

Reese nodded and took off with her friend. After she left, Patrick could now have the conversation he and Mira should have had Friday night, or Saturday morning. He noticed her pushing her plate aside and reaching for her notes. *Darn it.* She actually wanted to study.

"I was thinking we could talk before we get started." Patrick retrieved his notes and smiled at the waitress as she refilled his cup of tea. She winked at him as she left the table.

"What did you want to talk about?"

Patrick's thoughts flashed back to Friday in the parking lot, when he and Mira were almost in a passionate embrace, until Rico spoiled the moment. "I think you know what. How about dinner?" He waited for her answer.

"I can't, Patrick," Mira apologized. "I have Reese, and we have to get ready for the week." She darted a glance toward the entrance to the café. "I would feel awful leaving her with a sitter on a school night, anyway."

Patrick took her refusal like a champion, not letting her see that she'd broken his heart. "How about you help me find a gift for my mom while we wait for Reese?"

She hesitated. "I told her to meet me here," Mira said. "I don't want her to think I left her or something." She took a curly strand of her hair and twirled it around her finger.

Patrick smiled, noting her frustration. He leaned across the table and whispered, "You know, we can go find her right now and tell her where we're going to be, or we could just hurry and be back here before story time ends."

After Mira helped him picked out several books for his mother, they approached the checkout counter. Patrick watched Mira intently as she stood beside him. A plan immediately popped into his head. "Why don't we put these in my car and then head back to the café?" Patrick asked, reaching for his wallet as they were beckoned to the cashier stand.

After he paid for the books, they walked to his car. Mira exhaled, enjoying being out in the fresh air, and closed her beautiful eyes. She looked like a goddess. Her curly hair flowed gently in the wind.

"This feels wonderful, Patrick. I didn't realize how cold it was in the bookstore until we came outside." She stretched out her arms.

Patrick tossed the books in the car and took advantage of the relaxed Mira standing before him. He closed the short distance between them and wrapped her in a gentle embrace. He moved closer to her. His lips brushed hers in a tender kiss.

She gasped, stepping away from him. "Patrick!"

Maybe he had misread every single signal she'd sent him the last few weeks and she didn't find him attractive. Immediately he apologized. "I'm sorry. I was blinded by your beauty," he joked, trying to ease the awkward moment.

"B-but you—we've only been studymates two weeks."

She was flustered, he thought. Good. At least she felt the intense heat between them, too. He was more sure when she licked her lips in satisfaction, offering her mouth for another kiss. His tongue teased her mouth open, pulling her closer to him. Mira's hands crept up to circle his neck, deepening the kiss. He felt her full breasts flatten against his chest, touching off electric currents of passion in his loins. His arms caressed her back. He slowly realized that they were in front of the bookstore and Reese could possibly see them. Gently and regretfully, he ended the kiss.

Mira stared at him while his breathing returned to normal. "You didn't like it?"

"No, don't ever think that. It was wonderful," Patrick reassured her. "I don't want to belittle what could be between us by your daughter just happening to see us in an act of reckless abandon. There'll be other times when we can just go crazy." He rubbed her flushed cheeks with the back of his large hand.

"Other times?" She reached for his hand, grasping it in hers. "What do you mean?" Mira asked coyly.

He took a deep breath, hoping his body would cooperate. It didn't. His erection was still very noticeable. "I mean just what you think I mean. There will be other times, Mira. You'd better get back in there." He kissed her gently on the lips. "Or Reese might get to learn about the birds and the bees today."

Mira nodded, stood on her tiptoes, and kissed him hard one last time. "I'll see you tomorrow in class." She quickly walked back into the bookstore before one of them changed their minds.

A week and twenty cold showers later, Patrick walked into a nightclub ready to get rid of some major frustration. He'd never been as frustrated as he was that night. No one in his life, professional or personal, was cooperating with him.

It had been seven days since his first kiss with Mira. Their attraction was mutual, but every time he attempted to ask Mira for a date, it seemed something was always there to interrupt them, or she had the most believable excuses.

He needed to blow off some steam and get his life back into perspective. Luckily, he was going to meet some of his buddies tonight for some drinks and male bonding. Well, the guys were going to drink, and Patrick would probably just enjoy the camaraderie of his friends, since the doctor still forbade him from drinking alcohol.

He looked around the smoky room and smiled when he noticed his friends at a table.

"Hey, Callie." Danny Flanagan waved to him. "Over here." Patrick joined his friends and took a seat. "We thought you weren't coming. Maybe you had some homework or something," he joked.

"Very funny," Patrick said.

The waitress approached the table and took their drink orders. He listened as his friends all ordered imported beers, his favorite. The waitress stared at him, waiting for his drink order. The one part of the evening he was dreading. "I'll have a daiquiri," he said in a commanding voice. Then he whispered, "Make it a virgin."

"A virgin?" The waitress repeated loudly, waiting for clarification. "You know that's with no alcohol."

He nodded, acknowledging the young woman. Patrick waited for the guys to give him a good ribbing about not being able to drink. He watched the waitress retreat from the table and silently waited for the first joke at his expense, but it didn't come.

He couldn't stand the way the guys were looking at him with sympathy in their eyes. They were all agents, DEA, CIA, FBI, or some other covert operative, but he knew them all, and they were all quiet. When the silence became unbearable, he spoke. "Come on, guys. You know you want to say something. Say it. I can't stand this."

"Hey, man, it's okay. We know you've been through hell, and we're not going to mention the fact that you ordered a girlie drink." The men laughed as Patrick began to blush.

Patrick relaxed. "That's better. It would have been embarrassing to order a glass of milk."

"Yeah, you would be sitting at another table, by yourself," Danny joked.

As the night wore on and Patrick consumed all the strawberry daiquiries he could tolerate without getting a brain freeze, he thought about going home. "Well, guys, it's been great, but I'm going home." He stood and pulled out his wallet. "How much?"

"Man, you gotta stay," his friend slurred. "Look at the honeys that just walked into the club." He pointed to a group of women as they entered and were escorted to a reserved section.

Patrick watched as a familiar face appeared in the midst of the crowd. She looked perfect. Her silk pantsuit complemented her figure. Peach was good color for her. The women around her laughed as she sat down. What was she doing here? *I thought she couldn't make a move without her daughter?*

He sat back down. "You know, I think I'll stay for just a while longer." He stared at her until she was no longer in view.

"Patrick, who's she?" Danny asked.

"My assignment," Patrick said, smiling. His chance had finally come.

Mira sat at the table determined to have a good time. This was supposed to be a night out with childhood pals, but instead it reminded her of what she didn't like about her old friends.

Five girls from the neighborhood. How things had changed in just seven months.

"Did you see those fine men over there at the table in the corner when we walked in?" Shara asked. "Somebody will be buying me some drinks tonight."

Why am I even here? "Shara, haven't you heard of being independent and buying your own drinks?"

Shara stared at Mira. "You can say that because you have serious cash in the bank and you're not worried about the next day anymore. We normal working women have to worry about that. So if a fine brother wants to buy me a drink in return for a little small talk, I'm not turning him down."

"What if he wants more?"

"You were always Miss Goody Two-shoes. I probably wouldn't turn him down for that, either. It's been ages for me. You know if you don't use it, you'll lose it." Shara laughed uncontrollably at her own joke.

Mira didn't laugh. "Well, I guess I lost it years ago when my marriage ended," Mira whispered, hoping to keep the bad thoughts of her first marriage in the back of her mind where they belonged.

But Shara, being Shara, she pushed the very button Mira didn't want pushed. "You mean when you divorced Jonathan and moved in with your mom."

Mira nodded. She'd had dreams, but they went by the wayside several years ago when her mother became ill and her brief marriage broke up at the same time. "I don't regret any of the things that happened to me. I didn't mind postponing my dreams to help Momma. I think it was horrible that she died the way she did, and after the doctor told her that she was getting better. He was ready to stop her treatments." She wiped her eyes with a napkin. "Sorry, Shara. I'll stick to happy thoughts. I don't want to ruin the party."

Shara stared at Mira. "I'd probably be doing the same thing, if it were me. Why don't you go fix your face?"

"No, I'm good. I didn't wear any makeup." She watched as a black man approached the table and asked Shara to dance.

"See you later, girl. I'm gonna get my groove on." She winked at Mira as she headed for the dance floor.

Mira smiled at her and shook her head. She'd hoped her one night out would be memorable, but it wasn't shaping up that way. She thought this would have been like the old days, but people change. Or maybe just she had.

She watched as, one by one, each of the women got asked to dance. Except her. Some things never changed. She signaled the waiter as he neared the table.

He put a daiquiri in front of her. "A drink for the lady."

"I didn't order this," Mira explained. "I don't drink frilly drinks." She pointed at the highly decorated glass. Pieces of pineapple, orange, and strawberry dangled over the edge of the twenty-ounce tumbler, and the drink had at least three inches of whipped cream on the top.

"It's from your study partner." The waiter smiled as he placed a napkin beside the drink.

"My study what?"

"May I?" Patrick stood in front of the vacant chair next to her.

She was too stunned to answer. What on earth was Patrick doing in this nightclub, this night of all nights? She felt like she was back in high school and the captain of the football team had just asked her out. "P-Patrick, w-what a-are you doing here?"

He dazzled her with his smile. "I'm out with some friends, and I saw you sitting alone. It's nice to see you out in an adult setting," he hinted.

Mira cleared her throat. "Th-thank you for the drink." She watched as other women walked by and blatantly looked at Patrick. She started feeling a little protective of him when she noticed Keisha, the birthday girl, returning to the table. Keisha may have been her friend, but that meant little when there was an attractive single man in the vicinity.

Mira introduced Keisha to Patrick. She sighed, realizing she felt jealous as her childhood friend flirted with him. Her heart sank to her stomach as more of her friends came back to the table.

Her hands dropped to her lap as the conversation continued.

Shara sat next to Patrick. "So, you're Mira's study partner? You know, we have to watch after her so she doesn't make any mistakes. So, you just watch your step, or you'll have us to answer to."

Mira knew that Shara meant it in a loving manner, but Mira felt that Shara was insinuating that she was inept and couldn't tell a good man from a bad one. Suddenly, she felt Patrick's hand in hers, letting the tension flow easily from her body.

"I think Mira is more than capable of making her own decisions." He released her hand and rose from the table. "It was nice meeting you, ladies. I'll see you in class, Mira." He left the table.

The women watched him walk back to his group of friends. Mira's friends then turned their attention back to her. "Girl, he's cute. Those green eyes and curly light brown hair. What's he mixed with?"

"He's not a dog," Mira countered, "he's a human being. I would assume two humans."

Five astonished faces looked back at her. Shara laughed.

"Well, I guess we can see who wants him. He's too yellow for me. He looks like he's mixed with white."

Why did that irritate Mira so? She stood up, needing to collect her nerve before she totally lost it. "Well, I'm going to the ladies' room. I don't know what my father is or was, but he wasn't black. So I guess I'm a mutt, too. You can discuss it among yourselves when I leave." She stomped off.

As she entered the ladies' room, she realized she had overreacted. These were her friends. They never questioned her heritage, at least not to her face. She sat on a sofa, noticing there was a line for the two toilets. A club this size and only two stalls in the ladies' room—what were those idiots thinking when they designed this place?

After she exited the restroom she saw a face from the past. *What is he doing here?* Mira walked past him, hoping he wouldn't recognize her and she could get out of the club before he did. But Shara had picked her up, she remembered, and she needed to call a taxi to get home. She turned around to use the pay phone, but that was her mistake.

"Hey, Mira, you look good."

She stared at the man with objective eyes. She could see why she fell for him hook, line, and sinker over six years ago. Honey-brown skin, brilliant smile, and lips that uttered many lies. He always knew what to say to make a woman feel like no one else mattered. Much like Patrick. "Hello, Jonathan."

"How's my daughter?"

"You don't have a daughter. At least not in my family."

He stepped closer to Mira. "We were husband and wife, you know."

"Yes, I remember we were married. *Were* being the operative word here. You haven't thought about Reese in five years. Why now?"

"I want to know my daughter," he said flatly.

Mira tried her best to contain her temper, but was losing the battle. "So she can know all her brothers and sisters? Yes, I have been thinking about that, too. How many kids is it for you now?" She laughed at his shocked expression. "I met one of your girlfriends at the doctor's office just after the divorce, when you told her to get rid of it, and she was stupid enough to listen to you."

He grabbed Mira by the arm and led her to a quiet corner in the game room. He spoke in a whisper. "I think you owe me something, don't you?"

"What could I possibly owe you?"

A wide grin. "Money. I happened to know that you came into some serious cash recently, took my child, and moved by the lake in some stuck-up neighborhood. I think it's time I reacquainted myself with my daughter."

"You bastard," Mira spat through her clenched teeth.

"I think a hundred grand to keep my existence quiet isn't too much to ask. You are denying me my parental rights. I have a legal right to see her and to get that money."

Mira felt her world crashing in around her. Would he actually keep his word if she paid him? "Actually, Jonathan, you owe me about six years' worth of back child support, if you're trying to claim the daddy role. You still work for the city?"

He stepped back. "What are you talking about? Yes, I still work for the city."

For once, Mira had him off-balance, and it felt good.

"According to my attorney, I can have a portion of your check garnished since you have never paid me any money in child support since we divorced. Do you still want to play Daddy?"

He grabbed her by her hair. "You bitch! All I want is some of your money. You'll never miss it. What happened to that naïve, stupid girl I married?"

"She got a lot smarter after she left you." Mira tried to wiggle free from his grasp, but he had a fist full of her hair. "You're hurting me, let me go."

"Yell your head off, no one is going to care. They'll just think it's a couple thang and not—"

All of a sudden, he let her go. Mira, horrified, saw that Patrick had grabbed Jonathan's arm and twisted it behind his back.

"I think you owe the lady an apology," Patrick commanded. When Jonathan refused, Patrick gripped his arm tighter. "Apologize, or I'll really hurt you," he growled. "One more second, and it's broken."

Finally, Jonathan relented. "Sorry."

Patrick released him, and Jonathan scurried out of the club like a freed prisoner.

"Are you all right, Mira?" Patrick caressed her gently, concern evident in his green eyes.

His touch was so light, Mira fought the urge to buckle at his feet. She nodded and leaned against him. "He-he said awful things to me. I-I was married—" She wanted to cry but the tears wouldn't come. Jonathan wasn't worth it.

"Are you ready to leave?"

"Yes, but I came with Shara. I'll have to tell her something, but I can't face any of my friends now. Please tell them for me." Her voice shook with emotion. "They'll ask too many questions." Tears trickled down her face.

Patrick helped her to a chair. "Sit tight," was all he said, wiping her tears away. "I'll just be gone a second."

Mira watched him through her tears as he went and spoke

to a waitress and pointed at her. Then he walked away. Soon the waitress came and sat at the table with her.

"Mira, my name is Cassandra. I'll sit with you until Mr. Callahan returns."

Mira nodded but didn't speak. She watched as the waitress counted her tips as she sat in the chair. Several men tried to order beers, but Cassandra only shook her head. "Sorry, guys, it will be a few minutes."

How could Patrick persuade a waitress to give up tips to sit with a babbling woman? In any case, soon Patrick returned, and the waitress made her exit when he approached the table.

CHAPTER 7

Patrick concentrated on the drive to Mira's house instead of staring at the woman in the passenger seat. He wanted to reach over and hold her hand for comfort, but thought it would only make matters worse, so he did the next best thing. He turned on his stereo and tuned in to the local jazz station. "You'll have to give me directions to your house," he said as the music played softly.

Mira shifted position in the leather seat. "Take a left on Riverdale Drive, then a right on Canal Street. It's 4995 Canal," she whispered. She took a tissue out of her compact purse and blew her nose.

He pretended he hadn't been in her neighborhood at least a dozen times before as he asked the street name again. He was glad she was in such a mental state that she wouldn't ask too many questions.

Her cell phone rang, shattering the quiet atmosphere of the car. "H-Hello," she whispered into the phone. "I'm fine. Okay. Bye," she said in a short tone. She ended the call and took a deep breath, letting the phone fall to the floor.

Patrick wished he knew the whole story. He did know it had nothing to do with Paulo and everything to do with him. His mind quickly faded to the moment in the club when his practical side had left him and the man in him wanted to protect Mira. Patrick had happened to be returning from the men's room when he heard the end of her conversation with the tall stranger and he had reacted. All Patrick knew now was that she was upset and he would do anything to comfort her.

"Mira, if you want to talk, I'm a good listener," he offered. Knowing that she would probably send him home, he braced himself for the usual refusal.

"That would be nice, but not right now." She blew her nose again. "Thank you for rescuing me. I don't know what he would have done to me."

"Who was he?" Patrick turned down the street and soon parked in front of her house.

"I'd rather not talk about it, if you don't mind," she said with finality in her voice.

He did mind, but he nodded and climbed out of the car. He walked around to her side and opened the door. As he helped her out, the streetlights illuminated her face, making her look even more vulnerable. He fought the urge to take her in his arms and kiss away the hurt. "Are you sure you still want me to come in?"

She nodded and walked to the house.

By the time he caught up to her, she was inside the house. He locked her front door and joined her on the plaid couch.

"Mira, what's wrong? I know we haven't known each other long, but sometimes an objective ear is good." Patrick hoped she'd trust him enough to talk. He wanted so badly to help her.

She took a deep breath leaning back against the couch. "If I start babbling, I just might not stop."

"I don't have any other plans," Patrick said hopefully. He turned and faced her, picking up her hand. He gently caressed it with his.

Mira sat up and tried to compose herself. "Well, I wanted this night out to be fun, since I rarely get to go out with adults without Reese in tow. But it was anything but fun. Friends are supposed to be happy for you, aren't they? I grew up with them, but I never felt I belonged with them. They always try to make me feel guilty because I want to give my daughter a better life."

"Then they're not your friends," Patrick said simply. She

stared at him and Patrick thought she would tell him to get out of her house and mind his own business.

She smiled through her tears. "I know. They're friends, just not the ones I need at this moment." She sighed and looked at the square clock above the fireplace. "Thank you, Patrick."

"For what?"

"You don't how many times my mother told me that when I was growing up," Mira said. "But you know how it is when you're young. You think you know everything, and your mother doesn't know what she's talking about. But now as I look back on it, I just seem to want more than they do, from the way we treat our kids to our attitudes about men. I guess I have changed."

"What are your attitudes about men?" Patrick didn't like that phrase. Did she mean the kiss meant nothing?

Mira stood. "Why don't I fix us something to eat?"

Patrick nodded and followed her into the kitchen. He was amazed at the size of it, and it was immaculate. *Not even a dirty plate on the marble countertop,* he thought as he continued to watch her move around the large room. He sat at the small kitchen table. It contrasted with the large dining room she had. This was for just her and Reese. The butcher-block table was cozy and looked like it had seen better days. He realized it must have been her mother's. She opened the stainless steel refrigerator door, gazing inside.

"You didn't answer my question, Mira," Patrick persisted. What are your attitudes about men? Are you a man-hater?"

She laughed her cheery laugh that jump-started his heart and spoke. "No, I like men. I just think a woman should never depend on one. It can only lead to trouble. I did, and got swept into a marriage that was dead from the beginning. We were divorced just after Reese was born."

So that was who that guy was, Patrick realized. "So every guy is like that one man?"

"No, I don't judge by him, or you wouldn't be sitting in my

kitchen right now," she said frankly. "How about an omelet? You eat eggs, right?"

Patrick nodded and watched as she quickly made omelets packed with cheese, onions, and mushrooms. After she placed one in front of him, she also poured him a glass of milk. "Would you prefer orange juice?" After he told her no, she handed him the glass.

"Thank you, Mira." He tasted the cheese omelet. "This is delicious." A few bites later, he was done, and he watched her eat hers at a much slower pace. "This is a nice house."

"Thank you." She stood and put the plates in the sink, then led him back to the living room so they could sit on the couch.

He studied her. She was more relaxed and seemed like the Mira he had encountered in class. The woman who made him take cold showers three times a day. "I'd better get going," Patrick said, trying to make his getaway. He rose and started looking around for his car keys.

Mira stood also. "Please stay."

The way she looked, sensual mixed with apprehensive, he wanted to take her upstairs and make love to her many times, but he knew that wasn't what she needed. She was an assignment, he reminded himself. Not a date.

"No, I'd better go, for both our sakes," Patrick said. He picked up the keys and walked toward the front door. He spoke without facing her. "You know I want more than this study partner crap, but your hands are full right now. I don't want you to think that I'm like the rest of the men you've met." He turned and faced her. "Mira, I think you're special. I know your life revolves around Reese. I'm sorry you've had more heartache than one person should endure. When we're together, and we will be, I want it to be happy, not because I saved you, but because you care for me." He turned and took the remaining steps to the door.

"Patrick, please stay." She caught up to him just as he opened the front door, placing a gentle hand on his shoulder.

Her hand felt like a cattle brand on his body. He turned and faced her. Neither said a word. He leaned down and kissed her hungrily.

She moaned as he caressed her body. His hands had slipped under her top and were headed for the clasp on her bra when she spoke.

"P-Patrick." She massaged his shirt-covered chest. She slid her hands beneath his shirt, feeling his firm abdomen.

He abandoned her bra as his stomach muscles clenched with excitement as she glided over his surgical scars. She made eye contact with him, then lifted his shirt.

"My God! What happened to you?" She ran her fingers across the scars as she waited for his answer. "It looks like someone has been playing tic-tac-toe on your stomach with a knife."

"You should have seen it six months ago," Patrick said, determined to keep the moment light. He smiled down at her. *What a conversation to have at this moment,* he thought.

She hugged him and then stepped back from him, fidgeting with her silk blouse. "I was worried about a few scars on my stomach. I guess you can't judge a book by its cover."

"I usually don't. Things are rarely what they appear to be." He stepped toward her and unbuttoned the troublesome blouse. When he finished, he stared at her honey-brown skin. "You are beautiful. Inside and out." The one scar he noticed, evidence Reese had been a Caesarian birth, was nothing compared to the gunshot and knife wounds he had sustained over the years with the DEA. He took his shirt off and let her inspect his chest, stomach, and back.

Each time she touched him only made him want her that much more. There was no turning back, he knew.

Mira picked up her blouse and led him upstairs. She held Patrick's hand as she entered the bedroom, then took a shaky breath and sat on the bed. Even with all the scars on his body, he still looked beautiful.

He kneeled in front of her, taking off her shoes and helping her out of her slacks. She wasn't sure what was supposed to happen next.

She watched him take off his jeans, revealing boxer shorts and an erection that would probably make Shara blush. She waited for him to take off his underwear, but he sat beside her on the bed. "Mira, we don't have to do this. Why don't we just sit here and you can decide what's going to happen next?"

Surely, he was joking. A man not wanting to jump in bed at that moment? She started laughing. "You're kidding, right? I thought men were all experienced at this kind of thing."

"I never said I was inexperienced, but I got a feeling that you might be. You always seem to be so nervous when I touch you. I won't force you to do anything that you aren't ready for."

That sealed her fate. He'd taken her heart in one sentence. "How did you know? It's true."

He didn't answer her with words. He kissed her tenderly as he eased her down on the bed. "I want you to enjoy this," he whispered against her lips. "I want to make up for all the hurt you've suffered tonight."

Mira nodded and moved against the pillows. Patrick continued kissing her, and slowly his kisses descended south. She arched her back slightly when he unfastened her bra.

She laughed as he threw her silk bra in the air and it made a faint sound when it finally landed on the hardwood floor.

"Patrick!"

He smothered her breasts in erotic kisses that did silly things to her blood pressure. She had trouble breathing when his kisses continued traveling lower.

He chuckled as he slid her panties off her body. "If you like this now, just wait a few minutes." He stood beside the bed and took off his boxers, revealing his entire body to her. "I hope that smile means you're happy with what you see." He laughed as he moved next to her.

Mira shifted over as he got comfortable. "I don't suppose you brought any condoms with you?" Mira asked as she turned away from him.

He sighed, reaching for his jeans. "Don't tell me we went through all that and you don't have any," he teased.

"I didn't say that," Mira confessed. "You're supposed to have them."

"What happened to women's lib? You're kidding, right?" he asked, mocking her.

She turned over and faced him. "Yes, I'm kidding." She shook a gold box at him. "It was a housewarming present from Shara."

He laughed as he produced a foil wrapper from his pants. "One of the guys gave it to me before we left the club." He reached for her. "I guess we could see if we could use them all tonight."

Mira laughed as she willingly went into his embrace. "Not hardly. I told you I'm pretty much a novice at this. I was married long enough to get pregnant and not much else."

He didn't comment, but kissed her gently, easing away the disappointment of the evening. She couldn't get close enough to his hard, naked body. She caressed his hair as hot kisses translated their feelings for each other. Mira was more than ready for him, but he insisted on taking his time. He slowly descended down her body one inch at time. Tickling her ear with his tongue, he then trailed her jawline until he playfully bit her neck.

Mira moaned at the sensations taking over her body. Her hands fondled his muscular back, discovering new scars she had not seen earlier. She had trouble catching her breath as he kissed each breast thoroughly.

"Oh, Patrick," she moaned, her body writhing to the motions of his tongue as he proceeded down her stomach and to her navel. His hands gently brushed the patch of dark curls below her navel. She shuddered in anticipation.

He smiled at her as his fingers caressed her heat. Her lower body moved in rhythm to his fingers as they darted in and out of her body. She grabbed a pillow as his tongue replaced his fingers and entered her body. Mira rose off the bed, panting, whimpering, begging him to stop, pleading with him to continue.

Suddenly Mira couldn't see Patrick any longer because he had become a blur. She felt him still deep inside her, but now a wonderful strange feeling slowly came over her.

"Patrick!" she screamed as the climax tore through her body like a Texas tornado. "Oh, Patrick." She grabbed his hair in her fist and didn't let go until she heard him grunt in pain.

Finally, she could release him. "I'm sorry, it caught me by surprise." She couldn't look at him. He'd know she was more a novice than she'd admitted to.

Patrick laughed. "I was trying to make you comfortable, not make you pull out my hair." His hands were under her buttocks and he kissed her again. She shivered, but urged him to continue. Her moans became incoherent fragments of gibberish.

He rose above her and entered her body with one sure push. He kissed her as he moved in and out of her body. Instinctively, she wrapped her legs around him, driving him deeper inside her. He increased the tempo as his own orgasm neared. He closed his eyes and surged into Mira, enjoying the fact that she was right with him, stroke for delicious stroke. He gave in to the desire and let his body flow. Panting like a marathon runner, he faced her with a dangerous look of mischief in his eyes. He moved her legs.

"Patrick, what are you doing?"

"Well if you move a little to the right, you'll soon see, or *feel* might be a better word." She let him guide her body until it was in the correct position.

Soon gasps filled the air.

"Hurt?"

Mira shook her head. He felt good, she thought. Too good. She kissed him softly, loving the new position. To her surprise, he wrapped her in a tight embrace, crushing his body to hers. Mira shifted her position gently, making Patrick moan. His hands were at either side of her waist, controlling her movements. She moved against him, enjoying the sounds he made. He reached for her face and kissed her as their fight for control was nearly lost. When he positioned her legs around him and he surged deep inside her, Mira couldn't contain her joy as she had another orgasm.

"I hope you can handle another one," he growled. He increased his tempo, as his own release was near.

With each stroke Mira didn't think she'd be able to handle the next one, but she surprised herself. The weight of his body against hers made her feel oddly comfortable, like nothing could hurt her. Except the man that made her feel safe.

Later, as they cuddled each other and prepared to fall asleep, Mira wanted to clear the air. "Tonight, that guy was Jonathan, my ex-husband. I haven't seen him in over five years."

Patrick stroked her with gentle hands as they spooned. "Why? Reese seems like a great kid."

Mira tried not to walk down memory lane. That would only bring tears. "We married after dating a few months. At the time, I thought it was love. I should have known better, but I was blinded by his charm. But once Reese was on the way, everything changed. He said he was too afraid of fatherhood to stay married. I tried to make it work for a while, but in the end I filed for divorce and moved back home. Reese was six months old."

"That bastard. How could he say those things?"

"Jonathan is an immature man who doesn't want to grow up. I've heard he has more children around, but I didn't want Reese to think he didn't love her, so I don't talk about him." She turned over and faced him. "I don't regret having Reese. I would like her to know her father, but I just wish he weren't Jonathan."

"He's just her biological father. Any man can plant a seed. Honestly, I don't think Reese has missed anything by not knowing him. She seems like a happy little girl."

"I've worked very hard at making sure her life is as normal as it can be. After her seeing my mother die, it has been hard." She rested her head on Patrick's chest, massaging the scars.

His hands roamed her naked body. "Do my scars bother you?"

"No, I feel bad for the pain you suffered." She kissed each scar on his stomach and chest gently before moving to the next one. "You have a beautiful body." She continued kissing him, and was just about to head south when he stopped her. He pulled her back on top of him. "You can only have one lesson per session," he smiled. "We'll save that for the next time. But for now we'll review what we've learned tonight," he said reaching for another condom.

After he hastily slipped the latex onto his erection, he held his arms out for her. She climbed on top of him and he guided her onto his body and surged deep inside her, taking her straight to paradise.

CHAPTER 8

Mira watched Patrick as he slept. Instead of answers, she had more questions about him. How did he get all those scars? He seemed very intelligent, so why was he just now getting his bachelor's degree? Was he like her, and had too many family responsibilities to think about college until now? Why had she just made love with a man she barely knew? She didn't get to think about any of those questions nagging her because Patrick's body attracted her attention.

His still form started shaking. He mumbled something in his sleep. Mira leaned closer to hear.

He started to toss and turn, shaking the bed. "Please, don't shoot me! You don't want to kill me!"

Mira touched him and rubbed his back in a comforting motion until his taut body slowly calmed. She took a deep breath, pulled the covers over her nude form, and turned away from him. As she closed her eyes, she felt him turn over, moving closer to her.

"Thank you." He kissed her neck as he molded his body to hers. "I hope I didn't scare you."

"No, you didn't. I go through the same thing with Reese when she has nightmares." She turned and faced him. "Patrick, if you want to talk about what happened, I'm all ears."

He smiled at her, then kissed her forehead. "I wish I could, but then I'd have to kill you."

Is he kidding? Of course he was. He had to be. She rested her head on his chest, listening to his heartbeat settle down to a gentle rhythm. "We'd better get some sleep. Thanks for a wonderful evening," she said before sleep claimed her.

Sun crept into Mira's room the next morning. She opened her eyes and turned over to face the man who made her feel so many different emotions at one time. Was he dangerous? He was probably on the right side of the law, she hoped. The scars looked like they came from a bullet wound. Why would he have a bullet wound?

Mira eased out of bed and put on her robe. Patrick moaned but didn't awake. She wondered how much time she had before Shara brought Reese home. Remembering that her friend loved sleeping in on weekends, Mira reasoned that she had enough time to fix Patrick a large morning-after breakfast.

She walked into the kitchen and began making preparations for their feast. After she fixed some coffee, she started working on the eggs. What did a vegetarian eat in lieu of breakfast meat? She looked in the freezer and retrieved some hash browns.

The back door opened. Mira knew it had to be Shara and Reese coming home, mainly because Shara had a key. Mira smiled as they both walked to the table. Reese greeted her mother with a hearty hug as if they'd been apart for longer than just one night. Mira leaned down and kissed her daughter, suddenly feeling very guilty for the pleasure she'd experienced the night before.

"Hi, honey. Are you hungry?"

Reese shook her head. "Aunt Shara took us to McDonald's this morning. Can I go watch TV?"

Mira nodded and resumed her cooking. Reese took off for the living room, and Mira hoped that Shara wouldn't stay too long and find Patrick in the house. But Shara was nosy and she wanted details. Mira heard the scrape of wooden chair against the tile floor, signaling that Shara had made herself comfortable. Mira knew she wanted an explanation about last night.

"Where are your kids?" she asked, delaying Shara's barrage of questions.

"Mom has them," Shara answered. "What happened to you last night? You seemed out of sorts or something. I keep telling you, you just need to get you some." Shara glanced around the kitchen. "I know you didn't fix all that for Reese. Especially when you didn't know when we were coming home. And whose sporty Mustang is parked in front of your house?"

Shara leaned across the table so only Mira could hear. "Mira, are you going to look at me or what? I knew it. He was being too caring last night. Especially coming to table and giving us that song and dance about your not feeling well and his taking you home. So you finally got to use those condoms, huh?"

Mira sat down at the table. Finally she looked her friend in the eyes. "Yes. I know I don't have a lot of experience in that area, but he made me feel like it was the first time I had made love with a man. It was wonderful," she said dreamily.

"And here I brought Reese home early to surprise you." Shara smiled at Mira. "I could take her shopping while you guys have a morning-after breakfast."

It sounded like a sensible idea. Mira nodded and went to find Reese.

Patrick struggled out of a well-deserved sleep. He and Mira had just made love for the fourth time, but as he lay on the bed, spent, she pulled a gun and shot him. Dead.

He opened his eyes. The wound felt as fresh as the day he received it. Quickly he grabbed the covers and raised them, expecting to see a puddle of blood on the sheets.

Reese sat on the edge of the bed, staring at him. Her curly hair looked tangled, like it hadn't been brushed that morning.

"What are you doing in Mommy's bed?"

"Oh, I was taking a nap." Patrick looked around the room, spotting his pants on the floor. Reese was sitting on his boxer shorts. He was doomed. "Do you remember me?"

She nodded.

Patrick racked his brain for something to talk to the child about. "Did you have fun last night?"

She nodded again. "Why are you in my Mommy's bed?" She shifted her position, but she still stared at him. "Mommy says everyone is supposed to sleep in their own bed."

This was too much too early in the morning. "That's true. Shouldn't you be in the kitchen or something?"

She kept her seat. "No."

Patrick didn't have a prayer. He would have to keep her entertained until Mira came looking for her daughter. Or he could be a wimp and yell for Mira. He continued the conversation.

"What did you do last night?"

Reese watched him with those big brown eyes like her mother's. "We watched movies. Did you go to the party with Mommy?"

Why was she asking more questions than he was? "Kind of."

She smiled at him. "Why don't you ask Mommy out on a date?"

Maybe he'd found some help after all. "Do you think she'd go out with me?"

"How much money do you have? Aunt Shara says that you have to spend a lot of money to have a good time. We're going to the museum later. Maybe you could go with us."

Finally in the distance he heard Mira's voice. *Thank God.* She entered the room, looking like the sexy siren that had seduced him. The short silk robe came to midthigh. Her curly hair was just as mussed as her daughter's. She smiled at Patrick before speaking to her daughter.

"Reese, are you bothering Patrick? You know you're not to bother people when they are sleeping."

"It's okay, Mira. We're having a good conversation."

Mira smiled at him. "I'm sure you would love to get dressed." She grabbed Reese's hand and they walked toward the door. "Breakfast is ready."

He watched Reese and Mira leave the room. When he

heard their footsteps fading away, he jumped out of bed, grabbed his clothes, and headed for the bathroom.

After depositing her daughter in the den to watch cartoons, Mira entered the kitchen, shaking her head. "Well, Shara, you don't have to take Reese. She discovered Patrick in my bed. I just don't know how I'm going to explain that to her."

"Where's he now?"

"I think he's showering," Mira said returning to her task. She put the eggs in the microwave to reheat them. "I can't believe this. I had planned this romantic breakfast, and now look."

Shara stood by Mira. "Well, you just have to learn to balance the two. You'll see." Shara grabbed her keys. "Do I need to give my house key back?"

"No."

Shara smiled at her. "Well, I'll leave you to your to breakfast. See ya," she said, heading toward the door.

Mira had resumed setting the table when Reese entered the kitchen, followed by Patrick. Mira was about to tell Patrick to sit down, but Reese beat her to it. She marveled as she watched Reese volunteer to fix Patrick's plate.

Mira handed her a plate. "Don't put any meat on it, honey. Just eggs and hash browns."

"Why, Mommy?" Reese looked at her mother with those big, inquisitive eyes.

"He doesn't eat meat."

"Oh. There's a boy at school like that. He eats his hamburgers without the meat. I tried it, but it was nasty." She continued fixing his plate.

Mira laughed at the amount of eggs Reese piled on his plate. "Honey, that's too much."

Reese nodded, took some of the eggs off the plate, and placed the dish in front of Patrick.

Mira watched the interaction between Reese and Patrick. She thought Reese would be asking a thousand embarrassing questions, but she was fixing his breakfast, pouring him orange juice. *Orange juice. Oh, no!* "Honey, Patrick can't drink orange juice."

"What's wrong with you, Mr. Patrick?"

"Reese! That's not nice," Mira scolded her daughter.

"That's okay, Mira." He faced Reese and began speaking. "I had an accident a few months ago and my stomach is sensitive to certain foods, like soda and orange juice. So I drink a lot of milk."

Reese made a face that made the adults laugh. "That sounds awful."

"I bet you never had a six-year-old fix you a meal?" Mira asked Patrick as she prepared her plate. She imagined he'd had a lot of adult women make him breakfast, but never a child.

He smiled at her. "Then you'd lose. My niece always fixes me meals when I'm home. She and my mom fight over who can fix me food first."

Mira nodded and dissected the information. Did he mean that he wasn't home often? Why couldn't she take what he said at face value? She knew the answer to that question. He wasn't what he seemed.

"Mira?"

She snapped out of her thoughts and realized that Patrick was speaking. She looked down at her still-full plate and Patrick and Reese's empty ones. "Oh, sorry. I can't believe you guys are finished eating already."

He smiled at her, telling her that she had missed some vital part of the conversation between him and her daughter. "I was asking you what time you wanted me to come back and pick you guys up for the playdate."

Had she agreed to him coming to the museum with them? Where was her brain? "P-Patrick, you don't have to come with us. Did Reese put you up to this?"

He stood and put his empty plate in the sink along with the glass. "I love history, the museum will be fun." He winked at her. "You don't remember the conversation, do you?"

She hated when he could read her like a book. Well, this

time he wouldn't have the satisfaction. "Sure, I remember. I just didn't want to impose on you like that." She stood up and tightened the sash on her bathrobe. "Reese, honey, why don't you go watch television?"

Reese smiled at her mother, but winked at Patrick and skipped out of the room. Mira had the strange feeling she'd been had.

Hours later, Mira watched Reese sitting in the backseat of Patrick's sports car. As promised, he'd picked them up. Once Reese had taken a look at Patrick's car, she'd bombarded him with questions.

"Mr. Patrick, is there a hole in your roof like in Mommy's car?"

He smiled and answered most of her queries. "No, my roof comes off. My niece likes to let her hair blow in the wind. My sister gets so mad when I let her do that."

"Why?" Both mother and daughter asked in unison.

"Because her hair gets so tangled."

Mira watched him. She wanted to ask him so many things, but didn't think she had the right. But they had slept together, she thought. Surely that must give her some rights. Only one way to find out. "How many brothers and sisters do you have?"

He carefully navigated through the museum parking lot as he answered her question. "I have three sisters and two brothers."

"Wow, that's a lot of people."

"Yeah, try getting us all in one spot at the same time." He chuckled as he parked the car. "My parents wanted a big family. My mom got sick, so they had to stop at six." He stepped out of the car. "I'll get your door," he offered Mira.

Mira blushed as he came around to her side. "I didn't think men did that anymore. Thank you." Mira took his hand to get out of the car. She smiled as he also helped Reese out of the backseat.

Reese held her mother's hand as they walked to the

museum. Mira didn't know why Patrick wanted to attend, but she would get some answers to some nagging questions while the kids were on their playdate. He silently followed them as they entered the museum.

Reese's friends greeted her as soon as they were in the lobby. Mira also noticed some of the mothers and a few of the fathers. She introduced Patrick to everyone, and soon the kids were off exploring. Courtney, Ashley's mother, approached Mira with a sly smile on her face. Patrick was off talking with the fathers.

"Mira, I wasn't aware you were dating." She eyed Patrick. "He's quite a hunk of man. Where on earth did you meet him?"

Mira smiled at the tall blonde. "I met him at school, of all places. He's in my sociology and English classes. Just so happens we got assigned to each other as study partners for the rest of the semester."

"Well, obviously he's very interested in you. He hasn't taken his eyes off you since Roger Welsh cornered him twenty minutes ago. If you need a night off or an evening out or something, Reese can spend the night or even the weekend." She winked at Mira as Patrick neared the women.

Mira admired his attire for the day. He was dressed comfortably in slacks and a polo shirt under a sweater. There was no mistaking his athletic build under the layers of clothing. Mira felt herself blushing as she remembered the night before.

"Thank you, Courtney, we haven't gotten that far yet," Mira said.

"Yeah, right. A man doesn't look at you like that unless he's had a taste of good loving." Courtney snapped her fingers at her husband as he yawned. He immediately perked up, smiling at his wife. "Dave has the attention span of a two-year-old. He's already bored," Courtney complained.

Mira laughed at the couple. Since she'd first enrolled Reese at the school, Mira and Courtney had become instant friends. Still, she was touched at Courtney's willingness to help.

Courtney coughed loudly. "Why don't you and Patrick get better acquainted, while I usher the husbands to the sports displays?"

Gone in an instant, she didn't give Mira time to answer. She smiled as Patrick stood before her.

"Hey, there's a salute to Ireland on the fourth floor, would you like to see it?"

He had the enthusiasm of a child, she thought. "Why would you want to?"

"I'm part Irish," he said, pride evident in his voice.

Mira hadn't wondered about his parentage until that moment. Of course, she thought, what man would be able to resist an accent? "I bet your mom misses Ireland. It looks so pretty and serene in pictures."

Patrick smiled slyly. "Actually, my Dad is from Ireland. My mom is from Philadelphia." He guided her to the elevators. "Dad met Mom at the height of the civil rights movement. He said he fell in love with her determination and her willingness to fight for what was right."

Mira was silent as they entered the elevator. "Patrick, that sounds like a great love story. Are they still alive?"

"Yes, and getting ready to celebrate their forty-second wedding anniversary in a few months."

"That's wonderful. It's so nice to hear about people still being in love after all those years."

"Yes. I think growing up in that kind of atmosphere made us realize that love is the most important thing there is. My mom is great. She says what's on her mind, and usually Dad agrees with it."

Mira nodded and tried to swallow the embarrassment in her throat. She had assumed that his father was black, but it was his mother. Boy, did she have that backward!

CHAPTER 9

Monday morning, Patrick's undercover phone rang, interrupting his sleep. He sat up as he answered it. "This can't be good," he murmured. "Yes, Harlan."

"We got a problem," his boss said in his Southern drawl, immediately irritating Patrick.

Well, he was wide awake now. "What is it?"

"Rico's in the United States."

Patrick relaxed. "Is that all?" he laughed. "You knew he was coming." He also hadn't told Harlan he had previously spotted Rico. "This is a game to him. Does he know where Mira is?"

"Mira?" Harlan laughed. "What happened to *Kasmira*? Does this mean that you're closer to her? I was wondering how long she was going to be able to resist your charms."

"I wouldn't say I am that much closer, but it's getting better. Is there anything else going on?"

"Not that I know of. I hope we get to Paulo before he gets to Mira."

"Yeah. I've got a few leads, and I'll get back to you." He hung up the phone and dressed for class.

As he drove to the university, he devised a plan. He could call a few operatives in to do a little more aggressive baby-sitting. But he was jumping the gun. He knew Rico wouldn't do anything without Paulo's permission. As long as Paulo was still in Mexico, Mira was safe. Maybe all the notorious drug lord wanted was a chat with his only living relative.

Patrick took his seat and watched the students filter in. He noticed two of Mira's friends weren't in class. As the professor began handing back the tests, Patrick realized that Mira wasn't in class, either.

He was only with her all weekend. Not in the sense he would have liked, but he saw her Friday, Saturday, and Sunday. Not once did she take the two seconds it would have taken to advise him of her movements!

Whoa, Pat! Cool your heels. Just because she saw him naked and didn't run from the scars didn't mean she had to tell him where she was going. After all, she was an independent woman able to take care of herself and Reese. She didn't need a wounded DEA agent watching her every move. The professor handed him his test, showing a grin that made Patrick want to run for cover.

"Well, it looks like Ms. Brenton has had a good effect on your grade, Mr. Callahan. You had a perfect score to add to your almost perfect average," the professor said, a little too loudly. Patrick knew what he was doing. He wanted the class to know who blew the curve.

The teacher continued speaking as he walked back to the front of the room. "Well, class, our little experiment isn't going as I had planned. The only students whose grades have benefited from the study-partner theory have been Mr. Callahan and Ms. Brenton. Their scores were one hundred and ten percent and one hundred percent, respectively."

Moans filled the room. Patrick smiled as the student across from him gave him a scowling look. The professor wouldn't shut up. "Needless to say, there will be no curve."

Patrick smiled, wishing he had taken the day off, too, but he had to take the heat alone.

Not knowing Mira's whereabouts had begun to eat at him again by the time class was over. Why hadn't she told him? He entered his apartment and went straight to his computer to find her by way of the tracking device. She was at the Dallas Museum of Art. *Why?*

Quickly he called the museum and got the information he

needed. There would only one reason she'd be at museum in the middle of the day. Reese. Pretending to be a nervous parent, he asked the receptionist if the Kirkstone Preparatory Academy was still there. The woman assured him that they were scheduled for the entire day. Would she be mad if she knew he had tracked her down like a common criminal?

Hell, yes, she would be livid. He had to channel his frustrations into work. He checked with his friend at the Bureau of Citizenship and Immigration Services of Homeland Security to see if Paulo was still in Mexico. Luckily the drug lord couldn't travel as much as he used to because of his illness. But Rico and two of his men were in Texas. And Rico would do anything to prove his loyalty to Paulo.

What would Rico do first? Would he harm Reese in his quest to get to Mira?

After his mother gave him some much-needed female advice about Mira, he went against all that advice and decided to visit Mira unannounced. He drove through her neighborhood, just as he always did. Just to satisfy his own dark thoughts. He saw no sign of Rico or his henchmen as he parked in front of the two-story house.

He walked to her front door and rang the bell. The door opened, and he smiled instantly. Reese had answered the door still dressed in her school uniform of a khaki skirt, blue shirt, white socks, and black shoes. She looked adorable.

"Hi, Mr. Patrick. Mommy said you can come in."

"Hello, Reese." He watched as Mira joined them at the front door. She also looked adorable to him, in a much different way. Her slightly baggy jeans and tight sweater only reminded him what he had experienced only a few nights before.

"Hi, Patrick." She smiled at him. "I was just getting ready to fix dinner. Why don't you join us?"

"That's not necessary. I just stopped by since you weren't in class today. I thought maybe Reese was sick or something."

Mira waved him inside and closed the door. "Reese, go change out of your school clothes while I finish making dinner."

Reese stared at Patrick. "Are you staying for dinner?"

Mira watched him as he mulled over Reese's question. He could always just drink a glass of milk. "I would love some dinner."

Reese nodded and ran up the stairs. Patrick shook his head, "Man, where does she have all that energy stored up?"

Mira nodded. "I know. We were at the museum today with her class, and it was like they were all hopped up on chocolate. They couldn't be at a display more than five minutes before they were ready to run to the next one." She walked through the dining room to the kitchen.

Patrick followed her and took a seat at the breakfast table. "So you were on a field trip today?" he asked, like he didn't know that already.

"Yes. I was a room mother today." She sat at the table facing him, smiling. "I knew I should have mentioned it, in case you wanted to study for the next test or something," she said.

"You wanted to keep an air of mystery about you. I understand. We got our test back today," Patrick acknowledged, wanting to know every secret Kasmira Brenton had.

"How did you do? You always know the answer to the questions in class, driving the sociology professor crazy. You know more about sociology than he does. You probably made a perfect score, as usual. You should have taken that life-experience test to get out of that class or something. I can't see why they made you take it anyway."

He grinned at her. At first he wasn't going to tell her, but now he felt like teasing her. "Well, you should know the class hates us. We ruined the curve. You made a hundred."

Mira's beautiful face made a frown. "He told the class my score! What happened to privacy? Isn't anything sacred anymore?"

Patrick watched her as she ranted and raved, continuing to

prepare dinner. "He told them mine, too," he countered. "I made a hundred and ten. I got the bonus question."

Mira handed him three glasses, silverware for three, and pointed to the dining room. "That's good. I forgot about the bonus question. But I'm still happy with my grade. You can set the table while Reese is changing. That's usually her job."

"So you're just using me for my body." He laughed as he left the kitchen. "I can only guess the smaller glass belongs to Reese," he yelled so he could be heard over the clanging of pots and pans in the kitchen.

Mira walked in with a tray full of baked chicken. "I could never use you, Patrick." She headed back to the kitchen, then returned with several dishes of vegetables. She smiled at Patrick as she turned to enter the kitchen.

After he finished his task, he sat at the dining table, waiting for both Reese and Mira. As he glanced around the elegantly decorated room, he noticed the small wine rack in the corner. It probably could have held at least twelve bottles, easy, but it stood empty. The cherrywood china cabinet was full of dishes. Not special dishes; the dishes he had set the table with looked more expensive. Those protected dishes were obviously old and held a place in Mira's heart. He hoped he also had a place there, but he couldn't help but wonder how she would feel when he told her he was an agent and she was his assignment.

He'd never had a problem severing the ties formed with a suspect, but he knew after the first kiss he wouldn't be able to break the ties he had to Mira. He had always wanted a marriage like his parents, one full of strength, love, and honesty. But he hadn't been very honest with Mira about his past.

The loud stomping noise of Reese heading down the stairs snapped his brain back to the present. Reese soon entered the dining room. Her wiry frame was dressed in a sweatshirt and jeans.

She surprised Patrick by sitting next to him. As she wiggled in her chair, he reached around to his backside for a Glock 22 that wasn't there.

"What's wrong, Mr. Patrick?"

"Nothing." He took a deep breath. "H-how was school?"

She shrugged her shoulders and shifted in her chair. "I went to see Dr. Sid."

Who was Dr. Sid? He didn't sound like a run-of-the-mill doctor. "What's Dr. Sid's last name?"

Another shrug of her small shoulders was his answer. "Mommy knows. She goes, too."

Maybe he was a regular doctor, he thought. But before he could question her any more, Mira walked in with a pitcher of milk and a pitcher of iced tea.

After Mira put Reese to bed, she entered the living room and took a deep breath. Patrick was sitting on her couch, patiently waiting for her. With the memories of Friday night fresh in her mind, Mira sat at the opposite end of the couch.

"Why are you sitting over there? Can't trust yourself to be near me?" He smiled at her and leaned back in triumph.

"Patrick, I have a six-year-old upstairs. I don't want her seeing something she shouldn't. I'm not even sure of what happened."

"I don't regret what happened," he said, scooting closer to her. "Whatever I tell you is the truth."

"Even about your past? Every time I ask you about it, you clam up or give me vague answers. Before I involve myself or my daughter with anyone, I need to be sure of what we're getting into." She took a deep breath and relaxed. Still not believing she'd actually voiced her concerns, she smiled.

"What do you want to know? Just ask."

"That's just it. I shouldn't have to ask you. You should want to tell me."

"I don't think I'm the only one hiding facts about my past, if you want to get personal," he taunted.

She was offended. How dare he ask anything after everything she'd been through with losing her mother in such a cruel way, and having to handle Reese still grieving for her grandmother? "What?"

"What about your father? I know your mother passed away; was she sick? Was it cancer?"

He was good. She had planned to use the night as a get-to-know-him session, but he'd turned the tables on her, just like that. How could she expect information from him, if she wasn't willing to give him any?

"Well, I don't know who my father is or was. My mother never said. She said she was young and he swept her off her feet. I was always curious about him. I mean, I know I'm biracial, but Momma got so upset every time I brought him up. So after awhile, I didn't. I figured maybe it was better not knowing, that way I couldn't be disappointed."

"But would you like to know who he is—or was?"

"I don't know. Momma said she never regretted that summer."

Patrick caressed her hand and moved closer. She leaned against him. "What about your mother?" he asked.

Tears flowed down her face at the memory of her mother. "Well, my mom was the victim of a stray bullet."

"What?"

"Momma and Reese always stood outside and welcomed me home. You know that was the best part about work, coming home and seeing them. Anyway, that day as I was driving home, they were in the front yard waving at me. A shot rang out, and by some freak of nature it struck Momma." She sniffed as she tried to keep her composure. She lost the battle and started crying. "If I hadn't worked late that day, they wouldn't have been outside."

He comforted her by rubbing her back. "Mira, you couldn't have known. Was Reese hurt? She seems to have recovered well."

"No. She wasn't hurt. At least not physically; emotionally it's been a little bit of a rocky road. It's just that something like that has never happened before."

"My God! What you have had to live through."

Mira snuggled closer to him, seeking more of his comfort. "It hasn't been easy. I just think about what Momma must have gone through. She didn't die right away. She died a few hours later at the hospital." She sniffed, wiping her tears with the back of her hand. "The medical examiner was baffled at the bullet. He said he'd only seen one other one like that, and it was in Mexico a few years ago."

"What?"

Mira felt his heartbeat speed up, like he was excited or hiding something. "Yes, he said it was some kind of hollow-tip gold bullet that wasn't manufactured in the United States."

"Rico," he whispered.

"Who's Rico?" Mira asked, not liking the new direction of the conversation. "Do you know something, Patrick?"

His body language screamed tension. He took his arms from around her and leaned forward, staring straight ahead at the empty fireplace. "I don't know anything about anything. It just sounded weird to me, that's all."

Mira reached for him, touching his back, but he moved away. Why did him inching away from her hurt so much? "Patrick, you tensed up when I mentioned it, that's all."

He took a deep breath and leaned back on the couch. "It just reminded me of my cousin, and how I felt when he died. You just feel so damn helpless that you didn't do something else to prevent it."

Patrick kissed her forehead as she struggled to get closer to him. She couldn't believe that she had emptied her heart to a virtual stranger. She hadn't even told Shara the horrid details of her mother's death. She felt better talking to someone who understood her feelings. But why was that person Patrick? She knew more about him than she knew a few days ago, but she still didn't know much.

His voice shattered the quiet of the room. "Mira, no one should have to endure what you went through. Be thankful you still have Reese. At least you have the good memories of your mother," he said, leaning over to plant a soft kiss on her lips.

Patrick tried to slow his heartbeat down. It was giving him away. He gathered Mira and placed her in his lap. He couldn't get close enough to her, and he wanted so much more. But the new information Mira unwittingly gave him needed to be investigated, and security would definitely have to stepped up.

Mira gazed at him with her beautiful brown eyes, encircling his neck with her arms. "Patrick, if you want to talk about your cousin, I would love to listen."

He smiled. Grinning, he took advantage of her close proximity by covering her mouth with his own and exploring her willing hot mouth. "I think that was what I needed."

She stood and took his hand, leading him upstairs. Patrick was left alone in her bedroom while Mira checked on Reese. He sat on the bed, taking off his clothes and glancing at his image in the mirror across the room.

He laughed at the thought of him dating a woman with a child. Patrick rarely took second place to anything else in a woman's life, but this time even he was considerate of Reese. By the time Mira returned to the room, Patrick was undressed and waiting for her.

She grinned at him. "She was sleeping peacefully." Mira closed the door. "I'm not going to lock it, just in case," she explained, walking to the bathroom.

Patrick nodded, not that it mattered, since Mira was already in the other room. He turned back the covers on her side of the bed. Mira emerged from the bathroom in a black silk robe opened to reveal a black silk nightgown with bright red roses embroidered around the neckline. As she neared Patrick, she slipped off the robe and placed it at the foot of the bed.

She sat on the bed before scooting next to Patrick. She leaned over him, kissed him goodnight, and turned off the light.

Patrick stared at the ceiling as Mira got comfortable next to him. Her silk nightgown was rubbing against his side, doing crazy things to his blood pressure and making his mind think the most erotic thoughts.

Finally, as her breathing settled into a steady rhythm signaling she was asleep, his mind traveled to how Helen Brenton passed away. Harlan hadn't had any details as to how she died. But the stray-bullet crap sounded like something cops would say when they didn't have any other answers. That bullet came from one gun, and he knew who the owner was. One Rico Suarez, Paulo's second in command, who would do anything to please his boss, including cutting a sweet woman's life short.

CHAPTER 10

Reese's scream pierced the quiet night.

"Sorry, Patrick." Mira threw back the covers and left the room, not bothering with her robe.

He lay there, attempting to think. Reese's screams brought back unfortunate memories. Paulo was to blame for this, he thought. The drug lord should pay for what he'd done to his and Reese's lives.

As time wore on and Reese's cries quieted down, Patrick realized that Mira wasn't returning to bed anytime soon. Maybe she was making sure that Reese was sound asleep. His eyes drifted closed with the thoughts of how good a mother Mira was.

There was a time that thought would have kept him awake and figuring out the quickest getaway, but this time, he wondered what kind of father he would make.

His green eyes snapped open a while later. He focused on the red numbers of the alarm clock in the dark room. Two-thirty, and Mira still hadn't returned to bed. He sat up, swung his legs over the edge of the bed, and slipped on his boxer shorts and jeans.

He walked as quietly as a panther down the hall to what had to be Reese's room. Gently turning the knob, he opened the door and beheld the picture before him. Mira and Reese were sound asleep and clinging to each other. They were half covered with a Barbie doll comforter. The light from the hall illuminated them, making the scene even more peaceful.

Patrick closed the door and went back to bed. His body hummed with the contentment of knowing his family was safe. But Mira wasn't family, she was the suspect, he reminded himself. He also knew it was too late for him to think that way, and that he couldn't stomach the thought of something happening to her or Reese. He had a plan.

The next morning, Patrick eased out of bed and headed for the bathroom. The closed door should have alerted him that maybe Mira was in there, since it was actually her bathroom. But his brain was on overload from the thoughts running rampant in his head. In the bathroom, Mira stood before him, fresh from her shower and naked. Her curly hair was matted against her head and drying quickly. For a minute he was speechless. He gazed at her wet body and had lustful fantasies.

"Patrick! Get out!" she shouted, reaching for her bathrobe.

"Mira," Patrick tried to quell her fears, "it's not like we haven't seen each other in the nude before." Then he realized she didn't want Reese to catch them. "Okay, I'll use Reese's bathroom."

"No, you can't." She tied her robe securely before continuing. "I finally got her to take her baths in there. Use the guest one down the hall. There are towels in the hall closet." She walked to her large closet and retrieved a clean white terrycloth bathrobe and handed it to him. "If you give me your clothes, I'll wash them for you."

"That's okay. I'll go home after breakfast." He walked out of the room, leaving Mira to dry her hair.

As he walked to the guest room, he pondered the situation. How could he get Reese's description of what happened at the shooting without alarming her or Mira or sending Reese into a relapse?

For once, he wished he had paid more attention in those child psychology courses he'd taken in college. But since he hadn't, he needed to do a little research.

After he washed and dressed, he went downstairs and waited for the women. Thirty minutes later, he heard footsteps coming toward the kitchen. He smiled as Mira entered the room. She was dressed for school in those jeans he found so sexy, and a light sweater.

She smiled back at him. "Good morning. Sorry about earlier." Mira opened the refrigerator and began to take out things for breakfast.

"There's nothing to be sorry for." He watched her take out fixings for omelets, bacon, orange juice, and milk. "You cook like that every day?"

Mira turned around and faced him. "Yes, I want Reese to have a good breakfast. We used to eat doughnuts every morning, until I found out how much fat was in them."

"What about Mira?"

"What do you mean?"

Patrick hoped she wouldn't take offense at what he was about to say. "You take great care of Reese, but what about you? I think you need taking care of, too. So tonight, I will take the both of you out for dinner. I mean a real dinner, not fast food."

She sat across from him at the comfortable breakfast table and smiled. "So, is this your way of asking *us* out on a date?"

He shrugged. "Maybe."

She stood and began making breakfast. "Well, I didn't like the way you asked. It was more like a command. Plus, you have to ask Reese as well."

So she has a little bite to her. "Okay," Patrick relented, "I will ask again when the other Brenton woman appears at the table."

Mira smiled and handed him a mug of coffee. "Can you drink this?"

"Sparingly." He liked the way she tried to be sensitive about his condition without taking away his manhood. She took the mug back and poured half the contents into the sink, then filled the cup with hot water.

"There. That should be okay," she said, smiling at him.

Well, he thought she was smiling at him, but he noticed Reese was standing behind him. She was dressed in her school uniform and her curly hair was pulled back in a loose ponytail. She took a seat across form Patrick.

"Good morning, honey. How do you feel?" Mira asked her daughter, placing a large glass of milk in front of Reese.

"Okay. I'm hungry. Hi, Mr. Patrick, did you come over for breakfast?"

"Yes, I did." She didn't remember him being there last night. He watched her as she slurped down most of the contents of the glass before finally placing it on the table.

Reese trained her big eyes on him and became the watcher. She watched him with the same scrutiny that he had her.

"Reese, how would you like it if I took you and your mommy out for dinner tonight?"

Her brown eyes sparkled. "Where are we going? Can I have dessert?"

"That's up to your mommy." She didn't take as long as her mother, he thought. "On both counts," he amended his answer.

"She likes steak and potatoes," Reese offered as Mira put a plate in front of her.

"Well, it sounds like a steak dinner then," Patrick said, digesting the information.

Reese clapped her hands with joy and then began eating her breakfast.

Patrick watched Mira set a plate before him. His omelet had spinach in it. It wasn't his favorite, but he would eat it like it was. Mira soon sat down at the table with a ham and cheese omelet. The three of them ate together as if they did the same thing every morning. That odd feeling of contentment surfaced again. Why did he feel so content with the one woman who held the key to the end of his career?

Patrick shook off those feelings and reminded himself he still had a job to do and a score to settle. But one look in Mira's face made him forget about everything except that he had a date with two beautiful women later that night. "Well, I'll pick you guys up about seven. Is that all right?" They both nodded in agreement, smiling at him and melting his heart even more. Patrick knew his fate had already been sealed the day he walked into the sociology class, and that there was nothing he could do to stop his path to love and contentment. Even if he had wanted to.

Mira walked into her history class in a daze. After breakfast, Patrick had convinced her that he should drive her and Reese to school. So she had let him. Reese had been excited to ride in his sports car again and had chatted all the way to Kirkstone Preparatory Academy.

Mira's heart raced as Patrick drove to Fort Worth University. Would he kiss her? As he pulled up in front of the Student Union, he turned toward her.

"I'll pick you up here at twelve. Then we can have lunch."

"How did you know when I get out of my last class? I never told you my schedule," Mira asked.

He smiled a little too confidently, as if he already knew she would ask. "Because we always meet around lunchtime to study. So, naturally, I just assumed."

"All right, I'll see you at noon." She leaned over the console and gave him a quick peck on the lips, then scooted out of the car. She was determined not to look back as he drove off, but she couldn't resist. "Mira, what's wrong with you?" she muttered to herself. "He's Jonathan all over again." That reminder should have kept her guard up, but it was already too late. She was in love.

Patrick entered Johan's Jewelry store and was immediately greeted by a salesperson.

"Can I help you, Sir?"

"I'd like to speak with John Geiger."

"Yes, sir. I'll take you to his office." The man led Patrick to the rear of the store. "Mr. Geiger has been expecting you, Mr. Callahan."

Patrick nodded, entered a large room, and smiled. "Hey, Johnny." He glanced around the office. "Pretty good setup for doing a little snitchin', huh?" John Geiger had been one of the most notorious drug runners in Germany.

"Ah, Callahan. Who would think I'd be glad to see your face?"

"At least you're on the right sight of the law this time." Patrick sat down in a leather chair. "Doesn't it feel good to be an honest citizen for a change?"

"Yes, and it's all due to you," John remarked honestly. "So anything you ask is never too much. You increased my life expectancy by at least forty years by getting me out of Berlin and the drug trade."

Patrick nodded, remembering the first time he had run into John, almost five years ago. John was peddling heroin, and Patrick had arrested him. But a funny thing happened on the way to jail. Patrick convinced John to turn evidence against his supplier. At first, John told him to mind his own business, in not-so-kind words.

Patrick hadn't seen him for another year when it happened again. This time John was in Italy, the drug of choice was cocaine, and again, Patrick was one of the arresting agents. After a little persistent preaching from Patrick, John had turned in his supplier and the Justice Department had taken over. John was now in the witness protection program.

John laughed, also remembering. "I know you had my e-mail address, but how did you know I was there? I thought that was confidential." The older man looked at him. "I figured no one would find me here in Texas."

"I'm baby-sitting."

The man nodded, knowing it was DEA code for an easy case, and reached inside his desk drawer. He produced two small boxes.

"I've installed the device you asked for. You can track them with this watch." He handed Patrick a gold Rolex. "I know it's a little showy, but it's one of the classics. I thought it was a nice touch."

"Will I be able to track both of them independently?"

"Yes. The mother is the blue dot, and the child is the red one. If they are together, the dot becomes purple. It can track for about a thousand miles, give or take. I didn't have time to test it."

Patrick stood and shook the gentleman's hand. "Thanks, Johnny. I know you did your best."

"Let me know if I can do anything else to help." He waved as Patrick left the room.

Patrick parked in front of the Student Union and waited for Mira. He smiled as he imagined his plan taking shape. A knock on his window brought him back from his daydream. Grinning, he pushed a button to unlock the door.

"What are you thinking about?" Mira asked as she opened the door and slid gracefully into the front seat. "I'm starving." She threw her book bag in the backseat. "I sound just like Reese."

Patrick put the car in gear. "Well actually, I'm hungry too, but not for food."

Mira grinned at him, then shyly turned away. "Me, too."

"Whose house is closer?"

"I don't know where you live, so only you can be the judge," Mira said.

Patrick knew his apartment was closer, but he couldn't take her to his place. He hadn't secured all his DEA notes and didn't want Mira putting two and two together and coming up with a drug lord named Paulo.

"Let's go to your house. My apartment isn't clean."

Mira nodded and stretched. "Sounds great."

As they entered Mira's house, she glanced at her watch. Not wanting to ruin the moment, she put thoughts of Reese to the back of her mind. Hand in hand, she and Patrick almost ran up the stairs to her room.

They stood in the middle of her bedroom, embracing. Just holding each other. She touched his cheeks, with her hands enjoying the soft feel of his skin. Patrick's hands caressed her body, sliding under her sweater and feeling her heated skin.

Mira stood on her tiptoes, touching her lips to his. She teased his mouth open and eased her tongue inside his mouth. Her hands slid in his hair as he returned her hot kisses with just as much enthusiasm.

He picked her up with a little effort and, without breaking the passionate kiss, placed her on the bed with his body next to hers. She struggled with trying to get his shirt off his body, not having much luck. Finally, Patrick helped her by taking it off himself in one smooth motion. He smiled down at Mira, pointing at her sweater.

"Would you like me to help you?"

Mira couldn't speak, but shook her head. She sat up and pulled the sweater over her head, smiling as she reached into her nightstand drawer and retrieved a condom for him. "Here you go, Patrick." She leaned against her fluffy pillows, watching him as he rose to slip off jeans and boxer shorts, then stood by the bed, looking like the most beautiful thing she had ever seen.

He pointed at her. "I believe it's your turn."

Mira eased out of the bed and took off her jeans and underwear. She had always felt self-conscious about her body, but she was oddly comfortable being naked in front of him, even if it wasn't his first time seeing her nude.

They got into bed, and Patrick reached for her and gave her a burning kiss, igniting every nerve in her body. His large hands traveled her supple body, gently rubbing her most sensitive area. Mira thought she was going to burst into flames. Every place he touched, kissed, and caressed was on fire, and she wanted release, and fast. Then he stopped.

"What?" Mira opened her eyes, noticing that he was now

on his back and handing her the gold packet that she gave him earlier.

"You know, why don't you put it on me? This is your second lesson."

Mira gazed at his naked form as he lay on her bed, tantalizing her without doing a thing. "No, Patrick. We don't have that much time. Do you really want me to waste it putting the condom on?" she said laughingly.

He watched her as if he was actually thinking in terms of how long it was going to take. He sighed, then opened the foil packet with his teeth and took the condom out of the wrapper.

She watched as he slipped the latex on his male hardness, and turned toward her. Mira went easily into his arms, reveling in the feel of him against her, eager for their bodies to meet in a demonstration of what they meant to each other.

He leaned down, nuzzling her neck with hot, wet kisses, and inched his way down to her breasts. As he licked and savored each breast individually, he entered her body with one smooth motion. Her feminine heat welcomed him, and they moaned together in utter satisfaction as he filled her completely.

Mira groaned again, pulling him closer for a kiss. By the time he reached her face, her mouth hung open, waiting for his tongue to imitate the motions below. Her hands were on both sides of his face, bringing him as close as she could without them being one. Patrick thrust his tongue in her mouth just as passion overtook them both and was spiraling out of control. Mira's hands encircled him, wanting as much of him as possible as her body jerked out of control in a heated climax.

"I hope you know that we aren't finished yet. You're a pretty fast learner." He smiled as he rolled over, pulling her on top of him. "Need a rest?" he asked, patting her backside playfully. "You look a little worn out, maybe we should stop?"

Mira leaned down and kissed him. She liked being on top. It gave her a sense of power. "No, I'm fine." She brushed her hair back and settled over his erection.

He pulled her down for another kiss and wrapped her in a bear hug, crushing her body to his. Mira whimpered cries of pleasure as he eased her back to the moment of ecstasy she felt earlier. His tongue darted in and out of her mouth, making her only want more. She heard him cry out as she collapsed on top of him. Both their bodies were still for a few minutes before either spoke.

Finally, Patrick chuckled as he opened his eyes. "Now, that's what I call a study session!"

Patrick had the attention of the Brenton women as they sat on Mira's couch. They watched him as he paced the room. Why did they make him feel all warm inside? He should be at his computer doing research, but after they finished their dinner at the Land and Cattle Restaurant and he drove them home, he wasn't ready to leave them yet.

"Patrick," Mira called, interrupting his thoughts, "what did you want to talk to us about? Reese needs to get ready for bed."

"Of course," he nodded. He reached into his pants pocket and produced two small boxes. He handed one to each. "This is just a little something I saw and I wanted to get for you."

Mira opened her box and gasped. She picked up the one-carat diamond earrings. "Oh, Patrick. We couldn't take these. They are too expensive."

He had forgotten he was on assignment when he bought the gifts. He was supposed to be a somewhat struggling mature college student, not a man giving away diamond earrings to Mira and gold stud earrings to Reese. He had to think fast and come up with something believable. "I got a really good deal. Promise. They're not as expensive as you think. Try them on." Actually, they were a lot more expensive than she suspected. They were flawless one-carat diamonds.

Mira stared at the earrings, then at him. She put the earrings on, walking to the nearest mirror to survey her appearance.

"They are nice, Patrick. Thank you," she said, walking back to him.

Reese had also put hers on. "Thank you, Mr. Patrick. Can I wear these to school, Mommy?"

"Yes, now go get ready for bed. I'll be up in just a minute."

"Okay," she said before scurrying upstairs.

Patrick shook his head. "I wish I had half her energy. I'm ready for bed now." He yawned, emphasizing his point.

"I'll walk you to the door." She stood and started walking to the entryway.

He knew an invitation for a second night would not be forthcoming. He exhaled and stood. He met her at the house's entryway and kissed her goodnight. "Thanks for this after-noon." He winked at her. His fingers gently caressed her diamond-studded ears. "Wear those and think of me." He kissed her again and walked out into the night.

As he drove home, he tested the watch. He was glad he didn't wear it before because it made a slight beeping noise. He would have to talk to Johnny and get that worked out. It wouldn't do for Mira to hear the noise. Or worse yet, if Rico or one of Paulo's other henchmen could hear the tracking de-vice. That could mean the end of his life.

CHAPTER 11

Patrick looked around his apartment for any evidence that he could be anything other than what he claimed: an unemployed mature college student. Mira and Reese were on their way over for dinner. He smiled as he hid his gun, badge, and ID card in the top shelf of his closet. Never in his wildest dreams would he ever think he would seriously date someone with a small child, but here he was, childproofing his condo. He locked his file cabinet just in case Reese started exploring.

After a phone call to his sister, he ran out and bought several movies and games to entertain Reese. He also bought a box of condoms he hoped he would get to use, but the moon and the stars would have to be in perfect alignment.

A point in his favor was that it was a Friday night, so Mira and Reese didn't have to rush back home after dinner. Maybe they could watch one of the many movies he had purchased for Reese. But he knew Mira's practical side would remind her that Reese had some activity to go to in the morning.

His phone rang as he was making his bed.

"Hi, Mom," he said. "Why are you calling? You know I have company coming."

"Yes, I know that. I just want to make sure you're cooking something her daughter will like. This is the first time you've dated someone near your age or with a child."

"I'm fixing lasagna," Patrick said.

"I'm impressed. This girl must be a looker."

He smiled at his mother's tone. "I think she's beautiful.

She's a lot different from the women I usually date. I don't like being second place in someone's life, and actually I think I'm about third or fourth. It takes a little getting used to."

His mother laughed. "I like her already." She paused. "So, what's she like?"

"I know what you're asking, and I'm not telling you. You'll just have to wait until you meet her."

"You're going to bring her home to Turner's Point?"

Patrick had scolded his mother about speaking about anything relating to his real life on the phone many times, but she always forgot. "Didn't we have a discussion about locations? But yes, I was thinking about Christmas."

His mother's voice softened. "I know, I forgot. You shocked me. I'm old, I'm supposed to forget."

"Yeah, right. You're sharper than most of the kids in my classes! Some of the teachers, too!"

"All right, all right. You're starting to sound like your father. If you have any questions, call." She cut the connection.

Patrick laughed as he put the private phone in a dresser. He started back to the living room. *What was I thinking, inviting her over here?* He knew exactly why he'd invited her—because she mentioned how she'd never seen his apartment. A definite hint. The doorbell rang and he took one last look at his apartment, hoping it seemed as it should, before he went to answer the door.

Mira smiled at him. She looked like a vision of ebony beauty in corduroy jeans and a cashmere sweater. As she curled her hair behind her ear in a nervous gesture, he noticed the earrings. He also noticed Reese standing beside her mother. She wore a sweatshirt, jeans, and tennis shoes.

As he stood back to let them enter his apartment, he noticed Mira's nervous energy. Her hands clutched a bottle of apple cider for dear life. She sat on the couch and zoned out into space.

He sat beside her and gently rubbed her leg. "Mira, is something wrong?"

Before she could answer, Reese said, "A car almost hit Mommy."

Patrick's blood chilled. *Rico.* "What happened?"

Mira nodded at Reese. Patrick took the hint. "Reese, why don't you watch a movie until dinner's ready? It's straight back." He pointed to the small room right off from the living room. "There are some movies in there, or you could watch television."

"Okay." She scooted off the couch and ran to the room.

Once she was out of hearing distance, he asked Mira again, "What happened?"

"I don't know. When I left the house, I thought this car was following us, so I took a detour. The car stayed with us until we got to the interstate, and then it was gone. I was trying not to alarm Reese, but then another car got in front of us and started driving slow. Then I noticed a car was behind us. I've heard of them doing that on the interstate near Dallas, but I was going the other direction."

Patrick held her against him. "What did you do?"

Mira sniffed and wrapped her arms around him. "My uncle always told me to pull over to the side, pretend to stop, then speed off."

"Did it work?"

"Yes. Reese thought it was a fun ride. I was a nervous wreck. After I was sure they were gone, I pulled over to a lighted parking lot just to get my bearings."

Patrick hugged her, then kissed her hair. "I want you guys to stay here tonight."

She looked at him, eyes glistening. "Thank you. I think I'm too shaky to drive home now anyway. But I didn't want to sound pushy by asking."

"You're never pushy. Please stay."

As they sat on the couch, Patrick tried to slow his heartbeat down. Was Mira's incident on the highway an attempted carjacking, or Rico playing games? "I'll look at your car in the morning to make sure there are no dents or anything."

She nodded, then her whole body began to shake. *Delayed shock,* he thought. Mira started crying uncontrollably. He tried to comfort her and quiet her sobs before Reese heard. Too late. Reese ran into the room.

"What did you do to my mommy?" she yelled, hitting him with her tiny fists. "Stop making Mommy cry!"

Patrick had two emotional women on his hands. Who to calm down first? Mira solved that dilemma for him.

"Reese, honey. I'm all right. Patrick didn't hurt me." She sat up, wiped her tears, then grabbed her daughter. "Reese, did you hear me?" she said, louder this time. "Patrick wouldn't hurt me."

Reese finally stopped pelting him. She hugged her mother, and they cried together. "I thought he was hitting you. I didn't want him to hurt you like those men hurt Granny."

Of course, she likened anything violent to the death of her grandmother. "Reese, baby, I would never hurt you or your mommy," Patrick said.

"Don't call me baby. I'm not your baby!" Reese yelled at him, tears trickling down her face.

He looked at Mira for clarification. As she comforted her daughter, she whispered, "Momma called her baby. No one else can."

"I see I have a lot to learn." He tried a different approach to Reese. "Reese, I know you aren't my baby. But I care about you and your mother. I was only comforting her. Sometimes it's okay to cry. It doesn't make you a baby. You cry for your Granny because you miss her, right?"

She wiped her face but hung on to her mother tightly. "Yes."

"Well, your mom was crying because of what happened tonight. Do you understand the difference?"

She shook her head.

He tried another approach. "Your mom was afraid that something serious could have happened to you, and she wouldn't want that. So she was crying for you."

Reese stared at him, then turned her head away. "I'm sorry for hitting you," she said in a muffled voice.

Patrick smiled, encouraged. "Are you still my friend?"

"Yes."

"Can I have a hug?"

Reese didn't answer him. Tentatively she walked over to him and gave him a little hug, then returned to her mother. "What's that smell?"

Patrick threw his head back. "Dinner!" he shouted, running into the kitchen. He called back to them, "I guess it will have to be pizza or Chinese food or something that can be delivered. Sorry, my masterpiece has burned."

Mira and Reese looked at each other, laughing. "I'm sorry, Patrick," Mira said. "This is what happens when you date two Brenton women. Maybe I could fix something instead." She stood up and headed toward the kitchen.

"No!" Patrick yelled, rushing toward her. "No! I'll call and order something."

Mira looked at him, clearly puzzled.

"I wanted to cook something very special for you, so the kitchen is a mess." He counted the seconds until she walked back to the couch and sat down before exhaling with relief. He was definitely slipping with this assignment. He had just realized his message board was still on his kitchen wall, and it was full of notes on Paulo and her. He had forgotten to take it down and couldn't now because it would be too obvious.

"Okay, Patrick," she said with skepticism in her voice. "I'll let you take care of it."

"Patrick, are you sure Reese will be all right on the couch in the living room? What if she looks for me in the night?" Mira asked, walking toward the bed in one of his old Nike T-shirts and one of his pajama bottoms.

"She'll be fine," he assured her. He sat up in bed, waiting for her to join him. Mira looked as sexy as a model in his

T-shirt. It gave him an odd sense of comfort, watching her strut around in his clothes. While she had been in the shower and Reese had been watching TV, he had finally moved that message board to a safe location.

"Besides," he reassured her, "I have the intercom on. We'll hear her if she has a bad dream or calls out for you." He patted the space beside him.

Mira nodded, slid into bed with him, rested her head on his chest, and listened to Reese's quiet breathing magnified through the amplifier. "I think tonight has tired us both out. Thank you for talking to her. I think you did more for her than Dr. Sid has in the month we've been seeing him."

That name. Although he had another agenda for the evening, he needed to know about the doctor. "Who is Dr. Sid?"

"I probably shouldn't be telling you this, but I'm trusting my instincts. He's our shrink. Reese was having problems adjusting after Momma died, so I thought he could help her with her grieving process."

"Has he?"

"A little. We both have to see him. He says it would help her recover quicker."

Patrick knew Reese was troubled about her grandmother, but he would need to probe deeper to find out what she knew about the murder.

But for the moment, Mira claimed all his attention. As she struggled to find a comfortable position in his bed, every hormone in his body was wide awake and raring to go. He eased her on her back and began kissing her. He deepened the kiss as he felt her arms around him.

"Patrick, won't she hear us?" she asked between kisses.

"No." He eased her T-shirt above her head and took it off. He stared at her bare chest. "You are beautiful." He caressed her stomach and kissed her breasts.

As he slid out of his boxer shorts, he moved next to her, twirling a strand of her curly hair around his fingers. "You look so beautiful lying against my pillows." He leaned down and took her mouth gently before devouring it. As their kisses became more intense, Patrick knew that he had let his guard down and that somehow Mira had gotten through.

Before Mira, he would have never invited a suspect to his home, let alone to spend the night. But she wasn't a suspect, wasn't the enemy anymore. She was Mira, a beautiful, single parent with an adorable daughter. She just happened to be the biological daughter of the man he had been hunting the last five years of his life.

If it came down to it, and it probably would, would she pick her father over him? Did she feel they had anything in common but sex? How would she know? Would she feel a sense of family toward Paulo when and if she discovered his existence?

"Patrick?" Mira ran her fingers through his curly hair. "Is something wrong? You stopped kissing me."

He looked down at her and noticed she was smiling at him. "No, nothing is wrong. I couldn't decide what to do first. Which would you prefer?"

Mira licked her lips and kissed him lightly on his chest as he towered over her. "It doesn't matter to me. As long as you're next to me, I know nothing can hurt me."

He wasn't expecting such an open answer. That only made her more special to him. He crushed his body to hers and started his journey toward loving her.

Mira woke the next morning, exhausted and alone. Where was Patrick? She wanted to lie in bed and sleep the day away, but it was Saturday, the day she and Reese usually spent together. The memories of being in Patrick's arms the night before lulled her into a much-needed sleep.

She didn't wake again until she heard Reese's screeches of laughter. She glanced at the bedside clock and noticed it was past eleven in the morning. She threw back the covers, realizing that Patrick must have put her T-shirt back on for fear of Reese catching her undressed. He was so sensitive about her relationship with her daughter; not even Shara was that understanding.

She walked to what she thought was the bathroom, but it was a closet. But this closet didn't have any clothes in it. It was stacked with papers, files, and photographs. One of those photographs fell to the floor. A picture of a distinguished-looking gentleman in a mug shot. The label attached to it read *Paulo Riaz, drug lord, San Juan-Jimenez, Mexico.* She hurriedly placed the picture back on the stack and closed the door.

Was Patrick a bounty hunter? She knew bounty hunting was illegal in Mexico from those true-crime shows on television. What was Patrick doing with this man's photo? She walked to another door. Luckily, it was the bathroom this time.

After she showered, dressed, and finished her morning routine, she walked into the living room, ready to face her inquisitive daughter. But Reese was in the other room watching TV. Mira heard noises in the kitchen. "Patrick," she called out.

He came out of the kitchen with a tray in his hands. "I was fixing you a little brunch since you slept through breakfast," he teased. Patrick set it on his dining-room table and nodded for Mira to sit.

She glanced in the direction of Reese's laughter. "Did she already eat? I can't believe she didn't wake me." Mira took a seat and inspected the meal. She didn't expect to see any signs of meat, but he'd fooled her. Four slices of bacon accompanied eggs, toast, and hash browns. She smiled at him as she began to eat. "I'm shocked, you know."

He sat at the table with her. "Yes, I thought you'd be surprised. Reese and I ate earlier. She convinced me that you would be sleep for a while, so we went and picked up some food. I can't make omelets as well as you, apparently."

She laughed as she drank her coffee. "That's Reese's biggest fault. She's says what's on her mind at that minute. Her brain doesn't have a filter. I hope she didn't hurt your feelings."

He smiled. "She didn't. I like her brutal brand of honesty. Reminds me of my mother."

Mira nodded and resumed eating. "I guess we'd better get going in a little bit," she hinted. "I'm sure we've invaded your house long enough."

Patrick shook his head. "You guys can stay as long as you want." He got up and walked into the kitchen.

She watched as he retreated. Her mind buzzed. What if he was a bounty hunter? Maybe a private detective? Maybe an undercover policeman? But why was he in Fort Worth, Texas? Was the drug guy in Fort Worth? Was she putting herself and her daughter in the line of fire? *Okay, Mira, just calm down.* He could just be a student like he said, and everything else had just been a freaky coincidence. Not hardly, not with a near-perfect grade-point average in sociology. Something about him told her he wasn't what he seemed.

"Mira?"

"I'm sorry, I was daydreaming."

"About last night, I hope." He winked at her. "I was telling you that I checked your car, and there are no dents. It's fine. I think I will follow you guys back to your house just to be safe."

"That's very nice of you, Patrick. How about I fix you dinner later?"

He grinned at her. "That would be great."

Mira finished her breakfast and realized that she had invited him to her house for another meal. But she wanted to get to know him, and so far she only knew about his parents. She also wanted to know why he wouldn't let her go into the kitchen.

Mira watched her rearview carefully. Even though Patrick was behind her, she still felt the need to check for any suspicious vehicles. Her cell phone rang, interrupting her. She cringed as she heard Shara's voice.

"You could at least call me to let me know that you are still alive," Shara exclaimed. "I called your house ten times last night. You don't check your messages anymore? Did you have a hot date with Patrick last night? What did you do with Reese?"

Mira laughed at Shara's tone. "First of all, Shara, I tried to call you yesterday, and your mother said you were getting your hair done. Yes, Patrick cooked dinner for Reese and me last night. I was the victim of an attempted carjacking on the interstate and I didn't feel like driving home last night, so we stayed at his apartment."

"Oh, Mira. Are you okay? I told you the interstate was dangerous at night."

"I know you told me that, but I'm fine now. Patrick's following me home, and Reese is riding with him. She loves his car."

"Well, I see he's fitting himself in your life good," she said, sarcasm evident in her voice. "Has he put the bite on you for some money?"

"He knows nothing about the money. Anyway, he's been showering *us* with gifts, not the other way around."

"But for how long? If he's a student, where's he getting his money? I saw Jonathan the other day, he asked me about you."

"What did you say? You didn't tell him where I lived, did you?" The last thing she needed was her sad excuse of an ex-husband showing up and ruining things with Patrick.

"No. Why don't you let him see Reese? After all, she's his daughter, and she doesn't even have Jonathan's last name."

"The daughter he said he didn't want. That's why I changed her last name to Brenton when we divorced. He doesn't pay me any child support because I don't want him connected to us in any fashion. He doesn't want to have anything to do with her. Did you tell him about the money? At the club, he knew all about it. He thinks he's entitled to it."

"No, I didn't tell him," Shara said in a very peculiar voice. "Anyway, why can't you give him some, you'd never miss it."

"Shara, I can't do this right now."

"Well, we're going to come out later."

"I'm sorry, Shara. I completely forgot. Patrick is coming for dinner."

"So now you pick him over me," Shara said with a tight voice.

"Why not?" Mira countered. "You've certainly done it to me enough times. How many times have you left me stranded somewhere because you hooked up with some guy, and ditched me like a used paper napkin? Talk to you later." Mira pushed the "end" button on her cell phone and threw it in the passenger seat. Thank goodness Reese had begged to ride with Patrick. She had missed watching her mother lose it on a cell phone.

Too many things were happenings at once. Patrick was fast becoming a permanent fixture in her life. Reese didn't seem to be getting any better, even with the visits to Dr. Sid's. Patrick made more sense than the doctor did. And now Shara. Mira had always suspected Shara had a soft spot for Jonathan. Even when Mira was pregnant, Shara wasn't supportive of Mira during her marriage.

As she arrived at her garage, she shook off her bad feelings and forced a happy smile on her face for her child. She parked on the far right side so that Patrick would have enough room to pull his car in next to hers. Smiling, she watched him drive in. Reese jumped out of the car and ran to her mother.

"Mommy, Mr. Patrick said we could ride with his top down when it's warmer," Reese announced as she walked toward the door to the house.

Does that mean that he'll be around next summer? She hoped he wasn't the type to break a little girl's heart, or a big girl's, for that matter. She had to prepare her daughter for the heartache men could cause. "Honey, I'm sure that Patrick means if he's still here in the area. He might have to go to his family, and they live far away." She unlocked the door, and they walked inside the house.

Reese looked at Patrick with those eyes that made Mira say

yes to so many things she normally wouldn't. "Mr. Patrick, will you be here?"

Patrick looked at Mira, then at Reese. He knelt down so that he was eye level with Reese. "Even if I have to leave, I will come back, Reese. That's a promise." He stood up and faced Mira. "That goes for you, too."

CHAPTER 12

Mira, Patrick, and Reese settled on the couch to watch some afternoon TV. After they had arrived home, Mira and Reese went to change clothes while Patrick relaxed on the sofa. Mira didn't know how Reese would respond to Patrick hanging around, but she didn't seem to mind. Mira also thought Reese would object to Patrick sitting next to her, but Reese only winked at her mother. Another sign her little girl was growing up, and maybe healing.

Reese had fallen asleep by the time the movie ended. *Maybe she's just tired,* Mira thought. "She never takes naps anymore," she whispered to Patrick, as she stood, reaching for her daughter, but Patrick stopped her.

"I'll get her for you." He eased off the couch and picked Reese up as if she weighed only ten pounds. Quietly, he headed for the stairs, with Mira right behind him. He turned around and shook his head. "I can put her to bed."

She was so used to doing everything for her daughter, it took a minute for the statement to reach her brain. "Okay, Patrick," Mira said, watching him take her only child upstairs.

The red light on the phone attracted her attention as she waited for Patrick to return. She listened to her voice-mail messages. True to her word, Shara had called, wanting to go out. There were several telemarketer calls, but nothing earth shattering, as usual.

"Well," Patrick said as he stood beside her, "care to tell me why you were so upset earlier? You've been acting strange since we came back to your house. If you want me to leave, just say the word."

He was standing so close that she could inhale his cologne. Slowly she turned around and faced him, her arms slowly creeping around his narrow waist and hugging him for dear life. "No, you don't have to leave. I just had a bad phone call." She sniffed, trying to hold back tears.

His hands caressed her back in a comforting motion. "Your old friends. I bet they don't like the fact that we spend so much time together."

"How did you know?"

"It's my business to know people. And as I've said before, they may have been your friends once upon a time, but you've outgrown them." He guided her back to the couch.

After they were seated, Mira let him comfort her. *So this is what being in a family is like*, she thought. She imagined being a small child, having both parents at home. How different would her life have been? Loads, she surmised, since she didn't know her father's ethnicity. Her skin began to tingle. "Patrick, what are you doing?"

"Taking your pain away." He continued tantalizing her with kisses on her neck and whispers of lustful words in her ear.

She nodded, tilting her head to one side so that he had better access to her neck. Moaning, she leaned closer to him, letting her body relax against his. "You succeeded."

"That was my plan."

A faint noise woke Patrick from one of the most peaceful naps he had ever had. He lay snuggled with Mira on the couch, and he saw she was still asleep. He realized his phone had fallen through the opening between the cushions and was now ringing. "Callahan," he whispered.

Mira opened her eyes, smiled, and then closed them again. Snuggling closer to him, she melted away the final barriers around his heart. This hadn't happened to him before. This assignment had been a series of firsts. The first time he had enjoyed baby-sitting, the first time he had dated someone with a child. He knew he would need help to watch both Reese and Mira and not blow his cover.

He hadn't seen any evidence that Rico was still in Fort Worth, since he hadn't set eyes on him since that day of the near-kiss at school. But Patrick didn't know if Rico was still following him or Mira. For Rico, as well as Patrick, it was personal.

He spoke into the phone as quietly as he could. Mira moaned at the noise. He listened as a field operative reported to him.

"The shipment has left Mexico," a voice announced, speaking in DEA code.

"Where will the boat dock?" Patrick knew this would require a meeting.

"Riverdale and Canal."

Reluctantly, he eased off the couch and kissed Mira on the forehead. She still didn't move. Not wanting to wake her from a peaceful nap, he left her a note: *Be back soon. Patrick.*

He arrived at the rendezvous point. After glancing around at his surroundings, he opened his glove compartment and retrieved his Glock. He loaded it, then reached into the console and retrieved the holster. Taking a deep breath, he slid out of the car, slipping the gun inside the leather holster and attaching it to his belt. Hopefully the gun wouldn't be needed, but he could never be sure. He had let his guard down once and had received a near-fatal gun shot for his carelessness.

He hadn't walked more than twenty feet from his car when two Hispanic men approached him. Then one moved behind him and one stood in front of him. One of the men spoke, asking Patrick in fluent Spanish, "Is it always this hot in Texas this late in the year?"

"How would I know?" Patrick answered sarcastically, looking at two of his fellow agents. "I live in a normal state."

They three men looked at each other and began laughing.

"Yeah, I wish I was there right now enjoying some decent weather. Man it's damn near Christmas and it's still almost ninety degrees," one of the men told Patrick. "What I wouldn't give for some fifty-degree weather."

"Me, too," Patrick agreed. "We have Paulo to thank for this." Patrick paused as he thought of Mira. He also had the drug lord to thank for the woman in his life.

The men spoke in hushed tones as they watched a strange car drive by, entering Mira's neighborhood. Patrick noticed the car and relaxed. The black Mercedes belonged to Mira's neighbor. After the car parked by one of the houses, Patrick resumed the conversation. "Can you watch the school?"

The man nodded. "We finally got clearance; the background checks required would put the Department of Justice to shame. She'll never know we're there."

"I want to know if anyone approaches the child or tries to get her released from school for any reason. If so, call me."

"How will you handle the mother?" the other agent asked, making notes in a small pad as Patrick spouted orders.

"I've got her under control," Patrick stated confidently, for the operatives' sake, but he knew Mira really had him under control.

The men nodded and departed.

As Patrick entered Mira's house again, he met Mira in the kitchen. Her curly hair looked sensual in its disarray. She smiled as she took a carton of milk out of the refrigerator. She held up an empty glass for Patrick.

He nodded and sat at the kitchen table. "How long have you been up?"

She yawned and stretched her body. "Not long. All of a sudden I felt cold and lonely, and I realized you were gone. You could have woken me to tell me you were leaving."

He probably should have, but she would have asked too many questions. Questions he couldn't answer without compromising the entire operation. He couldn't let Paulo get away and laugh at him. "You looked so peaceful sleeping. I didn't have the heart." He smiled at her as she handed him a glass of milk. "Besides, I was coming right back. I thought you wouldn't miss me for thirty minutes."

She sat across from him, grinning. "Did you forget something?"

Patrick discreetly checked his pockets. The watch was in the car, his Glock was in the glove compartment, and his phone was on his belt. What could he have forgotten? "No, I don't think so."

She pointed to her cheek. "When you left, you kissed my forehead. I demand the same attention when you return."

"Of course." He rose and leaned over the table. He didn't kiss her forehead or her cheek; he aimed for her soft, tender lips. "Is that better?"

"Much."

Mira hummed as she prepared dinner for her family. Did she already consider Patrick part of her family? *Not really,* she thought to herself. Just because he was becoming a permanent fixture at her dining-room table was no reason to put the cart before the horse.

First, he needed to tell her more about his life, she thought. Then the other steps would come naturally. She hoped her heart wouldn't let her down like it had so many times in the past.

Jonathan had told her he loved her. Every day. Every time they were together, he told her he loved her. She believed him so much that she'd run off to the courthouse and married him. It wasn't until she was pregnant with Reese that his true colors emerged.

Even with that, she had tried to make the marriage work. She wanted her daughter to have a father, but Reese's father didn't want her. As the stress of a troubled marriage and a newborn wore her down, she filed for divorce and moved back home with her mother. She vowed to find Reese a father worthy of her love. Had she found that in Patrick?

Why did she feel differently but the same about Patrick? She knew he was nothing like Jonathan, but still a little part of her was suspicious of him and his vague past. She trusted him, no doubt. Reese adored him. But why weren't there any pictures on the walls of his apartment? How could a man with no visible means of income own such an expensive sports car that had to be specially ordered?

She still couldn't believe she looked up the price of his sports car on the Web. *Am I that nosy*? *Yes*, she thought. Other than the price of the car, her search proved fruitless. When she attempted to look up his name, she kept getting strange messages such as "The Justice Department retains this information." No further data was possible.

A sizzling noise attracted her attention. The hamburgers were burning! She was supposed to be frying burgers, not burning down the house! With a sigh, she emptied the contents of the skillet into the trash. One look at the ruined pan, and she threw it away, too.

"Hey, what are you doing?" Patrick asked as he walked into the kitchen with Reese right behind him. "I thought you said dinner was in five minutes."

"I burned the meat. Everything else is frozen. Want to order something?"

He smiled at her. "Why don't we go out to eat? My treat."

She shook her head. "Patrick, I couldn't let you treat us again. That's too much money."

He walked over to her with the determination of a tiger seeking its prey. "You let me worry about that." He turned off the stove. "Come on, let's go." He grabbed her hand and led her to the garage.

Mira tried to sound stern, but it was hard when Reese grabbed her other hand and was dragging her to Patrick's car. "Come on, Mommy."

Outvoted, she got into the car, and they left. She thought

they were going to Burger World, a popular kiddie restaurant. But apparently Patrick had learned about a few places in Fort Worth, and took them to the World of Burgers, a burger restaurant in the art district of Fort Worth. As he parked, Mira had to ask.

"How did you know about this place? It's kind of expensive." Mira glanced at the flags flying proudly in front of the restaurant. The large brick building demanded attention because it reminded everyone of a castle.

"The day we were at the museum, I saw it. You know, not a whole lot of places do veggie burgers right, but I hear this place is great." He climbed out of the car and went to her side, opening her door.

"Are you sure about this, Patrick?" Mira couldn't help asking because her practical side had taken over. The last thing she wanted was him being overextended on his credit cards.

He leaned down and kissed her as he helped her out of the car. "As sure as my name is Patrick Callahan."

They entered the restaurant and were immediately seated. He had both Reese and Mira's attention as he explained the menu to them in great detail. "They serve burgers that represent the different regions of the world. They do a great soy burger. You guys want to try that?" He winked at Mira, daring her.

She smiled that glorious smile at him. "No, thanks. I probably should because soy burgers have fewer calories, but I like meat in my burger."

"I think you look great." He blew her a kiss as Reese concentrated hard on reading her menu.

She shook her head. "I have the Brenton curse. We always battle the scale, and the last few times, the scale has been winning."

"Well, I guess I will have to get rid of those scales, huh?" Patrick winked at her.

She laughed as the waiter approached the table. Mira recited her order, then Patrick. When Reese finally stopped studying the menu, she looked at the waiter and froze; the large leather book of burgers fell to the carpeted floor.

"Reese, honey, the waiter wants your order," Mira prodded.

Reese was still silent. Patrick noticed she looked as if she had seen the man before, but she wouldn't speak. Giant teardrops rolled down her face. Then she started muttering.

"Bad man." Reese jumped out of her chair and ran to her mother. "Bad man will hurt me." She burst into tears.

Patrick watched Reese, then the waiter, who was clearly puzzled. "She'll have an American burger," Patrick said. The waiter nodded and left the table hurriedly. Patrick pondered the events that had just occurred. Just how much did Reese see when Helen Brenton was killed? He watched as Mira comforted her daughter. His heart went out to both women. Reese sat in her mother's lap, hugging Mira with an iron grip.

He would have to read the full police report and ask Mira some general questions without Reese in hearing distance. An educated guess would be that Reese Brenton saw more than anyone realized. As usual, with her being a child, the police probably didn't think to ask the only eyewitness.

Reese relaxed and returned to her seat. Soon the food arrived, and they ate their meal. After Reese's outburst, the waiter didn't return. Another took his place, and Reese was fine. What was different between one waiter and the next?

The only difference Mira noticed was the first one was Hispanic and the second one was white. But Reese had seen Hispanic people before. Why, all of sudden, was Reese so afraid?

As they finished their meal, a Hispanic woman neared their table. Mira watched Reese's reaction. Nothing. Reese smiled at the woman as she cleared the table. So it was just the men.

Patrick smiled as he scribbled his name on the credit card receipt. "What are you thinking about?" he asked Mira.

"How much money you're spending on us. We could have just ordered pizza, and it would have been half the price of this." She hated sounding like a broken record. "I know what it's like to be on a budget, Patrick. We wouldn't think less of you if you say you can't afford it," she assured him.

"Well, thank you, Mira. I'm glad to hear that. But I can afford it. So stop worrying. You could always offer to fix me breakfast in return for dinner."

He winked at her. Reese soon joined in the conversation.

"Yeah, Mommy. You can make pancakes for Mr. Patrick."

Those pancakes would cost me more than just breakfast, she mused. They would probably be an even trade for an evening of unbridled passion, but she was willing to pay the price, especially after Reese's earlier outburst. "Why do I feel like I'm always being railroaded when I'm with both of you?"

"Who, us?" Patrick winked at Reese. "I don't know what you're talking about." He stood, and they left the restaurant.

After a stop at the video store and a stop at Patrick's apartment for clothes, they headed to Mira's house. She should have objected when he suggested that he get some clothes to change into, but she didn't. Like a puppet on a string that he controlled, she agreed.

Reese became very quiet in the backseat. Mira shifted in her seat to see what her daughter was up to. She had fallen asleep, with the DVD Patrick bought for her clutched tightly in her hand.

"Patrick, you don't have to buy us things all the time. We're not those kind of girls," Mira reminded him again.

"I want to. Does it make you feel uncomfortable?" He glanced in his rearview mirror.

"No, I just don't want you spending your money on us when you don't have to."

"Mira, just because I don't have a job doesn't mean I don't have money or access to it. If I couldn't afford it, I wouldn't offer. You don't have a job, either, so where are you getting your money? You have a mortgage payment to make. Your daughter goes to an exclusive private school, and Fort Worth University is a private college. I know how hard it is to make it."

She was touched by his sincerity. She bit her lip, not wanting to tell him how she came into her life of unemployment. *Just let him think you're living off your mother's insurance policy*, she thought. "We're okay, too. Now that we've danced around the issue of money, what are we doing about our sociology test next week? We haven't studied in quite some time. Our last few study sessions have been in my bedroom." She giggled. "And we're not taking biology."

He laughed, then looked in his rearview mirror again. He cursed just as blue and red lights flashed behind them.

"You weren't speeding," Mira noted. "Why are they stopping you?"

"It's the car. This type of sporty Mustang always attracts cops. Mainly because my car is a racing model and can outrun them if I wanted to." He pulled over and stopped the car. He reached into the console, grabbed his wallet, and opened the car door. "Sit tight, I'll be right back."

Mira watched him as he walked to the two policemen. He shook their hands and began talking in a hushed tone. She strained to hear the conversation, but all she heard were muffled voices. "He'll need his insurance papers," she muttered to herself. She opened the glove compartment and reached in for the insurance card, but her hand hit some metal.

She pushed papers aside and gasped. "What is he doing with a gun?" She put the papers back and closed the door. She shifted in her seat, checking on Reese, who was still asleep, then on Patrick. He was pointing and walking toward the car, with the officers following close behind. "How's he going to explain a gun?" she whispered softly.

He peeked his head inside the car and smiled at her. "Mira, the police want to look at the interior of the car."

She thought they wanted to search the car. The officer glanced at the stereo system but stared at Mira. He smiled, noticing Reese sleeping in the backseat, then faced Patrick.

"That's a nice system. Did it come standard with the car?"

"No, it was an upgrade. It's a top-of-the-line Bose system.

It has six speakers and a CD changer. When I really crank it, it's awesome," Patrick added in a proud tone.

"Well, sir, have a good evening. Good luck. Let us know if we can be of service to you."

Patrick thanked them and got into the car, smiling at Mira.

She smiled back at him, but her mind buzzed with more questions than she knew she would ever have answers for. In her limited experience with the police, she never had had a conversation end like that. Was she in danger from Patrick, or was he protecting her from the danger?

CHAPTER 13

Mira yawned as she turned off her alarm clock. She reached over to tell Patrick he had to leave her bedroom, but he was already gone. "The things I do for my child," she muttered as she walked to the shower. There was no sign that Patrick was ever in her room the night before. They had agreed that he would sleep in the guest room since Reese had a habit of getting into bed with her mother in the wee hours of the morning.

Since Reese had had such a traumatic time at the restaurant, Mira had expected her to beg to sleep with her, but she hadn't. Reese had even volunteered to go to bed early the night before. Mira suspected she had been the victim of another plot hatched by her daughter and Patrick.

Reese hadn't joined her mother in bed that morning, either. After Mira finished dressing, she checked on her daughter. Reese lay snug in her bed, cuddling with a teddy bear. Mira smiled at the brown bear with its pastel bow tie. It was the last gift her mother had given Reese before she died. Mira closed the door and headed down the hall to the guest room. Patrick was asleep as well. He had kicked off the cover, revealing his pajama bottoms and his six-pack stomach. Giving in to the memories of the night before, she walked inside the room and closed the door.

As she started toward him, he sprang up in the bed. If his finger had been a gun, he could have shot her. Mira's adrenaline started pumping. Maybe he was a detective on the hunt for someone that she knew. Jonathan? She noticed they were both breathing hard; she leaned against the door. "I-I'm sorry, I didn't mean to scare you. I wanted to surprise you."

He rubbed his face with his large hand. "You succeeded. I guess I was having a nightmare." He patted the space beside him for her to sit down.

She steadied herself so she wouldn't skip over to the bed. *Slow steps*, she reminded herself. *Slow steps*. "I was just checking on you. I didn't hear you leave my room this morning." She sat down beside him. "Was your nightmare about how you got those scars?" She ran her hand over the scars that haunted her dreams, too.

"Partly. Hey, if your hands move any lower, my body might start to react on its own," he teased her. His hands traveled over her sweater, easing her down on the bed next to him. "Think we have time for a quickie?"

"No. Remember, you and my daughter conspired against me last night and demanded pancakes. What would you like to eat in lieu of bacon?" She was a breath away from his lips. Why didn't he kiss her? *Why don't you kiss him?* She listened to that voice, raised her head a few inches, and kissed him before he could answer her question.

Patrick's lips started a trail of fire down the column of her neck. Between kisses he spoke. "I was thinking I might try a piece of bacon until I can get a suitable vegetable or soy replacement." His kisses dipped lower, easing toward her breasts.

Mira felt herself drowning in his kisses. "Patrick, I have to get downstairs, or Reese is going to catch us." She gave him her best stern look so he would let her up. Finally, he relented and eased off her overheated body. As her body finally forgave her for not indulging in a little romp, she stared at the floor. Knowing that one look into his sexy face would have her jumping back in bed with him, she remembered why she was there in the first place. "Breakfast will be ready in thirty minutes." She straightened her clothes and left the room.

Patrick watched as she sashayed out. Why did he feel so comfortable in this house? Was he losing control of the situation?

He couldn't recall a woman he couldn't entice into making love in the early-morning hours. He also couldn't believe that he had left the comfortable position of being in Mira's arms to sleep down the hall, just so her daughter wouldn't catch them in bed together. *Yep. Pat, ole boy, you are definitely losing it.*

He stepped into the shower and sighed as the hot water hit his tired body. He had thought he was healed from all his injuries from the summer, but his stomach was still giving him trouble. Dreading seeing the doctor again, he turned off the water.

After he dressed, he went to check on Reese. He opened the door to her room and smiled. She was still asleep, hugging a teddy bear like it was a lost friend.

Patrick waltzed into the kitchen, his heart swelling at the sight of Mira making pancakes and attempting to set the table for breakfast. "I thought I smelled something delicious cooking." He walked over and hugged her. "Good morning." He kissed her. "Are we celebrating something?" He noticed the amount of food Mira was fixing. In addition to pancakes, there were also bacon and eggs, and hash browns.

Mira shook her head and broke the embrace, resuming her pancake making. "I cook like this because it's Sunday." She turned toward him and smiled. "I like cooking for my daughter."

He knew that. Mira's world revolved around Reese. Any invasion into that world would take a very concerted effort on his part. "Reese is very lucky. Hey, why don't you let me do that for you?" He walked over to her and took the spatula from her hand. "I've been told I cook some mean pancakes. Why don't you sit down for a change?" He pulled a chair out for her.

Mira took his advice. "I hope you know how to do smiley faces? Reese really likes those."

As if on cue, Reese walked into the kitchen. The hysterical little girl from yesterday was gone. She was all smiles, and she kissed her mother on the cheek.

"Hi, Mommy. Hi, Mr. Patrick." She sat down and took a

sip of orange juice. "Is breakfast ready? Why are you sitting down?"

Mira smiled at Patrick. "Mr. Patrick decided he wanted to cook this morning. What do you think about that?"

"Ashley's dad cooks all the time," she reported. "Her mom burns stuff."

Mira spoke in a whisper loud enough for Patrick to hear. "Let's hope Patrick doesn't burn the house down." The women giggled.

"If you want my pancakes," Patrick said as he placed a stack of pancakes on the table, "I would suggest no cracks about men cooking." He laughed, returning to the stove to continue preparing breakfast.

"Yes, Patrick." Mira laughed, causing Reese to speak in a happy tone as well.

The phone rang, interrupting their banter. Patrick was closest to the phone, but he felt he shouldn't answer because it wasn't his home. Mira might think he was overstepping his bounds as her lover.

"You can answer the phone." Mira put a stack of pancakes on her plate. "Hey, where's the bacon? You promised."

Laughing, Patrick placed a platter of bacon in front of her and Reese, then answered the phone. "Brenton residence."

"C-could I speak to Mira?" a stunned female voice asked.

Patrick gathered this was probably Shara. "She's having her breakfast at the moment. Would you like to leave your name and number? I'm sure she'll call you as soon as she's finished."

"Tell her Shara, her friend from the hood, called," she said in a surly tone.

"I sure will." Patrick hung up the phone. He sat down and began to pile pancakes on his plate. "Shara called," he said casually as he slathered butter on his food.

"These are good, Patrick," Mira said. "You can fix pancakes any time you feel like it. Right, honey?"

Reese nodded in agreement.

"Well, it's nice to know you aren't just using me for my

body." He winked at her and began cutting his masterpiece into bite-sized pieces.

"Patrick!" Mira scolded him, smiling.

"Mommy, why are you using Mr. Patrick's body?" Reese asked as she poured maple syrup on top of her pancakes.

She was too cute, quizzing her mother so innocently. Patrick's gaze went to Mira's horrified face. A slow blush rose to her cheeks. She was as adorable as her daughter. "She uses my body all the time. Isn't that mean?"

Reese looked from her mother to Patrick, not sure whom she should side with. "If Mommy uses your body, she has a good reason. Mommy would never do anything bad."

Patrick winked at Mira. "You got that right, kid." He stared at Mira until she looked in his direction, and then he blew her a kiss. She smiled back at him.

"Well, honey," she said to her daughter, "Mr. Patrick has to earn his keep."

Mira listened to the professor as he spoke about the upcoming test. She gazed around at the rest of the class. Patrick was twirling her hair with his finger, a little habit he'd picked up in the last few weeks. She wondered if anyone noticed.

"This is the second of three tests. I can only hope that the rest of the class has been studying as hard as Ms. Brenton and Mr. Callahan have."

Mira felt every student in the room staring at her. And Patrick was still twirling her hair around his fingers. They were caught. She felt a warm blush cover her skin. She slapped Patrick's hand.

"Okay, maybe not that kind of studying," the professor said, laughing along with the rest of the class.

She shook her head and hoped she could survive this humiliation. Sliding lower in her chair, she heard Patrick's chuckle. How could he sit there laughing with the class, like they hadn't just been caught like two teenagers in heat? Finally, the professor continued his lecture.

"You shouldn't let him get to you; the class, either." Patrick whispered in her ear.

It felt more like a kiss. *Mira, you know nothing about this man, except he can turn you on in the middle of a classroom,* she chastised herself. "I can't help it. Years of being insecure."

Patrick patted her shoulder. "I know."

The innocent gesture made her feel more secure than she had been in a long time. Mira wanted to turn around and face him, but she couldn't. She had an upcoming test, and since the entire class knew she had aced the first exam, the pressure was on.

She didn't relax until the class was over. As she talked with one of her friends, she noticed Patrick waiting for her in a corner of the room. He always looked incredibly sexy to her. Mira could barely hear her friend Abby speaking.

"Mira, how does Reese like gymnastics? Kelsey really likes having Reese there."

Mira gathered her books. "It's been great for Reese. But I was thinking about taking her out of it because she doesn't have much free time in the afternoon."

Abby stared at her. "Oh, that's too bad." She lowered her voice. "How are the sessions going?"

"Well, I don't know. It seems Reese shuts down when we go to Dr. Sid. Patrick makes her understand more than the doctor does." She turned toward Patrick and then back to Abby. "Sometimes I think I should be paying him for all the times he calms her down."

"It seems like he should be teaching this class, instead of the professor," Abby said. She looked at Mira with sympathetic eyes. "I'm sorry he embarrassed you. I didn't know you before, but you look better now than you did at the beginning of the semester."

Mira nodded. "Yes, this last year has been a wild ride, but it's calming down. Hey, I should get going, but why don't we have lunch tomorrow?"

Abby pointed at Patrick. "What about Mr. GQ over there?"

"He doesn't have class tomorrow." Mira picked up her bag and started walking toward Patrick. "We're having our study session today. I'll meet you in the lunch area about noon."

Abby nodded and waved good-bye as Mira approached Patrick.

"Where do you want to eat lunch?" Patrick asked as he put his arm around Mira, leading her out into the busy hallway. "I was thinking lobster sounds excellent."

"I think we'd better stay here." Mira smiled up at him. "Every time we leave this campus to study, we end up at my house. Now since everyone knows what my score was on the last test, I have to do well on this next one."

"Sounds like someone is full of herself." Patrick's hand left her waist and grabbed her hand, leading her through the crowd. "We can eat in the cafeteria."

Mira nodded. For the first time in her life, a man was holding her hand in public. When she was with Jonathan, he disliked public affection of any kind. At first she thought it was cute. Later, she found out it was because he had relationships outside of their brief marriage. She squeezed Patrick's hand.

"The cafeteria sounds fine. We can study upstairs."

After they picked their lunch choices, they settled at a table. Mira took stock of Patrick's very healthy meal of salad, fruit, bread, and milk. She looked at her tray of sirloin tips over rice, broccoli drowned in cheese, fried okra, soda, and cheesecake, and shook her head. "I should learn to eat like you."

"Why?"

"So when I tell Reese that she needs to eat vegetables, I can be her example."

"Well, I could always be the example of healthy eating to both of you."

Mira gazed at him. "Yes, milk has definitely done your body good." Even with all those scars on his stomach and back, he was still a fine physical specimen.

"Does that mean that you like my body?" He winked at her, heating her up a centimeter at a time.

She couldn't deny it. "Yes."

"Well, I like yours, too."

That surprised her. "How? My body isn't like yours. I still have baby fat, and Reese is six years old. Your body is all lean muscle mass, not one ounce of fat to be found, and I searched," she joked.

"I can't believe we're having this conversation here, but I'll tell you. I think you're beautiful on the inside and out. I guess I noticed your inner beauty first."

"What inner beauty?" Mira asked.

"Are you teasing me? I liked your smile. I thought it was great that you're completing your education. You are a survivor. A lot of people couldn't endure what you have and still have had the balls to go to school."

Mira always thought she was just living her life. "I never thought about it, I guess. I was just trying to make good choices. I was the breadwinner of my family, and before, college wasn't an option, but I didn't want to end up like so many of my friends."

"How?"

"Well, like most of my friends, I was from a single-parent home. I think Shara was the only one out of my friends whose parents were married. At least most of my friends knew who their father was. I have no idea who mine was, or what he was."

But Patrick knew. For the first time, he wanted to break the rules and tell his secret, but that wouldn't help his dead cousin or the countless other people Paulo had hurt over the years. "Is it important to you to find out who he is?"

"I don't even know if he's alive. My uncle knows his name, but won't tell me because he promised Momma he would never tell."

"Does your uncle know anything else about him?"

"Unfortunately, no."

Patrick wanted to tell her, just to set her mind at rest. But if he did, he would compromise the operation, and all his hard work would have been for nothing. And if he told her one part of the truth, he would have to tell her everything. Those sobering thoughts brought him back to the task at hand. He was an agent first. "You've done fine without knowing anything about him so far, why do you think you need to know his identity?" *Just you wait, you'll meet him in time,* he thought. Then she would really be sorry.

"Maybe. My mom was great. She just didn't talk about him at all. When she died I thought she would have had a picture or something, but I didn't find anything."

"What do you wonder the most about him?"

Her eyes took on a dreamy look. "Oh, I don't know. Maybe something about my mother. I can't imagine her being so carefree to have a summer affair. When I came along, she was very strict. She always told me she didn't want me to end up like her."

Patrick was more confused than ever. "What did she mean?"

"You know, that I didn't have a father. Still, between my mom and Uncle Harold, I felt I was loved. Yet I wanted so much more for Reese. I wanted her to have a father who would be proud she was his daughter. Not some idiot who didn't want any responsibility." She sighed. "But I'm smarter and stronger now. I'm determined to be best parent I can be."

"See, that's what I mean."

Mira looked up from her meal. "What?"

"You wanted to know why was I attracted to you. Your determination. No matter the circumstances, you persevere."

She looked at him with teary eyes. "Sorry," she said, wiping her lashes. "I didn't mean to start crying. No one has ever complimented me like that before. It felt nice."

"Reese compliments you all the time. She may not say it, but she shows it." He hadn't meant to start the waterworks. Now he felt like a heel for bringing back bad memories. He had a better grasp of his plan now.

So Paulo hadn't contacted his only living relative. What would Rico do to her? Would he kidnap her and Reese and fly them to Mexico to show his loyalty to Paulo by bringing his daughter to him? Or would he kill Mira and Reese and tell Paulo that they had somehow died before he could bring them to Mexico, and Paulo would therefore make him successor to the drug business? Rico was known for getting people out of the way. He had tried to do as much with Patrick when he had sent an innocent child to shoot him.

"Thank you, Patrick," Mira said, bringing him out of his dark thoughts. "She is the center of my universe."

He looked down at their untouched trays of food. "Since we didn't eat our lunch, why don't we go study for a little bit, then get a bite later?" He stood, and grabbed his bag.

She looked at her still-full tray. "Yeah, my appetite is gone, anyway."

"I'll get this while you get your stuff." He grabbed her tray and walked to the trash can.

Mira tried to collect herself as she watched him empty their trays. She grabbed her bag and stood, waiting for Patrick to return. She pulled out her cell phone to check her messages. No messages. She breathed a sigh of relief.

"Excuse me," a young woman said, approaching Mira.

"Yes." She glanced at the woman's flawless brown skin; she wasn't much darker than Mira. Maybe her father was of Hispanic descent, too, she thought.

"Was that Dorian Martinez you were talking to? I didn't know he was in the States," she stated in heavily accented Spanish.

"No, his name is Patrick Callahan. I think he's from the East Coast."

The young woman shook her head in confusion. "He looks just like this guy I knew in my village."

"Village?"

"Yes, I'm from San Juan-Jimenez, Mexico."

That place. It was listed on that picture at Patrick's apartment. "I've heard of that place. What is it?"

The girl smiled a prideful grin. "Well, it's a small village in Mexico. You've probably heard of it because of all the drug trafficking that goes on there. Dorian worked for Paulo. He's a drug lord in San Juan-Jimenez. The last thing I heard, Dorian had gotten shot in some kind of mixup."

The man in the picture? Was Patrick hunting this Paulo guy? Why was he in Fort Worth if Paulo was in Mexico? Mira noticed the girl shaking her head and walking away.

Mira watched Patrick as he approached the table. He looked startled. "Who was that girl?"

"No one special. She thought you were someone else."

He grabbed Mira's arm forcefully. "Who did she think I was?" he demanded. He took a deep breath, then let her arm go and apologized. "Sorry."

She looked at him, not recognizing this Patrick. "She thought you were a dope runner named Dorian Martinez."

CHAPTER 14

Patrick watched Mira as they settled down to study upstairs in the Student Union. His heart had almost dropped to his stomach when he had noticed Maria Cortez speaking to Mira. Maria was another victim of the Callahan charm, he mused.

He had chosen Maria to help him infiltrate Paulo's inner circle, not because of her exotic beauty, but because she was Rico's girlfriend.

Patrick had quickly seduced Maria, and she was soon ready to tell him everything she knew about Paulo's drug business. Patrick was the reason she was in the United States now.

After Maria had helped him as much as she could, Patrick knew her life was in danger. He had made it possible for her and her family to get to the U.S. It was ironic she was attending college in Fort Worth.

"Patrick." Mira's soft voice pushed him back to the upcoming test. "If you don't want to study now, it's okay. You can come over tonight, and we can study them."

He smiled. Everything about her warmed his soul. Seeing Maria had freaked him out, and he had to think of something to explain his sudden mood swing. He leaned toward her and gently brushed her lips with his. "That sounds like a good idea. I have to go visit my doctor this afternoon, anyway. I guess that's why I'm so preoccupied."

"Why are you going to the doctor?" Mira looked at him with her sincere brown eyes brimming with concern. "Would you like me to go with you? I'd have to pick up

Reese first, but if you don't mind an inquisitive six-year-old accompanying us to the doctor, I wouldn't mind."

It was a grand offer, he thought. "Well, my stomach has been giving me trouble. I would very much appreciate some company at the doctor's office." He tasted her lips softly before igniting into flames. He licked her lips with his tongue, teasing her mouth open and deepening the kiss.

Their sociology professor interrupted their smooching with his loud, boisterous laughter. "I hope you devote as much time to studying as you guys do to preparing to study." He walked away, laughing.

Mira covered her face with her hands in embarrassment. "Oh my God, Patrick. He's going to think we're in heat or something," she said through her hands.

She was so cute. He tried to peel her stiff fingers from her face, but she held firm. "Mira, it's okay. It's normal to display affection. I like being with you, and I don't care who knows it. Want me to kiss you again?" He leaned closer and puckered his lips, kissing her hands, which were still shielding her face.

Mira shook her head, speaking in a muffled voice. "Patrick, we've already been caught once." She dropped her hands and stared at him before she spoke. "Please kiss me."

He complied.

After they parked Mira's car at her house, Patrick drove her to Reese's school. "Since the school has never seen your car, they won't let her come near it," she said, opening the door. "I'll be right back."

Patrick, in both his capacity as a DEA agent and as the protector of Mira and Reese, wanted to get a look at the interior of the school. "Why don't I go with you? So they won't think I've kidnapped you or something against your will." He flashed his seductive smile at her, hoping that she hadn't seen the wheels working inside his head.

She nodded. Smiling, she reached back inside his car for her purse. "Okay, you can see where my money goes."

He walked beside her and grabbed her hand. "Does it bother you when I hold your hand in public?"

She shook her curly head at him. "You're the first man to ever do it. It makes me feel safe and secure. As if nothing bad can happen to me." She leaned against him.

He hoped he could keep her safe when the time came. They walked into the school, and Mira flashed her ID for the guard.

"Hello, Ms. Brenton. Reese is in the study room awaiting your arrival."

"Thank you, Mrs. Bastine. This is my friend, Patrick Callahan. We came in his car today."

The mature woman looked at Patrick and studied him. "Well, I'll just make a note on Reese's release list, just in case it happens again."

Mira nodded. "Thank you, Mrs. Bastine," she said, grabbing Patrick's hand as they continued down the hall.

A few things struck him as odd. "Is security really that tight?"

"Yes. If it's not my car, they won't let her go outside at all. No exceptions. Since this might happen again, I thought it would be a good idea for Mrs. Bastine to see you and get your license plate number."

"But she never asked me for it." He felt challenged. That was a mature woman of at least sixty. How could she get the plate number unless she physically went outside? And if she left her post, who would watch the door? Someone could sneak in while she was outside.

Mira laughed as if he had said something totally idiotic. "There are security cameras all over the parking lot. She doesn't have to ask you for it. She looks on the camera, gets your plate, has it run through Motor Vehicles, and gets your driver's license number before we get back to the exit."

"Wow. *The DEA needs that kind of security*, he thought. "I'm impressed. Reese is very safe here. I was worried for nothing."

"Why were you worried?"

"You know, you hear these stories on the news about some nut getting inside a school and going insane or something," Patrick offered.

Not to mention a drug lord in search of his only granddaughter.

"Well there's nothing to worry about here. This is one of the best private schools in Texas," Mira boasted proudly. "It should be for the amount of money they charge per year," she whispered. "Here we are."

They entered a room full of kids hopped up on chocolate. Patrick couldn't imagine his nieces and nephews running around like that. "I don't see Reese."

Mira nodded. "She must be in the cafeteria." She led him down another hall.

Patrick was amazed at how much the school didn't look like a school. It didn't even smell like a school. Probably because parents were shelling out a serious amount of money for their kids to attend, he figured. They entered the cafeteria, but it didn't look like his school's cafeteria. He couldn't imagine food fights here. The tables probably seated ten students each. Linen, not some cheap plastic tablecloths, covered the tables. It looked a restaurant for little people. "Why would Reese be in the cafeteria?"

"If the students are waiting for their parents, they can go to the study room to read or to the cafeteria for a snack. Knowing my child, she's getting a snack."

Patrick spotted her first. She was sitting at a table with Ashley, the girl from the bookstore. They were eating some sandwiches accompanied by glasses of milk. "There she is, Mira." He also noted one of his contacts walking around the cafeteria. "Where's the little boys' room?"

Mira pointed to the north end of the cafeteria. "Maybe you should save it for the doctor?" she giggled.

He laughed at her sarcasm. "Funny." He walked in the direction of the restrooms. After he knew he wasn't in Mira's line of vision anymore, he sneaked around a corner and waited for his contact. Soon the young man met him at the end of the hall, away from the innocent eyes of the children, teachers, and the rest of the staff.

"Well?" Patrick asked, keeping one eye on the entrance to the hallway and one on his field agent.

"Everything is on target," the agent answered. "I did notice a black Lincoln Navigator drive by slowly a few days ago, but this place is like Fort Knox. Did you think we couldn't handle it?"

Patrick smiled. Jorge Ortiz was one of the best field agents in Texas. There was no question he could handle the situation; Patrick had the utmost faith in him. "No, it's just that I saw a face from the past today. Maria Cortez. She attends Fort Worth University. Nearly blew my cover, or what used to be my cover, of Dorian Martinez."

Jorge changed the subject. "Seeing the mother, I would have preferred looking after her, rather than the daughter," Jorge teased. The man gazed at Mira as she glanced around the room. "You know I can't resist a beautiful woman. Especially one who looks like that."

"Then I would have to kill you." Patrick laughed, slapping Jorge on his back, then left to rejoin Mira and Reese.

As he approached their table, he watched Mira. She sat in one of the small chairs, talking to Reese and her friend. Ashley wanted Reese to spend the night. Patrick hoped Mira would say yes and they could have an actual date. But as usual, she put Reese's needs first.

"How do you feel about it, honey? Ashley could always spend the night with us," Mira hinted hopefully. "I need to talk to your mom first. Are you sure she doesn't have plans for Friday night?"

Ashley nodded. "I'm sure, Ms. Brenton."

Patrick knew Mira was hesitant to let Reese spend the night anywhere without her, given her emotional state. He would have to convince her that Reese needed to resume her

An Important Message From The ARABESQUE Publisher

Dear Arabesque Reader,

I invite you to join the club! The Arabesque book club delivers four novels each month right to your front door! It's easy, and you will never miss a romance by one of our award-winning authors!

With upcoming novels featuring strong, sexy women, and African-American heroes that are charming, loving and true… you won't want to miss a single release. Our authors fill each page with exceptional dialogue, exciting plot twists, and enough sizzling romance to keep you riveted until the satisfying end! To receive novels by bestselling authors such as Gwynne Forster, Janice Sims, Angela Winters and others, I encourage you to join now!

Read about the men we love… in the pages of Arabesque!

Linda Gill
PUBLISHER, ARABESQUE ROMANCE NOVELS

*P.S. Watch out for the next Summer Series **"Ports Of Call"** that will take you to the exotic locales of Venice, Fiji, the Caribbean and Ghana! You won't need a passport to travel, just collect all four novels to enjoy romance around the world! For more details, visit us at www.BET.com.*

ARABESQUE

SPECIAL OFFER! 4 BOOKS FREE!

BET★ BOOKS

www.BET.com

A SPECIAL "THANK YOU" FROM ARABESQUE JUST FOR YOU!

Send this card back and you'll receive 4 FREE Arabesque Novels—
a $25.96 value—absolutely FREE!

The introductory 4 Arabesque Romance books are yours FREE
(plus $1.99 shipping & handling). If you wish to continue to
receive 4 books every month, do nothing. Each month, we will send
you 4 New Arabesque Romance Novels for your free examination.
If you wish to keep them, pay just $18* (plus, $1.99 shipping &
handling). If you decide not to continue, you owe nothing!

- Send no money now.
- Never an obligation.
- Books delivered to your door!

We hope that after receiving your FREE books you'll want to remain
an Arabesque subscriber, but the choice is yours! So why not take
advantage of this Arabesque offer, with no risk of any kind. You'll be
glad you did!

In fact, we're so sure you will love your Arabesque novels, that we
will send you an Arabesque Tote Bag FREE with your first paid
shipment.

* PRICES SUBJECT TO CHANGE.

YOU'LL GET 4 SELECT ROMANCES PLUS THIS FABULOUS TOTE BAG!

ARABESQUE

Visit us at:
www.BET.com

life so she could find closure. And also that he wanted to enjoy some private time with Mira.

He sat down next to Reese. "Hi, Reese."

"Hi, Mr. Patrick. This is my best friend, Ashley." The girls giggled together.

He watched Reese return her tray to the bin and say good-bye to Ashley. Reese grabbed Mira's hand and led her down the hall. The child explained, "I have to get my books." Patrick followed them.

As Reese gathered her belongings, Patrick needed some answers. "Where's Ashley's mom? Do you want to take her home?"

Mira shook her head. "Well, Courtney takes college classes too. She doesn't pick Ashley up until three-thirty. Besides, you can't take someone's child without written and verbal permission from the parent."

Patrick nodded. Fort Knox, indeed. If Paulo did get inside the school, the cops would be there in an instant.

Mira, Patrick, and Reese sat in the waiting room at the Highpoint Sports Clinic. Mira glanced around the clinic, noticing some members of the Dallas Cowboys football team also in the waiting room. "Patrick, why do you come here? This has got to be an expensive place. What kind of insurance do you have?"

He shifted closer to her. "Are you worrying about me again?"

"What are you doing?" Mira asked.

"That guy is watching you." He nodded toward the large man in the corner smiling at them. "I don't want him getting any ideas. He might beat me up or something."

She leaned closer to him. "You have nothing to worry about. What are you doing after the doctor?"

"Taking you and Reese out to dinner. Before you start, yes,

I can afford it. You just concentrate on not looking at that football player." He kissed her gently on the forehead.

"Mr. Callahan, Dr. Evans will see you now," the receptionist announced.

Patrick nodded and stood up. "I'll be right back." His kissed Mira softly on the lips, marking his territory.

Mira nodded and watched him walk down the hall. She turned her attention to her daughter. "Honey, why don't you read while we wait for Patrick?"

"What's wrong with Mr. Patrick?" Reese asked as she opened her book. "Ashley's dad has an ulcer. Is that what Patrick has?"

"I don't know." *The perks in the military must be pretty good,* she mused. He can afford to go to a private university, have a sports car, live in a condo, and still have ample amounts of spending money. *Stop it,* she chastised herself. Not every man was like Jonathan.

"Ms. Brenton, you can join Mr. Callahan in room two," the nurse announced loudly. "You can bring your daughter with you." She smiled at Mira's confused face.

"Th-thank you." Mira helped Reese gather her books, and they went to the examination room.

The doctor was with Patrick, who was lying on the table with his shirt open. The stout doctor looked at Mira and smiled as if she had been coming with Patrick all along.

"Well, Ms. Brenton, what do you think?" He grinned at her. "Has he been eating well? He wants me to let him drink alcohol again."

Patrick turned his head in Mira's direction and smiled. "I told him we eat lunch together a lot, and that you're my witness that I have been doing well."

She couldn't deny it, even if the sight of his naked, muscular chest wasn't driving her mad. "Well, he has been eating well. He's a vegetarian, you know."

The doctor smiled. "Yes, I know, but Patrick's stomach still hasn't healed. So I'm trusting that you'll remind him that he needs to eat unseasoned food, soups, things like that."

Mira scowled at Patrick. "He never mentioned that. He told me only that he couldn't have soda and he didn't eat meat. But I will make sure he eats better," Mira added in her I'm-going-to-get-you-buster voice.

"Thank you, Mira. Finally, some cooperation. He's been my patient for three months, and this is the most cooperation I have gotten out of him." He motioned for Patrick to get dressed. "See you in two weeks." He handed Patrick a sheet of paper.

Mira watched the doctor leave the room. The minute he closed the door, she lit into Patrick for not telling her the truth. "How could you? If we're going to be together, you're going to have to be honest with me."

He watched her with those sexy green eyes as he sat up to button his shirt. "I was honest with you. I just didn't follow doctor's orders."

She stood directly in front of him, pointing her finger in his face. "You're going to follow Mira's orders." She kissed him. "If you don't, I'll have to cut you off. I'm sure I don't have to clarify, do I?"

Patrick shook his head. "No, you don't. Let's go." He grabbed Reese's hand and headed out of the office, and Mira quietly followed. He stopped at the nurses' window and handed the woman seated there the form.

"Billed to the agency as usual, Patrick?"

He nodded, and they left the office and headed to the parking lot. He opened the car door and let Reese and Mira get in the car before he slid behind the steering wheel. "Where would you like to eat?" Patrick smiled as he started the car.

"How about Soup and Salad?" Mira suggested, but she saw two very disappointed faces staring at her. "Okay, okay. How about The Steak Place, it has steak and salad."

"Better. Although soup and salad would have worked for me, Reese would have a hard time finding something to eat." Patrick reached across the console and caressed her hand. "You can't always get your way. Life would be too easy."

***

Patrick hummed as he got ready for his date. After a lot of debating with Mira, he had finally gotten her to let Reese spend the night at Ashley's. This was their first official date as a couple.

As he slipped on his cashmere sweater, he smiled. Even though Mira had given her permission for the date, he had to clear it with Reese too. After a private conversation with Reese, the child's only request to Patrick had been a doggie bag.

When he arrived at Mira's, he was hoping to see Reese before she left for her sleepover. But once Mira opened the door, all thoughts of Reese and her sleepover disappeared from his mind.

He had told her to dress casual, but her corduroy slacks were just tight enough to show off her hips, and her tight V-neck sweater emphasized her full breasts and showed off her cleavage. "You look great, Mira." He leaned to kiss her. "Almost good enough to eat."

She blushed, then turned her head away. "Th-Thank you, Patrick. You're wearing those slacks well yourself." She waved him inside.

After she closed the door behind him, the phone rang. Not wanting to eavesdrop on her conversation, he turned on the TV. Before he could get acquainted with the remote, she walked into the living room, laughing. Patrick asked, "What's so funny?"

She sat on the couch next to him. "That was Reese. She called to give me last-minute instructions. She mentioned something about a doggie bag."

He smiled, not wanting to give away his game. "Thanks for reminding me." He pulled her closer to him and kissed her with the longing he felt for her. "Do we have to go to the restaurant?" His fingers ran through her hair and he whispered in her ear. "We could whip something up in the kitchen, then go upstairs and whip something up."

Mira shook her head. "You're kidding, right? I never get to go out on an honest-to-goodness date, and you have the nerve to not want to go!" She stood up and grabbed her purse.

He should have known the night would be special for her. It was also the first time since they became a couple that they wouldn't have Reese with them. He shrugged his shoulders, stood up, and spoke. "I was just asking." He grabbed her hand, and they left.

Mira followed the waiter to the table, with Patrick close behind her. She had stopped walking twice in awe of the decor. The vaulted ceilings, the candles, the soft music playing—she felt like an adult. No clowns or other annoying people coming to your table and interrupting your dinner were to be seen.

"Madam," the waiter said as he pulled out her chair.

She loved the attention. Although Patrick had taken her to some nice places, no one had pulled her chair out for her. Happily, she sat down in the offered chair, smiling at Patrick as he took the seat across from her. "Thank you," she told the waiter as he left the table.

"So, do you like this?" Patrick asked.

"Yes, this is very elegant." Could he really afford the restaurant? He had taken them out quite a few times that week. She hoped he wasn't overextending himself. He always paid with a credit card. "Patrick," she began.

He held up his hand. "What do I have to do, show you my financial assets to set your mind at ease?"

She hadn't meant to upset him, only to reassure him. "I'm not trying to second-guess you or anything. But you've bought dinner for us at least five times this week. I was going to offer."

"That's kind of you, Mira. But this is a date, and there's no way in hell I would let you pay. My father would kill me."

Mira nodded, wanting to know more. "Tell me about your parents."

The waiter came and took the drink order. To her surprise,

Patrick ordered a drink for her. "The lady will have a glass of your finest champagne, and I will have a glass of water. I'd like that in a champagne flute."

The waiter nodded and scurried away. Patrick began, " 'My Parents,' by Patrick Callahan." He wasted time rearranging his gold-plated flatware to his satisfaction. "My parents are very cool, in my opinion. My mom, Amelia, has been a nurse for the last thirty or so years. She retired last year. My dad, Kieran, is a part owner of a pub in Turner's Point, Virginia, with his cousin. He arrived here from Dublin, Ireland, during the late fifties, and met Mom a few years later."

"How did they meet?" Mira couldn't help being drawn to what she knew was probably the most romantic story she'd ever heard.

Patrick smiled slowly. The smile told her he loved telling the story. "At the March on Washington. Dad couldn't believe the way blacks were treated, and he's always down for a good cause. So he and his cousin went to Washington. Can you imagine two pale, white Irish dudes among all those blacks?" He laughed. "My Mom was from Philly, and she went because one of her best friends had just died by the hands of the police. Dad said the minute he saw her, he had to get to know her. It took a little convincing since he was white, but he can be stubborn and he won the battle. He said when they first starting dating, his cousin, who is his partner, gave him grief about the trouble they would have. Dad didn't care. He said he had to have anyone with that much spirit."

Mira was amazed; that kind of love was once in a lifetime. It was the kind of love people hoped for, but rarely enjoyed. "Do you ever go to Ireland?" She watched as the waiter approached the table with their drinks and took their food orders. Mira ordered shrimp scampi, and Patrick ordered a pasta dish.

He laughed. "Yes, I usually go to Ireland once a year. My dad's parents are still very much alive. My paternal grandmother always insists that we kids make the trek annually, so we usually go at the beginning of the summer or late fall. My maternal grandmother isn't living. I see my mother's family more, obviously, since they're in Philly. But some of my dad's family are in Turner's Point, and we hang out. What about you?"

"I guess I have my uncle. But I don't see him as much as I would like."

"You know I have to ask."

"I really don't like my aunt much. She's very materialistic. She has to have the bigger, better thing. My uncle loves her, so I limit my visits to him. But he's my rock."

"How are things going with Shara?"

"She's says I've changed. I just want a good life for my daughter. We used to work together. I was a trainer, but she was content being just an associate. We've had bumps in our friendship before, I know it'll work out."

He nodded. "I'm sure it will, but maybe it's time to move on. Sometimes people in our past can ruin our future."

"Very eloquent and true. Has that happened to you?"

"Actually, yes. My cousin and I grew up together. I went into the military. He chose to stay home. Every time I went home on leave, he'd give me some song and dance about how I had changed. I don't think I did. He was a slacker, never applied himself, and got hooked on drugs. He died about five years ago."

"I'm sorry, Patrick."

He nodded. "For a while I was so mad at him for dying like that. It devastated my aunt. But he chose that life, I didn't."

As she listened to him, she realized that her friendship with Shara was much like that of Patrick and his cousin. "Thank you, Patrick."

"For what?"

"You helped me realize something. I shouldn't feel guilty about wanting to better myself. A friend is supposed to encourage, not discourage." She lifted her glass to him in a mock toast. "To our friendship. It's been one of the most fulfilling things in my life since I had Reese."

Patrick lifted his glass to hers. His green eyes seemed to take on a deeper hue with the candlelight. "I hope you consider me more than just your friend, Mira. I know you don't believe me when I say I'm going to be around for a long time, but I am. To us." He clinked his glass with hers.

CHAPTER 15

"So what are we going to do now?" Mira asked as Patrick started the car.

He smiled at her. "Well, you'll just have to wait and see, won't you? It's a surprise. So just sit back and relax. This will be a night to remember."

She reached across the console and gently rubbed his arm. "Dinner was great, Patrick. We really don't have to go any-where else."

He grinned at her, knowing she was again hinting about her concerns about his financial status. "No way," he countered. "We're doing the night right. Right after you call and check in with Reese."

"I don't know what you're talking about," she said, with-drawing her hand and turning away.

"What do you think? I'm blind? I know that's your phone in your purse. I noticed you kept opening and closing your purse during dinner. You know you want to call her, so call."

She sighed like a drama queen and pulled her cell phone out of her purse. After she pushed the appropriate speed-dial number, she waited as the phone rang. "Hi, Courtney. Just calling to check up on my little woman. Could I speak to her?" She put her hand over the receiver and stuck her tongue out at Patrick as he laughed. "Hi, honey. Are you having a good time? Yes, he's right here. Okay." She thrust the small phone at him. "My daughter wants to talk to you."

Stunned, Patrick took the phone and spoke into it. "Hi, Reese. How's it going?"

Reese giggled. "Great. Are you showing Mommy a good time? Don't forget my doggie bag. I will see you tomorrow. Tell Mommy, kisses." She hung up the phone.

He handed the phone back to Mira. "She hung up the phone. She said 'kisses.' What's that, code or something?" He smiled as Mira held the phone to her ear, then placed the phone in her purse.

"Well, if you must know, it means 'I love you, good night.' When Reese was younger we had our own little code. When I used to baby-sit Shara's kids when she had a date, they made fun of Reese and me saying the whole I-love-you thing, so we came up with 'kisses.' It was short and sweet, and they couldn't make fun of us."

He reached across the console and caressed her hand. "You've been dealing with Shara a long time, haven't you? You shouldn't feel ashamed that you and your daughter express love for each other openly. I know people in therapy who would kill to have the relationship you have with your daughter."

"You know, you're right." Mira smiled at him. "Thank you."

"Wait until later, when you really have something to thank me for." He pulled out of the restaurant parking lot.

Patrick led Mira to the lighted area of the River Gardens in the downtown area of Fort Worth. A fellow agent had told him how romantic the gardens were at night. As they cuddled together, watching the water and the lights, he would have to agree. A few other couples were scattered about on the steps around them. The only sound that could be heard was the soft caresses of the water flowing over the cement.

Mira exhaled loudly. "This is beautiful, Patrick. I've lived in Fort Worth all my life and have never been down here before. How did you know about this?"

"I read about it in the newspaper," he lied. "I thought this would please you. You're always worried about how much money I'm spending. This is free."

She snuggled closer to him. "Well, I love it. This is the best date I've ever had." She kissed him, then whispered in his ear, "Let's go home."

He wanted her to enjoy the evening, not think he had his mind on ending the date so soon. But his body began to wake up as her hands slowly glided up and down his leg. "No, remember, this is supposed to be the night you'll never forget."

"So, you don't want to go back to my house?"

"Mira, that's not what I said. I wanted us to enjoy this. Don't ever think that I don't want to be with you. I do, always." His lips brushed hers. "Let's just enjoy this and see where the evening takes us."

Mira sighed and leaned against him. "Okay, Patrick. Are you saving me from myself?"

"No, from me." *And possibly your father*, he thought. Patrick looked into her eyes and smiled. "Definitely me." He watched as her hands started crawling up his leg toward his throbbing erection.

"You know, we could always make out here," Mira whispered. "I've never done anything like that in a place like this." Her hands massaged him through the corduroy fabric.

The images in his mind were playing havoc with his brain and other parts of his body. "You'd do that for me, here?"

Mira unzipped his pants and massaged him more intimately. "Yes, I would and I could."

Patrick gritted his teeth against the images Mira provoked. If she stroked him one more time, he would burst in her delicate hands. He didn't want her like this. "No, Mira." He removed her hand. "Not that I don't appreciate your effort, because I do. But we're not teenagers, and I don't want to cheapen the feelings we have for each other." He took a deep breath and zipped up his pants.

Mira smiled at him, loving him more each time they were

together. She stood up and held out her hand for him. "I feel like walking now. What do you say?"

With the lights illuminating her face, Patrick thought only of one thing: sex. That would get him into more trouble than he was ready for. "How about some ice cream? I know it's a little chilly out here, but a little ice cream might cool us off."

Mira nodded. "Sounds great." She looked down at his affected area. "Are you sure you'll be able to walk?" Grinning, she headed for the street.

After he took a few minutes to calm down from the intense feelings of Mira's little game of foreplay, he caught up with her. He kissed her, grabbed her hand, and led her down the street.

Patrick discreetly surveyed the street. It was quiet. Too quiet for a downtown street near a tourist attraction, and it was only a little after nine P.M. But the street was desolate except for him and Mira.

He felt Mira's hand squeeze his tightly. She was scared. "What is it?" he asked. Patrick gazed around and he spotted it. Maybe it was nothing, he hoped.

She lowered her voice. "Those men look like they're looking for trouble, and I left my purse in your car."

Along with my gun, my knife, and my phone. "Don't worry, Mira. I'll protect you," he said with confidence.

"With what?"

"Now that's a good question," Patrick whispered, trying to think of a decent plan that wouldn't get either of them killed. "Just keep walking normally."

They continued down the street. *Three men,* he noticed. He could take them, but what would Mira think? Maybe they just wanted his wallet, or something else minor. As the men neared them, Patrick could tell they were looking for something else. He listened as they spoke in Spanish.

"She's got a nice rack," one man said to another in Spanish. "We can knock him out, throw him over the bridge, and take her."

Patrick couldn't maintain his poker face. "Apologize to the

lady and keep moving, fellas," he told them in their native tongue.

They continued to speak in Spanish. "There are three of us and one of you. How can you defeat us and keep the lady safe at the same time?"

"You don't want to know. Why don't you guys go sleep it off?"

One of the men looked at Mira, licked his lips, and made a smacking noise translatable in any language. "I'm taking the lady with me. They'll find her body tomorrow."

Patrick sized up the situation. He decided on his course of action and hoped Mira would understand later. "Leave," he said, pushing her out of the way.

"Patrick!" Mira yelled as she ran to the car. Then she realized she should be hiding and not watching him.

Knowing she was safe and out of the way, Patrick could focus on the men before him. Catching them in a moment of shock, he used the full force of his body weight and knocked the first man out with his fist. The second man pulled a knife and attempted to stab him. Patrick stepped out of his way, and the man ran into a parked car. He hit his head on the outside mirror and then kissed the pavement. Patrick stared at the third man. "What are you going to do? You want to join your friends?" he asked in Spanish.

The last man shook his head and ran away. Patrick watched him as he ran right into a pair of police officers waiting at the end of the street. He walked to Mira as she met him.

"Patrick, are you all right? Did you get hurt?" She embraced him the in warmest hug he had ever had in his life. She dotted his face with small kisses. "I thought you were going to get beat up, but you took care of all of those guys."

He wrapped her in his arms, attempting to bring her closer to his body. His adrenaline was pumping at an enormous speed, and for the first time in too many years, he was scared. Not for himself, but for Mira. What if one of those inept men had succeeded in taking him out?

This supposedly easy assignment was fast turning into a full-charge one, complete with bad guys following Mira and almost succeeding in taking her. Luckily, the idiots tonight were not as adeptly trained as Patrick. He could tell those guys were hired morons. Which only meant Rico was on his way.

Mira continued her soft, gentle stroking of his back. "Why did you do that? Pushing me out of the way like that," she clarified.

Patrick hugged her and kissed her on the forehead. "I didn't want you to get hysterical, and I couldn't tell if they were loaded or not." He couldn't tell her that those men could have been hired killers sent by her father.

"You thought they were drunk, so you pushed me to a car?" Mira attempted to clarify his statement.

"No, I mean I couldn't tell if they had guns or any other kind of weapons," Patrick clarified.

"Oh." Mira looked down at the two men on the ground. She hugged him tighter as the realization hit her. "You mean they could have killed us?"

"Yes. Look, Mira, I know you're not naïve about situations like this. They didn't have good intentions toward you."

"You speak Spanish?"

"A little here and there," he lied. Actually he was fluent in the language as well as German, Italian, and his father's native language of Gaelic. Patrick noticed the police car as it neared them. The officer hopped out of the cruiser and approached them.

"Were these guys bothering you?" The officer smiled at Patrick. "Nice work." He bent down and handcuffed the men.

Patrick watched the police officers put the men in the car and drive off. He stared at Mira, hoping that she didn't question him about the police and why they didn't ask any questions. "Why don't we skip the ice cream and go back to your place?" He gently rubbed her face.

"I feel fine. I still want ice cream, and since I'm walking

with Mr. Universe, I feel pretty safe." She grabbed his hand, and they headed down the street.

Patrick shook his head. "Mira, don't you want to talk about what happened?"

"No. I just want some ice cream and a little TLC."

As they sat across from each other eating hot fudge sundaes, Mira thought about the events of that evening. Patrick had knocked those guys out and wasn't even winded. That could have been his military training, she told herself. Those men were just street vermin, and they were drunk. It wasn't like they were sober, healthy men, or hit men.

"What are you thinking?" Patrick devoured his sundae in a matter of minutes. "Are you still thinking about before?"

"No," she lied. "I was just thinking about how you're going to make all this up to me. I think it's time for another lesson, don't you?"

He leaned back in his chair and stared at her. He stared so long that she completely missed her bowl and was trying to spoon up the table instead of the sundae. "You gonna eat the table, or what?" Laughing, he signaled the waitress.

The woman approached the table, smiling at him. "Yes, sir."

He winked at Mira. "Do you have a larger spoon for my friend, or a larger bowl? She's having problems reaching the bowl with her spoon."

The waitress was dumbfounded and stared at the couple. "I'm sorry, sir, I don't understand. That's the biggest spoon we have, unless you want the ice-cream scooper."

"No," Mira shouted, then softened her voice. "This is just fine. My friend was trying to be funny."

The waitress shook her head and walked away from them.

Mira shook her finger at Patrick. "You are in so much trouble! I can't believe you chose to embarrass me like that." She concentrated on not looking at his face, but at her ice cream.

"Oh, Mira, it was a joke. How many times was I supposed to watch you hit the table with your spoon?" He smiled at her, melting what little resolve she had. Reaching across the table, he caressed her hands. "Now, you know I would never embarrass you unless you really deserved it."

She was overreacting; she knew it. He'd never done anything like that before. Maybe he was trying to lighten the mood. "Okay, maybe I deserved it a little."

He grinned and stood. "You look just like Reese, when she's done something she isn't supposed to. I think it's very cute." He held out his hand. "I think it's time for that lesson."

"It's about time!" Mira's hand slid into his, and they left the ice-cream shop.

Later, Mira sat on her bed dressed in her most desirable lingerie, waiting for Patrick to come out of the bathroom. Something wasn't right. Since they had returned to her house, he'd been in the bathroom, supposedly changing into his pajamas. "Patrick, are you okay?"

"Yes," came his reply, but he still hadn't exited the room.

"Are you looking for condoms?" She'd heard him open the medicine cabinet.

"I was looking for indigestion tablets," he called to her.

"Look under the sink," she called to him. Why did he need tablets? They had eaten dinner over three hours earlier. They had only had sundaes later; she wondered why his stomach was upset. She heard him opening the cabinets again. Finally, he came out of the bathroom, rubbing his stomach. "What's wrong?"

He sat on the bed. "Well, there's something I should have told you earlier."

It's about those scars, she guessed. "What is it? We can forgo tonight."

He held his head down in shame. "I'm allergic to chocolate."

Mira turned toward him. "Why didn't you say something? You didn't have to have a chocolate sundae. You could have just had plain old vanilla ice cream."

"I like chocolate. So it's a trade-off. I eat chocolate and then take some tablets, and I'm fine." He kissed her.

Mira held his hand. "We don't have to make love tonight. We could just cuddle."

Patrick looked at her and licked his lips. "Cuddle, hell!" He reached for her, wrestling her until she was pinned beneath him and breathing hard. He lowered his head and nibbled her lips before engulfing her mouth with his.

The phone rang early the next morning, waking Mira from a much-deserved sleep. As she answered it, she heard her daughter speaking but couldn't understand her. Reese was chattering a mile a minute. "Honey, let me speak to Ashley's mother." Soon she heard the calm voice of an adult. "Hi, Courtney, what's going on?"

"Well, we were going to the mall later and wanted to know if it's okay to take Reese with us and bring her home later today."

"Oh, that's sounds fine."

Courtney's voice dripped with innuendo. "I'm sure you probably have to let Patrick come up for air." Laughing, she ended the call.

Mira laughed as she replaced the phone in its cradle. If she only knew, she mused. All her hopes for a night of romance had been dashed with a bad mixture of over-the-counter medicine and chocolate.

Patrick awoke at the slight move Mira made to replace the phone. He noticed that their feet were entwined. Grimacing as the events of last night came to mind, he moaned. "Sorry about last night." He drew her closer and began to nibble on her ear. "I didn't mean to pass out." His hands began traveling over her body as he felt her inching closer to him. "Was that Reese? How much time do we have?" His kisses moved to her cheek, then toward her mouth.

"We have practically all day. Ashley's mother is taking them to the mall. Usually that's an all-day excursion. How do you feel?"

"I feel like making up for lost time," said Patrick, easing her against the pillows. He nibbled her lips as if they were the plumpest, ripest strawberries in the world.

Mira moaned, wanting more of him. She wrapped her arms around him and moved her nightshirt-covered body in rhythm with his. Finally, their lips broke contact, and Mira reached for a condom.

Patrick took the foil wrapper from her. He stood, took off his pajama bottoms, and slid back into bed. She watched as he unbuttoned her nightshirt and glided it off her shoulders.

She looked like a goddess to him. His eyes bathed in the beauty before him, and his lower body told him he was more than ready. He leaned against her, the condom still in his hand. Her full lips beckoned for another soul-stirring kiss, and Patrick couldn't help but comply. But he felt something strange as soon as his lips met hers. Mira was biting his lips, and not in a good way. "What is it?"

"Put the condom on first." Her hands glided down his stomach, and they didn't stop until she heard him moan.

He liked the way she played with him. His lessons had paid off. Mira was a quick study in lovemaking and she knew what pleased him, but he'd also learned what pleased her. He slipped the condom on and leaned down and kissed her. Just as their kisses were getting too hot to handle, the phone rang again. Patrick refused to let her go, but Mira squirmed against him.

"It could be Reese," she breathed as she attempted to put space between them. Panting, she reached for the phone. "Patrick, if you don't move your hand!"

"All right, all right." He leaned back against the pillows, taking a deep breath and watching Mira's nude form reach for the phone. "Tell Reese it had better be important."

Mira nodded and answered the phone. "Reese, honey, what's wrong?"

Shara laughed. "Well, I can't believe you actually let her go somewhere without you. Where's Reese? The kids and I thought about coming out for the day and they wanted to spend the night."

Mira dissected the innocent sentence. "So in other words, you have a date and your parents won't watch the kids." Mira sat up in bed, hugging the sheet closer to her. "I'm sorry, Shara, Reese had a sleepover last night. She's at the mall with Ashley as we speak." Mira giggled as Patrick moved closer to her.

"What are you doing later?"

Mira took a deep breath as Patrick began kissing her back and moving his lips up to her neck. "Well, I have plans for today as well. You should have given me more notice." She eased against Patrick as his hands began wandering over her body.

"So, in other words, Patrick is over, huh?" Shara huffed. "I can't believe you let Reese spend the night with someone. You hardly ever let her spend the night with us, and we've known each other for ages. Is he that good in bed you pawned your fragile child on the first person that offered?"

"That's not fair. Reese and Ashley go to school together. Courtney isn't a stranger."

"Ashley, Courtney, what is going on with you? You forgot where you came from, Kasmira Brenton. Just cuz you have curly hair and live in that snooty neighborhood, don't forget where you came from! Does Patrick know that you're from the hood?"

"Yes, he knows where I'm from. Reese is happier here than she ever was at home. I won't ever forget where I came from, because you'll always be around to remind me."

"Oh, no, I won't. I don't associate with sellouts." Shara hung up the phone.

Mira beheld the phone as it buzzed at her. "What's with her?" She asked the room. When Patrick or the room didn't answer her, she turned and faced him.

"What was that?" he asked.

"Shara wanted me to baby-sit for her tonight. When I couldn't, she lashed out. It's okay, I'm used to it."

Patrick encircled her in strong arms and kissed her. "Mira,

I know I have said this before, but she's not your friend. Regardless of the fact that you grew up together, you've outgrown her."

Mira laughed. "I don't care about that, I care about you and what you're supposed to be doing. Whether Shara and I remain friends is immaterial right now. What I want is to be loved by a certain green-eyed study partner."

Patrick smiled, drawing her closer to him. He kissed her forehead gently, not knowing if passion was what she really needed. Maybe she just needed comforting. And he wanted to comfort her as much as possible.

He placed gentle kisses on her cheeks and closed eyes, and then nuzzled her neck. "Mira, maybe we should wait. You just had an argument with your childhood friend. Your emotions are out of control right now, and I won't take advantage of you." He moved away from her.

Mira sat up, looking at him with those eyes that drove him crazy. She let the sheet fall from her body, not bothering to hide her nudity. "Patrick, Shara and I have disagreements all the time. It's only because I'm hanging on to a friendship that should have ended long ago."

"But Mira," Patrick started, "I don't want you looking back at this and going 'What was I thinking?'"

She crawled over to him and settled in his lap. "What I'm thinking, Patrick Callahan, is why this man won't make love to me right now." She teased his mouth open with her tongue, showing him exactly what she wanted.

CHAPTER 16

A few hours later Mira woke up feeling refreshed. Patrick was gone from the bed and she wondered if her fantasy would come true—the one where he would walk in her bedroom with a tray of all her favorite breakfast foods, and feed her breakfast. Since he was a vegetarian, that fantasy would probably remain just that. She wouldn't subject him to making her bacon a second time.

Glancing at the phone, Mira thought about calling Shara. That thought went directly out of her mind as she watched Patrick enter the room with a tray of food. Maybe her fantasy would come true after all.

"I thought you might be hungry after our little workout this morning." He grinned as he placed the tray in front of her. "Here you go. A breakfast of champions."

Mira looked down at the tray. "I have to give you an A for effort. Eggs, toast, hash browns, milk, and juice. Did you forget something?"

Patrick gazed at her, confusion evident on his sexy face. "I don't think so." He sat down on the bed and started eating. "Remember, you said you were going to give up meat for me, you know, to help me stay on track."

Mira snickered. "There are not enough condoms on this earth to make me say something that crazy. I want bacon, Patrick Callahan." She crossed her arms in front of her chest. "I want it now."

He winked at her. "I don't think that was a wise word

choice, do you?" He sipped his milk, trying to mask his laughter.

"Yes, it was. You just have a filthy mind. I want bacon."

"I was afraid you'd say that." He stood and left her room. Soon he returned with a plate of bacon and sausage. "Happy?"

"Extremely." She picked up a piece of bacon and put it in her mouth. "I know you don't eat meat. It must have been an ordeal for you to cook this, especially since this is the second time you've done it. Much like when I fix dinner with you in mind."

He also picked up a piece of bacon and popped it in his mouth. "When in Rome . . ." Patrick smiled as he guzzled down the last of his milk.

Mira shook her head and continued eating her breakfast.

Later, Patrick stood in the kitchen, a feeling of contentment running through him like a lazy river. Mira was upstairs, taking a shower. They were going shopping and then picking up Reese at the mall. He finally understood what his parents had been drilling into his brain all those years about family and responsibility. He felt personally responsible for Mira and Reese. It was no longer an assignment, and she was no longer a suspect.

The phone rang, interrupting him as he cleaned up the kitchen. Absentmindedly, he answered the phone, forgetting where he was. "Hello."

"P-Patrick?"

"Yes. Who's speaking?" He recognized the voice, but wanted her to admit who she was.

"So you're Mira's personal phone screener now? It seems every time I call, you're answering her phone like you own the joint or something," Shara complained in her whiny voice.

"I was near the phone, so I answered it. Who's speaking, please?"

The caller spoke through gritted teeth. "This is Shara Hilliard, Mira's friend."

Patrick wouldn't use the term *friend* when he thought of Shara. "Yes, Shara. How can I help you?"

"You could help me by telling me what you plan on doing with Mira."

"I'm sure I'm not following you."

"Ever since you popped into the picture, Mira's been acting strange, and I don't like it. You're always there. Don't you have a place of your own?"

"Yes, I do. Why does it bother you that Mira is dating? You don't want her to have some of the happiness you've shared with your children's fathers?"

"How do you know my kids have different fathers?"

"I didn't. Just took a wild guess." Patrick smiled as Mira walked into the kitchen, silently asking who was on the phone. His eyes immediately went to the cleavage of her sweater.

Placing his hand over the mouthpiece, he whispered. "It's Shara. Did you want to talk to her?"

Mira nodded.

He released his hand and spoke into the phone. "Shara, Mira just walked into the room. Hold on." He handed the phone to Mira as she leaned against him.

Patrick rubbed Mira's arm in comfort, knowing that the phone conversation would probably end in a fight. He was startled as Mira started giving Shara one-word answers. Mira's body tensed up more with each response.

Mira hung up the phone. "Well, at least that's over for now."

Patrick turned her in his arms so that she faced him, and hugged her. "Honey, was it because of me?"

"No, sweetie." She grinned up at him. "If it hadn't been you, it would have been some other man or something. She was trying to guilt trip me into baby-sitting tonight. See, after she had John four years ago, her parents refused to baby-sit for her anymore for a date. Her father said if she had time to get pregnant a second time, then she could keep her own kids. She still lives at home."

"You did, too," Patrick reminded her.

"Yes, I did, but the situations were quite different. Shara's father still works. Not that I begrudge her the comforts of living at home, but I think she should move out, and she won't."

"What did she say to you?" Patrick didn't really care about Shara, but wanted to know why she was so against Mira dating.

"That you will leave me."

"Well, tell her that I will be around for a long time."

She smiled, snuggling against his chest. "That's good to hear."

His arms automatically encircled her in a tight embrace. "I mean it. So you just tell Ms. Shara, or better yet, we can call her right now." He reached for the phone, but Mira took it out of his hand.

She replaced the phone in its cradle. "You just leave her to me. Whether we remain friends or not isn't important, as I said before. Like you said, I have outgrown her." She offered her lips for a kiss.

Patrick liked the confidence Mira exuded. Nothing reminded him of that woman he saw that night at the club. The woman in his arms was strong and could handle her own situations. He just hoped she would be strong when it came to her father. "What do you say we go back upstairs?"

Mira smiled. "Unless we're going up there to get your wallet, the answer is no. I'm ready to go shopping."

Mira glanced at Patrick as she drove to the mall, knowing how uncomfortable he was sitting in the passenger seat. He was definitely a man who liked being in control.

"Hey, red light at twelve o'clock," Patrick warned as he adjusted the seat belt. "I knew we should have taken my car."

"And be stopped by cops so they could look inside? No, just sit over there and be a good passenger. I promise I won't kill you." She had a fit of giggles. "Or at least until our test on Monday."

"All right." He adjusted his seat belt again. "I think my car has better seat belts."

"No, it doesn't. All seat belts are made the same. If you don't stop fiddling with it, I'm going to make you go in Victoria's Secret."

"You don't have to force me to do that. I love that store."

Mira wiped that smug smile off her face. She knew he was not inexperienced with women; he had told her that. But for him to admit that he loved the lingerie store was just a little too much for her.

Patrick was enjoying his temporary victory. "Mira, I know you know that I wasn't a virgin when I met you. Remember, I was teaching you about sex." He leaned across the console and kissed her on the cheek.

"I know," she whispered. "It just rattles me to hear that you like that store." She turned into the parking lot and parked the car.

After they got into the actual shopping mall, Patrick moaned at the amount of shoppers. "Why is it so busy? It's not even Thanksgiving yet."

She couldn't contain her happiness. Shopping at the mall with Patrick had to be a sign. Jonathan had always refused to shop with her. "Sweetie, it's Saturday. It's always crowded during the weekend." Patrick stopped walking. Mira stopped as well. "What's wrong, Patrick?"

He looked down at her, smiling. "You have to find a more manly term of endearment for me than sweetie."

"Can I call you Pat?"

"Not if you plan on living after today." He grabbed her hand and they started walking again. "Hey, Victoria's Secret, let's go in."

Mira realized that she had to go in; she didn't have a choice. Although she had never shopped there in her life, she would never let him know that. "Sure," she said with a fake air of confidence. "I shop here all the time. I'm surprised the salesclerks don't know me." She started to walk inside the store, but Patrick stopped her.

"They might know you at Victoria's Secret, but this is the bubble-bath place." He laughed as she backed out of the store and entered the correct one.

"Honest mistake. I do that all the time." Mira lied as she went to the first rack she reached. Unfortunately it was skimpy lingerie. *Oh, great!* "Why don't we look at something else?" Her suggestion came too late, though. Patrick had already picked up a red lace number.

"What about this one?" He held it against her body. "I think you'll look hot with this on."

Mira could imagine everyone was staring at her and laughing. "Patrick, you've seen what I wear to bed. I don't think I could wear that to sleep."

He picked up a royal blue one. "Who said anything about you sleeping in it?" His innocent question was anything but.

How could he make her feel all toasty and warm in the middle of the store? "Patrick."

He didn't hear her because he was heading for the checkout counter. Mira rushed to stop him purchasing the items in his hands. "Patrick, have you lost your mind? I can't wear that."

His green eyes danced with mischief. "Not even for my birthday?" He nodded to the salesclerk.

Mira knew she was walking into the lion's den. "When is your birthday?"

"Today."

"Not."

"Is too." He handed his credit card to the salesclerk.

"All right." Mira watched the salesclerk complete the transaction. As he grabbed the shopping bag she noticed it was too large to contain just a skimpy baby-doll nightie. "What else did you get?"

"You'll have to wait and see." He winked at her and grabbed her hand, and they left the store.

Mira intended to go through that shopping bag at her first

opportunity, but her cell phone rang. She looked at the display, praying it wasn't Shara. Her prayers were answered—it was Courtney. "Hi, Courtney. Is everything okay?"

Courtney's soft voice erupted in laughter. "Man, you are a nervous mother, aren't you? I called because the girls wanted to go skating after lunch, do you mind?"

"Actually, Patrick and I are at the mall. I can meet you at the skating rink."

"That'll be great." Courtney ended the call.

Mira pushed the "end" button on her cell phone, placed it in her purse, and faced Patrick. "Hey, how about some lunch? My treat."

He nodded, smiling at her.

"What are you grinning at?" She fished in her purse for her wallet.

"You," Patrick said. "You went through all this let's go to the mall business, when all you had to say was that you missed Reese. We could have picked her up hours ago instead of making love this morning." He winked at her.

She hated when he could figure her out, before she could herself.

Patrick eye's scanned the crowd at the food court as Mira attempted to get some money from the cash machine. Satisfied he didn't see any of Paulo's henchmen, he turned his attention to Mira as she muttered some not-so-kind endearments to the ATM. Patrick asked, "What's wrong?"

She inserted her bank card again. "It's saying I don't have enough money in my checking account. I know I transferred money last Wednesday." She pushed the buttons and waited.

Again the card popped out of the machine. Patrick noticed the brand of machine. He had the same problem whenever he was out of the county. A simple computer programming error. If the card was signaling the wrong network, the card wouldn't work, which had to be the case here. A buddy at the FDIC had told him the banks weren't willing to fix the problem. "Let me see your card."

Mira looked at him for a minute. If she was like most people that card was her lifeline. "I promise I won't ask for your PIN number."

"How will you get it to work, then?"

"You'll just have to trust me." He held out his hand for her card. Finally, she gave it to him, and he inserted it into the machine. He punched the numbers. "How much?"

Mira gasped. "You got it to work! How? A hundred dollars." She looked up at him with awe. "Usually, it takes me at least two attempts before it will take my card."

"Well it's a secret to making them work. If you're a good girl, I might show you." He handed her the money and her card. "See, and you didn't have to give me your PIN."

"Yeah, I'm very impressed. You're my new hero," she said, grinning. "What would you like for lunch? There's a health food place across the way." She pointed across the crowded food court.

"I'll have what you're having," Patrick said, glancing around the food court area.

"You're just trying to put me on the spot. Well, you're not. You think I'll eat vegetarian food, but I won't. I'm having Chinese food." She pulled him to the line and ordered for them both.

After they got their meal, they sat in the corner as Patrick surveyed the room. His glance rested on a Mexican man of medium height who looked directly at him while talking on a cell phone. Rico was watching Patrick and Mira intently. But did the bad guys know about Reese?

Patrick tried to control his breathing so as not to alarm Mira. "Hey, why don't you call Courtney and see where they're at?" An uneasy feeling had settled in the pit of his stomach.

Mira stared at him before she reluctantly pulled out her phone and called her friend. She mumbled a few short responses, laughed, and hung up the phone. "She says that the girls are just getting on the ice. We can go there when we're finished eating."

Patrick nodded and concentrated on trying to finish his food in record time. He didn't want to arouse Mira's suspicions, so he tried to intersperse a little conversation between his rapid bites. "So, what's on tap for tonight?" He shoveled a spoonful of rice in his mouth.

"I don't know. It pretty much depends on Reese. She needs to read a story by Monday and I need to study for that sociology test. What about you?"

"Nothing. I thought I would keep you company. Maybe break in that lingerie I bought for you."

"I don't think it's your size," Mira said sarcastically.

"You're my size."

"Patrick! Your word choices sometimes," she scolded.

He grinned as her face turned a cute shade of red in embarrassment. "Aw, Mira. You're about the only woman who can get me hot and bothered in a crowded mall." Just imagining her in that teddy did serious things to his body temperature.

They continued eating and trading barbs until Patrick couldn't wait any longer to make sure Reese wasn't in any danger. "Hey, let's go see how Reese is doing." He stood up and grabbed his bag. "Come on, we can surprise her."

"My, my aren't we in a hurry? Are you just trying to see what Reese has going on, so you can plan accordingly? Is that it?" She smiled as she stood also.

"No, I just haven't seen my new best friend in a few days. She might not recognize me," he teased her as they walked downstairs to the skating rink.

As they entered the area, Patrick noticed screaming children of all ages raced all around the skating rink, a merry-go-round, and a train ride. He feared a headache would be his undoing tonight. The noises got louder as they neared the rink. A short, blond woman met them as they entered the stands to take a seat.

"Hi Mira, Patrick, we could have brought Reese home." She sat beside Mira. "I see you have been shopping at my favorite store. I usually get something from there on my husband's birthday, my birthday, you know." She winked at Mira.

Patrick couldn't help laughing at Mira's nervousness. It made her seem more adorable. He joined the women's conversation. "Yeah, she forced me to go there with her. I couldn't help it. Where are the girls?" He scanned the crowd but couldn't see Reese anywhere.

Courtney looked out on the ice. "That's funny, they were just waving at me. Oh, there they are. Dave is out on the ice with them. I think he sometimes wishes he were a figure skater. I think he uses the girls as an excuse to skate."

Patrick relaxed as he saw Reese wave to him and Mira. Reese reminded him of a figure skater. Her thin build was certainly a plus in that respect. "Honey, there she is. Look, she's waving." He also spotted Rico, leaning against one of the stands. Patrick would have to step up security. Rico in attendance meant only one thing. Past experiences taught him that Paulo was on his way.

CHAPTER 17

Reese ran to Patrick and jumped into his arms. Automatically, he wrapped his arms around her in a tight hug as if they had been doing that forever. Her light body in his arms felt like as comfortable as his Glock did. Why would someone else's child have that kind of effect on him?

Easy, he thought, as he placed Reese back on the floor, you love her, too. "Hey, how was the sleepover?" He watched as Reese hugged her mother. Smiling, Mira stroked her daughter's hair. Mira felt the same contentment he did. "How was your party?"

"It was fun, Mr. Patrick. How was your date?"

"It was fun, too. We had ice cream sundaes." He winked at Mira, getting a laugh from Ashley's parents.

"With whipped cream, I hope?" Ashley's father asked.

"Of course," Patrick said, with a conspiratorial wink.

Mira shook her head in disbelief. "Man, this is getting more embarrassing by the minute. Honey, are you ready to go?"

Reese nodded, running to collect her shoes. Courtney talked to them as her husband ran in the same direction as Reese. "One of the kids in their class is having a birthday party here next Saturday. If you like, I can pick up Reese and she can spend the night, to give you Patrick a little, you know," she teased Mira.

Patrick wanted to laugh, but Mira had started twirling a strand of her hair, a sign she was nervous and embarrassed.

She spoke in a quiet voice. "I'll have to think about that, Courtney. How did she do? Any nightmares?"

Courtney laughed. "Yes. Mine. They kept me up until four this morning, watching movies. I'm looking forward to a nap."

Patrick could definitely relate. Who would think a little six-year-old would have that kind of energy? He watched the kids return. "We'll stop by and get her things later, if that's okay," he told Courtney.

Mira gave him the look of a woman about ready to lose it. He had overstepped his bounds. He wasn't the head of her household. They were merely study partners, and occasional bed partners. "Sorry, that's not my call," he amended.

Mira laughed. "That's better. Yes, we'll come get them later."

As they drove back to Mira's house, Patrick struggled to think of a believable reason to make a private phone call. For every excuse he thought Mira would believe, he reversed the situation and found that he would have questioned her motives and demanded an explanation.

He settled back and listened to Reese go on about the previous night until his cell phone rang. "Callahan," he answered.

"Patrick, I need to talk to you."

He heard the anxiousness in Harlan's voice, definitely a bad sign. This would be tricky. "No, I can't party with you guys tonight. Do you know where Ricky is?"

Harlan laughed, instantly irritating Patrick. "I take it you are with Kasmira. Is Rico in Fort Worth? Where did you see him?"

"I've been at the mall in Fort Worth. They were having a sale at Victoria's Secret."

"Got it." Harlan ended the call.

"Are you sure you should let Reese go to the skating party next Friday night?" Patrick asked as they settled on the couch later that night.

Mira stared at him with fury in her pretty eyes. "Any other time, you would be telling me I should let her spread her wings and play with other children. She likes Ashley and they play well together, why shouldn't she go?"

He knew it was risky suggesting that she not let Reese go. It would mean one of the rare times they could have an evening alone would be lost. He had been fighting a battle with his brain and his manhood for the last ten minutes. Looked like his brain was going to win. "I just don't want her thinking that we're always trying to send her away. Haven't you been going on and on about how you're trying to balance her time with other people and you? It just seems like you're jumping at the chance to get rid of her."

Mira became defensive instantly, reminding Patrick of his sister when she didn't want him to know he was right. "That's not true! I love Reese with all my heart, and I make all my decisions with her in mind. How dare you sit there like some master of all things related to children! You don't even have any! I'm sick and tired of everyone trying to tell me how to raise my child! I think I have done pretty good, considering the circumstances." She snatched a tissue out of the box and blew her nose. "I'm doing the best I can. I have a daughter who's having some emotional problems dealing with the fact that my mother was shot in our front yard *in front of her*."

Her voice trembled with desperation, frustration, and a whole lot of anger. Patrick tried to smooth her ruffled feathers. "Mira, I know you're dealing with a lot. So is Reese." He rubbed her back in a comforting motion. "I didn't mean to upset you. I was just concerned about Reese. I'm not trying to upset your schedule with her. I just don't want her to think that you're choosing me over her."

"I'm sure she doesn't think that. But we will ask her if she wants to go to the party when she wakes up from her nap. I will let her decide what she wants." She smiled that dazzling smile that always made him grit his teeth against an erection.

"That's all I'm asking." Patrick knew he would have to step

up security. He'd already lost all control of the assignment, and could already hear Harlan's comments about how Patrick had let everything go to hell without a return ticket.

Mira inhaled and leaned against him. "I'm sorry about just now. It's just that lately, that's the same argument Shara is always throwing in my face. I think I have balanced a relationship with you and my time with Reese well."

"Yes, you have," he agreed. "We have even managed to study a few times. Speaking of, when are we going to study again? The test is Monday."

Mira smiled as she turned and faced him. She eased onto his lap. After she wiggled into a comfortable position, she grinned in satisfaction. "I think you have more pressing matters than the test, Mr. Callahan."

Patrick was enjoying the agony, but didn't know how long he would last. "Mira, come on. You know how bad our timing is. The minute we get into bed, Reese could knock on the door."

She slid off his lap and gave another dramatic sigh. "I know. But I don't have to like it."

After Patrick fell asleep in the guest room, Mira decided to confront Shara, her latest demon, and wanted to get it over with as soon as possible. She sat at her large mahogany desk in the dedicated study room she never used.

Shaky hands dialed the phone number. After a customary greeting to Shara's father, John Hilliard, she was able to talk to her friend. "Shara, what was that about this morning?"

Shara's harsh voice quickly answered her. "What do you mean? The fact that you are letting your daughter spend time with anyone but your best friend, just so you can have a little mattress time with Patrick? What is going on with you? You know what kind of mother that makes you?" Shara taunted.

"That's not true," Mira countered. "If you had given me a decent enough warning, I could have made different provisions and would have enjoyed seeing you guys," Mira lied.

"Provisions. You're using all those big words, like always. You always thought you were too good for us. Your mother, too, and now your daughter is going to grow up the same snobby way. On another note, what about Jonathan? Are you going to ever let him see Reese?"

"Why should I? Remember, he wanted me to have an abortion. Even though we were married, he picked that moment to tell me he didn't want any children. We have been divorced over five years, and he hasn't made one effort to see her or offer any money. He has never sent her a birthday card or present. I don't think it would do Reese any good to see him now."

"Are you going to give him the money?"

"Why should I? The minute I found out I was pregnant, he wanted nothing to do with me, let alone Reese. Momma always said he was no good."

"He's a good man," Shara defended Mira's ex-husband. "He just wasn't ready for a family, but you got pregnant anyway. He told you how frightened he was of fatherhood."

Mira snorted in disgust. "Were you in the room with us when he gave me that sob story? When our daughter was just born and, instead of my relishing the first moments of motherhood, I had a grown man telling me how he couldn't stand to hear our daughter cry, and that I ruined his life?"

"John said you told him you were on the Pill," was all her childhood friend could say.

"Shara, what are you talking about? I never told him I was on the Pill. We were only husband and wife, for goodness' sake. He didn't mention he didn't want any children until I told him I was pregnant." Mira was beginning to see the whole picture, and it was ugly.

Shara had become very quiet on the other end of the phone. Mira continued her line of questioning. "Why do you

call him John? He had always told me to call him Jonathan.
He said he hated being called John."

"What?"

Mira hated rehashing old history, especially when she hadn't
wanted to have this discussion anyway. But something about the
way that Shara was defending Mira's loser of an ex-husband
didn't sit well with her, and she had to know the truth.

"Have you slept with him, Shara?" Mira asked, already
knowing she'd been the victim of betrayal.

"Of course not, don't be silly," Shara sputtered, guilt em-
bedded in her soulful voice. "I couldn't sleep with someone
that you were married to. We're friends, you know me better
than that," she answered in near whisper.

I used to, but not anymore, Mira thought. "Well, either way,
it doesn't matter to me. He'll never see Reese as long as I have
any say in the matter. Since he's never given me one red cent
for child support and the divorce was final when she was six
months old, I don't see how he could even demand anything."

"But Mira," Shara pressed the issue, "you won't miss the
cash. You could think of it as a gesture of forgiveness."

"Forgiveness for what?" Mira looked at the phone as if it had
sprouted another head before she continued the conversation.
"What are you, high on drugs?" Mira asked sarcastically. "He's
not getting one red cent from me. As far as I'm concerned,
Jonathan doesn't exist, and neither do you!" Mira hung up the
phone. She stared at the ceiling. "Momma, I hate it when you're
right all the time. Sorry I wasn't listening all those years ago.
Thanks."

Shara paced nervously in front of the stop sign down the
street from her parents' one-story frame house. After making a
feeble excuse to her mother about needing to get some fresh air,
she waited patiently for Jonathan in front of their spot.

She glanced at her watch again. It shouldn't have taken this
long, she thought. Finally in the distance, she saw his car.

He always had a nice car, to go along with that nice body, she figured. The car stopped directly in front of her.

"Get in," was all he said. No *hello* or *hi honey*, no terms of endearment, just cold, heartless words he could have spoken to a stranger.

Feeling like she was back in high school, she slid into the car, and they took off for their spot. But Shara knew they wouldn't be making love that day, or probably any other, thanks to Mira's revelations. "John, we need to talk."

Jonathan took his eyes off the road for a millisecond. "Oh, hell, not you, too. I get enough of this crap at home from my wife. I certainly don't need it from you."

Shara didn't feel like fighting with her son's father. "I want to talk to you about Mira."

Jonathan suddenly pulled to the side of the road and stopped the car. He didn't turn the engine off, but he shifted so he could face her. "Look, whatever that bitch is saying is a lie! I haven't seen or talked to her since that guy threw me out of the club that night. Whoever he is, he must have some kind of cop training. He used some moves on me that I never saw coming."

Shara thought that Patrick wasn't what he seemed. But he had a better position in Mira's life than she had. "Is that what happened to you that night? We were supposed to meet. I figured you were with your wife."

"Well, you were wrong. That wall of a guy manhandled me and threw me out of the club. Later I saw him and Mira leave in his car. I attempted to go back in the club, but four guys gave me an incentive not to."

John had always been able to take care of himself. That was one of the things she liked about him. He was muscular and tall, and nobody ever messed with him. It was like she had her own personal bodyguard when they were together.

With the exception that she could never be with him in public, or tell Mira that her son and Reese had the same father.

"What did they do to you?" Shara cursed herself for feeling

a weakness for this man, who had caused so much hurt to her friend.

John laughed. "Those four bastards took me to some secluded area and beat me up like I was a punk. I was almost unconscious when they left me. I overheard one of the them say something about someone named Callie should be thanking them." He rubbed his arm, pulled up his sweater and thrust his arm at her. "See. This took five stitches. My wife was on my case for weeks to tell her how it happened."

Shara looked at the mark that the stitches left. "My gosh, I can't believe it." Her mind shifted back to the reason for this meeting. "Why did you tell me that Mira told you she was on the Pill and that you had told her you didn't want any children? How do you expect me to convince her to give you money if you don't tell me the truth?"

Licking his lips, he watched her with those eyes that would have normally had her stripping her clothes off for some quick action. "Hey, I thought we came to have sex, not to discuss how you're not doing what you promised you would."

Tears escaped Shara's eyes. This baby-making machine couldn't even say *make love*. Granted, they usually did it a couple of times a week, and maybe the moves were now automatic, but the least he could have done was make it sound less dirty than it already was. She couldn't count how many times they didn't even go to a motel anymore. They did it in the backseat of his car.

"What are those for?" He nodded at her face. "You know that doesn't work on me."

Shara wiped her eyes, determined to be strong, and took a deep breath. "You didn't answer my questions."

"I guess I better if I want to get some, huh?" He inhaled as if he were thinking of a plausible excuse that she would appreciate. "I told you that because I had to tell you something. Yeah, we were married, and I just didn't want the responsibility of a child."

The last words slapped Shara in the face so hard they left

a mark on her soul. "How could you tell her that you weren't ready for fatherhood when you've got all these kids running around now?"

"Baby," he inched toward her, "you know that was a different time. We got married too soon, but I had to do something. She wanted to remain a virgin until we were married. It was a challenge. Yeah, I did love her in some way, but when she got pregnant, I just felt like my life was slipping away and I had to get out of a bad situation."

The man who faced Shara in the car was a stranger. A cold, calculating jerk of a stranger. She didn't know him at all and wished she'd never met him. Now she could understand why Mira was so staunch about not giving him money. But if Shara ever hoped to get out of her parents' house, she had to complete their insane plan. "So is that why you told her that, so she would leave you?"

"Yes," John admitted. "I know she didn't love me, not really. But I knew she'd stay in the marriage because of the baby. I did both of us a favor."

Shara still wanted to believe that he had a good heart. "So, what about your wife? You married her right after I—"

"Got pregnant with John," he finished the sentence for her. "I know, Shara." He took a deep breath, continuing the conversation as if he could ever fix this debacle.

"Shara, you know we got this good arrangement going, and now you're trying to mess it up with all these questions and stuff. You know we jus' kickin' it. I am not leaving my wife, and you know that." His shoulders sagged with the realization that he wasn't going to get any that night. "Look, are we going through with the plan or not?"

Shara wanted to say no, but the word wouldn't come out of her mouth. "Are you sure Reese won't get hurt in the process? She's been through so much already."

John shook his head. "I knew it. I knew you'd get cold feet or a conscience or something. Don't you want your own place, so that we won't have to have sex in my car? Don't you want us to be together? We could live together."

She wanted her own place, but not for that reason. She craved the independence that Mira had, and she wanted to get rid of Jonathan. This was the only way. God forgive her for what she was about to do.

CHAPTER 18

Shara walked back into her parents' house, wishing she'd never met Jonathan, let alone him being the father of her son. Her mother sat on the couch, shaking her head in disappointment at her as she put her purse on the counter. Shara really didn't have the time to have a fight with her mother right now, but the look in Geraldine Hilliard's eyes told her that it was exactly the time.

Shara walked to the flowered couch that was probably as old as her daughter and took a seat by her mother. "Okay, Mom, what is it? Where are the kids?"

Geraldine put down her latest issue of her favorite tabloid magazine on the wooden coffee table and stared at her daughter. "Your father took them to the movies. Something you should be doing instead of always running after those no-good men. Why don't you tell me where you've been?"

"Mom, I'm 27. I think I can go for a walk without having to report to you."

"I know how old you are. I also know you went to meet Jonathan Handley. You know he's not good enough to spit on. I knew he wouldn't stay married to Mira long. She was too smart to put up with his mess. But you, on the other hand, are still seeing him after he married someone else. Does Mira know?"

Shara's mother was a lot sharper than Shara gave her credit for. "I didn't know you knew. I know I need him out of my life, but who's going to look at me now? I have two kids and I still live at home with my parents."

"So who are you trying to blame for that? Us? You can move any time you want. You control your destiny, not some sorry man. Look at Mira; she took control of her life. She raised that baby on her own, helped her mother, and still advanced at work. Now she's living the life she deserved."

"But I don't have that kind of money." *Not yet*, she thought. The conversation only cemented her need for the plan to work. "You know, you have always thrown Mira up in my face." Her voice imitated her mother's voice. "Why can't you be more responsible like Mira? Mira doesn't have two children with two different fathers."

Her mother cleared her throat. "Shara, I only meant that you and Mira worked at the same place, and she advanced and you didn't. She was a trainer, and you are *still* an associate at that place. It just seems she knew what she wanted from life and wasn't waiting for someone to hand it to her on a silver platter."

Shara knew that. People were always comparing her to Mira, and she hated it. Another reason her plan had to work. "I know, Mom."

"When are you going to tell her that John and Reese have the same father?"

"How did you know about that?"

"Well if you don't want her to figure it out, I would suggest not having them in the same place. Reese took after Mira a lot, with the curly hair and the honey complexion, but I can see the subtle likeness to John. I thought Mira was your best friend. And you're sleeping with her ex-husband. I didn't raise you with those kinds of loose morals. You should treasure your friendship with her, but you don't. I've heard some of the things you've said to her, and you're always putting her down. One of these days she's going to tell you where to go and how to get there."

Shara smiled ruefully. "That day has arrived. She has a boyfriend now and they spend all their free time together. I tried to get her to keep the kids tonight, and she couldn't. We got into this big fight. She's never fought with me like that until Patrick came on the scene. I don't understand it."

Her mother laughed. "You'll learn one day. The things you think are important, aren't. The people you think are your friends, aren't."

Patrick stood at Mira's dining-room table, staring at both Mira and Reese. Mira took a small bite of the lasagna and chewed slowly. Reese took a bigger bite and made smacking noises. He couldn't stand it any longer. "Well?"

Mira still hadn't finished chewing. Finally, she swallowed. "It tastes good, Patrick. It just doesn't have any meat in it. I'm used to a dead animal of some sort in my food."

Reese loved it. "This is yummy, Mr. Patrick. Can I have some more?" She lifted her small plate up to him.

"Well at least someone appreciates healthy cooking." He sat down at the table and scooped up another helping for Reese before fixing a heaping plate for himself. He smiled as Mira took another bite, then another.

Mira offered her plate for a second helping. "You know, it's not so bad once you get used to the no-meat thing."

"You'd better get used to it, Mira. I plan on cooking a lot of meals like this." He laughed as Mira's expression changed to one of disbelief. She looked so cute. "Thanks for letting me cook today."

Mira gave him that hundred-watt smile that made him forget about all his good intentions. "Patrick, you didn't have to cook for us."

He watched Reese as she finished a second helping of the lasagna and started working on the salad. "I like doing things for you, Mira. Reese too." It gave him a feeling of contentment, that he'd finally gotten it right. "How about we go get some ice cream for dessert?"

Reese clapped her small hands in approval. Mira nodded.

He hoped he'd be able to make his appointment and not rouse their suspicion.

As they settled down at the table at Baskin-Robbins, Patrick and Mira sat across from Reese. He glanced around the room, feeling like a parent. This wasn't what he had envisioned for a rendezvous point, but he had had few options that wouldn't raise too many questions.

"Patrick, why did you want to come here? I had ice cream and stuff at home," Mira asked as she read the menu board.

"Are you still worried about my money? Mira, it's okay, I promise. Besides, I cooked dinner. This is way cheaper than taking you out for dinner. So what are you having, sweetie?"

She scooted her chair closer to his. "You know how that turns me on when you call me sweetie."

He winked at her. "You can show me later." This innuendo stuff was hard, especially with Reese being so smart. They had to talk in code most of the time if the subject remotely pertained to sex, which was most of the time lately.

Mira's hand slipped under the table and ended up in his lap. She fluttered long eyelashes at him. "I think I could show you now." She winked at him.

"Oh, my, I think I've created a monster!" He laughed, taking his wallet out of his pocket and handing it to Mira as he stood up. "Why don't you order for us while I go to the restroom?"

She took his wallet and nodded. "Don't do anything in there that I can," she said loud enough for his ears only.

"Funny," he said, walking to the restroom.

Once inside the men's room, his contact was waiting for him. Brandon Martinez stood at the sink with a silly smile on his clean-shaven face. Patrick shook his head. "Man, you need to grow a mustache or something. You look twelve."

"Thanks, Dad. Don't think I didn't see her trying to give you a hard-on at the table. I thought you said she was so reserved. She looked pretty laid back to me."

"I know. I think she just does that to get under my skin."

"Yeah. I wished I could get an assignment like that."

Brandon smiled as he took out his Palm Pilot. "You wanted to see me."

"Yeah. I spotted Rico at the mall. He was watching Mira, me, and Reese. Reese is attending a skating party at the mall next Saturday night. We need to step up security. I have the school covered, and I'll be with Mira at the university. At the mall, I need someone close to Reese at all times. That means someone will need to be on the ice with her."

"Could you persuade Mira not to let her attend the skating party?"

"I couldn't," Patrick confessed.

"What?"

"I know, a woman immune to the Callahan charm. I think I'm losing my touch."

"I think it's something else," said Brandon.

Patrick ignored his comment, though truth be told most days he felt Mira was in control, not him. "I need you to run a check on a few of these names," he said, handing Brandon a list of three names. "E-mail the info to me ASAP."

"Got it."

Patrick nodded and left the men's room. When he returned to the table, Mira and Reese were giggling with another couple sitting near them.

"I was ready to send a posse in there for you," Mira teased, returning his wallet. "I ordered you a strawberry shake."

"You know I love chocolate."

"But chocolate doesn't love you."

Patrick realized he was so not in control anymore.

CHAPTER 19

After Patrick, Mira, and Reese left the ice-cream shop, Patrick drove back to Mira's. He breathed a little easier knowing that the skating rink would have more coverage. He could focus his attention on Mira.

She sat in the passenger seat quiet as a mouse. Reese chattered in the backseat about how much she liked eating ice cream and how she wanted to go to the shop again. Was there a food she didn't like? Probably not.

He wondered about Paulo. According to his source at the Bureau, Paulo hadn't entered the country yet, at least not through legal channels. They wouldn't have a record, though, if he flew one of his many private jets in. Patrick hated to admit it, but Paulo was a financial wizard. He had an investment portfolio that would have rivaled any of the Fortune 500 companies. He had jet planes, yachts, mansions, vacation homes, and that was the stuff the DEA knew about. There was probably an incredible amount of money in Swiss bank accounts, Patrick thought.

"Why are you so quiet?" Mira and Reese asked in unison.

Mira laughed. "You seem to be on another planet." She lowered her voice. "If you don't want to stay, I won't feel slighted."

Was she kidding? Even if she weren't his assignment, he would be with her any chance he got. "No, that's not it. I was thinking about what we could do next Saturday night." He glanced at her as they entered her neighborhood. "We could have a real date again."

Mira nodded. "Yes, I have to attend my uncle's birthday party earlier that day, so I know I will need something to cheer me up."

He knew she didn't get along with her aunt and Mira's going to the party showed only how much she truly loved her uncle. "I like birthday parties," he hinted, wanting to be there for her comfort.

"Patrick, it's in my old neighborhood, and Shara will probably be there, along with some of the women that were at the club. You might not feel comfortable there."

"I'm going to be moral support for you, not get into a heated debate with Shara about how she's not being your friend."

She touched his arm. "Thank you."

Electricity traveled up his arms, through his bloodstream and straight to his lower body. But strong determination would win out this time. He knew that making love would not be on the agenda, especially with the amount of food they had shoveled down at the ice-cream shop. He knew that tummy-aches would be the order for the evening. Patrick would happily settle for cuddling.

"What's so funny?" Mira asked.

Patrick couldn't tell her that he was laughing at the fact that he was willing to spend a night of not making love. What happened to Callahan, the woman-slayer? 'The slayer' had fallen in love with a woman whose father happened to be the man he vowed to kill.

"Patrick," Mira prodded softly.

"Oh, nothing. Just thinking." He pulled into her driveway and pushed her remote-control button to open the garage door.

Mira looked at him, puzzled. "Hey, how did you get my remote?"

This is where the agent part came in, he thought. *Think fast, Patrick.* "Remember that time I needed to leave when you were sleeping? I borrowed your spare opener and forgot to return it. Sorry." He didn't tell her this remote was actually a copy of her spare.

He expected her to ask for it back, but she only smiled. "Why don't you keep it? We spend a lot of time together, and we wouldn't broadcast to the neighborhood when you're spending the night if your car isn't parked out front."

Patrick nodded as he got out. He hadn't thought of that. If he could catch Paulo or one of his employees off guard, Mira and Reese wouldn't be harmed, or worse. He opened the door for her. "You mean the neighbors are asking for sex tips now?" he asked, helping her out of the car.

"No, not yet." She laughed, helping Reese out of the backseat of the car. "But you just never know!"

"Mommy, can Mr. Patrick read to me tonight?" Reese asked as she settled in her bed.

Mira was a taken aback by the odd request, but as usual was not able to deny her daughter anything. "Sure, honey, if he doesn't mind reading to you. I'll come say good night when you're done, okay?" Mira smiled as Reese pulled the comforter closer to her and plopped her head on the Barbie doll–covered pillowcase, barely missing the wooden headboard. Excitement was evident in her small face.

"Yes, Mommy," Reese said as she reached for her favorite storybook.

Mira nodded and walked downstairs, not knowing if she should feel excited that Reese wanted Patrick to read to her or rejected because Reese wanted Patrick to read to her, and not her mother, who had read to her every night of her life.

Patrick was flipping through the channels with the remote when she reached the living room. He smiled as she stood in front of him. "Hey, I found a good movie on cable. It's got everything. Romance for you, some action for me, and sex for us," he said, lust dripping with every word.

Mira nodded. "Reese wants you to read to her."

He couldn't contain his surprise. "Are you sure, Mira? Maybe you misunderstood her."

"I think I can understand my own daughter," she said shortly. Was she jealous that her daughter had asked for someone else, and that that person had no ties to her whatsoever? "She specially requested for you to read to her tonight. If you don't want to, I understand."

But Patrick was already up and headed for the stairs. "Mind, are you kidding? This is like getting an A in sociology. This is major in a child's world." He took the stairs two at a time.

Mira sat on the couch, trying to handle the conflicting emotions going through her mind. She should enjoy this private moment, but why did she feel like her world was crashing in around her?

Patrick entered Reese's room with a little apprehension. He wasn't sure what he was supposed to do, since he never dated anyone with children.

He could pretend she was like his niece, and he could relate to her a cartoon version of his latest mission. But Reese and her mother were his mission, so what was he supposed to do?

"Hi, Mr. Patrick," Reese said, when he was silent too long. "I'm glad you could read to me."

"Any time, Reese." She was already dressed in her Barbie nightgown and was holding a small book.

She looked at him with her those big eyes and placed the book on the nightstand. "I wanted to ask you a favor."

"Sure."

She whispered, "You can't tell Mommy or she'll tell Dr. Sid."

That sounded like some big shoes she was asking him to fill. "Well, Reese, you're asking a really big favor, but I'll do my best," he told her, not really giving her the answer she wanted to hear.

She studied him for a few minutes as if deciding if she should continue. She motioned for him to come closer with her skinny forefinger.

When Patrick finally sat on her bed, she spoke. "Granny visits me in my dreams."

Patrick fought to maintain his poker face. "That's perfectly natural, honey."

"Did Mommy tell you how she died?"

Patrick knew this was painful for Reese to talk about. "Yes, it was an accident."

Reese shook her head, contradicting his answer. "No, it wasn't. The man said, 'That's Helen.'"

"How do you know that?"

"One of Granny's friends, Mrs. Hawkins, can't hear. You have to speak slowly so she can make out what your lips are saying."

She can read lips, Patrick surmised. "But honey, why didn't you tell your mother or the police?" Rico could have been under the jail by now.

"Nobody asked me. Everybody told me to forget it, but I can't. Then Granny told me she was happy. I don't know what to do."

"If your Granny says she's happy, then it's okay to forget it," Patrick hoped her testimony wouldn't be needed when it came time to take Paulo to court. "Why didn't you tell your mom?"

"She thinks I'm crazy. I heard her tell Aunt Shara that the doctor wanted to give me some medicine so I wouldn't hurt for Granny. But I have to." She wiped her tears with the cotton sheet.

"Why do you have to hurt for her?" Patrick's curiosity got the better of him, wanting to understand the logic of a six-year-old.

"I didn't protect her then, so I have to hurt for her."

Patrick reached for her hand, wanting to comfort the little girl who had eased her way into his heart. "Honey, your Granny understands and she told you she was happy where she was, right?"

She nodded.

"Well, I don't think she wants you to be unhappy for her.

Just think, she's up in heaven, smiling down on you and your mom. I know she's proud of you. Just like I am." He reached and kissed her on the forehead.

"You're proud of me, Mr. Patrick? As much as your nieces?"

"Yes, Reese. I'm very proud of you."

That seemed to please her immensely. She scooted down in her bed, smiling and preparing to go to sleep. "I won't have dreams tonight." She winked at him.

Patrick laughed at her hint. "Why are you telling me that?"

"Just in case you and Mommy want to watch a movie or kiss." She giggled. "You can send Mommy in."

Patrick knew he had been dismissed. He stood, left the room, and was about to head back downstairs when he heard noises coming from Mira's bedroom. He walked softly, hoping like everything it wasn't Rico sneaking into the house. But breaking and entering wasn't Rico's style.

Patrick stood quietly by the doorway, listening. He relaxed as he heard Mira's voice mumbling something about bedtime stories. She was upset Reese asked for Patrick. He sighed and entered the room.

Mira sat on the bed, wiping her eyes. She was also dressed for bed in a white silk bathrobe and matching lace nightshirt that buttoned down the front. It was only buttoned halfway.

"You must read pretty slow," she said, reaching for a tissue from the bedside table.

Patrick stared at the sight of exposed breast and forced himself to think. "Well, we actually didn't get to read. She wanted to talk."

"What could she possibly want to tell you that she couldn't tell her own mother?"

"Well talk about it later. She's waiting for you to tell her good night."

Mira instantly scooted off the bed and headed for the door. "At least that's something," she mumbled, walking down the hall.

While Mira was gone, Patrick busied himself with getting

dressed and wondering how he was going to tell Mira about Reese's dreams, or if he should. Would Reese view it as a betrayal of trust?

Mira entered her bedroom and shook her head. Patrick strode past her in nothing but a pair of silk boxers.

"Oh, no, you don't! You are supposed to wear pajamas, remember?" Mira took off her robe and placed it on the end of the bed.

Patrick groaned, staring at her with those eyes that made her weak with desire. He eased toward her and wrapped her in his arms. He gave her a quick kiss before answering.

"Reese isn't coming in tonight, she promised," Patrick said as he continued kissing her and easing her closer to the bed.

"How can she promise you something like that?" Mira sat on the bed and he sat beside her. "What did she want to talk about?"

Patrick took a deep breath and grabbed her hand, gently rubbing it. "Well, she told me something earlier in confidence, but since you are her parent, we do need to talk about it. But you've got to promise me that you will not do anything rash like call Dr. Sid on Monday."

She didn't like the sound of that. "Okay, Patrick. I promise. How bad is it? You think I should just let him put her on medication?" Her heart melted at the thought of her beloved daughter having to take medication just to be happy. She'd been through too much for that. Teardrops fell on her comforter. "I've failed my baby!" Her hands covered her mouth, stifling her cries.

Patrick took her in his arms. "Now, Mira, you're getting ahead of the game, okay? No, I don't think Reese needs to be put on medication of any kind. Honestly, I'm against that. She can work this out for herself. Reese told me that the last few nights your mother has been visiting her in her dreams."

"Oh, no!" Mira gasped. "I have failed her. I've tried very hard to fill that void Momma left, but it's hard."

Patrick nodded and whispered, "She told me that your

mother always tells her that she's happy where she is, and that she's proud of her two ladies."

"Mama used to call us that. Her two ladies that were going to change the world." She sat up and looked at Patrick. "It sounds harmless enough, what do you think I should do?" Maybe he knew something she didn't. He had helped with Reese that dreadful night of that attempted carjacking.

"I think you should let Reese tell you herself. She wanted to, but she thought you would think she's crazy." He watched Mira's expression. "Her exact words, promise."

"I know she doesn't tell Dr. Sid very much. She clams up the minute we get into session. I had been thinking about stopping them. You make better sense. I'll bring it up tomorrow. Are we still studying?"

He pulled her into his arms. "I left my book at home. I'll go get it after breakfast. You know, give you a little time to talk to Reese alone."

"You know, you are awfully brave to willingly keep coming back to the crazy Brenton women. I'm sure there are some sane women you could date."

"Yes, there are. But none have your smile and sweet personality." Patrick kissed her softly on the lips. "And you are not the crazy Brenton women, you are the cute Brenton women."

They slipped in bed, nestling close to each other. He was still in bed with her and hadn't run for the hills, she thought. That had to mean something. Mira turned out the light and snuggled against him. "I love you, Patrick."

Silence filled the dark room. As her head rested on his chest, she heard his heartbeat speed up. She realized she had frightened him. "You don't have to say anything in return. You've helped me through some incredible times with Reese and Shara. Before, I wouldn't have been able to cope. I just appreciate you being here for us."

Patrick's heart was so full of love at that moment that he thought it would burst. She had said it first. *Damn it!* He had intended to say it next week when they had their next official date.

His mother's voice popped into his head. She was always telling him that love didn't run on his schedule. In the past, he had always been able to control his emotions. Why couldn't he when it came to Mira? Any other assignment, he would have been able to tell the suspect what to do and when to do it. But Mira wanted Reese to attend the skating party coming up and stood firm against Patrick's objections. He'd make an awful husband.

As he felt Mira's body getting comfortable against his, he gritted his teeth against his growing erection. If she moved just a few more inches to the left, he hoped, all he would have to do was . . . She stopped before she got to the hoped-for position. He tried to relax, but it was becoming more difficult with each of her moans. Each time she moaned, her legs and hands would travel. Patrick began to feel that he was a pawn in the game of sex and could do nothing but let Mira work her magic.

She caressed his flat stomach; then, opening her sultry eyes, Mira smiled at him. He thought he had been considerate by not asking for a passion session, but obviously Mira had different plans.

He took a deep breath as her lips grazed the scars on his stomach. For some reason, that act of tenderness seemed to do ridiculous things to his hormones. All he could think about was the sensation of her tongue against the flatness of his abdomen. *Lower,* he thought to himself. *Lower, please.*

"Do you really want me to?" she asked, looking up at him with seductive eyes.

He didn't realize he had said it aloud. "Only if you want to." He lay flat on his back, letting Mira work her magic on his tired body.

She pulled on his boxer shorts, sliding them down his legs. "Well, looka here," she said, laughing as she threw his underwear across the room.

The boxers hit the wall and fell to the floor. Mira leaned over and kissed Patrick on the mouth, then moved lower, and then lower still. Her hands were at his waist as if she had to hold on to him. She took him in her mouth and Patrick thought he had taken flight. He couldn't think straight with the things she was doing to him with her tongue. She was a pretty fast learner, indeed. This almost made up for her saying the L word first.

Enjoying the sensation, he realized he just had to stop; he didn't want to explode in her mouth. He grabbed her gently, and she crawled up his body and reached in her nightstand for a condom. "Would you like me to . . . ?" She looked at him, mischief obvious in her eyes.

"Yes, honey. Why don't you? Show me what I've taught you these last few months." He dared her, knowing how much she hated being challenged, but was amazed as she unrolled the condom and slid it onto him.

He pulled her down for a kiss as he rolled over so she was underneath. Feeling her insides surround him, he increased his tempo and took them both to paradise. Patrick swallowed her screams of pleasure as he fought off his own release. But he couldn't hold it off for long. He kissed her with the fire he felt in his body.

Slowly their gasps faded into the air. Patrick took a deep breath as he rolled beside her and she settled her head onto his chest. Patrick said, "You get an A for tonight."

"Thank you, Patrick. I had an amazing teacher. He is really a hands-on kind of guy." She snuggled against him. "How about a shower?"

She couldn't mean together. "You can go ahead."

"I meant us showering together."

Did she really understand the implications of an after-lovemaking shower? He always wanted to have one with her, knowing that she would love sex in the shower, but didn't want to press his luck. Especially with Reese in the house, he didn't think it would be wise. "What would happen if Reese caught us? I know she promised that she wouldn't come in, but that's no guarantee."

She nodded. "The door has a lock, Patrick." Rising from the security of the comforter, she walked to the bathroom door. Oozing with sexual confidence, she stood at the bathroom door as if she were daring him to take a shower with her. "But if you're afraid of getting caught, that's fine. I understand completely." She leaned against the doorway, letting him take a good look at her nude body.

His body betrayed him instantly. Blood had ceased flowing to his brain and had headed south. Patrick stood up, revealing a fresh erection, and walked toward her with the purpose of a man with a severe need. "Understand, hell. We'll see who can last underwater." He gently pushed her into the bathroom, locking the door and turning on the shower.

CHAPTER 20

Sunday morning, Mira fixed Reese's favorite breakfast—lots of everything. Patrick had left to get his books so she could have a private conversation with her daughter. Usually Reese woke before her mother, but that morning she slept so late Mira was beginning to get worried.

Mira was getting ready to go upstairs and wake her when Reese emerged in the kitchen, already dressed for the day in a sweatshirt paying homage to Harry Potter, and blue jeans. Her hair was a curly mess and would definitely take some time fixing later. "Reese, are you okay? Hungry?"

She nodded and sat in her chair, looking around the room. "Where's Mr. Patrick?"

Mira sat at the table staring at her small child, not knowing how to start the delicate conversation. She also didn't want to jeopardize the fragile relationship Patrick had with Reese. "Is there something you need to tell me? You know nothing you can say will make me ashamed of you."

Reese looked at her mother, then looked down at the floor. "He told you," she muttered.

Mira took a deep breath. "Now, don't be mad at Patrick for telling me about your dreams. You could have told me yourself. Why were you so afraid to tell me?"

After a few deafening minutes of silence, Reese spoke, "Well, when I spent the night with Angie, she said that she had overheard you saying that you thought you were going to have to put me in a home because I couldn't let Granny go.

Then when Granny started visiting me in my sleep, I knew that you would send me away, like they did Mr. Tucker."

Mira wiped away her tears as she remembered Mr. Tucker from the old neighborhood. A few years before, a white van had come and taken Mr. Tucker away. It wasn't an ambulance, and the van was unmarked, but it did have bars in the back window. Mrs. Tucker never explained it. When asked about her husband, she merely said he was on vacation and wouldn't be returning. It wasn't until much later, when he died, the neighbors found out what actually had happened to him.

Mira sat next to Reese and hugged her. "Honey, that was a special case. Mr. Tucker wasn't well. He thought he was in the war and Mrs. Tucker was a German soldier. He wanted to kill her. You're not like that," she said, brushing back the errant stands of Reese's hair. "There's nothing wrong with you," Mira reiterated, as much for Reese's sake as well as her own. "You just miss your grandmother." Damn Angie for always making Reese feel she was less than perfect!

"But Mommy, if Granny says she's happy where she is, does that mean that she didn't love us at all?"

"Honey, you know Granny loved us. Don't you ever think that she didn't!"

"But Angie said—"

"I don't care what she said! She doesn't know everything. She especially doesn't know how special you were to your grandmother. Angie is not the authority on everything, don't you forget that!" Mira covered her mouth. Reese's big brown eyes had immediately filled with tears. Mira reached for her, and Reese got in her lap. "I'm sorry for losing my temper, I'm not mad at you." She comforted her daughter and spoke in a whisper. "Just because Angie says something doesn't necessarily make it true. I know Momma loved us both. So if she visits you again, tell her I miss her, too."

"Granny told me that something bad was going to happen to us and we needed to stick together." Reese looked down at the floor, slowly raising her eyes to Mira's. "Mommy, would you be mad if I said that I didn't want to play with Angie anymore?"

"No, honey. You can be friends with whoever you want. But why?"

"She called you snobby."

She must get that from her mother, Mira thought. "Well, we have to attend Uncle Harold's birthday lunch next week, and I know they will be there, but we're going to leave as soon as he opens presents. We'll show them how mature we can be, right?"

Reese looked at Mira like she had taken what was left of her brain out of her head. "How?"

"We will show them how real women behave. We will be polite and not cause a scene, okay?"

"Okay, Mommy. Then I get to go skating."

"Yes." *And I get to have a date with Patrick.* "Why don't you tell me about those visits from Momma?"

Reese stared at her. "Are we going to eat breakfast?"

Mira blinked her eyes. The wonderful breakfast she'd fixed was now cold. She didn't want to reheat it or cook again, so she thought of something she knew her daughter would enjoy. "Why don't we go out for breakfast?"

"Yes!" Reese slid out of her chair and walked to the door leading to the garage. "I'm ready."

Mira laughed. "I just have to get my purse."

Patrick walked into his apartment and looked for any signs of forced entry. Everything seemed in order. He heard the distant ring of his satellite phone. His mother? Maybe something was wrong.

"What is it, Mom?" he asked, sitting in front of his computer and turning it on.

Her laughter instantly calmed him down. "Oh, nothing. I wanted to see how things were going with Mira. Have you told her that you love her or that you're a DEA agent?"

"No, but it's been hard not to. I don't really have time to chat, things are heating up here." He read his e-mail as he spoke to his mother.

"I know. Some guy was on your answering machine at your apartment here in Virginia. I know most people know the routine. His message was odd."

"What did it say?"

"He said you can't break up his family. He'd break up yours first."

Patrick laughed, but he didn't really find the message funny. *Paulo.* "This was on which phone in my apartment?"

His mother hesitated. Patrick knew the answer. As usual, his mother cleaned his apartment when he was out of town. He had told his mother repeatedly not to mess with the special phone. As was customary, she hadn't listened to her son. He heard her take a deep breath before she answered, "The same one you told me not to bother with."

Patrick relaxed. His cover as Dorian Martinez was still intact. "I love you, Mom," he said, ending the call.

He found the book he didn't need to study for a test he didn't have to pass since he already had a college degree. He grabbed fresh clothes for the next day and a little gadget for Mira's back door, and headed back to Mira's. He'd plant the tiny camera in the doorknob to test it tonight. He wanted to know if anyone had been checking out her house during the day while no one was home.

If the tests were successful, he would place a camera by her front door as well. He had a bad feeling about Shara, and if the reports he had received about her were true, Mira was in for the heartbreak of all heartbreaks.

But it wasn't his place to tell her. It was Shara's. But *he* would probably be the person who would lose the most. Maybe if he thought of a plan to make Shara confess her secret to Mira, he could still come out the winner. Who was he kidding? This was like getting shot. No matter the how small the entry wound was, you still bled.

Patrick entered Mira's garage and got the surprise of the day. Her PT Cruiser was gone. Where was she? Had she left voluntarily? Had Rico snatched her the minute his back was turned? He took the Rolex out of the console and activated the tracker.

After he located Mira with the aid of the tracking device in the watch, he backed out of her garage and proceeded to restaurant row, which was where Mira and Reese were eating breakfast. The dot on the watch was purple, so they were together, and since food was involved, Mira and Reese were probably just getting something to eat. But wasn't Mira supposed to fix breakfast so that she and Reese could talk about the dreams?

Think, Callahan, think. Patrick took out his cell phone and dialed Mira's cell. He could pretend he was somewhere else and wanted to know what Mira wanted for lunch or something else equally stupid. He waited as the phone rang.

He was about to hang up when he heard Mira voice's. "Hey," said Patrick. Okay, he lost twenty cool points for that lame opening. "I just wondered if you wanted me to pick something up for lunch?"

Mira laughed. "Why don't you just come into the restaurant and join us?"

"How did you find us?" Mira asked later as they entered her house.

Patrick walked behind her into the living room. "I have a better question. How did you know I was outside in the parking lot?"

Reese sat on the couch, watching the couple and smiling.

Mira shrugged her shoulders. She liked when she rattled him. Like today, she had noticed him the moment he drove onto the parking lot. She'd know his car anywhere, never mind the fact that she had memorized his license plate. A car with Virginia plates wasn't too hard to find in Texas.

"Mira, are you going to give me an answer?" Patrick was standing in front of her.

"I just knew."

"Not good enough."

"Mommy recognized your car, Mr. Patrick," Reese said. "We know your car."

He smiled. Mira thought he would be upset, but he smiled at her. "What was that about honesty?"

"Oh, all right," she finally confessed. "I know your car. There aren't many Mustangs that have Saleen emblazoned on the windshield. There are only three black ones like yours around here. Yours is the only one I've seen with that kind of top. Speaking of honesty, how long were you in the military?"

Patrick stared at her as if she had just asked him to name names, like the government had done in the fifties during the Red Scare.

"I was in the military ten years," he said.

So much for that great pension plan, she thought. "How could you retire from the Navy with only ten years of service?"

"I don't recall saying I retired. I said I left the Navy." He sat on the couch by Reese as if dismissing her last question, but Mira was not to be deterred. "Patrick. Answer me."

"All right. I was honorably discharged. Remember the scars?"

Mira nodded, not wanting to bring up the scars and how she saw them in front of her daughter. "Okay, I'll drop it for now." She sat on the other side of Reese, willing her nerves to calm down. But something was bugging her. What was it?

She watched as Patrick whispered something to Reese, and her daughter giggled. Mira knew that meant she was in trouble somehow, especially when Reese nodded her head in agreement to whatever sinister plan Patrick had involved her in.

Mira kept waiting for him to play out his hand, but it didn't happen. Leaning back against the couch, she relaxed, closing her eyes in contentment. But she felt airborne, which wasn't possible.

"Patrick!" she yelled, opening her eyes. Just like that, without making any noises, he had picked her up and lifted her over his head. She was at least ten feet off the floor. "Put me down!"

"Do you doubt my strength?"

"No. Put me down."

He obliged her and slid her down his body. He did that on purpose, she knew it. It didn't mean she had to enjoy it. But she did. Every cursed inch.

CHAPTER 21

Mira held her breath as the professor passed back the tests. She heard many groans in the room. True, this test had been harder than the first one, but still she held out hope that she at least hadn't failed it. Even if she made a sixty-five, she would still have a B average in the class.

"I wonder how we did," Patrick whispered in her ear.

Mira smiled as she turned around. "I'm too afraid to look. I know I wasn't focused on the test." She glanced at her friend Amy as the professor handed back her test. "How'd you do, Amy?"

Amy quickly scanned the paper; her thin lips frowned. "Not as well as I'd hoped," the woman answered. "I only made an 85."

Mira nodded, not really knowing what would make her friend feel better. Amy was always studious, but she complained of her partner not wanting to dedicate the time and usually not showing up for their study sessions. "I just hope I did that well," Mira said, knowing that wasn't likely. She watched as the teacher continued handing out the test. Finally he handed her her paper.

He looked down at her with that annoying smile, which told her he was about to embarrass her again. "Well, Ms. Brenton, kudos," the professor said, a little too loudly. Was her giving her a hard time for getting the lowest score in the class?

Mira was confused and knew she couldn't hide it. "I'm sorry."

The professor didn't answer, but handed Patrick his test. As the professor walked toward the front of the room, he began speaking again. "Well, these test scores were marginally better than the last ones. The highest score was a hundred and ten, as usual. I'm sure reasonable deduction would tell you who the culprit is."

"Patrick," someone called out.

The professor laughed. "You would be wrong. The overachiever for the test was Kasmira Brenton."

Mira gasped. "What?" She turned and faced Patrick. "What did you make?"

He smiled at her. "I made a ninety-eight."

She couldn't contain her smile. "I made a perfect score! Oh, my God! I was so rattled, I didn't think I passed it at all." She turned around and faced the teacher as he continued talking.

"Needless to say, the curve has been cancelled for this test."

Mira sank deeper into her seat as the moans got increasingly louder. These people were going to get her after class, she just knew it. This was the second curve the class had missed out due to her test scores.

"How about a celebratory lunch, Ms. Overachiever?" Patrick whispered.

Mira nodded and sank deeper in to her chair.

Later, Mira could finally relax. She sat across the table from Patrick at the Irish Pub. "I thought when you mentioned lunch, you had something else in mind."

"I did, but I thought this would be better." He smiled at her. "If we really celebrated the way we wanted to, we might not have enough time before you have to pick up Reese."

"Plus, we're having an actual date this Saturday. Save your energy for this weekend," she teased, glancing at her watch, making a mental note of when she had to leave to pick up her daughter. "Have you been to this place before? It doesn't look like your kind of hangout."

"What, exactly, is my kind of place?" He reached across the

table and took her hand. "Do you mean because it looks like a hole-in-the-wall kind of place rather than the linen-napkin kind of restaurant?" He raised her hand and kissed it gently. "This has the best authentic Irish food I have found around here. You should try something. The potato scones are really good, or the potato-and-leek soup, or the cheese pudding."

Mira nodded and decided on the potato-and-leek soup, trying to get her heartbeat to slow down. It was just a kiss, she thought. "I've heard this Irish stuff has nothing but fat in it," she told him. "You know I have the Brenton curse." She reminded him of her daily battle with the scale.

He shook his head. "You do not have the Brenton curse. I happen to think you're beautiful. Besides, the food is good, and you probably won't even eat dinner, it's so filling." He winked at her. "Unless you want to work it off later."

Mira waved off his not-so-subtle hint about how to work off the heavy meal. "I think I'll settle on the potato scones. Reese would be mad if I didn't eat at least one hot dog at dinner."

"I like hot dogs. At least the non-meat ones," he hinted.

She didn't know when it happened, but lately every meal she planned, she planned with Patrick in mind. "You won't believe this, but when I was grocery shopping last week, I found some made out of tofu."

Patrick watched her as the information sank into his skull. A large, happy smile crossed his face. "I would love to come to dinner tonight."

"Wow, did I ask?" she giggled.

Patrick was about to reply, but her cell phone rang.

"It's Reese's school," she said, looking at the caller ID. "I hope nothing is wrong." She flipped her cell phone open and spoke. "Hello."

Patrick watched with growing alarm as concern crossed Mira's face. The hair on the back of his neck stood up. His adrenaline started pumping something fierce. In short, he felt like he was getting ready to take somebody down.

Tears sprang instantly in Mira's eyes. "No, do not release

her. I'm on my way. Yes, detain her and call the police." She stood as she snapped her phone shut.

"Mira, what's wrong?" Patrick stood also. "What happened to Reese?" Mira sat back down. Then stood up.

"Patrick, drive me to Reese's school. It's an emergency."

"Mira, what's wrong?" Patrick raised his voice, attracting the attention of the other lunch customers. "You need to tell me something, or I'm calling the school." Just then his phone rang. It was his contact from the school. "Callahan," he said into the receiver, as a thin sheen of sweat ran down his back, his internal alarm that something big was about to happen. He grabbed Mira by the arm, and they left the restaurant.

"Sir, you need to get here immediately," the agent told him.

It was all Patrick needed to hear before he ended his call. He sped up his steps, dragging Mira with him. After they got into the car, he peeled off and headed for Reese's school. "Mira, what's going on?"

He could barely understand between her bouts of sobs and hiccupping. "Shara was at Reese's school trying to check her out. Why would she check Reese out of school without my permission? Is she trying to get back at me for the other day?"

Patrick knew why. But he wasn't going to tell Mira. "We'll find out what is going on. You promise to be strong and not crumble?"

Mira attempted to dry her eyes and failed; the tears were just coming too fast.

Patrick pulled up to the school parking lot, and they rushed inside. A tall official-looking man in an Armani knockoff suit met them just inside the entrance.

"Ms. Brenton, I'm Detective Harris," he said, flashing his badge quickly, almost too quickly for an average civilian to inspect it, but not too fast for Patrick's agent eyes. It wasn't a fake. "We've been able to solve some of the riddle." The detective glanced in Patrick's direction.

Mira nodded and held Patrick's hand. "This is Patrick

Callahan, a friend. What's going on?" Mira's soft voice trembled with emotion.

The detective didn't answer but motioned for them to follow him. He spoke over his shoulder, "It appears that Ms. Hilliard and a Jonathan Handley had devised a scheme to kidnap your daughter and ask for a ransom. I found the note in her car when I searched it earlier. They were asking for a hundred thousand dollars. If you want to file charges against her, the FBI will have to be called in."

Patrick nodded in agreement. If he had his way, Shara would be carted off to jail right that second. But he knew Mira wouldn't go through with it, just because they were childhood friends and Mira felt some kind of loyalty to Shara.

"Where is Reese?" Mira asked, "Is she okay?"

The detective nodded. "She's fine and has no idea that this has happened due to the efficient security guards here at the Kirkstone Preparatory Academy. We're going to pick up this Handley fellow, though."

Mira shocked everyone else in the room, including Patrick, by asking to speak to Shara.

Patrick insisted on accompanying her, right after he talked to the detective. Once Patrick had the officer alone, he flashed his DEA badge and explained what he could to the plainclothes detective, then returned to Mira.

He held her hand as they walked to the room where Shara was being detained. Shara looked surprised to see Mira and doubly surprised to see Patrick.

"What are you doing here, Mira?" Shara snapped, as if Mira were the criminal and Shara hadn't just tried to kidnap her friend's daughter.

Mira took a seat across from her childhood friend. "Why don't you tell me why you felt compelled to take my child without my consent?" She took a shaky breath. "We grew up together, we worked together, my God, our kids grew up together. Did my coming into money cause all this?"

Shara focused on the floor instead of meeting Mira's discerning gaze. *Good,* Patrick thought, *she should feel like dirt.*

"I didn't want to do it. I mean, at first, I thought I could do it, but then I realized what it would do to Reese. How it would probably scar her, and I didn't want to be the cause of that."

Patrick couldn't help stating the obvious. "But you attempted to kidnap her."

Shara wiped her eyes but still focused on the floor. "John said that we deserved that money."

"How on earth could he think that?" Mira stared at Shara, but she kept a tight grip on Patrick's hand. "I told you he was an idiot."

"He's not an idiot!" Shara defended him. "You would never miss that money!" Shara cried.

The light finally came on in Mira's brain. "You're seeing him, aren't you? He talked you into the harebrained scheme, and now you're willing to risk jail time for him. You deserve him."

Shara looked at Patrick for clarification. "Yes, Shara, you can get Fed time for this. Kidnapping is a federal offense. Even if Mira doesn't file charges on you, the school still can."

"This wasn't my idea," Shara whined. "I'm just as innocent as Reese in all this."

Patrick would have throttled Shara right in front of Mira, but it wouldn't have really solved anything. He tried to get a hold of his temper. "But you walked in here and attempted to take Reese without Mira's permission. What do you call that?"

"Maybe I was just doing her a favor and wanted to pick up Reese," Shara suggested in a cold, calculating voice. "Maybe I was trying to give the two of you some time together."

Patrick rubbed Mira's tense shoulders. There wasn't an easy way out of this. "I don't think you've ever had Mira's or Reese's well-being in any of your thoughts. Why don't you admit everything?"

Shara's dark eyes finally met Patrick's. She knew exactly

what he was saying and what he knew about her children. She shook her head and resumed looking at the floor. "I can't."

Patrick contemplated the consequences of telling Mira himself, but changed his mind.

Shara raised her head again and looked at Mira. "Mira, all my life, people have compared me to you. Even my own mother. She's always at me about why I didn't advance at work like you did. I wanted freedom. That's why I agreed to this plan, which I knew wouldn't work. I wanted to move out and be on my own like you are."

"But Shara, I gave you money to do just that, if that was what you wanted."

"I know you did. Once my mom found out about the money, she made me put most of it in a college fund for the kids. She said she knew I would blow it or give it to some worthless man. Funny thing, she was right." Finally she made eye contact with Mira. "I'm sorry."

Patrick didn't want Mira to feel bad about the life she had now. "Mira, you could still file charges against Shara and her partner."

Mira shook her head. "The only reason I'm not filing charges against you is your parents," she said to Shara. "This would devastate them. Don't you ever call my house again or talk to Reese. Saturday should be the last time I'll ever have to see you."

"Mira, please—"

"No, Shara. The Mira that used to listen to you is gone. Just like our friendship." She stood and led Patrick out of the room. The detective followed them.

"Ms. Brenton," the detective said once he had closed the door to the room, "are you sure about not at least filing a report? I'm sure the school will still charge her with something."

Mira nodded. "I don't want to be the reason her parents freak out about what she's done. As long as she didn't hurt Reese, I don't see any reason to hurt her parents or children for something she didn't think through."

Patrick agreed. But as they walked down the hall to Reese's classroom, he realized that Shara still hadn't told Mira what an awful person she really was.

As the trio entered Mira's house after retrieving her car from school, Patrick knew he had a difficult task on his hands. Being a government agent, he was often faced with the challenge of helping victim's families cope with a tragedy.

But this wasn't a stranger he could offer a generic sympathy. This was Mira and Reese, the two most important women in his life at that moment and he hoped forever. He watched Mira as she and Reese sat on the couch side by side without so much as air getting between them.

He knew Mira was a mass of nerves. He noticed the occasional defiant tear escape her control and slide gently down her beautiful face. She sighed and hastily wiped it away, hugging her daughter. Patrick realized she was thinking *what if.* . . .

What if Shara had succeeded in her insane plan? What if they had decided they didn't want a witness and had killed Reese? What if they didn't kill Reese, but she was so scarred she would have to go into therapy again, or worse?

"Mira why don't you take a nap?" Patrick suggested, wanting the dazed look in her eyes to disappear.

Mira stared at him, then finally agreed. "Maybe you're right." She stood and reached for Reese's hand. "Let's take a nap honey."

Reese nodded and took her mother's hand and they headed upstairs.

Mira woke up from her nap smiling. Reese was lying beside her in Mira's king-size bed. With the day's ordeal, Mira hadn't thought she would be able to close her eyes, but somehow she was able to take a well-deserved nap with her daughter next to her.

She sat up and looked around the room. Noticing a blanket covered them, she realized Patrick must have come in to check on them. Still not believing Shara betrayed her in such a way, she sighed. "Okay, now what?" She rose from the bed, straightened her clothes, and went downstairs.

"You know you really didn't have to cook dinner," Mira said as she sat at the dining room table across from him.

He was scribbling in a notepad, and she really couldn't see what he was doing. It looked like a chart of some sort.

"I know I didn't have to fix dinner. But you have had an unusual day, to say the least." He reached across the table and grabbed her hand. "I didn't make hot dogs. I made something special."

Mira didn't like the tone in his voice. That meant he made something that didn't have any meat. "So, what did you fix for dinner?"

He put away his chart and rose from the table. "Well, since you guys were asleep so long, I had time to make my mother's favorite recipe."

She knew his mother was black, and she could only hope it was a soul-food dish. "What is it?" She held her breath, awaiting his answer.

"Well," he started.

She hated when he started a story about his family. It never ended like she thought it should.

"When my mom and dad were first married, she tried to make only Irish dishes to make my dad feel more at home, since he had only been in the States a few years. But turns out my dad wanted American food. He actually loves soul food and can make some mean collard greens. So I made a pot roast with potatoes, mushrooms, and onions. Fooled you, didn't I?"

"Yes, you did," Mira admitted. "Actually, what are you still doing here? I thought you would have gone home."

He looked at her with those green eyes that made her do so many things she'd sworn she would never do, like fall in love with a gorgeous man. He sat in the chair next to her. "I'm here because your best friend tried to snatch your daughter and ask for ransom. I'm here because right now I want you to feel safe. I'm here because I want to be. What I'm trying to say under all that Irish blarney is that I love you."

Mira's heart skipped a beat. "I know you love me, Patrick, just like I love you. You make me feel safe, very safe. Even with all the crazy things going on around me, you are like a beacon in the night."

She reached for his hand, caressing it gently. "Today has shown me how much you care for me and Reese. A lesser man would have hit the road a long time ago, but you stayed." She raised his hand to her lips and kissed it gently before continuing with her speech. "Each time you have had every reason to run and not look back, but you're still here and you helped us through an emotional crisis."

She took a deep breath and said simply, "What I'm trying to say, badly, I might add, is that I have loved you from the first time we kissed."

CHAPTER 22

Patrick snuggled into Mira's heated body, wanting to get a few more minutes of rest, but he knew they had to get up soon. The day would be a test for them all. Mira, Reese, and he were going to attend Mira's uncle's birthday party, and Shara and her family would also be in attendance.

He heard Mira moan at his movement, but she didn't get up. Her hand traveled his body slowly, lingering in all the right places. She opened her eyes, smiling as her gaze met his, asking a silent question. He answered her with a deep, slow kiss.

The night before too many charged emotions were in the house for them to make love. After they had both admitted their love for each other, Patrick was too shaken to do anything but sleep. But he didn't sleep—his heart wouldn't allow him that luxury.

For the first time in his thirty years, Patrick was actually in love, and the worst part was when Mira actually found out who he was and why he was there, she just might not love him anymore, and that would break his heart.

He felt Mira's hand unbuttoning his pajama top and nuzzling his chest with her nose. She let out a moan and moved closer to him.

Helpless to do anything but help her in any way he could, he eased out of his silk pajamas, then helped her out of her nightshirt. He couldn't get enough of looking at her body, especially when she was hot with desire and ready for him.

He kissed each of her full breasts, then suckled each nipple gently until Mira writhed against him, the heat building in both of them at an alarming speed. But Patrick wanted her to feel what he was feeling. He continued his assault on her willing body.

As he moved down her body, kissing her stomach, dipping his tongue inside her navel, and easing lower, Mira's hands slid into Patrick's hair. He tasted her and she screamed. She tried to get him to stop for fear of waking Reese, but Patrick shook his head, ascended back up her body, and planted a kiss on her mouth as he hurriedly donned a condom and entered her in one smooth motion.

She wrapped her legs around him, holding him tightly inside her. "Oh, Patrick!" was all she could muster between their heated kisses.

He knew she was close to release and he wanted her to enjoy it for as long as possible. He stopped moving against her, but kissed her hard and long as if his life depended on the bond. In many ways, it did.

Hours later, Patrick awoke to the sound of the bedroom door opening. He thought Mira had locked the door, but she hadn't. He didn't feel comfortable with Reese seeing them in bed together in an obvious state of undress. He pulled the comforter to cover Mira more effectively. Reese smiled at him as she came to his side of the bed. *Please don't let her lift up the comforter*, he prayed silently.

Reese stood by the nightstand looking like an angel. An angel with pillow hair and dressed in her Powder Puff nightgown. "Mr. Patrick," she whispered, "when are you and Mommy getting up? I'm ready for breakfast." She looked at him with those adorable brown eyes, and a smug grin on her face. "I know Mommy doesn't think I know that you sleep with her, but I've known for a while."

Patrick feared what was going to come out of her mouth next. "Reese, I can explain."

She shook her head. "I know what you do in here. Ashley told me," she continued.

Oh no. Mira was going to be upset when she found out. "Honey, it's not what you think."

Big brown eyes stared at him. "Aren't you taking a time-out? That's what Ashley's mom said. Mommy seems happier when you take a time-out with her."

He knew he had tears in his eyes, but he couldn't do anything about it. "I love you, Reese. Why don't you go get dressed, and I'll make breakfast?"

She nodded and walked softly out of the room, so as not to wake her mother. Patrick shook his head in disbelief.

After a shower, Patrick dressed in his favorite pair of worn Levi's and a worn denim Ralph Lauren shirt, and headed for the kitchen. Reese soon joined him, dressed in a red sweatshirt and jeans. He asked, "What do you think we should fix?"

She looked at him as if she were actually deciding. "Pancakes and bacon," she said with confidence. She walked to the refrigerator and took out the milk and orange juice.

He watched her set the table for breakfast with practiced precision. He searched the cabinets for the pancake mix. After he was successful, Reese helped him find the electric griddle. Then she reached into the refrigerator to get the bacon. "Mommy likes a lot of bacon." She handed him the meat.

He took it from the little girl. "Yeah, I noticed." Patrick started making the pancakes. At first, he thought about two each, then he remembered Reese's adult-sized appetite and decided on three.

By the time Mira came downstairs for breakfast, he had finished cooking. She was already dressed for the day in a V-neck sweater and hip-hugging jeans. Quickly, she took her seat and began eating.

Patrick sat down as well. He knew she had overheard Reese's conversation with him earlier that morning. "No 'good morning, stud'?" he joked, wanting to see her smile. "I slave over a hot stove all morning. I even cooked bacon." He made a retching sound. "I handled a pork product for you. Nothing?"

Reese, who was sitting by her mother, leaned over and whispered, "Mommy, I think Patrick wants you to kiss him."

Mira tried to keep her sanity intact as she, Patrick, and Reese neared her uncle's one-story wood frame house. Cars lined the street leading up to the house. Mira could only imagine how many people her aunt had invited. Her simple birthday parties involved no less than fifty people. How had Uncle Harold coped with her need to be the center of attention all these years?

Patrick helped Mira out of the car, carried some of the presents for her, and still managed to hold her hand. Reese held her other one. Mira smiled at her daughter. She felt enough love for Patrick and Reese to endure whatever put-downs her aunt hurled in her direction.

They reached the front door, and Reese rang the doorbell. Soon Matilda Brenton was opening the screen door to let them in. She wasn't very pretty, Mira thought, wondering what her uncle had ever seen in her. Perhaps she was a looker back in her day.

Matilda looked Patrick up and down before shaking her head in disappointment. "Well Mira, I see you brought your gentleman friend with you. I wish you would have told me beforehand."

"If you're worried about the food, we'll leave before you pass out the entrées," she offered her aunt bitterly.

Her aunt shook her head. "And have your uncle read me the riot act for not feeding his precious nieces? No, ma'am." She shooed them inside the small house. Mira gazed at the crowd that had already assembled. Finally she spotted her uncle, the man who had been her lifeline those horrible months after her mother died. He didn't look like the strong man that she was accustomed to seeing. He looked beaten down and tired.

"Uncle Harold. Happy birthday." She kissed him on the cheek. "How have you been?" She glanced around the room and sighed with relief. No Shara.

He took her hand in his and kissed it. "You know I miss you girls since you moved away. How's Reese adjusting?"

"Fine," Mira lied. Not wanting to burden her uncle, she repeated her answer. "Fine."

"I know you, Kasmira Brenton, you're lying. She'll be fine. You'll see." He glanced in Patrick's direction. "I see you brought a man with you. Good. He looks like a good one. I like the way he stands. Like he owns the world."

Mira looked at Patrick as if she were seeing him for the first time. He did have that look. "He was in the military."

Her uncle nodded. "I need to speak with you. Privately."

"Why?"

He flashed that smile that always made her feel like all was well with the world. "Well, you won't know until I tell you." He grimaced as he rose from his chair and started walking to the den.

"Harold, where are you going? Mira shouldn't make you walk," Matilda scolded her husband.

He looked back at his wife with a glint of danger in his eyes. "I'll be back. I just need to talk to Mira, alone."

For the first time in her life, Mira watched her aunt shut up and return to her guests. Mira followed her uncle.

They entered the den and he closed the door, muffling the noise of the still-growing party. He sat down and let out a sigh, then reached for a folder. "Kasmira, I have something to tell you."

She was only Kasmira when it was totally serious. "What is it, Unc?"

"Why don't I start with the hard stuff first?" He took a deep breath. "I'm sure you've realized that Tilda has felt a little resentment toward you and Reese."

"Yes."

"Well, it all started when your mother met your father. He had met Tilda first, but once he took a look at your mother, he threw Tilda over for her. Granted it would have been Tilda who would've gotten pregnant. But it was your mother. Tilda didn't like the fact that I felt responsible for Helen."

Mira nodded. Funny, her mother never mentioned any of this.

"I felt responsible because as Helen's brother, I should have been there when Helen went off with him, and then when he left town without a word and she found out she was pregnant. It was my fault. Helen was my responsibility, and I failed to keep her out of harm's way. But later he came back, trying to find her. He even came by the house looking for her."

"Why?"

"He'd heard about the baby—you. He wanted to do the honorable thing, but Helen refused after she found out he was involved with drugs. Soon he left and never returned again. But a few years later on your birthday, an envelope arrived full of cash. Helen didn't want to keep it, calling it the devil's money, but eventually I persuaded her to keep it, though she refused to use it."

"That explains the money in the bank." Mira realized that her uncle was careful not to say her father's name or what race he was. "What was my father's name?"

"I promised your mother I would take that secret to my grave. I intend to honor that promise. It would do you no good, anyway."

"But Uncle Harold, I think I have a right to know."

"Yes, you do. But I promised, and Tilda knows she can't tell either."

"How will you ensure that she won't tell?"

"Because if she does, she doesn't get any money when I

die. She will be cut off without a dime. That's how serious I am about keeping that promise. I know you'll find out one day, but I want to keep my promise to my sister."

"But you're not going to die anytime soon."

"Yes, I am."

Tears streamed down her face. Her only living blood relative outside of her daughter was leaving her. It just didn't seem fair. "How?"

"I have cancer. Like your Momma. I probably just got a few more months left." He took a deep breath. "I want you to promise me that you will take good care of Reese."

Mira nodded. "What will I do without you? You helped me find the house I bought, the school for Reese. Who will help me now?"

"Now, now. I don't want all these tears at my party. I'm ready. Don't ever be afraid when it's your time." He patted her knee.

"Maybe there are other alternatives. I could give you money to get better help."

He shook his head. "No, honey. It's time."

"This has been the worst week in my life." Mira blew her nose. "Shara had some harebrained scheme to kidnap Reese."

"What?"

Mira laughed; now the incident seemed unimportant. "Luckily, Reese attends a very secure private school. They wouldn't release her without my permission."

"Baby, I'm sorry. I know those are trite words when you think about the outcome if that school hadn't called you. You pressed charges?"

"No, I can't do that to her family."

"But what about you?"

She laughed. "You sound like Patrick. I'll be fine." She hugged her uncle. "I love you."

"I love you, too." He rose and brought her with him. "Don't you ever forget that. You've done well with the money. You moved yourself and your daughter out of this neighborhood and enrolled her in a private school. You've always had a level head, and I know you want only the best for Reese. Helen would be proud of your choices."

Mira embraced her uncle again. There were so many questions she wanted to ask her uncle, but she knew she probably wouldn't get the answers she wanted. If he had only a few months left, she didn't want to harp on the past.

Later the party was in full swing. Mira sat on the couch with Patrick beside her. Shara and her family had also arrived, but Shara kept a safe distance from Mira and Patrick. Reese was playing with some of the other children. Both Mira and Patrick were keeping a discreet eye on her.

"Mira, who's that woman? She keeps waving at you," Patrick whispered in her ear.

She leaned closer to Patrick, whispering back, "That's Shara's mom. I wonder what she wants." She glanced in Reese's direction, then back at Patrick. "Keep an eye on her."

Patrick nodded as she stood up and walked to the kitchen.

"Hi, Mrs. Hilliard. How are you?" She leaned against the refrigerator, trying to look relaxed and failing miserably. How does one start a conversation with her daughter's wannabe kidnapper's mother?

Geraldine Hilliard shook her head at Mira. "Don't you try to act like nothing happened. I know what my stupid child has done. Aren't you angry? You should have pressed charges."

"I didn't want to hurt you or Mr. Hilliard. I thought it would devastate you."

Shara's mother looked at Mira with sorrow in her eyes. "Mira, you're the one who's devastated. I'm sorry that Shara wasn't a better friend to you. I don't want you to think that you can't call and talk to me. You call me if you ever need to talk."

What would she need to talk about? "Thank you, Mrs.

Hilliard, but I'm fine. Reese is fine. I just want to forget about the whole matter."

Mira didn't like the look that crossed Mrs. Hilliard's face. "Mira, we need to talk."

"It's not necessary, Mrs. Hilliard. I know Shara was listening to Jonathan and she wasn't using her head."

"This has nothing to do with that. It has to do with you."

Well, Mira didn't like the sound of that in the least. But how much bad news would she take today? "Okay, Mrs. Hilliard. Let's go to the den." Mira walked down the hall with Shara's mother behind her.

Once they were settled in the den, Mrs. Hilliard began to speak. "Mira, I know you. You're a good person and have a big heart. Patrick seems very nice. I'm only going to say this once, because it hurts me so."

Mira started to grip the arm on her uncle's favorite chair. "What is it? Please tell me."

"Remember when Shara got pregnant with John? Well, to put it in a nutshell, Jonathan Handley is John's father."

Mira placed a hand over her rapidly beating heart. "What did you say?"

"Yes. You heard correctly. Reese and John have the same father."

Mira shook her head in disbelief. "What is this? Let's-see-if-we-can-push-Mira-over-the-emotional-edge day?" She was too shocked and hurt to cry. "I asked Shara if she was seeing him, and she said no."

"She told me the same thing. But I dug a little deeper. I noticed the resemblance between Reese and John. It's subtle, but you can see it."

"I thought they looked a little alike, but I just pushed it out of my mind. Momma also said once that she thought something along those lines."

"Yes. I told Shara she should have told you, but I don't know why she didn't." She looked at Mira with those hurt eyes. "This will stay between us. But I feel you should at least confront her. Let her know how her misdeeds have hurt you."

Mira stared at the floor, summoning up the strength that she needed. "I just want to get through this day. I've had too much sorrow today."

"I know. But I wanted you to know."

She stood up. "Thank you, Mrs. Hilliard." She took a deep breath. "I know many years from today, I will look back on this day and I'll be glad that you told me."

Shara's mother stood and hugged her. "You'll see. When life gives you lemons, make lemonade."

Lemonade indeed, she thought. Mira exited the room. She glanced at Patrick and headed straight for Shara. By the time she reached Shara, Patrick was by her side.

She faced her former friend. "We need to talk. Now."

Shara looked shocked at Mira's tone. "What do you want? Do you want to rub how stupid I am in my face again?"

"No. This is about our children." She exhaled as she felt Patrick's strong hand in hers, giving her comfort.

For the first time in her life, Mira had Shara right where she wanted her. Shara sputtered, "Oh my God! You know?"

Mira was outraged. She spoke through clenched teeth. "Yes. I know. You betrayed me! So I suggest you get your ass into the den now."

Shara nodded and walked down the hall. Mira held on to Patrick's hand as she followed her. The minute she closed the door, she lit into Shara.

"How could you? Check that. I know how you could. It's the way you operate. Like with Angie's dad. He was Lisa's boyfriend. You remember Lisa, don't you? She was our childhood friend."

"Oh, man. You knew that, too?"

"Yes, I knew. You betray your friends. Everyone warned me over the years, but I hung tough and defended you. I shouldn't be surprised about Jonathan, but I am. You're trying to get money out of me for Jonathan. I should have realized he was putting you up to that. What did he tell you? He'd share the money with you? You know he's lying to you. I don't even want to think about what the kidnapping would have done to Reese emotionally. You were willing to cause my daughter grief, for what? Was he going to leave his wife for you? I don't think so. You know he's probably got six kids, including the ones from his marriage."

"He has more than that. He told me he had ten."

"And still you haven't learned anything, have you?"

"Yes. I don't regret what I have with him. I know he loves me."

"You deserve him. Come on, Patrick. We're leaving this place." She pulled Patrick by the hand, and they started for the door. Mira looked back at Shara. "I can't see how I stayed friends with you. I can't understand what you see in a man who treats women like used tissues."

Mira and Patrick continued down the hall. The walls were closing in on Mira, and she needed to get out of the house. "Help me find Reese. I've got to get out of here."

He grabbed her by the hand. His eyes were a dangerous green. "Mira, you have got to calm down before you find Reese. The last thing she needs is to see you upset."

She knew he was right, but she was also angry. She couldn't decide whom to be mad at first—Shara, for betraying their lifelong friendship by having a relationship with Mira's ex-husband, or her uncle, for taking the secret that could ease some of her heartache to his grave.

CHAPTER 23

"Patrick, could you get the door? It's probably just Courtney and Ashley," Mira called from upstairs. "We're almost ready."

Patrick nodded as if Mira could see his answer and rose from his comfortable position on the couch. Mira and Reese had retreated upstairs so Mira could help Reese pack for the sleepover.

He opened the front door and sure enough, Courtney and Ashley stood in the doorway, smiling at him. Courtney winked. "Well, hello Patrick," she said, her voice full of mischief.

"Hi, Courtney, Ashley. Mira said they'd be right down," he said, waving in the direction of the living room. "Would you like something to drink while you wait?"

Courtney shook her head and raised her hand, showing him a large white gift bag. Patrick laughed as he noticed the bag was from the local condom store, Condom Sense.

"I have a present for Mira. We know the way." She grabbed her daughter's hand and headed for the spiral staircase.

Patrick shook his head, closed the door, and headed back to the couch. Courtney might look all innocent and everything, but he knew she was anything but. He could only imagine what was inside the bag.

After Reese left with her friend for the skating party, Patrick had the task of trying to cheer Mira up. He knew exactly how she felt, being betrayed by so many people at one time. He had felt like that himself when he lost his cousin so many years ago to a drug overdose. It was his reason for tracking Paulo and vowing to get him.

Patrick had planned a romantic dinner, then a carriage ride in the park in downtown Fort Worth, but now he thought something that would occupy Mira's mind would be better. Something fun.

While she finished dressing upstairs, Patrick called his contact at the skating rink. To his dismay, Rico was at the rink, blatantly watching Reese, but he hadn't made any attempts to go near the child. That made Patrick breathe a little easier, but he knew a big move was coming. As long as Paulo hadn't made an appearance, things were just fine.

Finally, Mira stomped down the stairs. Her velour slacks hugged her hips gracefully. He frowned as he noticed the slacks were a little loose. "Hey, you're not dieting on me, are you?"

She smiled for the first time that day. "No, but with the incidents of the last few days, food has lost its appeal for me. But the good news is that I finally won the battle of the scale, for today at least."

He nodded, grabbing her hand as they headed for the garage. "I noticed you didn't eat a thing at the party. No matter. We'll make up for it later."

She looked at him with sadness in her beautiful brown eyes. "Patrick, we don't have to go out. Actually, I would like to stay home."

Patrick shook his head. "And have you brooding over the conversations you've had today? No way. We're going to have some fun." He led her to his car and opened the passenger side for her. "This evening is all about Kasmira Brenton and nothing else." He smiled as she slid into the seat, closing the door. He settled behind the wheel, and they were off.

As he started driving, Mira fidgeted in her seat. "Where are we going?"

"We're going a place where you can forget your troubles," he answered, liking that it would be a total surprise to her.

"I could have gotten drunk at home," Mira said in a quiet voice.

"That's what I thought. Tonight there will be no alcohol. So when you throw yourself into my arms, you'll be stone-cold sober." He caressed her hand gently when they were stopped at a red light. "I know today was awful for you and you just want to crawl under a rock, but you've got to face your demons." He started driving again.

"I know. I'm just upset that my uncle won't budge on the promise he made to Momma. I wish there was some other way to find out my father's name or origin or something, but he and Aunt Tilda are the only ones who know. It's hopeless."

Patrick nodded. He could make her life so easy by saying something like 'I know who your father is, and he's a drug lord.' If he did that, he would compromise everything. Even trying to avenge his cousin's death would be lost. Who knew how many DEA rules he had broken on this tour?

He pulled into the parking lot of the Horseshoe Arcade. "Are you ready for some fun?" he asked, hoping a diversion would keep her mind off her problems.

Mira stared at him incredulously. "My child is at a skating party, and this is my romantic date? An evening at the arcade?"

He unbuckled his seat belt and faced her, feigning disgust. "Man, I'll never be able to figure women out. I thought this would help forget your troubles. If you want to go somewhere romantic, we can."

Mira sighed, giving in. "No, this is fine. It's just that after the week I've had, I just wished for something quiet and cozy," she whispered.

"So you could brood about the things that have happened to you? No, ma'am, get ready for noise, and lots of it. You won't be able to focus on anything but fun." He climbed out of the car and walked to her side to open her door. Offering his hand, he helped her out.

They fell into a companionable silence as they approached

the arcade. Patrick had an ulterior motive for wanting to go to the entryway—he had to meet his contact. "Why don't you look around and I'll get some tokens?" Patrick nudged her to the video games. He nodded to the attendant. "I'll have fifty dollars' worth."

"Feeling lucky, eh?" The young man smiled at Patrick, then lowered his deep voice. "I can't thank you enough for this assignment, sir. It was worth all those weeks at Quantico, training to be a DEA agent, and look, I'm working at an arcade. My parents will be so proud," he said sarcastically.

"I know. I just wanted to see if Rico had someone following us, too. You do good work." Patrick laughed, leaving the counter with his bucket of tokens and joining Mira at the virtual snowboard ride. "Can you ski?" he asked, watching her read the instructions on the screen.

Mira looked at him, laughing. "Me, heavens, no," she whispered to him. "I haven't been out of Fort Worth my entire life. It doesn't snow here very often, and there's almost never enough to actually ski on."

Patrick inserted the coins in the ride. "Well, we'll have to change that. There's a big world out there, Mira. It's just waiting for you to explore it."

She grinned at his words, more so when the meaning of those words finally filtered through. "Well for right now, I'll settle for learning this thing," Mira said, stepping onto the snowboard and slipping on the virtual glasses on her perfect face. "Okay. How do I ride this?"

Mira listened carefully as Patrick explained the ride to her. She felt glad he had brought her, but she couldn't tell him that. He would start planning on this kind of date all the time. Variety was the spice of life, but a little predictable romance didn't hurt.

She watched as he walked over to a shooting type of game. "Patrick, I don't really like shooting games." If she never saw another gun again, not that she had seen the one that killed her mother, it would be too soon. But Dr. Sid had told her that she needed to face this particular fear or it would get the best of her.

Patrick's large hand engulfed the mounted pistol. "Oh, come on. Just one game. Let me see if I can beat you."

He looked so cute with that excited gleam in his gorgeous eyes. He reminded her of a little boy with a new toy. She couldn't resist. "All right. I bet you learned to shoot in the military, didn't you?"

"Of course. But that was only training," he said, glancing around the room.

"So are we betting or something?"

He gazed at her with those green eyes, and she thought she knew what his wager would be: the loser would fix breakfast in the morning. "Of course."

"Okay, what? Breakfast?"

He grinned at her, putting the coins in the machine. "I was thinking of more than breakfast. I was thinking along the lines of a massage. A hot-oil massage."

Mira couldn't stop the smile that tugged at her lips. "I like your idea better."

He aimed the gun at the screen, grinning at her. "Did I mention that I was a sharpshooter? I have several medals."

Damn. "No, you didn't, and now is a fine time to tell me." Mira tried to act upset but she wasn't; at least she was finally learning something about his past.

"Just to show you I'm a good sport, I'll spot you a game," he said with confidence. He quickly aimed at the target.

Mira's heart sank at the sight of the word *winner* on the screen. One round, and he had already won. She prepared to shoot. But her hands shook from the terror of holding the plastic gun. Breathing became something impossible as she tried to squeeze the trigger. She just couldn't do it.

Patrick stood behind her, speaking softly and wrapping his long arms around her, as if he knew that she was scared to death. "Mira, just hold steady. Look at the center of your target.

Don't see a face or a body, see a target. Complete with a big red circle on it and a dot in the middle. Aim for the dot."

Mira nodded and imagined what he said, and her hands stopped shaking. She had to grip the gun with both hands to squeeze the trigger. Finally she hit the target. The screen lit up with the word *winner* on it. "Oh my God. I hit it!" She hugged Patrick and pecked him on the lips. "Thank you, Patrick."

He kissed her back, only harder, deeper, and longer. "Don't thank me yet. In your jubilation, the enemies have taken you down." He pointed to the screen. He pumped some more coins into the machine. "How about one more round?"

"You got it." Mira gripped the gun and prepared to shoot, but Patrick hadn't started the game yet. He was staring at the entrance to the arcade. Mira asked, "Hey, are you scared that I'll take you down this time?"

He blinked his eyes, turning his attention back to Mira. "I think that sounds like a dare to me. How about double or nothing?"

"How can you have double or nothing with a massage?"

"I think there's something called a full-body massage."

"A what?" Mira couldn't talk to him and shoot at the same time. She chose the latter. "Look, I shot something!" She repositioned the gun and shot more targets. Soon the winning phrase came up on the screen. "I won! I won!" She jumped in celebration until she realized that all the youngsters in the arcade were watching her in confusion.

"That's great, honey. It's a tie."

"No it's not. You said you'd spot me a game. So that makes two games for me and one for you. Would you like to play again?"

"Don't give me that smirk on your face. I think we should play for higher stakes."

"What are the stakes, Mr. Callahan?" she cooed.

Patrick put some coins in the machine and laughed at her expression. "I spent some time in Spain a few years ago and got this wonderful massage called what translates loosely into

English as the sensual-lover massage. I can't even describe it without breaking some of Texas's indecency laws." He winked at her as he started shooting the targets and hitting each one. "Years of military training, baby," he said, oozing masculine confidence.

Soon the dreaded phrase appeared on the screen: Winner. Patrick led her to the counter to redeem the last of their tokens.

"Boy, I'm glad that I didn't take that last bet," Mira admitted. "I'd be in a whole lot of trouble right now." She grinned at him as he handed the remaining coins to the attendant. "We didn't play very many games, did we?"

He winked at her. "Not as many as I had thought we would. I think I'm ready for some adult entertainment."

Mira couldn't face him or the attendant at that moment. She walked down to the other end of counter to look at the stuffed animals.

Patrick laughed until she was out of earshot. He whispered to the attendant, "I saw Rico in the corner."

"Yeah, I saw him watching you. I thought he would have confronted you."

"No, that's not his way. Besides, it's personal between him and me. He's still mad because I took his woman and she turned evidence on him. But he's not going to do a thing until he gets the word from Paulo."

The young man looked at Mira. "I think she would have made a good agent. She was getting into the shooting game."

"Yeah, and I think she'll get her chance pretty soon. Be in touch." Patrick left the counter and walked toward Mira.

She was admiring a three-foot-tall teddy bear. He walked up behind her. "Hey, I bet Reese would love that."

"Yeah," Mira nodded, "but her birthday isn't for a few months, and I want to get something really special. You think I'd be spoiling her if I got this for her now?" She looked up at him, waiting for his opinion.

He thought Reese deserved to be spoiled after the hellish year she had had. But would he be overstepping his bounds as a lover if he offered to buy it for Reese? He grabbed Mira's hand, bringing her body closer to his. "No. I don't think you're spoiling Reese. You love her too much to do that. How about I get it for her?"

She shook her head. "I couldn't allow you to do that."

"Well, I was only being polite by asking. I'm getting it for her regardless." He pulled her to the counter before she could protest.

Patrick pointed to the bear in the corner. "I'd like to buy that bear."

The attendant winked at him. "Well, sir, since you redeemed your coins and hadn't picked out anything, you can get the bear for half price."

Mira laughed. "Talk about the luck of the Irish!" She reached in her purse for her cell phone. "I'll just call Courtney and check on Reese."

Patrick nodded. "She's fine. Probably skating all over the place and eating everything in sight."

"Not my daughter." Mira struggled to keep a straight face and failed. "Yes, my daughter would do exactly that. They'll probably have to drag her off the ice."

Patrick nodded. He didn't tell her that he'd just gotten a text message on his cell phone from the one of the agents assigned to the skating rink, stating that very information. Reese was safe and unharmed, but she was being watched. Patrick knew that Mira's strength would soon be tested. He hoped that she would be able to forgive his betrayal.

The attendant handed him the bear, and they left the arcade. After he helped Mira into the car, he put Reese's present in the backseat, then sat behind the wheel.

Once he started the car, he glanced at Mira. She wanted to ask him something, but didn't have the nerve. She fingered the strap on her purse. "Out with it, woman."

Brown eyes stared at him. "What?"

"What's up with you?"

A deep breath. She was biting her lip. Twirling her hair. Something had her rattled.

"I know there's a reasonable explanation for that guy and that bear. But he gave it to you almost for free."

"Remember, I turned my tokens back in. He hadn't exchanged my money yet, so that's why." He hoped she didn't realize he was lying through his teeth.

Mira studied his statement and dissected it with a sharp razor. He could tell the minute the question formed in her brain.

"Another thing," she started.

"What?" He dreaded what she was going to say next. He could always distract her with a kiss, but then she would be really mad.

"I've never heard of an arcade letting you cash out tokens that you didn't use."

He leaned over the console. "Honey, didn't your mother ever tell you anything about not biting the hand that feeds you?"

"I guess that means you're not going to tell me, doesn't it?"

He put the car in gear. "Yes, it does." He took off for a restaurant.

Patrick had just pulled into Mira's garage after their date when his cell phone rang. "Callahan."

"Just wanted to report, sir. The kids are preparing to leave the ice-skating rink, did you want us to follow?"

"Yes. Anything odd?" He glanced at Mira. Why hadn't she gotten out of the car yet?

"Rico was there, and he watched the girls. He never approached Reese, but he followed all the girls to the food court area when they all went to eat."

Mira coughed indiscreetly. "Patrick," she said, loud enough to be heard by his caller.

He smiled at her veiled attempt. "Tell me when Richard gets home." He ended the call. He turned to Mira who was looking the picture of innocence. "That was my mother," he lied. "You have me all to yourself." He leaned over the console and kissed her. "Isn't it time for that massage?" Patrick opened the door and got out of the car.

Mira laughed and raced to unlock the back door before Patrick came any closer to her. If he so much as touched her, they would be making love in the garage, giving her neighbors quite a show.

She had barely unlocked the door when Patrick captured her in his arms. She giggled, floating in the happiness of the moment.

"Gotcha!" Patrick yelled, slamming the door and locking it. He smothered her neck with kisses as he guided her through the kitchen, the dining room, the living room, and up the stairs.

Mira eased out of his embrace and slipped into the bathroom. She opened the cabinet drawer and retrieved the bag Courtney had given her when she came and picked up Reese earlier that night.

Mira opened it and immediately closed it. *Courtney and Patrick must be related or something,* Mira thought. There were candles, oils, and a few other things that Mira would never use in her lifetime.

She changed into her nightshirt, took the candles and oils out of the bag, and placed them in a basket. With a last glance in the mirror, she left the bathroom. "I have a surprise for you."

Patrick stopped struggling out of his shirt when he saw the basket in her hand. "What's in there? Condoms? I hope you bought extra, I'm feeling frisky." He smiled and finished taking off his shirt.

She placed the basket on the bed. "Courtney bought me a surprise tonight, and I think you might enjoy it."

He hopped on the bed, clad only in his boxers. "Well, I'm ready."

Mira smiled at him. She would never tire of looking at his body. His stomach was flat and toned. Despite the scars, it was a sight to behold. "Your body is beautiful," Mira whispered as she sat on the bed. "I believe you said something about a massage."

He smiled. Those green eyes sparkled with mischief. "Yes. Why don't you take off those heavy clothes, and I'll give you a massage that will have you wondering why we didn't do this a long time ago."

"That's my surprise, but I think it's your turn to scream."

He held her gaze as he slipped out of his boxers and stretched out on the bed. "I see someone thinks she's ready for another lesson."

Mira finally broke the gaze by looking at the oils. Courtney and Dave must have been some kind of freaks, she thought. The label on the small bottle of oil stated it was ingestible. Why would it matter if she could eat it or not? Oh, she thought, as the sexual light went on. Yes, Courtney and Dave were freaky. They look like such a normal couple. Who would have thought they were into all this stuff?

She opened the bottle of banana oil. "Where would you like me to start?" She scooted closer to his naked form.

"By taking this off." He pointed to her favorite nightshirt. "I want a body-to-body massage." He grinned at her, then pulled up her nightshirt. He sent it sailing across the room.

Mira hadn't planned on him turning the tables so fast, but he had. Now that he had her naked, he stared at her body as if he'd never seen it before. "What?"

He smiled. "You are one beautiful woman, Kasmira Brenton. How did you get your name?" He gently caressed her breast.

"Hey! I'm supposed to be seducing you." He didn't move his hand. "I got my name because my mom met this woman, Kasmira, at the hospital who helped her a lot. I think it's Slavic. I looked it up once. I can say that I've never run into anyone else with that name."

He watched as she poured some oil on his stomach. Automatically, his abdominal muscles contracted and relaxed.

"How did Reese get her name? Did you know someone name Reese?"

Did he really want to talk about that now? She rubbed the oil into his skin, liking the feel of hard muscle under that skin. She leaned down and licked the oil to test the edible guarantee. It didn't taste too bad. It reminded her of bananas and Crisco with a little something else added to it. "Well, after I got over the shock of being pregnant and my husband telling me he didn't really want any children, I turned to food for comfort. By the time I went into labor, I had formed an addiction to Reese's peanut butter cups."

He gasped as her hands glided over the planes of his body. "No," he moaned. "You named your daughter after a candy bar?"

"So? Men name their kids after athletes all the time. I don't really see the difference." She held the bottle above her head.

Patrick's green eyes watched her intently. "Mira, what are you doing?" Really, he was hoping that she was doing exactly what he thought.

She let the oil drizzle over her body slowly. After she was suitably drenched in banana oil, she straddled his body. "I thought I was doing it right." She leaned so that she was stretched out on top of him. "Do you want me to get up?"

Patrick answered her with a passionate kiss and pulled her slippery body closer.

CHAPTER 24

Patrick woke up first. Initially, he couldn't remember how he and Mira ended up in the guest room. Slowly, their night of unbridled passion came back to him. Using the oil was great at the time, but they had gotten it all over the sheets and kept slipping out of the bed and onto the floor, so they had decided to sleep in the guest room.

He gazed at Mira as she snuggled against him, looking like the siren that seduced him many times he night before. Her curly hair splashed against his chest contrasting against his golden skin, and she wore a contented smile in her sleep. She was beautiful. When he could finally tear himself away from her, he slipped from the bed, threw on a bathrobe, and walked down the hall to Mira's bedroom to retrieve his clothes.

He entered the room, looking at the disaster before him. It reminded him of the aftermath of a tornado or a hurricane. The mattress was dangled precariously off the bed. He picked up the sheets from the floor and confirmed they were covered in slippery banana oil. If the bed linen was a mess, he could only imagine his clothes. His jeans were in another oily pile on the floor. There was no way he could wear those. Luckily, being an undercover agent taught him to always be prepared for events such as these, and he was. He had a change of clothes in the car. As he turned to head downstairs, he took another look at the room. It was a mess. The least he could do was clean it up.

He finished cleaning, then headed downstairs. He retrieved

his clothes from his car, dressed, and then started making breakfast.

A strange feeling came over him, not a feeling of contentment. This felt like something bad was about to happen. Walking to the front window, he saw that the feeling was not wrong.

Rico, the number-two man in Paulo's organization, was sitting in a black Navigator across the street from Mira's house. "Come on, Rico. Could you be more obvious?"

Patrick walked back to the kitchen, dialing his cell phone at the same time. He called his field operative. "Hey, it's me. Why is Rico across the street?"

"I know he is, sir. But he hasn't broken any laws. We're on him."

"Good. I have a feeling Paulo will make his appearance soon."

"Yes, we just got confirmation that Paulo has left Mexico."

Patrick muttered a curse. "I thought I would have more time. Is he headed here?"

The agent sighed and shuffled through some papers. "His flight plan listed the final destination as Canada."

Patrick knew exactly where the drug lord was heading. "Let me know the minute he arrives in Fort Worth."

Patrick heard the young agent mutter a curse. "Follow him," he told his partner, momentarily forgetting that Patrick was on the phone. He let out a string of expletives before he composed himself. "Sir, Rico has just peeled out in a hurry. I'll get back to you." The call disconnected.

Patrick sighed and finished making breakfast. As he decorated the tray, Mira's phone rang. He knew there wasn't a phone in the guest room, so he answered it. "Brenton residence."

"Well, hello, Patrick. I hope you and Mira enjoyed last night," a feminine voice purred at him.

He smiled as he recognized the voice of Courtney Cable, Ashley's mother. "Yes, we did. I take it that you were responsible for the oils."

She laughed. "Yes, I am. Not that I thought you need any aid in that department, but everyone can use a little fun."

He couldn't help but laugh. Those oils had brought out the seductress in Mira. He still had vivid memories of Mira's body rubbing against his and them almost falling out of the bed when the sheets got too slippery.

Courtney joined in his laughter. "I know. It's horrible cleaning that stuff up, though."

"It's okay. Everything is under control. Did you need me to come and get Reese? Mira is still asleep." He had hoped he and Mira could at least have a few more hours of couple time before they had to get their chaperone.

"Actually, I was just calling to check on you guys."

"What do you mean? Has someone approached you?"

He could tell that last question caught Courtney off guard. "No," she paused. "Usually when Dave and I use the oil, it's a day or two before we're back to normal. I can tell you're already up fixing breakfast, but then again, you're in a lot better shape than Dave. I'll bring her by after lunch. That way, you still have a little time." Courtney ended the call.

Patrick laughed as he hung up the phone and finished loading the breakfast tray. After he double-checked the locks on all the doors, he took the tray upstairs.

He entered the room quietly because Mira was still sound asleep. A large wicked grin split her face, and that made him smile. He set the tray on the floor beside the bed and sat next to her.

Patrick nudged her awake. "Hey, are you hungry?"

Her eyes immediately opened. She sat up hugging the sheet to her nude body. "Starving. If I had known we were going to have a marathon, I would have had something to eat for dinner last night."

He placed the tray in front of her. "Hey, that was you with all those oils and marital aids. I had planned a nice evening of seduction, but when you produced a box of scented oils and lotions, all bets were off." He placed a napkin in her lap. "Like you weren't begging for more."

Mira took a sip of coffee. "I didn't say I didn't like it. You should have told me to build up my strength."

Patrick tried to keep his hands to himself. But when she said things dripping with sexual innuendo and looked at him with those deceptively innocent-looking brown eyes, he just lost control. "You know," he started, "when you say things like that, the thought of breakfast leaves my mind faster than the answers to one our tests."

She knew what he meant. She pulled up the comforter over the sheet. "I want breakfast, Mr. Callahan," she stated in a voice brimming with confidence.

He gazed at her second layer or armor in the form of a goose-down comforter. "Okay, you got it, Ms. Brenton." He removed the lid, revealing breakfast.

She dug into it with gusto. "This is so good. Almost as good as . . ." She let the sentence hang in the air, taunting him.

"You're saying I cook as well as I make love." He winked at her and removed another lid, revealing his meatless breakfast of eggs and hash browns.

"I haven't decided which you do better. But I think I'll keep you." She smiled at him as she continued eating.

Patrick nodded, not knowing if he could swallow another bite of food because his heart was now in his throat. *Now what, genius?*

Later that afternoon, Mira and Patrick were deciding what to do after they picked up Reese.

"Why don't you go see your uncle?" Patrick asked as he navigated the traffic in the neighborhood.

"Why should I? I'm still mad at him for not telling me he is dying sooner. I can't believe he waited until his birthday party to tell me," said Mira.

Patrick picked up her hand and kissed it. "Honey, a lot of

people don't get the chance to say good-bye. I know you. When he does pass away, you would regret not seeing him. You said he's the only family you have, and you don't want to be there for him? You know when my cousin died, I was in Germany. I would have given anything to have seen him one last time."

"I really hate when you make me feel bad. But you're right. He's all I have, and Momma would be upset at my behavior. That sounds like a good idea, and I want Reese to see him again before . . ." She couldn't bring herself to say more. It was unfair that her family had been taken away from her. Now she and Reese would be all alone, with no one to help them but each other.

Patrick looked at her. "And," he prodded.

"I won't ask about my father," she added. I know he knows, but he said he promised Mama. He won't tell me, anyway." She both admired and hated her uncle for keeping his word to her mother.

"Mira, maybe you haven't missed anything by not knowing him. Maybe he was a criminal. Would you want a criminal in your life? Reese's life?"

"I think I should have had the chance to make that decision. Can you imagine your life without knowing your father?"

"No."

"I know our situations aren't the same. But we are both products of multiracial families. You know your heritage. You're part Irish. I would just like to know what I am part of."

He drove in silence. "I see your point. Yes, I know my heritage. I don't know all of it, just like every other black person born in this country. But, Mira, that doesn't make up all of you, your personality does. I can tell you are good mother, and you're making sure your daughter has all the love you can give her. That is not defined by a heritage or a race. You're a good person, you're beautiful, and I love you. None of that is defined by ethnicity."

Tears fell out of her eyes. "Thank you. Mama always said it doesn't matter what you are, it matters who you are."

CHAPTER 25

Patrick's eyes quickly scanned the neighborhood of Courtney and Dave Cable. There was no sign of any strange vehicles, and frankly, he was surprised that no one had followed them. Then again, it was another sign that Paulo was expected soon. He liked an audience when he landed, which would explain Rico's absence.

Mira pointed to the two-story brick house. It reminded Patrick of a miniature castle and looked just like Mira's house. "Patrick, there it is."

He nodded and pulled in front of the large house. "Hey, she doesn't live that far from you. You could walk here," he said, turning off the engine and getting out of the car.

He met her as she opened the door. "I know. That's probably why we bonded so fast. Most of the other parents at Reese's school live much farther away."

Before they could walk to the front door, it swung open and Reese ran to greet Mira. Ashley followed behind her almost as fast.

"Mommy!" Reese yelled, jumping into Mira's capable arms. "I missed you. Did you and Patrick have fun last night?"

Patrick smiled as he remembered last night. He noticed Reese sniffing Mira's neck and became nervous. Please let that be soap that she smelled. He knew it wasn't.

Reese faced her mother. "Mommy, why do you smell like bananas and Crisco? You know, that kind Granny used?"

Mira looked at Patrick. He could only nod his head, because

if he opened his mouth, laughter would erupt, and Mira would be more than upset.

Mira released Reese. "Well, honey." She looked at Patrick with squinting eyes. "Patrick and I made banana pancakes this morning. Didn't we, Patrick?" Mira shot him a look. "I must have gotten batter in my hair or something."

He loved watching her squirm. But she was the love of his life and he had to save her. He squatted down so that he was eye level with Reese. "That's right. We made breakfast this morning." Just not the kind of breakfast Reese imagined.

Reese nodded and took his hand, leading them all inside. "Come on, Mommy, Patrick."

Patrick couldn't remember when he had gone from Mr. Patrick to Patrick, but Mira didn't seem to mind that Reese dropped the "mister," so he wouldn't mention it.

Courtney met them as they entered the living room; she was already dressed in a corduroy jumper. Patrick tried hard to keep a straight face as Courtney winked at Mira and asked her how the night went.

Mira sighed, sitting next to Patrick on the sofa. She didn't speak until the kids were headed upstairs to collect Reese's things, and were out of earshot. "It was different. But fun."

Courtney nodded as Dave walked into the room. "You wouldn't believe that someone from his stuffy office told us about the oils."

Patrick knew Dave had some kind of desk job. He couldn't remember what. "What do you do, Dave?"

"I'm an accountant," Dave answered blandly.

Patrick nodded. Yeah, that was definitely a desk job. He wondered, if Mira had to pick between a DEA agent and an accountant, who would she choose?

Dave laughed. "I know. Don't say it. My wife reminds me constantly of how boring I am. That's why my partner told me about those oils."

"Well, tell him thanks for me," Patrick said, grinning mischievously.

* * *

Mira practiced her speech to her uncle as they approached his house. Patrick must have an excellent memory, she thought. He'd only been to her uncle's house once before, and he remembered the way. Not once did he ask for directions. But what man would?

She glanced back at Reese to make sure she knew where she was. "We're going to see Uncle Harold, Reese. He's not feeling well."

Reese nodded. "He told me he was going away soon. When will he be back?"

Mira was mad at her uncle for telling Reese that. "It might be a long time, honey." It seemed so unfair that now that Reese was getting over her grandmother's death, she'd be faced with another one.

"Granny said that he would come and see her soon."

Mira and Patrick exchanged shocked glances. "Shocked" was a mild way of stating it. Startled, flabbergasted, or frightened would have been a better choice of words. Mira was very careful not to say anything about him dying. "What did she say?"

Reese shrugged. "Just that she and Uncle Harold would be together again and they would be able to look after us. But if Uncle Harold was joining her, doesn't that means he's going to die? Will those bad men come and shoot him, too?"

Mira took a deep breath. Whoever said kids didn't know anything? "No, honey. The bad men won't come back. Uncle Harold is going to leave us, but he has cancer. Cancer is an illness. Remember when we took Granny to the hospital and they took pictures of her insides to see where the cancer was?"

"You wouldn't let me go in the room with her. I could have protected her," Reese said quietly.

Mira remembered that day well. Reese had thrown a fit to accompany her grandmother into the room, but she couldn't.

They could only watch from the next room. "Yes, Uncle Harold has that. But he's much worse."

"Oh. We should have brought him something," Reese said in her matter-of-fact way. "Gifts always make me feel better."

"Not to mention food," Patrick added in a whisper. Mira reached over and pinched him, expecting to hear him yelp in pain, but he didn't flinch. He didn't make a sound.

She was amazed he didn't let out one groan of discomfort. Something left over from his military training. But what was his breaking point? Did she really want to know?

He grinned at her as he parked the car. She watched him walk around to her side of the car, open the door, and help her out of the car. "Thank you, Patrick." She reached into the car for her daughter. "I don't know if you could have helped Reese out since she eats so much," she said sarcastically.

"Oh, Mira, I was kidding." He put his arm around Mira's waist and planted a kiss on her cheek. "We both know Reese has a big appetite for a kid."

Mira knew he was right. Again. Thank goodness Reese had inherited Jonathan's slender frame, or they would both would be having daily battles with the scale. "That comment will cost you."

His hand slipped from her waist and he took her hand. Reese grabbed her other hand and they walked to the front door.

"All right," he said, ringing the doorbell. "But actually, I think we're even."

Mira was just about to answer him when the wood door swung open. She braced herself for her aunt's usual harsh comments. "Well, Kasmira, how nice to see you," she said bitterly. "Since you left the birthday party with out so much as a good-bye to your poor uncle," her Aunt Tilda said, waving the trio inside. "I'll tell Harold you're here. I see you brought your young man and your daughter with you. Sit down."

Soon her uncle ambled into room and took a seat. "Hey, Mira. It's good to see you." He nodded at Patrick. "Hey, Reese.

Come give your uncle a hug, girl." He opened his arms wide, and Reese obliged by running to him.

Mira's heart swelled at the sight of her daughter giggling as Uncle Harold hugged her. They would both miss this man more than life itself, and Mira didn't know how she would fill the void. "I'm sorry we left so abruptly yesterday, but the walls were closing in on me. I had to get out of here."

He nodded at her. "I know. Geraldine told me. Can't say that I'm surprised."

She glanced at Reese. "Honey, why don't you go see if Aunt Tilda has a snack?"

"Okay, Mommy." She rushed into the kitchen. Mira stared at Patrick, remembering their earlier conversation about Reese's appetite. "Don't say one word."

Patrick held his hands up in a motion of surrender. "I wasn't going to say anything."

Harold laughed, meeting Patrick's gaze. "I like you. You learned fast about those Brenton women." Then he turned to Mira. "Mira, Helen told you that girl wasn't nothing but the devil. You thought your Momma was being a snob. She wasn't. That girl has been caught with all the wrong people, and you always try to defend her, even when you're the one getting hurt. See where it got you; she tried to kidnap your daughter. You should have pressed charges against her."

"I know I should have, but I just couldn't," Mira whispered. "I just couldn't do that to her family."

"But you see," Harold pointed out, "she doesn't give a second thought about what she does to you."

"No, she doesn't. It was a costly lesson, but I figured it out."

Harold smiled at her. "That's my girl. I know you're smart, and you guys will be able the move forward from all this. I'm glad you came back today, we got some unfinished business."

Those words made Mira nervous. "What kind of business?"

"I have some papers of your mother's that she wanted you to have. Before you get all your hopes up thinking it's something about your father, it's not. It has something to do with the money he sent."

Mira wondered where all this talk was leading. "I closed that account when she passed away."

He shook his head. "No, before she started saving it, she gave it to me for safekeeping. So I invested some of it. I have a check for you." He stood, walked to his den and returned with an envelope. "I know this will tide you over when that other money runs out."

She took the envelope and looked at the check. It was for fifty thousand dollars. "Uncle Harold, are you sure? This could help you."

"No, it's time. You just take care of my baby."

"This just paid for Reese's college and mine." And probably college for any other children she could have. She kissed her uncle on the cheek. "Thank you, Uncle Harold. You've helped me more than you will ever know."

Uncle Harold looked at Patrick as he sat quietly on the couch next to Mira. "I know I'm leaving you in capable hands." He shook his weathered hand at Patrick. "I know you will watch after my girls."

"Yes, I will," Patrick answered with no hesitation.

Mira smiled at Patrick. She wondered if he would stay in Fort Worth or if he would move after he was finished with school. How could she ask him to stay in a strange place forever?

Shara spied on Mira and Patrick as they left Harold's house. She needed to meet Jonathan if it was the last thing she did, but didn't want to risk the chance of being seen. Today she was fixing all the messes that she had created, or at least some of the larger ones.

She watched Patrick help Mira and Reese into the Mustang. When was the last time a man helped her into a car? Probably when she had had her son, four years ago. To make matters worse, it was her father who had helped her.

She watched Patrick speed off. Finally, she could resume her jaunt. Jonathan was already at their meeting place, waiting. He had had the nerve to come in his wife's car.

She stood in front of him and folded her arms. "What are you doing here in her car? You know how I hate that."

He licked his lips with his tongue. "Girl, don't start. Haven't you got me in enough trouble by blabbing about our plan? You should have known that Mira wouldn't turn you in. You didn't have to tell her anything. But you sang like a canary, and I got a visit from those dudes who beat me up at the club. They're cops."

She stared at him, not believing him. "You're lying. How could Patrick know cops? They didn't look like Fort Worth's finest that night at the club," said Shara, gazing at the man she once thought she loved.

Jonathan grinned at her as he continued explaining. "I didn't say they were city cops. Those guys were government cops. The kind that can snap your neck and make it look like an accident. If they had wanted to kill me that night, they could have."

It didn't make sense. Patrick didn't have a job, or did he? Shara's curiosity was piqued. "Did they say Patrick was with them? He knew a lot about federal law. Like, that kidnapping was a federal offense. Did you know that when you came up with that brilliant idea?"

"Yeah I heard something about that," Jonathan said with no remorse. "But I didn't think you'd get much time if Mira pressed charges. Which I knew she wouldn't."

Shara shouldn't have been surprised. Why was she? He used women all the time. Her, his wife, and in some way Mira, he used them all. "You know, when it goes to the federal level, it's no longer up to Mira, you idiot. We can still be charged," she told him. She hoped he was scared. He should be.

He stared at her. "You mean, you could still get time?"

"And you too, genius," Shara said.

"B-but I wasn't there," Jonathan whined, like the sorry excuse of a man he was.

The sight of him made her stomach hurt, especially when she thought of all she'd given up for him. She'd alienated Mira for probably the last time. "But it was your idea. You confronted Mira at the club about the money. So you're in this, too. You think I'm going to take the fall for you?"

"What's wrong with you?"

"I just realized how many times you've lied to me over the years. About Mira, about your wife, about those other kids. I've been with you for over seven years. I can't believe I was with you when Mira gave birth."

He watched her rant and rave, smiling. "You know you got off on the fact that I was with you the night Mira had Reese. Hell, I was with you the night I married Mira. So don't try to act all innocent. I was also with you the night I got married three years ago."

Shara remembered that last night all too well. With just a few well-placed words and some booze, she was having sex with the groom in a closet at the church. She was the devil, as her mother called her. "Yes, I did. I'm not necessarily proud of that, or the fact that you're John's father."

He grinned at her with his sexy smile. It was that smile that had talked her into things she knew weren't right, but she did them anyway. "Like I said before, you knew what you were doing. Save that innocent act for someone who will believe it, like Mira."

"She's not speaking to me."

"What? I thought you could tell her what to do and when to do it."

"That was before Patrick. She is a different person now. Mama told her the truth about John *and* you."

He muttered a curse. "Why can't your mother mind her own business?"

"I'm glad she told her. I'm so tired of all these lies and half-truths. I'm making a clean break with you. If we don't get charged, I don't want to see you ever again. I'm also filing for child support from you."

He tried to grab her, but she moved out of his reach. "You can't. You didn't put my name on the birth certificate."

"I'm sure once we do the blood tests, it will be more than evident that you're John's father. Or we can do this another way."

"What?"

Bastard, always wanting to take the easy way out, she thought. "You could just pay me five hundred a month."

"No way. My wife will divorce me. I can't explain how five hundred dollars is missing from my paycheck."

"All right. You need to be at Fort Worth General Hospital to take the blood test on Friday at one o'clock. Room 219. And if you decide that you're not going to show," she stated, in a voice she had to work hard to keep steady, "a deputy will show up at your house and bring you by force."

"Shara, baby," Jonathan said, stepping toward her. "What are you doing to us?"

She stepped farther away, making sure that she evaded his grasp. "That sweet talk won't help you now," Shara said with a surge of confidence she hadn't felt in years. "I'm getting rid of your sorry ass."

CHAPTER 26

Mira took a deep breath and sat next to Patrick on the couch, giving him an affectionate hug. "Thank you, Patrick."

"What are you thanking me for?"

"Because I'm glad we went to see my uncle. I probably would have been kicking myself for not going after he passed away. We got a lot settled." She leaned against him, taking advantage of Reese napping upstairs, by reclining against the wall he called his chest.

"I know how important family is," Patrick said. "I think it was drilled into my head when I was growing up." He kissed her forehead softly. "My mom always said family is your link to the past and your hope for the future."

Mira nodded and held his hand. Her only link to her past was dying, and he wouldn't help her find her future. She wanted to know who her father was, but how? Maybe she should just let it go. Reese didn't know her father. How would Mira react if Reese asked her about Jonathan? It was then Mira realized that she didn't need to know about her father. She trusted her mother's judgment and hoped that Reese would trust hers.

"Mira?" Patrick asked, scooting closer to her. "What's wrong?"

"Nothing is wrong. In fact nothing could be more right." She sat up and then moved to sit in his lap. "I thought we were going to study for the last test. It doesn't feel like you want to study. Not sociology, anyway."

He laughed, kissing her neck. His hands started unbuttoning her shirt slowly. "I think you're the one that doesn't want to study. You're just using my body," he said, punctuating each word by undoing a clear button on her blue shirt.

When her shirt hung open, he reached inside it and squeezed one of her breasts gently.

Mira felt her plan spiraling out of control. She had just meant to have a little fun with him, but knowing that Reese's naps were unpredictable at best, there was no guarantee of how long they'd have. Now, as desire had taken over, she had to get her hormones under control.

She slid out of his lap and put space between them, while buttoning up her shirt. He watched her, chest heaving. "I'm sorry, Patrick. I was just trying to have a little fun, not trying to send you the wrong message. You know we can't."

"I know," he agreed. "I was just playing along." His breathing still hadn't returned to normal. "It must be something about you that just excites me, and I lose control." He shook his head in amazement. "Why don't we watch a movie until Reese gets up? Better yet, why don't we go wake our little chaperone?"

Mira laughed, but the idea had begun to appeal to her. Reese would keep them in line. But just as she headed for the stairs, the phone rang. After she answered, she almost dropped the receiver as she recognized the caller.

"Mira, it's me. Shara. I know I'm not supposed to talk to you ever, but I wanted to clear the air."

Mira didn't speak.

"I know you're mad at me," Shara continued. "You have every right to be. I screwed up. I just want the chance to apologize and explain why I have been such a fool about Jonathan."

Mira's first thought was that Shara knew about the money her uncle gave her. "What do you want?"

She laughed, frightening Mira. "I don't want anything, girl. I just wanted to you to know that I'm truly sorry about Jonathan."

"Okay. Was that all?" Mira asked shortly, wanting to end the conversation as quickly as possible.

Shara muttered something under her breath. "You know, we've been friends since we were little girls. The least you can do is be a little forgiving. Nobody's perfect. Not even you," Shara shot at her friend.

"I've never said I was perfect," Mira countered. "What would you like me to forgive you of? Trying to kidnap my child? That you slept with my ex-husband? That your son and my daughter are siblings, and you weren't going to tell me?"

Shara was silent. Mira was getting ready to hang up the phone when she finally spoke. "I've done worse than that. That's just scratching the surface. For the record, I have severed my ties with Jonathan, and if I don't go to jail for that stupid plan to kidnap Reese, I'm filing for child support from him. I just want to talk to you face to face. I think you owe me that much."

"I don't owe you anything."

"Mira, please, I want to make a clean slate. You've been a good friend, and I know I blew it. I just want the chance to come clean about everything."

Mira felt herself weakening, wondering what other little surprises her childhood friend could have for her. How many more could she take? "Shara, I'm really busy." What would it hurt to meet her and get this over with?

"Mira, I want us to be friends. Please, give me another chance."

"No. We can never be friends again. You betrayed me more times than I want to think about. You knew Jonathan was awful when you introduced me to him. But you still pushed him on me, knowing what kind of man he was."

Shara wept softly. "Mira, please meet me so I can explain. You're the last friend I have."

"Then you don't have a friend." Mira hated the way she sounded, but this was one time she actually saw the light. "Okay, Shara, I'll meet you tomorrow at one. I'll be in the lobby at work. Don't be late, or I'm gone." She hung up the phone.

When she turned around, Mira discovered Patrick was

standing behind her, his eyes a dangerous dark green and his large arms folded across his chest. "You're going to meet her! How could you even entertain the idea of meeting that woman? Have you gone mad?"

Mira walked back in the living room, not wanting Reese to hear them. "Patrick, she said she was sorry and wants to explain. Don't I owe her that?"

Patrick paced the length of the couch. "Personally, I don't think you owe her anything. She causes you constant pain, and yet you're giving her another chance? What does she have to do? Kidnap you, or worse?"

"Patrick, she's not going to hurt me. She just wants to make a clean slate."

He sat next to her on the couch. "I just want to know, if I did all this to you, would you be as forgiving?"

Mira didn't think she was being a sap. Maybe her expectations were just too high. Patrick should be encouraging her to mend the fence with Shara so she could move on, she thought, watching him rant and rave with his temper. "I think I'd have been the same with you."

"What are you talking about?" Patrick stopped pacing, his back completely up and ready for a fight.

Mira sighed, finally saying all the things plaguing her for the last few months. "Patrick, why are you in Fort Worth? You have no ties here, no friends outside of the guys I heard you talk about but have never met. I know you didn't just move here because of them. What about your car?"

He faced her with the darkest green eyes she'd ever seen. He took a deep breath. "I will answer you, not because of your accusations, but because I hope that we have something stronger than this fight. Yes, it's an expensive car. I think I deserve it. I worked hard for it and I got it. The only ties I have are to me. Why does it matter where I decide to live? How are you paying for this house?"

"That's not your business." He was good at turning the tables on her. "This isn't about me. It's about you."

"No," he said simply. "This is about us and you trusting the wrong person."

"Patrick, I'm just meeting her for lunch, and then she's out of my life forever. Why can't I get closure with her?"

He rubbed his hand over his face, clearly trying to rein in his temper. "So, when you get closure with the person who betrayed you on a daily basis, are you going to find closure with that loser of an ex-husband?"

Mira didn't answer.

"You know what? You just got closure with me." He stormed out of the living room, through the dining room, and slammed the door to the garage.

Mira stood to run after him, but before she could start, she heard his car speed away. She sat back on the couch and cried.

Mira woke up the next morning on the couch. Thank goodness for small favors, Reese must have thought she was tired and didn't bother her last night. She wasn't tired, but she had spent the night crying over Patrick. She had tried to call him several times, and he never picked up the phone.

She'd cancel lunch with Shara so she could make up with Patrick after their class. Wiping her eyes, she got up and headed upstairs. Reese met her as she went to her bathroom.

"Mommy, can I watch cartoons? I already brushed my teeth and washed my face." She opened her mouth to show her mother.

Mira was too tired for this. It was too early for an active child. "Okay. Let me know if the phone rings or anything."

Reese nodded and headed downstairs. Mira went into her bathroom and took a shower. As the water pelted her body, she decided to wear something special to give Patrick a little incentive to make up. She clung to the hope that he would be in class that morning. It was the only thing that would keep her going.

She dressed in an ankle-length corduroy skirt with a silk

shirt, and boots. Although she didn't like the idea of trudging around campus in high heels, she knew Patrick liked them. The things she did for her man. She checked herself in the mirror one last time, then headed downstairs.

As she fixed breakfast, she contemplated calling Patrick again. What would she say? "Sorry, I think I'm right, and you're being a real jerk about the Shara thing, but since I love you, I'm willing to cancel lunch and make love with you." Why don't you just wear a sign, she chastised herself. She was worse than a lovesick teenager.

She and Reese ate breakfast in silence.

"What's wrong, Mommy? Is Patrick coming over later?"

Mira finished the last of her coffee. "I don't know, honey. He might have other plans. We'll see."

"Were you fighting yesterday?"

"We just had a little disagreement. That's all. Nothing to worry about."

Reese nodded. Sometimes she made Mira feel like she was the child, not the parent. "When Ashley's mom and dad talk like that, Ashley's dad usually sleeps downstairs and her mom sleeps with her."

Why did that commentary make Mira want to scream? But she didn't get to because the doorbell rang. "Why don't you get your stuff ready for school? Maybe that's Patrick."

Reese nodded, then left the kitchen with Mira behind her. Mira just knew that it was Patrick coming to apologize for being a jerk and for not listening to reason. Her heart was beating so fast, she didn't think she would be able to make it to the door. She flung the door open and immediately realized that was a mistake. It wasn't Patrick. "Can I help you?"

"Are you Kasmira Brenton?"

"Yes. Can I help you?" She watched as the men nodded to each other. They weren't salesmen; she knew that, and one of them looked familiar. Where had she seen him before? Around the neighborhood?

Each man was dressed like a funeral director, or an FBI

agent. Dark suit, sunglasses, and a gun. One man opened his suit jacket. "Can we come in?"

Like she had a choice. She stepped back and let them inside her house. Reese entered the room and started screaming.

"Mommy, that's him!"

Before she could finish her sentence, one of the men was at Reese's side, telling her to be quiet, but Reese was screaming bloody murder. Mira ran to comfort her daughter.

"What do you want?" Mira looked up at the stranger. She noticed her purse was behind Reese. If she could reach her purse and dial 911, they would be safe. She inched Reese closer to her purse, but she didn't get very far.

"Ow!" Mira shouted. Suddenly, she felt funny, and Reese went out of focus.

CHAPTER 27

Paulo Riaz sat in his large office at the warehouse Rico had found for them to set up business in. It would do for now. He listened as his right-hand man told him of the day's events.

"We went to speak with her, and she refused to speak with us, sir."

Paulo's attention was diverted to the monitor. He watched his daughter and granddaughter as they both lay huddled on the floor of the room.

"Why did you have to knock them out? I didn't want her hurt, I just wanted to talk to her."

Rico adjusted his tie and coughed. "The child started screaming, and we had to do something, or someone would have called the police."

Paulo leaned back in the leather chair and took a liberal drink of wine. "I am grateful that you brought them here, but I didn't want it under these circumstances. I wanted to meet her on neutral territory, not as a kidnapping attempt. How long will they be out?"

Rico looked at his gold watch, then at his boss. "At least four hours."

He nodded. "I will straighten this out later." He pointed toward the door, signaling Rico to leave.

Paulo watched his daughter on the screen. "Very soon, my child, we will have the talk we should have had ten years ago."

Mira awoke out of a drug-induced sleep to the stench of cigar smoke and a realization that almost took her breath away. She slowly opened her eyes and gazed around the room. She didn't see her daughter anywhere in the small, dank area. Where was Reese?

She gazed down at her rumpled shirt and skirt. Her boots were missing. Memories of being kidnapped from her own home in broad daylight were fresh in her mind. How could she have been so stupid to open her door without checking to see who it was first? Just one more area where she had failed her daughter.

She heard a faint moan in the corner. "Reese?" *Please let it be her*, she prayed. Mira crawled over to the mound under the blanket. She lifted the blanket and gasped. Her daughter's usually unblemished face now had a purple bruise above her left eyebrow. She shook Reese awake.

The young girl opened her eyes and stared at her mother. "Mommy, what happened?"

Mira gathered her daughter in her arms and rocked her back and forth gently. "I made a horrible mistake. I let strangers in the house and I shouldn't have. I will get us out of this."

"That man shot Granny," Reese said, hugging her mother. "What man?"

Reese pointed her finger toward the door. A tall man paraded in the hall. "Him. He shot her. He was hiding behind a car, but I saw him." She stared at her mother. "Is he going to shoot us?"

"Not as long as I have wind in my lungs, baby. I let you down once, and it won't happen again." She gently touched the purple bruise. *What does this man want with us?* Her heart skipped a beat as the man entered the room.

He walked toward the women and sat on the floor next to Mira. "Well, Ms. Brenton, I see we meet again." He caressed a strand of her curly hair. "You have something that I want, and I will get it."

"W-what do you want?" Mira's skin felt as dirty as the implication he made.

"You will find out soon enough."

"Did you kill my mother?"

"I was under orders." He stood and formed a sinister smile that cut through Mira's heart like a sharp knife. "Just feel lucky you had to work late the night your mother was killed." He left the room.

She watched him as he stopped at the door and whispered to the man standing guard. His last words were quite clear. "If they move, stop them any way you have to."

Her mind flashed to Patrick. Where was Patrick in all this? Any other time she was in danger, he was always near. How could he let this happen to her? Maybe he was working for these people, she thought.

Feeling despair, she hugged Reese tighter. "Mommy has really made a mess of things."

That afternoon, Patrick paced his apartment, waiting for his computer to reboot. Mira hadn't called him and she wasn't in class. He had tried her at home several times, but with no luck. The tracking device earrings had been removed, and he couldn't find her. Hopefully, she had her purse with her.

His computer crashed just as he was getting ready to bring up the tracking device. He watched the blank screen stare back at him in defiance. When the landline rang, he ran to get it, praying it was Mira.

"Baby?" he answered, hoping against all hope.

"Patrick. This is Shara. I couldn't reach Mira at home. I called her cell phone, and a man answered, then turned the phone off. I'm worried about her."

He tried to contain his anger. "Well, now is a fine time to think of Mira, isn't it? You didn't think about that when you betrayed her as you did."

Her soft, fragile voice spoke, abruptly ending his tirade. "I know my friendship with Mira is pretty much over, but we did grow up together, and I still care about her and Reese, no matter what you may think. We were supposed to meet today, and she never showed. That's not like her. Even with the strain I caused on the relationship, she would have still called to tell me that she couldn't make it or something."

He used his calming agent voice. "Shara, you're right. It doesn't matter what I think. The important thing is we find Mira and Reese. When was the last time you talked to her?"

Shara sniffed, holding back tears. "Last night."

He remembered that call. He and Mira had their biggest fight ever over it. He had wanted Mira to sever all her ties with Shara, but Mira had refused and had agreed to meet her one last time. "Did she sound strange?"

"Not really. But a few days ago, two men came by our house and asked where she lived. My mother didn't know any better, so she told them. I hoped it was a friend."

Patrick's heart started pumping faster. "Can you describe him?"

"Not really. My mom talked to him. He was Hispanic and he was dressed all in black. Momma said he looked like an undertaker."

In some ways he was, Patrick thought. "Thanks, I'll let you know if I hear something." He hung up the phone, thinking now the game had begun. Paulo had arrived, as he had feared.

His computer finally cooperated with him. The device came up. What was she doing in the warehouse district of Fort Worth? Then he realized what was happening: Paulo had her!

He grabbed his keys and headed for Mira's house. As he drove, he called the deputy manager at the DEA.

"Callahan, code nineteen," he shouted into the phone.

"Whereabouts?"

"Looks like the edge of the warehouse district on the border of Fort Worth and Arlington."

"Got it."

Patrick pushed the "end" button on his cell phone and

dialed another number. "I'm calling in a favor. I'm going to need backup. Paulo is here."

"Got it on the computer now," the voice told him.

Patrick hung up his phone and floored the Mustang. "Let's see if I got my money's worth." He watched as the speedometer easily went past a hundred miles per hour. "Mira, I sure hope you're strong enough for two," he prayed.

Several hours later, Mira watched a heavyset tanned man enter the room with a tray. The aroma of food toyed with her stomach. When was the last time she ate? She didn't know the time, but knew it was way past lunchtime. Closer inspection of the meals revealed a steak, baked potatoes, pizza, a glass of milk, and tea.

Poison was her first thought. But why go to all this trouble just to poison her and Reese?

"I know what you're thinking," the man said, eyeing Mira, "but it isn't poisoned. I thought we could chat while you eat."

Mira wanted to be strong and not give in, but they hadn't eaten since breakfast, and they were starving. She passed the pizza to Reese, picked up her plate, and began eating. For prison food, it was delicious. "Why are you holding us against our will?" Mira asked with her mouth full of the tender ribeye steak.

"My dear lady, I am not holding you," he said in a voice that had a thick Spanish accent.

"There are men with guns walking around, and we can't just walk out of here. I would believe that constitutes holding someone against their will."

"Well, I like to call it involuntary freedom. You can go when I say so. You might as well continue to eat, your food is getting cold."

With a sigh, Mira another took a bite of food and watched the man. He was very distinguished, and his neck and wrist dripped in gold and diamonds. His dark hair sprinkled with gray contrasted with his tan skin. His clean fingernails and smooth hands indicated to her that he probably didn't lift a finger to do anything. Somebody probably laid out his clothes for him, too. Looking at him carefully, she gasped as she realized where she had seen him before. He was in the picture at Patrick's apartment!

"Who are you?" she asked, staring directly into his dark brown eyes.

The man smiled. "I guess it won't hurt to tell you that. After all, it's been twenty-seven years. I'm your father."

She shook her head in disbelief. "My father is dead," she lied.

"Was that the story Helen told you? As you can see, I'm very much alive."

Mira watched him. She couldn't imagine her mother with this man. She knew her father wasn't black, but never in her wildest dreams would she have imagined being the daughter of the person sitting in the room.

He waved his heavily jeweled hand around the room. "What do you think is in those boxes?"

She shrugged her shoulders.

"Product. You're right in the middle of my factory. I have been trying to break into Texas for some time. You were my last hope."

The word product meant only one thing with all these gun-toting men around, Mira thought. "I want nothing to do with drugs."

"Self righteous, just like Helen. After I found out about you, I started sending her money for you. At first she sent it back, and I returned it again. Then after about three years she started keeping it. I don't know what she did with it. I saw the house you lived in."

Mira instantly realized where that money went, and why her mother had never touched it. Her mother, being a proud woman, saved the money but refused to touch it because of its origins. She smiled in satisfaction. All his dirty drug money was being put to good use now. It had bought her a house, a car, a private-school education for Reese, and a lifestyle her mother should have enjoyed. She needed to think of a plan to get out of there, but first she needed some answers. "How did you meet my mother?"

He smiled as if he actually remembered. "I met her at the park. She was so pretty and womanly. It was quite a remarkable summer. I could talk her into anything."

"Do you have other children?"

"No. You're my only child. I was in an accident a few years after you were born, preventing me from having any more children."

"I'm not your child. You didn't raise me." She tried to contain her temper so Reese wouldn't know their peril. Luckily, Reese was concentrating on the pizza.

"Those were your mother's wishes, but you are my seed. Like it or not."

"Why did you have Momma killed?"

He looked puzzled. "I didn't have her killed. I was told she died of cancer."

"She would have, if your goons hadn't shot her down in cold blood in the front yard," Mira stated.

"She was shot?" He asked for clarification.

"Yes, by your men."

"I didn't order a hit, especially not on Helen. I only wanted to meet you. But Helen made me promise never to come near you because of my occupation, and I kept that promise."

Tears sprang from Mira's eyes. Her mother wanted to shield her from her father, just as Mira wanted to do with Reese and her father. "Why did you wait until now to meet me? You could have sent a letter any one of my twenty-seven years."

"And tell you what? I am your father, but your mother wanted nothing to do with me?"

"But I was your child. You didn't want to see me? You weren't curious?"

"I tried. Once, when you were probably five years old. Helen denied me that chance. But I'm a patient man, I knew the chance would come, and it has."

Mira realized Patrick was right. Her mother was right. Did it really matter who her father was? All her life she had dreamed of this moment. Now that it was staring her in the face she wished she'd never met this man.

CHAPTER 28

When Patrick arrived near where Mira was being held, he stopped the car, loaded his Glock. He threw open the door and climbed out, closing it as quietly as he could. He tucked the gun in his back holster. Ducking behind the car, he noticed his fellow agents huddled about fifty feet away from the building, hiding behind one of Paulo's delivery trucks. He hunkered down and slowly made his way to the other agents.

"What's going on?" Patrick asked as he reached for his gun.

The nearest agent answered, "Well, looks like Rico has Mira and Reese in one of the rooms. But Paulo is in with them talking to them right now. We've been looking through a telescopic lens. They appear to be fine, except the child does have a bruise on her face of some sort."

"Reese," he muttered as he stood.

The agent pulled him down. "Okay, Pat. Calm down. We don't want them to know we're here just yet. So pull in those hormones."

He knew the agent was right. He would endanger both Reese and Mira's lives instead of saving them. "I know. Thanks, man. What's the plan of attack?"

"Right now, we wait. If we rush them, it could turn into a bloodbath. Then everything we've done so far would have been for nothing. Once night comes, we'll make our move. You think you can wait three more hours?"

Patrick nodded. "As long as I will have the joy of eventually killing Rico and Paulo, I can wait indefinitely." Patrick smiled for the first time that day. After all this was over, he would take Mira in his arms, tell her he loved her, and reveal most of his secrets.

Hours later, Mira watched Reese as nightfall crept into the small room. Mira now understood so many things that had puzzled her for so long in her life. Why her mother cried every time Mira brought up the subject of her father. Why her uncle wouldn't break his vow to his sister. She had finally met her father, and for all the good it did, she wished she hadn't.

Her biological father was a drug lord, infecting innocent people with horrible drugs. *Well*, she mused, *at least you know*. Another chapter of her life would soon be closed. Mira looked down at Reese, who'd fallen asleep in her arms. She wanted so much more for her daughter. "Honey, I will find you a proper father."

Reese opened her eyes at her mother's words and watched her mother with those big soulful brown eyes. "Why can't you marry Patrick?"

"Well, for one, he hasn't asked me, and two, I don't think Patrick is father material for you." Was he husband material? Mira hoped he was, but she knew he was a wanderer and Reese needed stability.

"Ashley's mom says that Patrick is handsome. So I think he'll make a good daddy for me."

Mira smiled; she couldn't argue with the logic of a six-year-old. She hugged her daughter, and they snuggled under the blanket, hoping they would be home soon.

A solitary shot rang through the night air. Patrick instantly panicked. He looked at his fellow agents as they scrambled for their bulletproof vests. But he couldn't spare the time it would have taken to put on a jacket. And knowing Rico, Rico would shoot him in the head anyway. Patrick took off in the direction of the fired gun.

Ignoring the shouts from the agents, he entered the building. Sliding into the first hallway he could, he tried to listen for voices. All he heard was mumbling from some of the guards as they neared him. He darted into one of the rooms for cover. After the guards passed him, he continued looking for Mira and Reese.

He noticed Paulo walking in his direction. Patrick leaned against the wall, hiding in the shadows, hoping not to be discovered. Paulo walked past him with a gun in his hand, followed by two men dressed in black suits. Where was Rico?

"That's what happens when my word is not followed," he told the men as they continued down the hall.

Who was shot? Patrick entered another room and found his answer. Rico was on the floor. Blood trickled out of his mouth and he lay taking his last breath. Patrick rushed over to him.

"Where are Mira and Reese?"

He watched Rico's lips move, but no sound exited his lips. Patrick moved closer, still not able to hear a sound. Rico closed his eyes and faded away.

Patrick walked out of the room and headed down the hall. He noticed the guards at the same time they noticed him. He aimed his gun and shot first. Patrick smiled as a guard fell to the floor. "I still got it." He aimed at the second guard and shot. The man went down with a thud. *Seven more shots to go,* he thought. One of those bullets had Paulo's name on it. Continuing down the hall, he heard a moan.

The door stood open, in invitation. He opened it wider, but the room was dark. His eyes adjusted to the darkness, barely making out a figure. "Mira?" he called out.

"Patrick!"

He knew instantly that it was her voice. He looked for a light switch, but instead found a flashlight. Light cascaded over Mira's form, then to the smaller one beside her. Mira was holding on to Reese for dear life. He holstered his gun and went to them.

He kissed her. Her lips were as soft as ever. "Are you okay?" He caressed her face and wiped away her tears.

"F-fine. I don't know what they are going to do with us. How did you find us?"

"Long story. I'll tell you as soon as we are safely out of here. Can you stand up?" He gazed at Reese. He lifted the girl in his arms and extended one hand to help Mira up.

He led them out of the room, and they started down the hall. "You'll have to take Reese." He let Reese down from his arms. Reese automatically reached for her mother's hand. "When I tell you to run, run as fast you can, and go to the brown van outside. Ask for Danny Flanagan."

"But—"

"Don't ask questions, Mira. The less you know, the better." He led her into the room where Rico's corpse lay. "Be quiet," he commanded when he realized Mira was getting ready to scream.

Mira swallowed her fear and nodded. She nestled Reese closer to her. But a deafening noise halted their movement to safety.

Patrick reached for his gun, but it was too late.

"That's right. I've got you, Martinez."

Patrick didn't have to turn around. He knew that voice. It was the same one that had tortured him since the day he was shot. Rico was dead, but the number-three man wasn't.

"Trey. So nice to see you haven't been killed or anything good like that." Patrick held his arms up in the air. "What happened to Rico? Lover's quarrel?"

"Funny, Dorian. I'd kill you right now, but I've got some pressing matters with Ms. Brenton."

Patrick ran toward the man and wrestled him to the floor before he could arm his pistol. Mira watched in horror as the men tussled over the gun, hoping with every fiber of her being that it wouldn't go off accidentally.

A gunshot pierced the air, and both men were still. Mira held her breath and prayed that Patrick would get up and finish Trey off, and that they could go home. She shielded her daughter from the violent act by standing in front of her.

Trey moaned and moved, leaving Patrick's very still body

on the floor. Blood trickled from his head in a steady stream down his face. He was out cold.

"He's Dorian Martinez." Mira couldn't keep the wonderment out of her voice.

Trey looked at her with scrutiny. "Yes, at least that's the name he used in Mexico. Do you know him by a different name?" He pointed the gun at Mira. "I'd hate for something else to happen to your little girl because you knew something and didn't come clean with me. I should have run you off the road when I had the chance."

Something else now made sense. That night, she thought it had been just an attempted carjacking, but it was these goons. She had to think of a way to get out, especially with Patrick out of commission. He moaned; he was slowly coming back to consciousness. But Trey wouldn't have that. He hit Patrick with the butt of the gun, then called for the guards.

Two uniformed men entered the room. "Take Dorian where all snitches go."

The men nodded, picked up Patrick's limp body, and left the room. "Now," he pointed the gun at Mira and Reese, "you follow me."

Mira did as she was told and followed him down a dark hall into an even smaller room than before. At least this one had one bare bulb hanging from the ceiling, providing a dim light. The man left, locking the door. She settled in the chair with Reese in her lap.

"Where are we, Mommy? Where's Patrick?" She yawned, but hugged her mother closer. "When can we go home?"

She smoothed her daughter's hair as she rocked her silently. "I hope soon." Her hand stilled at the sound of the door opening. She noticed the older gentleman from earlier that evening. "What do you want from us?"

"I want you to take over my business."

"Never."

"I have men in my organization ready to kill for the chance to take control. They're ready to kill you right now, if I say so."

"Like they killed my mother in cold blood."

"That was an accident. I respected Helen's wishes all these years. Why would I have her killed? Call it misguided loyalty. The situation has been righted."

"How? You can't bring her back to us," Mira pointed out.

"No, but Rico will be seeing her soon." Paulo left the room.

Mira exhaled when he closed the door. "My God. He killed that man," she said to the night air.

Patrick slowly came back to consciousness. He was strapped in a chair, and his hands were bound behind him. *Mira*. He had to get to her somehow. He had to save Mira and Reese, but he didn't have a clue as to how. Wiggling his hands slightly, he tested the strength of his confinement.

With the will of his African and Irish ancestors, he stretched his fingers until he was able to retrieve the blade from his belt. He patiently sawed through the ropes that bound him and freed his hands. Quickly, he untied the other ropes and moved the chair. Hiding behind the door, he waited for a guard to make his routine check.

As if on cue, the guard walked into the room. Patrick sprang into action. He held the chair above his head, and with all the force he had, he crashed the chair over the guard's head, knocking him out. He tied the guard up and relieved him of his gun. "You won't be needing this."

Patrick eased into the hallway and spotted Paulo. He was talking with Trey and another guard. Patrick knew his time was limited before they realized he was free, and that they might do something to Mira to get back at him. Patrick walked in the opposite direction, searching each room carefully. He came to a locked door. "Mira," he whispered. "It's Patrick."

He heard a faint whimper through the door. "Mira. It's okay."

"Patrick, the door's locked, and it's dark in here. The light bulb burned out," she told him, her voice trembling as she spoke.

"Stand away from the door." He stood back from the door, hoping it hadn't been rigged with dynamite or some other explosive, pushed the door with all his strength, and knocked it down. "Mira, say something. I can't see you." He walked inside the room, waiting for his eyes to adjust to the darkness.

"Patrick, I'm scared," was all Mira could say before the tears consumed her.

That was all he needed to hear. He shouldered his way through the darkness to them. He kneeled at the sound of sobs. "It's okay, Mira. I'm going to get you guys out of here." He grabbed Reese's hand and told Mira to follow him.

They walked out of darkness and into the hall. He saw a guard at the end of it. There was only one option if he hoped to get the safety. Carefully aiming the gun, he fired one shot. The guard went down in an instant. The man never had time to call out for help.

Patrick looked at Reese's little face. Knowing what she went through with her grandmother, he hoped she wouldn't get hysterical. "Reese, I had to do it for your safety."

She nodded. "It's okay. He was bad."

They continued down the hall. Patrick looked over his shoulder, and he saw three armed guards heading straight for them. He pushed Mira ahead of him. "Keep heading for the lighted doorway. No matter what happens to me, don't stop until you get to the van."

"But, Patrick, we're not going to leave you."

"Mira, you'll have to."

A single shot rang out, and Patrick hit the floor.

"Patrick!" Mira yelled as she went to him. She touched his forehead and blood drenched her hands. Where was it coming from? He moved, startling her.

"Move!" he shouted, pushing her out of his line of fire. He raised his arm, aiming his shaky hand at Paulo. He squeezed the trigger.

Mira watched her biological father fall backward as the guards continued to fire at Patrick. She huddled Reese closer to her.

"Mommy, why is Patrick's leg bloody?"

Mira looked at Patrick. Blood trickled down his forehead, and his pants leg was soiled with fresh blood. *He should be writhing in pain,* she thought, but he still fired back at the guards. Finally the gun fell out of his hand and into the puddle of blood beside him.

He opened his mouth to speak, but nothing came out. Mira realized that he had lost a tremendous amount of blood. His honey-beige skin had paled with pain. She leaned over his bloody body to hear him. "Mira. You will have to shoot."

"I can't shoot at those men, Patrick. I just can't handle a gun."

He strained his voice to speak. "Mira, we will be killed if you don't. My vision is blurring. I can't aim.

"Just pretend we're at the arcade. Just imagine a target." He turned his head. "They're getting closer. He's not a person, just a target. Close your eyes and imagine," Patrick prompted.

She made a split decision, one that she hoped and prayed would not get her killed. Picking up the gun with a shaky hand, she aimed it. Her hand shook as she tried to remember what he had taught her at the arcade. She squeezed the trigger, but nothing happened. She failed not only herself, but also Reese and Patrick.

Patrick could hardly speak. He was barely conscious. "Squeeze the trigger with both hands." He passed out.

Mira looked at Patrick, then at Reese, and then gave it one more try. The trigger released, but the force of the gun sent the bullet astray and it hit the wall instead of the gunmen.

Trey was almost upon them. "Looks like I get to kill three people and take over the business after all. Too bad I don't get to make you suffer like you did me last year, Dorian."

Mira's shaky hands still held the gun. She wasn't going down without a fight.

Trey stood over Patrick's body and aimed his gun. "Well, Dorian, guess I'll see you in Hell."

Before he could shoot, Mira closed her eyes and pulled the trigger.

CHAPTER 29

Mira didn't open her eyes until she heard the thud of a body falling to the floor and Reese shrieking in terror, or so she thought.

"Mommy, you got the bad man!" Reese threw her arms around her mother in jubilation.

Before Mira could react to anything, another voice intervened and she noticed Trey struggling to his feet. Apparently, she had only winged him.

"D-E-A! Drop your weapon," a loud voice commanded.

But Trey wasn't going to give up. He aimed his gun at the voice. The next noise Mira heard was a hail of bullets and a thud.

Mira opened her eyes and gasped. Trey was dead, and men were coming toward her. Five men, outfitted in black shirts covered by bulletproof vests, slowly walked the hall. Their guns were still aimed and ready in case any surprises happened. Mira watched Patrick's limp body. She caressed his forehead, not caring about the blood covering her hands.

"Kasmira, are you all right?" A man asked as he squatted down near Patrick. "Is he dead?"

"No, he was shot, but I can't tell where," Mira said.

He lifted Patrick's limp wrist. "Good, he still has a pulse. It's faint but it's something. Callie, come on." He opened Patrick's shirt and yelled, "Agent down. Call an ambulance, pronto!"

"Is he an agent? What's his name?" Mira watched the chaos around her as agents sprang into action.

The man looked at her. "Yes, he's an agent." He took a handkerchief out of his pocket and wiped Patrick's bloody forehead. "Looks like he took one near the ear."

Memories of the last few months flashed through her mind. The signs were all there; she had just chosen to ignore them. *I am stupid and I endangered my daughter!*

Hours later, Mira woke up in a hospital bed. "Reese," she called. She sat up and looked around the room. The bed next to her was vacant. Just then a nurse walked into the room. "Where's my daughter?"

The nurse stared at Mira. "Well, she was here a few minutes ago. She was asking about someone named Patrick. I'll get security to search for her." The nurse left the room.

Mira attempted to stand but was having trouble. A tall man in a business suit appeared at the door. "Ms. Brenton, I'm Agent Daniel Flanagan. I need to ask you a few questions."

She rubbed her head, remembering the red-haired man from the warehouse. Just how much time had passed since the commotion? "Yes, and I have some questions for you."

He walked inside the room, settling in one of the chairs. He took out a pad and began scribbling in it. "I will try to answer your questions if I can."

"Where's my daughter? Why is there a bandage on my arm? I wasn't hurt when I got to the van."

"Ma'am, if you could calm down, I will give you as much information about this evening as I can, provided you do the same."

Mira nodded, rubbing her arm.

"Security is looking for Reese. More than likely she's in Patrick's room. He's still unconscious. She's been asking about him constantly while you were asleep. How did Paulo and his gang get you?"

She hated thinking about her lapse in judgment. "I thought they were salesman and opened the door for them. Then they forced their way into the house." She didn't want to admit she didn't check before opening the door.

"Had you ever seen those men before?"

Another bad judgment call. "I hadn't, but my daughter recognized one of them from the shooting last summer."

The agent nodded in understanding.

That only infuriated her more. "You knew, didn't you? You knew that he would come looking for me, and no one lifted a hand to protect me or my daughter."

He raised his hand. "First of all, he hadn't broken any laws we could nail him on. Yes, we knew that he wanted to contact you, which was why Agent Callahan was around. Why was he not with you at the time in question?"

We had a fight and I let him leave, she thought. "It was morning. He didn't live with me. Let me ask a question. When can my daughter and I be dismissed?"

"You're not being held against you will. You can leave as soon as your doctor dismisses you."

Mira wiped her eyes. "How is Agent Callahan?"

The agent studied her as he stood. "Well, he was shot three times: in the back of his head, in his thigh, and in his back. That bullet pierced several internal organs, and also his spine."

He had almost died trying to save them from the danger. "Would it be possible to see him before I leave?"

The agent nodded and told her the room number. Without another word, he left the room. Mira stood and ventured down the hall. The armed guards at the entrance to Patrick's room frightened her. There was no way Reese would have gotten by these walls of steel, she mused.

She approached the room; to her surprise, one of the men opened the door for her. He nodded to her as she walked inside the room.

Nothing could have prepared her for what she saw. Reese was lying in bed next to Patrick, but he was asleep or in a coma. He didn't look like the Patrick she knew and fell in love with. This Patrick was fighting for his life, and it was her fault.

"Mommy, Patrick is sleeping," Reese informed her mother.

"Reese, you shouldn't be on his bed. You might hurt him.

He has a lot of tubes running in and out of body, and you might accidentally disconnect one. Get down." She offered her hand to her daughter.

She shook her head at her mother. "No, he needs me."

Mira didn't have the strength to fight any more. She sank in the nearest chair and decided to wait her daughter out. "We can sit with him a few minutes, honey. I'm sure his family will be here soon."

Reese nodded and snuggled closer to Patrick, ending the conversation with her mother. Mira watched them, Patrick mostly. He didn't moan or let out any noises of any kind, but he lay there, still as death. She sighed with relief as she noticed the rise and fall of his chest. The nurses came in and checked his vital signs, but never asked her or Reese to leave the room.

Mira heard someone whisper her name. She sat up and noticed Patrick had opened his eyes. "How do you feel?" She scooted closer to the bed and caressed his arm.

He smiled at her. "I see my favorite girls were looking out for me as usual. I'm sorry I couldn't tell you sooner who I was, but it was my job."

They both glanced at Reese as she lay next to Patrick. Mira wanted to talk to him, but she couldn't talk honestly with her daughter in the room. This time there was no one to leave her with. They only had each other. But Patrick must have been thinking along the same lines.

"Hey Reese, I bet those guards will take you to get something to eat."

Her little eyes widened at the mere mention of food. "Really, Patrick? Anything I want?"

"Anything, honey. Tell them I said so."

She jumped off the bed and ran into the hall.

Mira laughed at her offspring. "You think you can always bribe my daughter with the lure of food?"

"It's worked so far." He patted the space Reese vacated. "What do I have to do for her mother?"

Mira looked at him. He looked so frail and weak. Even breathing was taking an effort. "Giving me a few straight answers would be a nice start."

"I'll do my best."

"What's your name?"

"Patrick Callahan. My undercover name was Dorian Martinez when I was working for Paulo."

"Whom do you work for?"

"DEA until I get well."

"What?"

"This is my third time being shot in the line of duty. I will be forced to retire or take a desk job."

"How many lies have you told me?"

Patrick studied her. If he told her the truth now, she would leave him forever. But he wanted her to be with him as a man, not as an agent. "They have been necessary lies. I have a Ph.D. in sociology. The DEA forged my records so that I could be in your classes and get to know you. I knew that Paulo would try to contact you."

"What did you do? Hack into the college computer so that you could be my study partner?"

He was silent, counting the seconds until she blew her top. When she was silent, he pleaded his case. "Mira, I had to get to know you. That was the only way."

She slapped her forehead. "Well, it all makes sense now. Why people were always so accommodating to you. That's why Shara disliked you so. She can smell a cop a mile away. I'm such an idiot!"

He reached for her hand, but she snatched it away. "You have betrayed me, just as Shara did. You both took my trust and abused it. You knew what a difficult time I had with Reese's father, and you still used me."

"Mira, please listen to me. Yes, I did fiddle with the computer to become your partner. But everything we did together was real. Those were my feelings, and they still are. When we made love, that was me. I love you."

"Mighty big words from a man who lies for living."

"Would you marry me?"

"No. You're just trying to rid yourself of the guilt you feel. Well, Reese and I will be fine, if not better, without you. We need someone who's not afraid to tell us the truth." She stood and ran out of the room.

Patrick barely had time to react to Mira when his parents walked in. "Well, I see you have upset another woman," his mother commented as she took a seat. "I guess this means you have retired from the drug business. Was that Mira?"

He smiled through his pain. "Yes, Mom on all three counts. I just told her most of the truth, so she's a little upset with me."

His mother agreed. "Well, I think you have some crawling to do. But it will be a while before you're able, according to the doctor." She gazed at her son with teary eyes.

"What did the doctor tell you?"

His mother watched him. "I'm going to stay here with you a while when you get out of the hospital. Then we'll go back to Virginia together."

It was a sure sign something was very wrong—she had avoided answering his question. "Mom?"

She touched his leg, but he couldn't feel anything. His earlier suspicion was correct. He couldn't wiggle his toes earlier. He couldn't hold back his tears. "What is it?"

"The bullet that hit your back grazed your spine. They won't know the extent of your injuries until the specialist comes in tomorrow. Let's just wait until the specialist arrives before we start jumping to conclusions."

She was using her nurse voice, that calm, soothing voice that meant impending doom was just around the corner. This wasn't good at all. "So can I walk or not?" His mother looked away from him. For the first time in his life, she wasn't telling him the truth. That meant only one thing. "Oh my God, I am paralyzed!" He began hitting his leg with his fists. "Nothing, I can't feel a damn thing!"

"I'm sorry, Patrick. There's nothing I can say that will make you feel any better. The doctor did say there's a probability that you could walk with lots of rehab. Now, about your hearing—he said that was temporary."

"What, I'm going to be deaf too? I thought I heard a ringing in my left ear." He wiped his eyes. "It's a good thing Mira's mad at me. It will make it easier for me to make a clean break. I can't stay with her."

His mother nodded, but still offered her opinion. "I think you should let her make up her own mind. But tell her the truth, the whole truth."

"I can't."

His mother grabbed her purse and nodded to her husband. "Then I guess I will." She walked out of the room.

CHAPTER 30

Mira walked to the lounge area of the hospital and plopped down on the leather sofa, crying uncontrollably. What would she do now? Patrick had lied, and lied well. She should be used to people betraying her trust, but it hurt more this time because she was in love with Patrick.

"Mira?" A tall, brown-skinned, mature woman sat beside her. "I'm Amelia Callahan, Patrick's mother. I know you've had quite a shock and you're probably feeling really hurt and betrayed right now."

"Sounds like you've given this little speech before." Mira sniffed and wiped her face. "You don't have to worry, I'm not a stalker. I'm just waiting for my daughter, the guards took her to get something to eat."

Patrick's mother shocked Mira by letting out a boisterous laugh. "I knew he had finally met his match when he told me about you. I like the fact that you put Reese's needs first."

"How did you know her name?"

"I told you, he told me about you. But I'm not here for niceties; I think there's something you need to know about Patrick's condition. I know you're mad at him for not telling you everything, but he had his reasons."

Something about the sorrow in her voice set Mira's nerves on edge. "What are you saying? You can tell me. I'm good at taking bad news." She braced herself for his mother's words. "I've had a lifetime of practice."

"Well, when he got shot, one bullet hit the back of his head, but his head is so hard it did minimal damage." She laughed, tensing Mira's already rigid nerves. "The second bullet was a little tricky. It hit him in the back and grazed some organs and his spine. The third one hit him in the upper thigh."

"W-what do you mean?" Doom was reaching out to her. "He's paralyzed?"

Amelia shook her head. "Right now, we just have to wait and see. I know that you love him."

There was something about this woman that made Mira want to confess her feelings. "How do you know?"

"I know my son. True, he's had his share of women, but you're the first one he's loved. How does he treat Reese?"

"Like his daughter. They do stuff together. He helps with her homework to give me a little time off. When we're together, I feel like we're a family."

"Well, that sounds like love to me." A mature white man joined the conversation. He sat by Amelia and kissed her cheek. He offered his hand to Mira. "Kieran Callahan, Patrick's father," he said in his Irish accent.

"What are you doing out here?" Amelia asked her husband.

"He kicked me out. He's having his own pity party."

Mira's heart broke at the thought of Patrick feeling sorry for himself. She should be waiting for Reese so they could leave, but she wanted to talk to Patrick first. She stood as she made her decision. "If you could tell me when the guards come back with Reese, I'll just go speak to him."

They smiled and nodded. Mira walked on wobbly legs to the room. She opened the door; tears immediately clouded her view. She ran to his side. "Oh Patrick, I'm sorry for upsetting you. I didn't know."

He wrangled his hands free from hers. "I don't need your pity. I know you don't want a cripple, so leave me alone!"

Mira stood back from the bed, shocked. "Patrick, I don't think you're a cripple. How could you think something so small?"

Tears ran down his face. His voice was tight and soft, filled with despair. "Just leave, please."

Mira's world tilted again. "All right." She walked out of the room.

A month later, Patrick just wanted his old life back. He couldn't do anything for himself. His mother had been with him since he got out of the hospital two weeks prior, and was hell-bent on driving him crazy.

He watched her bring in his breakfast tray. As usual, she made enough to feed two people. Instantly, he thought of Reese and her adult-sized appetite. Smiling, he sat up in bed.

"What are you grinning about? That's the first time you've smiled since you've been home." She placed the tray across his lap.

"I was just thinking. That's all." He noticed her face. "Don't say it."

"Say what? That you sent away a woman who loves you because you're feeling sorry for yourself?"

"Mom, please. It was hard enough making her leave. Don't bring up those memories."

She sat on the edge of the bed. "You know, when your father and I met, was a very bad time for both of us. He could have been with any white woman, and his life would have been fine. But he picked me and even after I sent him away, he was still persistent and proved he was willing to do whatever it took for us to be together. Knowing the difficulties ahead, he still picked me. I don't regret it for one minute. You should let Mira decide what she wants."

Patrick was silent, thinking about his parents. They had a strong marriage; now he knew why. They worked for their happiness. "Mom, she's been through too much for me to ask her to spend the rest of her life with a man who can barely walk."

"But you can walk. And you're getting stronger every day.

No, you won't be running any marathons, but you can walk. Your hearing is coming back, so I think you should be thankful your injuries are workable. That little girl saw her grandmother die right before her eyes, and now you're trying to desert her. Which pain hurts the most?"

He hated when his mother made sense with her twisted logic. "I have to get over this before I can be with her and Reese."

The doorbell rang before she could answer him. "Is it the therapist already? He's early." She stood and left the room.

He sighed as she exited. He didn't know when or if he would ever be able to face Mira again. After he ate a forkful of eggs, things didn't look any better. Now the damn therapist was early. Not looking forward to the painful workout he was about to endure, he pushed the tray aside and swung his feet onto the floor.

"Patrick."

He turned his head in the direction of the voice. Mira was dressed in a sweater and jeans. Her curly hair hung loose about her shoulders. He was happy to see her but couldn't let it show. "What are you doing here? I told you I'd call when I was ready to see you. As you can see, I'm not."

"Patrick," Mira continued as if he hadn't spoken, "Reese wanted to see you. So before you get on your high horse about being a cripple, I'm only here to please my child. I just wanted to make sure you were decent before she burst in on you." She left the doorway.

A few minutes later, Reese appeared with a bouquet of balloons and huge gift bag almost as big as she was. "Hi, Patrick." She walked slowly to the bed. "Mommy said you were still sick and I shouldn't talk to you too long. But I wanted to make sure you were okay." She handed him the bouquet and the bag. "Mommy hasn't been feeling well, either. She cries every night. I sleep with her, but she still cries. I think she misses you."

"I miss you guys, too, but I'm not well enough to go anywhere." He opened the bag; it was filled to the top. It contained movies, books, pajamas, magazines, and a teddy bear. It was

Reese's favorite sleep partner, and she'd given it to him. That small gesture touched his heart. "Thank you, Reese, for thinking of me."

"It's from Mommy, too. We can always come visit you here."

He caressed her curly hair. "How can I make you understand? I have to have help now. That's too much of a burden to place on you and your mom."

"That's funny, I don't recall you asking me." Mira stood at the door.

"Reese! I have some fresh cookies for you!" Amelia called out. Reese ran out of the room at the sound of Amelia's voice, leaving Patrick and Mira all alone in his bedroom.

"I recall you telling me to leave and not giving me many options about that," Mira continued, still standing in the doorway.

"Mira, I can barely walk. I can't drive."

"So?"

"You have a daughter who's still grieving for her grandmother. I won't be in your life unless I can—"

"Unless you can what? Control it? Lie about your past?"

"Protect you."

"You killed my drug-dealing father, you exposed my old friends for what they were. Just what are you protecting me from?"

"Me."

"What?" She leaned against the doorway for support. "I don't understand."

"Mira, I'm going to be needy for awhile. I will probably have rehab for the next three years." He stood, walking to her. Each step took concentration, but he wanted her to see how bad he was hurt.

She met him halfway. "Patrick, I don't care if you had to crawl to me. I want be with you. I can drive you wherever you have to go." Tears fell to her hand, but she made no attempt to wipe them away. "Reese and I have come such a long way since you came into our lives. It doesn't matter what's wrong or not wrong with you. I love you."

"You love me? After all that's happened, you can still find it in your heart to love me?" He had given up hope of that happening. He kissed her with a built-up hunger. "I wanted to tell you so many times, but I knew the consequences of that, and as much as I wanted to, I couldn't compromise the investigation and risk Paulo getting away again. I wanted to get Paulo before he got to you."

"Well it cleared up a lot of the mysteries about him. I think I'll stick to my mother's story." She grabbed his hand and led him back to the bed.

They sat on the bed, holding hands and forgetting the trauma of the last month. She gently touched his leg. "How does your leg feel?"

"Stronger now that you're here. I was so afraid that you'd stay with me out of gratitude instead of love."

"Patrick Callahan, I've loved you since that night you rescued me at the club. I've only felt gratitude for a month." She kissed him. "Oh, wait, I guess I was grateful for what you did for Reese. So maybe I have felt gratitude for more than a month. But love is the more powerful emotion here."

He gazed at her with love in his eyes. Never had he felt love for a woman as he had for Mira. He kissed her softly, then whispered against her lips. "I just need one little favor."

"What? I don't think we should, especially with your mom and Reese in the next room." She smiled at him.

He tweaked her nose and kissed her lips. "No, I want to marry you. If you think you can handle a man that may have a little trouble walking, I would love to be your husband, and I would like to adopt Reese."

Her mouth hung open in surprise. "Why? How?"

"Stop asking stupid questions and kiss me," he said, inching closer to her. "I want to be there for you as you continue your education. And since I was shot again, I will more than likely have a desk job. Do you think you can handle that?"

Mira smiled, love dancing in her eyes. "I can handle anything as long as you are by my side and let me into your life."

"You're already there, baby." He kissed her again.

He watched as Reese bounced into the room and hugged her mother.

Mira watched her daughter. "Reese, what do you think about me marrying Patrick?"

Reese smiled at him. "Does that mean that you're going to be my daddy?"

Patrick smiled with tears in his eyes. "Yes, baby, it does. And my mother will be your grandmother."

"Can I call her Granny?"

Patrick knew at the moment that she had let her maternal grandmother go and she knew it was time to move on. "Yes, you can."

He hugged Mira and Reese, then looked at his mother as she stood in the doorway to his bedroom, watching them. "You're right, Mom, having a family does feel good."

EPILOGUE

Two years later

Patrick laughed as he watched Mira race around preparing the house for Christmas dinner. "Raced" might have been a strong word considering she was six months pregnant.

"Honey, why don't you rest for a minute? My parents won't be here for another couple of hours." He sat down on the couch and propped his leg on the table.

Mira watched him, smiling and with love in her eyes. She looked as beautiful as the day they were married in the small intimate ceremony at her house, with Reese by their side and all of their friends and his family wishing them well. The last two years almost seemed like dream to him. Reese finally had a father. Every time she called him "Daddy," it made him all misty-eyed and content. Mira usually laughed at him and told him that he'd get used to it. But he hadn't, and he didn't plan to.

Finally, she sat beside him on the couch. "I must have been crazy inviting your entire family to a holiday dinner. We've only been in Virginia for three months, and we haven't even finished unpacking our stuff yet, and Reese—"

Patrick silenced her with a soft, tender kiss. "Reese is just fine. She's at my sister's and enjoying being around her new cousins. As for you, I want you to slow down or I will be forced to hire a maid. Remember what the doctor said, you're supposed to be resting." He rubbed her stomach. "My mother said she would make the dinner and we agreed, remember?"

"I know, Patrick, but—"

He silenced her with another kiss. "Look, if I have to take you upstairs and make love to you until they get here, I will. You're supposed to take it easy. You're carrying my son in there."

Finally, she gave up all pretense of cleaning and leaned against Patrick, sighing in contentment. "You know, when you first brought up your new job at the DEA as deputy director, and moving to Virginia, I didn't think I would like it here, but it's pretty and your family has been amazing, welcoming us with open arms and filling the void since Momma died. It's so nice to see snow at Christmas, and Reese loves it," she said, yawning. "You know, going upstairs does sound like a good idea."

Patrick smiled. "Good."

Mira hoisted herself up and stood in front of Patrick. "Not for that. I was thinking in terms of a nap. Your son has already tired me out, and it's not even lunchtime." She glanced at the wall clock. "Maybe I should call your sister and see when Reese is coming home."

Patrick grinned. "Reese will be here with the rest of the brood. Come on, you're going to take a nap." He took her hand and led her upstairs.

"You're taking one too, right?" Mira looked up at him as she sat their bed. "You know how I hate sleeping alone."

Patrick watched her get settled in bed and crawled in beside her. "Me, too."

They snuggled together, and Mira was soon asleep. Patrick watched his beautiful, pregnant wife as she snuggled against his body. He thought about the changes Mira and Reese had endured, and it only made him love them more, if that were possible.

Dear Readers,

I hoped you enjoyed the journey of Patrick, Mira, and Reese as much as I did writing it. I am a huge fan of James Bond movies and I love spy gadgets, so it was only fitting to try to fit some intrigue into a book.

I would like to hear from you. Please don't hesitate to e-mail your thoughts about Patrick, Mira, Reese, and even Shara. You may e-mail me at author@celyabowers.com

Thank you for your support, and God bless you!

Celya Bowers
www.celyabowers.com

ABOUT THE AUTHOR

CELYA BOWERS was born and raised in Central Texas, and attended Sam Houston State University. She now resides in Arlington, Texas, where she works at a mortgage company in the tax department. She also is a member of several writer groups locally. Her hobbies are reading, writing, attending cultural festivals, and listening to classical jazz and just about any other kind of music. An avid traveler and seeker of fun, she hopes to finally get her wish and visit picturesque Ireland.